ADVENTURES OF THE
KARAOKE KING

ADVENTURES OF THE
KARAOKE KING

Marilynn —
I hope you
enjoy this
adventure!

HAROLD TAW

PUBLISHED BY

amazon encore

The characters and events portrayed in this book are fictitious. Any similarity to real persons, living or dead, is coincidental and not intended by the author.

Published by AmazonEncore
P.O. Box 400818
Las Vegas, NV 89140

ISBN-13: 9781935597568
ISBN-10: 1935597566

For Katie, whose piquant temperament and long, lively torso inspire my adoration.

CHAPTER 1

My main competition was Irma Johnson. She could lull you with Ella Fitzgerald and roundhouse you with Janis Joplin. Months before the competition, when Mori would drop by to watch, she'd call out, "Now, Mori, you know your queen's going to bring the crown back to the Lily Pad. I *hope* that's going to mean more than just *one* free drink a night."

That was her weakness—excessive showmanship. If she was lubricated, she put annoying Mariah Carey flourishes into the most atonal of songs. We clapped for one another but rarely spoke. Irma shot me smug "top that" stares on the way back to her seat.

Before I purchased the Troy Bobbins *Personal Path* series, her gamesmanship might have intimidated me. Now, I reveled in it. If you couldn't snatch what someone else valued, what was the use of wanting it in the first place? Jimmy—who cued up the songs—took wagers on the competition and, a week before the event, I was the favorite at 1:3. Irma was second at 1:5. She complained to no avail. Jimmy danced around her table to someone's rendition of "La Isla

Bonita," shaking his souvenir maracas from Tijuana, his lazy eye cocked up at the ceiling. "Jimmy doesn't make the odds," he said, speaking in the third-person. "Money does. Invisible hand. Blame the market."

Odds of 1:3 do not mean, by any stretch of the imagination, a done deal. Imagine, however, how many variables are involved in a multi-round, countywide competition. Theoretically, Irma or I could be knocked off at the outset when the pre-screened field moved from sixty to nine, bumped off by a specialist destined to embarrass himself later. But with each successive round, my chances of winning would improve. Jimmy and the invisible hand of the International District's underworld knew karaoke, and they were rolling out a red carpet for my coronation.

A week before the competition, Mori hopped onto a neighboring barstool. For a seventy-year-old, he still had spring in his step, and his short legs dangled like a boy's. He reeked of cognac—his drink of choice—and his bald pate was flushed red. His wife let him come to the Pad only on weekends and he made the most of it.

"Hey, Guy," he said to me. "I got a call from the editor-in-chief of the *Seattle Asian Herald*—you know, that free rag I keep out front—a Norene Wong or Woo, something Chinese. She wants to do a feature story on the upcoming karaoke competition, you know, handicapping the race. I told her you and Irma were the favorites."

I sipped my drink with what I hoped was suitable Asian humility. "That's awful kind of you, Mori, but I'm sure there are singers out there we don't know about who'll knock the judges' socks off. And Irma. I don't know if I can hang with her."

Mori nodded. "I think Irma's got better song selection and a more expansive vocal range, but you never know. I told the reporter to talk to you both, but she wasn't interested in Irma."

I should have guessed Mori's feelings about the competition. He never bought *me* free drinks. "Why's that?" I said.

"Oh, who knows? Probably because your last name's Watanabe and Irma's is Johnson. Though I swear, if you straightened Irma's hair, she could pass as Southeast Asian. She looks like a village beauty from Cambodia."

Irma, who was sitting at a table near the stage—too far to hear what we were saying—eyed our conversation with suspicion. She was five-foot-ten, about 180 pounds, wore her hair in corn rows, and was about three shades darker than I was. I had a hard time picturing her wading through rice fields in a straw hat.

"This, what's her name—Norene?—wants to interview *me?*" I said. "Why not just interview the champion?"

Mori stood on the rungs of the barstool and waved at Irma, nearly tipping over in the process. Irma's anxious expression brightened into a smile. Mori flushed redder than he already was. "Makes no sense to me either. Says she wants to do a story called 'The long road to the karaoke crown.' Do me this one favor, will you, Guy? We're still reeling from that nasty column she wrote about our food. It's a good thing so many of our customers are on fixed incomes and can't read English."

"No problem, Mori. I'll give her a call tomorrow morning."

"Thank you, Guy. Hey. Good luck on the competition." Mori gave me a swift pat on the back. He then had Josie mix a drink that he brought over to Irma.

On the telephone, Norene said she needed exactly thirty minutes of my time, that day. I suggested we meet at the House of Hong for dim sum to spend a leisurely hour talking. I'd even treat.

"I'm a journalist. I don't have time for things like that. You think you can sway my impartiality by buying me a meal? You can't. Did you ask because I'm a diminutive Asian woman you presume to be submissive and meek? I'm offended."

I rubbed the sleep out of my eyes. Ten o'clock in the morning is way too early for an argument when you stayed through last call. "How about Gossip, the bubble tea place on King Street and—"

"I publish *the* paper for the Asian American community. You don't think I know where that teeny bopper hangout is? We're the reason its competitor bit the dust. I'll meet you there at 2:17 p.m. Don't be late."

At two o'clock, I ordered a drink and took a seat near the window. At the neighboring table, four Asian kids, dressed baggy, played cards. I have a weakness for a good iced milk tea with tapioca balls, even if drinking milk gives me gas. Why don't bubble tea shops, which cater to a population that lacks the enzyme to break down dairy products, offer a soy milk option?

I recognized Norene by the way she surveyed the room in a military fashion. She was in her fifties but well-kept, her sensible, blue business suit clashing with the ominously sharp points of her pumps. I stood and waved. She stared at me for a full five seconds before she marched over.

"Hi there, Norene. I'm Guy Watanabe."

She left my hand dangling in midair. "No you're not," she said, staring straight at me through the thick lenses of her wire-rimmed eyeglasses.

"Um, yes. The last time I checked, I was Guy Watanabe."

"You're no Watanabe. Your skin's too dark. You're *pinoy*."

"No, I just look Filipino. It's a common mistake. My father's half-Japanese. Did you want to get a drink? I can wait."

"What are you then?"

"Oh, a little bit of this, a little bit of that. Mostly Asian, Chinese, and Japanese. Some Yakima, Norwegian, black."

"*Mostly* Asian? What percentage? Which type?"

I scratched my head. "We're not talking hybrid pea plants here. Seventy-five percent? Eighty-five percent? I guess it depends on whether you count my Yakima blood. Personally, I think being part-Native should count toward my 'Asian' quotient because of the Ice Age land bridge theory. If my Indian ancestors hadn't chased wooly mammoths across the continents, who's to say I wouldn't be more Chinese?"

Her eyes narrowed. "I didn't come here to be insulted. I'm a journalist working on behalf of the community." She set her Prada purse on the table and sat down. "I'm not going to have one of those nasty milk teas. I'll just have water."

I looked around, but a waiter had not suddenly materialized. She was talking to me. I joined a long queue of customers and returned ten minutes later with a cup of water.

"This isn't really an interview," she said, leaning forward.

"But Mori said—"

"Moriuchi can't be trusted. I'm convinced he pays off public health officials to keep that kitchen open. And I have several trustworthy sources who tell me he's running numbers in that joint. He's nothing but a middle-man capitalist profiteering off the most vulnerable members of our community. Who do you think drinks, smokes, gambles, and eats bad food? The immigrant underclass. You should care about this. You're Southeast Asian."

I used my oversized, pink fluorescent straw to siphon up tapioca balls, chewing them contemplatively. "All right, then. Why is it that you—"

"You're wondering why I wanted to contact you. Very perceptive." She looked down at her plastic cup. "Is this tap water?"

I nodded. She pulled a bottle of Evian from her purse, unscrewed the top, and took a sip. "I've heard from sources more reliable than Moriuchi that you're a frontrunner in the King County Karaoke Competition."

"Right. And from what I understand, you wanted to write an article—"

"Are you thick? That was a ruse. A cover story. Sometimes you have to deceive people in the name of the greater good. There are lives at stake here."

I stroked the stubble on my chin. Over a karaoke competition? Did the Yakuza have money riding on someone else? Did they plan to slit my vocal cords behind a local nail salon? "Maybe if you could be a little less vague, I—"

"Look." She pushed her glasses up though they hadn't been sliding down. "I'll put this in language you can understand. I'm one of the judges for the upcoming competition."

I sucked up another tapioca ball. She was one of the "celebrity" judges? Who else had they invited? My eighth-grade chemistry teacher? "Fantastic. You must be quite the karaoke fan then. Do you have a particular song you like to sing? Something you'd call 'your' song?"

Her nostrils flared. "I don't have time for small talk. I'm the editor-in-chief of the *Seattle Asian Herald*. Look, Wa-ta-na-be." She crinkled her nose skeptically. "Karaoke, regardless of its questionable merit as an art form, is *our* tradition. Asians were the first to emulate famous singers in public, long before the wide-eyed *guilos* began renting karaoke machines for office Christmas parties. We invented karaoke. We produce the machines, the discs, and those tacky videos. We spend the most karaoke dollars. Dominant white culture marginalizes our place in this rich history. We need to move from margin to center, but it won't happen unless we erase that little pink line and tear up the page. How would it look if at the inaugural karaoke event in western Washington, a non-Asian took home the crown?"

My stomach began to roil in lactose intolerance. "I don't think I follow. Is this a motivational tool? Win one for the team? Or are you suggesting that as a judge—"

She held up her palm. Colored stones adorned three fingers. "Stop right there. I hope you're not impugning my integrity."

Thank goodness. "Well then. There's bound to be a sleeper who pops up, but I've put in the prep time. I feel confident. Not overconfident, but—"

"I've fought long and hard with the county executive over this. I've made sure that three of the five judges are Asian American. There's me, Chinese; there's Joon Kim, artistic director of the Northwest Asian American Theater, a Korean; and there's Tetsuro Taniguchi, the Japanese supermarket owner. *He's* obviously Japanese, though I question his progressive credentials. Sorry there aren't any Southeast Asians, but there weren't any prominent ones to appoint. The other two judges are Charlene Styles, a mezzo-soprano for the Seattle Opera—African American—she can be counted on to go black or for an unquantifiable 'quality' rating; and a vice-president of the Miller Brewing Company, which is owned by one of the sponsors. Miller's trying to up sales of malt liquor in our community so she might go Asian, but since she's white just presume she'll vote white. They can't help it—it's subconscious."

I looked out the window. An elderly Asian man leaned hard on his cane as he crossed the street. He wore a tweed blazer with patches on the elbows and a cross-hatched Ivy cap. His precise ethnicity was hidden within the deep creases of his face. Was this a karaoke competition or an election in Pakistan?

"Norene, a true karaoke aficionado wouldn't vote one way or another based on ethnicity. That's the beauty of karaoke. Go to a bar here, Buenos Aires, Beijing, or Moscow—if you can warble 'Pretty Woman' with Roy Orbison's warmth, you'll have friends forever. It has this *purity* that can't be understood in objective terms but has to be experienced firsthand. Some might compare it to sitting in the right field bleachers at a baseball game, peanut vendor cocking his arm to throw you a—"

"Shoeless Joe Jackson."

"What?"

"Pete Rose. Bud Selig." Norene looked down at her wristwatch, the band of which was so golden it looked fake. Norene shared the love for 24-karat gold that middle-aged Chinese women have regardless of how far from the mainland their ancestry takes them. If there was such a thing as 35-karat gold, they'd wear it, even if it was as pliable as tin foil. "I don't have time for this. I'm paying you a courtesy visit. All you have to do is not embarrass our community. Remember that without our blood, sweat, and tears, you'd never have the opportunity to sing for public access television. Oh, and we get an exclusive. Don't talk to the *Seattle Times* or the *P-I.* They quote *our* article."

The competition unfolded exactly as I'd visualized. Irma and I were neck and neck, but after two rounds and forty percent of the scoring, I held the top spot. Mathematically, whichever of the top three seeds took the finals would take the crown, but my voice had never sounded better. Domination was supposed to exhilarate me. Instead, a numbness that began in the morning as a trickle in the back of my throat had branched out into my limbs and head and I had to pinch myself hard, until the broken, nearly purple skin on my forearm verified that I was me.

"Don't you start getting cocky," Irma whispered. We sat next to each other at the competitors' banquet table. Not a single dessert had been touched. The party favors—bundles of cigarettes tied with crepe-paper bows, compliments of sponsor Philip Morris—remained unsmoked. "Don't count me out. I'm still nipping at your heels."

Irma didn't mean to sound desperate, but her rushed cadence gave her away. Her entire extended family seemed to be in attendance, about half of whom had flown out from North Carolina and Georgia. Little boys in ties and girls in ribbons; uncles with round bellies and aunts with wide hips; elders who talked while no one listened—they populated three tables in the center of the room. In the midst of this well-dressed black family was diminutive Mori, wearing a beige suit and a powder-blue bowtie.

The competition would be won or lost in this final round, in front of a heavily liquored, majority Asian crowd determined to get the most of the free booze provided by the event sponsors. You couldn't move a plate without knocking into two-liter bottles of King Cobra Malt Liquor. But far more popular were the pony-keg-sized bottles of Remy Martin cognac. They were planted next to the tables in chrome stands that pivoted forward to pour with a light press of the finger. At first, it seemed odd to be singing karaoke in a ballroom at the Washington State Convention Center: the high ceilings, advertising banners, and jumbo-sized everything created a Costco warehouse ambiance. Then I realized that for Asians, Heaven was waking up in Costco with someone else's American Express card.

In Round One, the competitors had free rein over song selection. In Round Two, we selected from a pre-screened list of songs. In the Finals, the judges selected a song for us out of the entire karaoke universe, the only limitation being that it could not come from one of the genres we had chosen during the first two rounds.

The competition rules set forth five established karaoke genres: rock, pop, R&B, country, and "world music." Due to the three-round structure, each competitor had to sing from three different genres. The catch, and it was a big one, was that a person couldn't choose the genre for the most important song of the night.

That didn't mean a cagey performer couldn't narrow down the available universe by gaming the system. Irma knocked off her *weakest* genres early—world music and country—gambling that she'd luck into her favorite genres—pop and R&B—when it counted the most. I played more conservatively, singing pop during the first round, when the chance of falling prey to specialists was the greatest, and bagging my weakest genre, rock, in the second round.

No one-hit wonder could usurp the Karaoke King's throne. Round Two exposed two pretenders, including one from the Lily Pad—Tony Nguyen, a jeri-curled Vietnamese refugee who idolized Marvin Gaye. Murmuring "mercy, mercy me" couldn't save his rendition of Twisted Sister's "I Wanna Rock!" The Finals were sure to double his, and our, pain.

Neither the competitor nor the audience knew what was to be sung until the title flashed on the singer's monitor and the RealNetworks jumbotronic screen. Novices complained for fear they'd encounter a song outside their limited range. Purists relished the gun-slinging nature of the challenge. It was like walking into an unfamiliar bar and being called to sing first. Who knew what the crowd was hungry for? You plunged ahead on adrenaline and instinct.

We ascended the stage in reverse order, starting with the ninth seed and ending with the first. Irma clenched my forearm as the title for Tony's song flashed on-screen: "I've Got Friends in Low Places" by Garth Brooks. I craned my neck to see the expressions on the judges' faces, but my view was obstructed by the stage. It was as if they were trying to chase the audience out of the ballroom.

When I first met the other finalists, I'd suspected a Norene-instigated diversity arrangement—only three were from the Pad (Tony, Irma, and me) and, unlike the audience, fewer than half were Asian. But after Tony Nguyen, the performances ranged from passable to superb. The fourth seed, a youngish redhead with multiple piercings and a latticework of tattoos that snaked up her bare arms, sang a rendition of "Mad About You" that brought the crowd to its feet. The third seed, a scrawny white guy from Bellevue named Leo, appeared to be channeling Louis Armstrong's soul in "What a Wonderful World." On any other night, I might have worried. As Leo finished his number, I noticed that Irma, beneath the yards of yellow taffeta covering her ample frame, was shaking. What did she have to worry about? She wasn't going to win, no matter how well she sang.

I leaned over to her. "Whatever happens up there, you deserve to win. You're an amazing singer."

Irma's eyes widened. "You think I can hang with *him?*" She pointed with her chin at Leo, who was descending the stage to deafening applause.

"Absolutely."

Her eyes darted from mine to the center of the room. Mori had his hands raised with his fingers crossed. Irma's mother muttered to herself. Irma smoothed out her skirt.

"You're right. I'm gonna whoop his bony ass."

Leaning back in my chair, I took a sip of cognac. Disgusting. Too smooth, too aged, too something. Onstage, the spotlight was on Irma. Up close, her taffeta dress looked like overkill, given all its folds and bows. But up there, she looked like a much larger, darker version of her idol, Whitney Houston. She took the microphone in hand and smiled. The RealNetworks screen flickered and her song appeared: "The Greatest Love of All."

Irma's gasp was amplified by the microphone. What were the chances of that? Irma had gamed for the off-chance she would luck into the pop diva genre, and she got her *favorite* song, the song she ended every night at the Lily Pad singing.

She killed that song—clubbed it, cremated it, and threw its ashes into the breeze. She resisted the urge to put in flourishes until the very end, in the same places the real Whitney starting going up and down the vocal ladder like a window-washer with dysentery. The Franklin Company representative, who was to present the karaoke medallion later in the evening, was mesmerized. He silently mouthed the words, clutched the velvet presentation box to his chest, and swayed from side to side. He was hammered.

Norene was sure trying hard to make it look as if the competition wasn't rigged. If I were fixing a competition, I wouldn't make the runner-up look so strong. She wouldn't have to look terrible, just not quite at the top of her game. How could anyone compare to Irma singing her trademark song? I felt relieved that Irma was allowed to go down swinging.

I didn't have a trademark song, unlike everyone else at the Pad. That itself was my trademark. Like water, my voice could fill any container. If Norene had known her karaoke, she would have asked me what I wanted to sing in the finals. Though even now, I wasn't sure what I would have chosen.

I gave Irma a standing ovation, calling out "Encore! Encore!" along with Mori. Her father, a graying gent who looked like a dark-skinned Ernest Borgnine, yelled over and over, "That's my girl!" Her mother dabbed her eyes with a dinner napkin. My stomach clenched in pain, but only for a moment, and then the soothing numbness, that confident objectivity, returned. I stayed on my feet until Irma returned to the table. Even before I could congratulate her, she enfolded me in a fleshy embrace.

"That felt so good. That felt so *good*! All that anticipation. All that doubt. And now…" She crushed two more of my vertebrae, and finally released me. "You go show them who's King, Guy. Bring this house *down*!"

The lights were so bright I had to shield my eyes to make out the judges' silhouettes. They sat at a long, low table, behind laptop computers that allowed them to enter their scores immediately. The only reason I could distinguish Norene was the light bouncing off her Coke-bottle glasses.

The talk amongst the drunken crowd receded as I grabbed the microphone, nodded in acknowledgement, and waited for the song title to appear. Norene would know, at very least, that Asian crowds don't take much to country no matter how well-sung. It was possible she would have chosen an English-language, Hong Kong pop song under the guise of "world music," but the safe bet was she had ensured a contemporary R&B selection, something safe and poppy. I grimaced, caught myself, and smiled.

I wasn't prepared for what actually happened. One second the video monitor was a neutral blue, and the next moment it contained a title placard I didn't understand:

Oxalá

by Madredeus
(contemporary-traditional Portuguese)

A ripple of murmurs washed across the auditorium, but they were mere echoes of the voices inside my head. Madre-who? How could someone hyphenate the words "contemporary" and "traditional"? Portuguese? Not even *Portuguese* people sang karaoke in Portuguese.

I blinked repeatedly, suspecting, for a moment, that the DJ would soon cue up the real song. Instead, the lilting arpeggios of classical guitar strings filled the room. The title screen dissolved into a market scene at the port of an old, European city, the sky and sea a steely gray. Thick-waisted women in peasant garb haggled with customers over produce while scruffy fishermen stared curiously into the camera lens.

Sweat dripped down my spine. An acoustic song without percussion? This competition was rigged all right. Rigged against me.

For six measures of music, I stared at the video screen, wondering what went wrong, wondering whether, at the last minute, Norene had switched her allegiances and traded a black victory at the karaoke competition for an Asian triumph as Seafair Queen. And then something peculiar happened. My stomach unclenched, as if a block of ice had cracked and melted, as I realized that I was going to lose, and lose big—so big I wouldn't even catch Tony's Marvin Gaye–loving pantleg on my slide over the precipice. Months of preparation would be rewarded with public humiliation. A giddiness welled up within me so intensely I began to tremble. I was going to lose and it felt good. No one was going to understand a word I sang, not even me, and I didn't give a damn.

The camera moved on to an organ grinder whose monkey was dancing about in the center of a cobblestone square. The lyrics appeared onscreen.

Oxalá, me passe a dôr de cabeça, oxalá
Oxalá, o passo nâo os moreça

I'd never sung like that before. The auditorium disappeared. The crowd dissolved. In fact, if it weren't for the physical fact that I must have been there to follow the cryptic syllables scrolling across the screen, I would have said that I had vanished completely too. There was just sound, lush, layered sound, and I couldn't distinguish where it ended and my voice began.

At times, it felt as if I were swimming; at times, it felt as if I were drowning. I didn't know whether it was "good" or "bad"; it simply was. The song lasted a moment and forever, and when I finished I forgot to bow. I stood there regaining the sense that I was onstage. The audience was silent.

One person clapped, then two, then twenty, then a hundred until, like raindrops becoming a storm, a single, collective roar saturated the air. I waved and they roared louder. I bowed and they wouldn't stop. There was a lull as Irma hugged me. Then applause burst forth redoubled when the scores were posted on the RealNetworks scoreboard. I had won.

It took me hours to get home that night. Mori's congratulatory pat on the back was more than cursory and Irma's family seemed pleased by her second-place finish. The judges lined up to greet me. Mezzo-soprano Charlene Styles—elegant, mocha-complexioned, and slim—held onto me until I began to feel uncomfortable. She rubbed her palm in circles on my back.

"Norene protested violently against giving you that song," Charlene said. "But I told her you were holding back.

You were capable of so much more than *pro forma*, pop trash. And you were. You are. Do you know that?"

Norene tugged me away from the others. "Remember who you owe for that victory, Watanabe. Our paper gets the exclusive. Photo shoot, tomorrow, 10:19 a.m., our offices." She pointed to my chest. "Wear that gaudy metal thing and some dressier clothes."

I fingered the ridges on the medallion, warm from my body heat. It had a reassuring heft.

CHAPTER 2

I noticed Megumi as soon as she walked into the Lily Pad. In Seattle, dressy means a new T-shirt. Megumi's outfit—a tangerine orange slip with a neckline millimeters away from revealing the nubs of her modest cleavage—made her stand out. But it was more than her looks and regal demeanor that captivated me. She listened to me sing as if my voice pained her, picking at her paper napkin until it was in tatters. And the more she resisted, the more she held me in her thrall. Her date's fierce expression showed that I was doing something right. It was as if Megumi and I shared a secret song no one else heard.

We ran into each other again at Pike's Place Market. The main drag was closed and filled with tourists and organic fruit stands. Somehow Megumi had gotten a hold of an old Seattle guide book and kept on passing the same corner in search of a nursery that had closed years ago. I watched her walk up and down the block three times before I worked up the nerve to step in front of her.

"I'm looking for a plant that won't die easily." She acted as if our conversation had been interrupted.

"That would be a cactus," I said. "Or some other succulent. They don't need to be tended. They take what moisture they need from the air."

A cup of coffee at the original Starbucks and a bag of freshly fried doughnuts later and we'd arranged to leave together for a weekend getaway. Megumi's fiancé—the man I'd seen with her at the Pad—had left her behind while he attended a conference in Vancouver. Maybe he had a mistress up there, or a favorite brothel, or just didn't want to be encumbered. A grown man, especially an affluent one, doesn't need looking after. All I cared about was that Megumi and I were instantly familiar though we'd never spoken before that day. My grandmother says that such acquaintances mean you've met in a past life. That may be superstitious mumbo jumbo, but we shared something, and it would have been wrong not to figure out what that was.

Megumi asked me to take her somewhere I'd never been. I suggested Lake Chelan, a four-hour drive just east of the mountains, warmer and sunnier than Seattle in June. Why Chelan, vacation resort for bargain-hunting Seattleites, host to sales conferences and business "retreats"? It was where my marriage ended without me.

Mid-morning on a weekday Tanya had called from Chelan to say she was leaving. She ticked off her reasons— "growing apart," "different paths," "the absence of something that was once there"—and then told me she had to go. The conversation lasted less than three minutes. Afterward, I thought I might have nodded off while reviewing a real estate contract and dreamt the whole thing. The other paralegals typed, stapled, and collated copies. Tanya's cubicle looked the way it always did, not a pen or paperclip out of place.

Since that day, I had replayed the conversation in my head a hundred times. Not to find a hidden meaning—her words, though banal, were clear—but because it was wrong for her to end our marriage while in-between sessions at a land-use law conference. Had she scribbled an outline of what she meant to say on the back of her conference agenda?

Sometimes I pictured her calling from a cheap motel, the kind with cowboy prints on the walls, a stagnant, pee-filled wading pool, and moths swarming around the light above the outdoor ice machine. Other times I put her in a bathrobe, hair still wet from the shower, lounging on a king-sized bed while a faceless man massaged her shoulders. What about Chelan had impelled her to call immediately instead of, for courtesy's sake, for the sake of a seven-year marriage, waiting to see me in person, or at least until I had returned home from work?

Megumi met me thirty minutes late at the service entrance of the Westin Hotel. She wore pink sunglasses, a pink half-tee reading "Sporty Girl," and perfectly ironed, white denim shorts. Without makeup and in broad daylight, she looked suspiciously under-ripe. She said nothing for most of the drive; she dangled her hand outside the window to feel the rushing wind. Two-thirds of the way to Chelan, we rounded a curve at the outskirts of a single gas-pump town and nearly ran over the carcass of a deer. I braked hard and turned, and still the car thumped its muzzle.

I stopped on the shoulder of the highway to examine the damage. The front panel was crooked and deer fur was lodged in my bumper. Why hadn't the driver who'd hit the deer pulled its corpse off the road? We might have swerved into a tree, ended up dead or crippled. There was no plumbing the depths of human selfishness.

Megumi hadn't been wearing her seatbelt and didn't put it on now. She was turned around in her seat, staring at the deer. Crows had alighted on it, picking away with sharp, dark beaks.

"Do you ever feel sorry for animals left dying on the road?" she said. Her voice was pitched like a little girl's, but her tone was flat and expressionless. She had a light accent.

"I suppose I've never given it much thought," I said. The deer stared at us blankly. It's a shame no one travels the highways shutting the lids of deceased animals. "It's like when you hear about the death of someone you didn't know. You feel bad the person died and you feel bad for the family. But it's too distant to muster much feeling about."

"When do you suppose you 'muster' enough feeling for a...creature...to care whether it lives or dies?" she said.

"Oh, I don't know. My emotional litmus test might be, would I miss it if it were gone?" I thought of Tanya and felt a twinge of irritation. This was a weekend getaway. What were we doing staring at a dead deer lacerated by tire tracks?

We checked into Progresso Resort, the same place Tanya had stayed. It didn't look like anything I had imagined, yet was generic enough to feel familiar (a trait to which all good resorts aspire). A nouveau rustic lodge housed conference rooms, an espresso bar, and an overpriced restaurant. The rooms were in long, sprawling buildings, and ours, like every other, had a view of the lake through sliding glass doors. The room was stuffy—as if the late-afternoon sun had burned away the oxygen molecules.

My energy ebbed as I sat at the dinette set and watched a group of boys dive off of the dock. Their puffy, pink parents watched from reclining lawn chairs. Megumi flipped through a *Welcome to Lake Chelan* magazine.

"I'd like to shower first," she said.

She disappeared and I soon heard the squeak of knobs and water pelting skin. Steam wafted out through the open bathroom door as if emanating from another world. Why anyone insisted on taking a hot shower on a hot day was beyond me.

I waited patiently for fifteen minutes before I realized she was the type of woman who showers until her skin puckers. At a loss for something to do after turning on the air-con, drawing the curtains, and switching on the side-table lamps, I unpacked our bags.

Her clothes were so impossibly tiny I hardly needed to fold them: an XXS sunflower-print summer dress; black slacks that looked as if they had been washed and dried on high heat; cotton panties, the size of my palm, covered in stars and little duckies. Japanese women worship at the altar of cute—Hello Kitty, Pochaco, et cetera—a cultural trait that is as alluring as it is alarming.

At the forty-minute mark, she scurried in an oversized terry cloth towel to the bed. I caught a glimpse of her bare, flat frame before she slipped under the covers. The sheets were pulled up to her chin and her eyes were neutral.

I folded my socks and placed them inside my right shoe. I peeled off my T-shirt and draped it over a chair. I slipped off my khaki slacks, careful to keep the belt in the loops. I placed my wallet, car keys, and medallion on the side table. I removed my briefs and burrowed under the sheets.

She kissed me back, caressed me like a mirror image, moved her hands downward when I moved my hands downward. But in the end, she was met with flaccidity. There was nothing to do but lie on our backs and stare at the ceiling. She held my penis in one tiny hand. As if it were a frightened bird.

"So," she said. "Do you think you'll be able to do it?"

I followed a dust mote on its descent to my eyes. "No. Sorry."

"Would it help if I sucked you off?" she said. A hypothetical question, like, "Would we get there faster in a taxi?"

"No," I croaked again. My body felt like another's. A golem body. Numb.

"That's okay," she said. "It's been a long drive and your car doesn't have air conditioning. Besides. I think I prefer it this way."

She curled into my body, tension releasing like a rubber band returning to its natural shape. But is that natural shape slack or taut? She petted my hair absently.

"What is that?" she said, motioning to the bedside table.

"That," I said, reaching for the medallion's ribbon, "is just something I carry around for good luck."

She dangled the gold disk before her eyes. "'King County proudly recognizes GUY WATANABE as its first-ever Karaoke King. May his reign be a long and prosperous one.' Did you win this in a contest?" she said. She fingered the ridges of the county seal.

"Three months ago." Since then, good fortune had rained down from the sky. Summer came early. I rarely drank before dark. I had revised my resume. I was moving on with my life without Tanya. As Troy Bobbins would say, little steps taken every day will cross great divides.

"A big deal," she said.

"I suppose in karaoke circles. There are so few serious competitions. The only ones that matter take place in the karaoke capitals of the world. Tokyo. Seoul. L.A. New York. Seattle's just starting to break onto that list."

"So that's why the DJ introduced you as the Karaoke King! My fiancé said it must be sarcastic. That you must be a real loser if everyone called you that."

I winced. Her fiancé was the superior kind of Asian you met at weddings. Ethnicity? His light skin suggested Japanese like Megumi, but you never could tell with those transcontinental businessmen. Baggy, tailored suit from Hong Kong. Megumi would soon be his trophy wife. For their first anniversary, he'd buy her breast implants.

She stared into my eyes. "Your voice made me weak, you sang so beautifully that night. I looked down and anywhere else except at you so my fiancé wouldn't notice how much I was moved. I don't know if it was the alcohol, but it was as if you'd opened a door in me and stepped inside. I pretended to laugh when he made fun of your clothes, but it was just to humor him. He is jealous. And violent. I can't speak to another man without him present."

Her animal-eyes were moist and her face flushed pink. I *was* singing just for her. I *knew* she had been afraid to meet my eyes. Tell me the shape of the pain you hide, I wanted to say. But I couldn't get the image out of my mind of her immaculately dressed fiancé laughing at me.

"What was so funny about my wardrobe?" I said.

"Your wardrobe?" she asked. "He was talking about your sweatshirt and old running shoes. He said, 'Why does the Karaoke King shop secondhand?'"

What a superficial prick. His first time in the Lily Pad and he cracks on me? The kitchen was closed but he slapped down a few bills, and suddenly it was open. Why did women like Megumi settle for guys like him? Money. It's the way of the world.

"Watanabe," she said, looking at the medallion again. "Wa-tan-a-be. You're Japanese? You don't look Japanese. Your skin's so dark. You look Thai." She traced her finger on my cheek as if testing whether the color would rub off.

I'd never been described as Thai. "I'm a mishmash of Asian and some non-Asian. But no group to which I belong claims me. On the other hand, Filipino gas station owners offer me free car washes. I should change my last name to De Costa."

Her brows knit. "Can you guess what I am?" she said gravely.

Let's see, besides her *first* name and her accent, she had the light complexion and delicate features of a Japanese person, wore the cute-cute outfits of a Japanese teen, and toted a tiny, leather backpack purse. "Japanese?" I asked.

She looked down for a moment then nodded slowly. "You are perceptive," she said.

She threw off the blankets and sat bold, nude, and cross-legged atop the bed. She slid the medallion's ribbon over her head and let the large, golden disk rest between her tiny breasts. Her chest showed light pink bumps—a heat rash from the forty-minute shower.

"Is this medal very important to you?" she asked in her woman-child voice.

It meant everything and nothing. Everything, because it was a sign that my life was back on track. Nothing because it was, after all, just a trinket, albeit a high-quality one.

"I suppose I'd miss it if it were gone," I said.

She flashed her slightly buck-toothed smile and pressed the medallion against her cheek.

"Let me wear it tonight," she said.

"I'm not sure if it matches your clothes. You look like Kerri Strug at the Olympics."

"Barry who? You don't like the way it looks on me, I can tell by your expression. I'll take it off if you're sensitive." Her hands paused while gripping the ribbon.

"I think it looks gorgeous on you. Wear it if you want. Tonight or the whole weekend." Just make sure to give it back.

She threw her arms around my neck. "It's like we're married, isn't it? Except I have a secret wedding medal instead of a ring."

I half-nodded and half-shook my head. But I wasn't displeased.

At dinner Megumi ate with the appetite of those blessed with truly high metabolic rates. We said little until dessert. She finished off nearly the entire, monstrous slab of chocolate-pecan cheesecake and then squished back into the leather seat like a snake that had swallowed a gazelle. Her eyelids drooped and I wondered whether we should head back to our room. I could perform sleep with ease.

"Are you excited about getting married?" I asked as we waited for the check.

She shrugged, the points of her shoulders reaching almost above her seashell ears. "It's a long way off. Who knows what will happen?"

Time for some shut-eye, I thought. But she perked up when we rose to leave. "Can we go karaoke singing?" she asked.

Karaoke singing? Perhaps that would put us both in the right mood.

The concierge—a wide-hipped, pimply twenty-year-old blonde about twice Megumi's size—said there was an upscale karaoke lounge forty-five minutes drive from the resort. Megumi frowned.

"Isn't there anything closer?" I asked.

"Yes. Um. No," the concierge said. I arched an eyebrow. She added, "Yes. Mr. Frog's is just down the street. But you don't want to go there. It doesn't have the right, um, ambiance." She chewed on the tip of her ballpoint pen.

I glanced at Megumi; her face had brightened. Mr. Frog's it was.

CHAPTER 3

Although the resort's pub teemed with Seattle conference-goers laughing over their microbrews, Main Street, only paces away, was deserted. A solitary teen in an apron swept the sidewalk in front of a café. Mr. Frog's windows were blacked out and only the faintest aroma of music seeped from the battered doors. No cars were parked out front, but a raised pickup truck clattered out of the neighboring alley.

I could imagine square dancers whirling around Mr. Frog's cavernous main room, do-si-do-ing around the wooden pillars gouged, discolored, and reeking from years of absorbed hamburger grease. At the far end was a dance floor, a stage, TV monitors, and an enormous projection screen, but the clientele looked as if it had been plucked from a nineteenth-century daguerreotype of the western frontier. The men at the bar had the hunted, haunted look of lumberjacks, their own brutal efficiency killing their profession. The ones at the tables were in better spirits—there was enough alcohol to make their desiccated girlfriends seem attractive for a few hours.

Megumi made a beeline for a vacant table in the center of the room. I chased her, weaving between chairs, legs, and large posteriors, sensing predatory eyes upon us. I lowered my voice.

"We're the only non-white people here," I said. "I think we're the only tourists too."

"Oh?" Megumi turned her chair around to face the stage.

A peroxide blonde was singing "Like a Virgin." She swayed like a listing ship tied to dock by the microphone cord. She rubbed her jeans and moaned the words.

"Do you want to go somewhere else?" I said to the back of Megumi's head.

"I would love a drink," she said.

I sighed. "Any drink in particular?"

"I'll have whatever you're having."

"Then I'll be right back."

She waved dismissively. "Could you see if they have nachos?"

As I picked my way across the room, another performer took the stage. He was a boar of a man, squat with a receding hairline that resembled a monk's tonsure. When the keyboard refrain of "Centerfold" boomed out, the crowd roared.

She was pure like snowflakes
No one could ever stain
The memory of my angel
Could never cause me pain

The television monitors displayed thirty-something cheerleaders bouncing in slow motion. The bartender, a bulky man in a dirty apron, was riveted to the karaoke video.

"Pardon me," I said. "I wanted to get a drink if I could." I gave him a confident, masculine nod.

He ambled away to the other end of the bar. He began wiping mugs with a filthy rag.

I looked at the other men. No one looked away from the video. Pursuing the bartender, I noticed the eyes of a man with a handlebar mustache following me in the mirror. I cleared my throat twice. The bartender craned his neck to watch the video over my shoulder.

"Barney," the man with the handlebar mustache said. "Why don't you get the man a drink? Can't you see he's come a long way?"

Barney opened his mouth, then thought better of it. He grimaced at the other man.

"What'll it be, Seattle?" the bartender said.

"Two Vodka Collins, please."

"All right. Two vodka tonics."

"Actually, I said 'Vodka Collins,' not 'vodka tonics.' I understand the confusion, they sound similar." I chuckled conspiratorially. And alone.

"We don't do Vodka Collins here."

"They're simple. Vodka, sour mix, and a splash of soda. You can leave off the garnish if you want." I anticipated the drink's cool tart bite.

"Would you like to choose the vodka?"

"Belvedere?"

"All we have is Fleischmann's."

"I guess I'll have that then." My stomach clenched as he poured vodka from a two-liter, plastic bottle.

"Two vodka tonics," he said, shoving the glasses forward. Paper umbrellas floated on top, one pink and one blue.

"Thanks. Keep the change." I placed a twenty-dollar bill on the bar. The bartender ignored it, as if it were a soggy paper napkin.

"I got you a vodka tonic," I said, slipping into my seat. Megumi snatched the drink and returned her attention to the stage. She clapped so enthusiastically for pig-man the people around us stared. A discerning karaoke fan she wasn't.

Well, I thought, flipping through the karaoke menu, at least the bar had an extensive song list. The key was picking the right song for this audience. Prince was a definite no-no. I picked up a pencil and a request slip.

When a tall, solidly built blond man took the stage, the crowd grew silent. He had movie-star good looks—a square jaw, a broad smile. He was dressed like the others but strutted like a bantam rooster to the microphone. Megumi's body stiffened.

I jabbed the ice in my drink with the blue umbrella. Good-looking men don't always sing well. Sure, he had stage presence, but that's just charisma and genetic good fortune. My drink tasted like alcoholic mouthwash mixed with silt. I spit out what I could on a deteriorating napkin. Onstage, Mr. Goodlooking said, "This song is for you lovers out there."

I expected a sappy karaoke standard to drip from his mouth—"Unchained Melody" or "Smoke Gets In Your Eyes." He surprised me.

The familiar chords of "Sundown" by Gordon Lightfoot filled the room. Great song, though infrequently sung in karaoke bars. I clapped in appreciation, but no one followed suit. Odd. I would have pegged the song to be a winner here.

Sundown, you better take care
If I find you been creepin' 'round my back-
stairs

A drunk couple stumbled to the dance floor and were tongue-wrestling immediately. Good old Gordon. Nothing like Canadian country music, eh? I chewed the end of the stubby pencil. What song would impress Megumi?

"I'm going to the ladies' room," Megumi said.

"I'm going to submit 'Brown Eyed Girl.' Get it? It's for you." I touched her hand. It was cold.

"Thank you." Megumi drained her glass and walked off. Her empty tumbler contained a soapy residue. A cast-iron stomach, I decided. Which reminded me: I had forgotten to ask about nachos. How could she still be hungry? A few songs to put us both in the mood and we could retire to our room to order room service.

I can picture every move
that a man could make
Getting lost in her lovin' is your first mistake

Sundown, you better take care
If I find you been creepin'
'round my backstairs
Sometimes I think it's a sin

When I feel like I'm winnin'
when I'm losin' again

Well, he could definitely sing—pitch-perfect, as if he were lip-synching. He had a way of making you feel he was singing directly to you.

"D'ya wanna dance?" a smoke-choked voice said. Her bilious breath made my eyelids flutter. It was the blond Madonna fan. Up close, she looked to be between thirty and fifty. Fifty in terms of alcohol consumption; thirty in terms of calendar years. Her mammaries strained against her T-shirt like eggplants yearning to breathe free.

"I'm waiting for a friend to return."

She swung her face to within an inch of mine. There was a scab on her right eyelid. "I don't need this SHIT!" she shouted. She stumbled off.

I looked around in embarrassment, but no one appeared to have noticed. A few tables away, she tripped and fell across boar-man's lap. He shoved her to the ground, where the crack of her bouncing head was drowned out by the music. A brunette splashed beer on her upturned face. Moments later, the handlebar-mustache man was there. He slipped his arm under her shoulders and led her away.

Not my type of karaoke bar, I decided. I was accustomed to more Asians and less violence.

The next song was new country, maybe Tim What's-his-name. The song after that was more of the same. What was taking Megumi so long?

Someone slipped into Megumi's seat. It was Mr. Good-looking. His complexion was perfect and his stubble was a uniform length. The inner creases of his face were as tanned as the rest of his face, neck, and hands—an almost orange hue.

"I'm sorry," I said. "My lady friend will be returning from the restroom at any moment."

He folded his arms and leaned back. "I know whose seat this was." A smile twitched at the corners of his thin lips. "You look thirsty. Let me buy you a drink. Vodka Collins, right?"

Recognition tickled the nape of my neck. He must have eavesdropped on the debacle at the bar. You can't back down in places like this; I should have insisted on the right drink. Now this joker was trying to rub it in.

"Barney," he called out. He waved, but the bartender was already shuffling over with a tray. As the two glasses were set down (*sans* umbrellas but *avec* orange slices and cherries), the man said, "Barney makes the best Vodka Collins in the Pacific Northwest. Don't you, Barney?" Barney waddled back to his station without uttering a word. "He does, you know," he assured me.

"Look, um . . ."

"John," he said.

"Look, John. I would be much obliged if you moved over to that empty seat."

John sipped his drink, a broad smile spreading across his face as he closed his eyes. "Barney has outdone himself. This Vodka Collins is truly delish! Please, Guy, take a sip. You won't be sorry."

How did he know my name? Delish? Who was this fruitcake?

"I don't know who you are or how you know me, but I'm serious…"

"John."

"What?"

"You know who I am. John. Please, Guy. Don't deprive yourself. Take a sip."

Was he mentally unstable? I scooped up my drink. What did they say about paranoid schizophrenics? Don't look them in the eyes. Move slowly. But he hardly looked prepared to attack me. He acted as if we were sipping iced tea on a veranda instead of in a karaoke bar that smelled like a human barn.

The Vodka Collins was just the right mixture. Refreshing. Tangy. Okay, so it was the best Vodka Collins I had ever tasted. And I had tasted a lot.

"Better," he said. "Isn't that better? Let's just take it easy now. One step at a time. We have so much to cover and so little time."

"Look, John, I…"

He waggled his finger. "The recipe for a Vodka Collins is simple, but so few can mix one well. The bartender's personal predilections intervene and then what do you have? Gasoline. A Vodka Collins is a Vodka Collins is a Vodka Collins, whether it's served in Chelan or Shanghai. Am I right, Guy? But without people like me, the uniform quality standard suffers." He sighed into his drink, broad shoulders drooping. I couldn't help but feel a touch of sympathy. Whatever his professional duties were, they weighed heavily upon him.

"Although," he continued, brightening again, "without challenges there would be no *opportunities*. Am I right, Guy?"

"I really wouldn't know," I said noncommittally.

"No, no. I suppose you wouldn't. Nothing you've done has shown you understand that. From what can be gathered, you haven't done anything of significance since your divorce and maybe since your birth. Except running off with my employer's fiancée. And that was a grave mistake."

A bead of sweat dribbled down my neck to join the puddle at my lower back. I sipped my drink as coolly as I could manage. My hands were perfectly steady, but pressure was building in my sinuses.

"I'm not sure I understand what you're talking about," I said.

"Don't fuck with me, Guy," he said in a low don't-fuck-with-me tone. "You nearly killed her on the highway earlier. What are you, blind? Was there something about the big '35 M-P-H' sign you didn't understand?"

"It was only two hundred yards to the end of the speed zone," I said.

"What kind of answer is that? You're not even pleading a technicality. You just admitted you were wrong."

"Legally wrong. But the act wasn't wrong in and of itself. It was made wrong because of an arbitrary speed limit posted on a deserted stretch of highway." It felt as if my head was filling up with molten lead. This was a bad time to start getting migraines.

"Whatever, Guy. The fact is you were wrong in more ways than one. And now you must pay. Cause and effect. The law of karma. Surely you can understand that." His teeth were perfectly even, white enamel scored with black pen.

I wanted to knock those teeth in. In fact, as I drained my glass, I gripped it more tightly in preparation of doing just that. "Cause and effect I can believe in. I don't believe in karma. It's just superstition. People do all sorts of bad things that go unpunished. Pointing to some kind of cosmic balance in a next life is a cop-out. You can't displace sins and good deeds onto eternity, as if anyone would change their behavior for fear of being reborn as a frog instead of a king. Punishment and reward are entirely personal and are never distributed fairly."

"Call it whatever you like, Guy. But you're going to pay." He steepled his hands. His nails were perfectly manicured.

"Megumi came here because she wanted to. She's an adult. This is a free country. She's not even married yet. Mess with me and I'll call the police. You and your boss will be the ones in trouble." Right across the bridge of his perfectly shaped nose. As soon as he twitched to reach for me.

"Let's play out your scenario, Guy. The police arrive to question her, let's say, at a five-star hotel in Los Angeles. Or at her penthouse condominium in Shanghai. She'll say, 'Thank goodness you're here. I wanted to run away with that unemployed divorcé. The one who spends all day doing nothing and every night at a dumpy, neighborhood karaoke joint.'"

"I suppose you have a point," I said. The bastard. The Lily Pad wasn't dumpy.

"By the way, Guy. How are you feeling right now? I mean physically."

I was feverish, out of breath, couldn't focus. But I wasn't about to tell him the truth. Make one move, I dared him mentally. I could feel his cartilage crumpling beneath the glass tumbler. "I feel feverish and out of breath. I'm having a hard time focusing on your words."

"Good." He rested his cheek in his palm. "Now why don't you put your glass down on the table. That's it. Now unclench your fists. That's a good boy. Concentrate on what I'm saying. I don't like to repeat myself."

"You've drugged me, haven't you?" I said. I wanted to spit the sentence out venomously, but my voice was a tinny transistor radio playing in the park.

"Isn't that obvious? Barney's never mixed a Vodka Collins in his short, dim life. Though, to be fair, who really needs to in a bar like this? For future reference: anything containing more than two ingredients is a sissy drink." He glanced at the Cartier wristwatch tucked beneath the cuff of his ironed flannel shirt. "Time's almost up."

"What is this?" I said. My brain tissue felt abraded, my consciousness a peel being torn from the fleshy fruit.

"Scopolamine. Quite popular among home robbery gangs in Colombia. It's more of a date rape drug here—those crazy college kids. Zombie effect: a compliant stupor. Only a mild risk of recurring psychotic episodes or brain damage. Just relax. Don't get distracted by the background noise. Focus on my voice so you hurt only yourself."

I concentrated on the air moving shallowly in and out of my chest. Stay present, I thought as the cords tethering my consciousness snapped one by one.

"Where are you taking her?" I croaked.

"Back to where she belongs." He leaned forward and peered at me, as if I were under a microscope. "Let me ask you a question, Guy." Bright blue eyes. Are they real, I wondered, or colored contact lenses? "Don't you ever get tired of the way you live? Day to day with no purpose? It's not a judgment. Live and let live, I say. I'm just conducting market research.

44

"Guy? Keep your focus, Guy. Don't you ever feel like an insect? Buzz, buzz, buzz. Not knowing, not caring when you'll be swatted. What difference would it make?"

I buzzed about the reeds of a stagnant pond. Countless grubs wriggled in murky fluid. From whose eggs had they sprung? Would they live or be swallowed by lizards? Who cared? Live and let live, I say.

He snapped his fingers. "Guy! Stay with me, Guy! For goodness sake, I've seen girls half your size take larger doses and still have more fight in them. We better get this show on the road. Stand up. That's it. Follow me and stay close behind."

"What if I don't do as you say?" I mumbled, following him as closely as I could.

"Then I'll shoot you, of course."

At the edge of the stage, just before taking the micro-phone, I managed, "Why are you doing this?"

"Weren't you listening? I'm sure she told you her fiancé is a jealous man. Violently jealous. She always tells them that. Makes her feel better somehow. It's like a warning label on a pharmaceutical bottle. Who's to blame if you were fully informed?"

The spotlight was so bright the room appeared to be populated by shadows, vague murmuring creatures flitting about an echo chamber. But as the wait for the next song became longer, they grew quieter. Until sound was swallowed by their humid collective breath.

Sing-sing-sing, said the voice in my head. Why wouldn't I sing, I replied. I lived for singing and a bottomless well of Vodka Collins. Or was it vodka tonics? Vodka gimlets? Whatever it was, I liked singing. What had I requested tonight? The TV monitor flickered and the first karaoke video rolled.

"Chains of Love," by Erasure.

Nothing wrong with that song. Eighties flashbacks are always popular. "Chains of Love" had spent weeks at the top of the charts, back when synth pop was fresh.

Come to me, cover me, hold me
Together we'll break these chains of love

I'd never sung it before but it felt good coming out. I was loose, relaxed. Could hit the high notes at the edge of my range, "*To-GE-ther with ME and my baby break these chains of love.*" I would have brought the house down at the Lily Pad with that rendition. But when the video ended—it was set in a factory where shirtless, sweaty men cranked cylindrical machines with enormous wrenches—the room was silent.

Sweat stung my eyes and dripped into my mouth. After a moment, a husky male voice said, "Well, that really sucked!" The crowd hooted and clapped.

"Why don't you sing another one just like that, sissy-boy?" said a man with the voice of a pig. Or was it a pig with the voice of a man?

I had no choice. The next karaoke video was already flashing on the screen.

"Karma Chameleon," by Culture Club.

Funky, opening guitar riff. Distinctive harmonica run. I've never much cared for the song as a whole. It always struck me as too, too…cloying? No, that wasn't the right word.

A loud rumbling grew among the shadows—it became a grating screech like the shifting of a tectonic plate. The sonic tide of song swirled about me and I had to stay focused on singing.

I'm a man without conviction
I'm a man who does not know
How to sell a contradiction
You come and go
You come and go

Karma karma karma karma
karma chameleon

Wasn't I just talking about karma with someone? What about karma? Oh yeah. I didn't believe in it. The video monitor flashed chameleons in red, gold, and green. With long, sticky tongues, they snapped up insects.

Something cold and hard struck my cheek. Another caught my top lip. Another my chest. I found the right nouns. "Ice." "Coins." Those would have hurt if they had struck me instead of striking me.

The end of the song brought not quiet but a jumble of voices. As if someone had unmuted a television set and the volume was set for ten.

"Go back to Seattle, you fudge-packing faggot!" squealed the man-pig.

"Get off the stage before I beat your fairy ass, you goddamned Chink!" another said.

Only part-Chinese, I thought as the next song cued up. To white people, I was either a Chink or a Jap. Ah, well. I had a song to sing.

"Do You Really Want to Hurt Me?" by Culture Club.

Had I committed this karaoke club *faux pas?* One *never* sings two songs by the same artist in a row. I swiveled my hips to the Boy Georgean, bossa nova beat.

This time it wasn't ice and coins that pelted me; it was elbows and fists. I was a rock buffeted by waves, a bee hive struck by a rake. I gave myself up to the crowd and floated to the top like foam on beer. Yelps of anger; squeals of pain; hairy, pink faces filmed in sweat.

My consciousness receded on a muddy riptide. Focus, Guy. Focus. On the words? No. On the song? No. On the girl?

The air outdoors was bracing after the farm sauna. The mud flap of a pickup truck showed the silhouette of a naked lady. Where had all these cars come from? Fluid filled my mouth, as if I'd bitten down on a balloon filled with sea water. Focus, Guy. On asphalt? No. On hard, riveted boot heels? No. On the girl. On the dark cavern into which I was tumbling.

CHAPTER 4

Hovering above was the face of a man with a handlebar mustache, the ends waxed into curling commas. The sun had scored lines on his forehead and brackets around his eyes.

"Are you back with us for good?" His breath was a puff of freshly ground coffee.

I gagged. The man put a tumbler to my lips, the fluid dribbling onto my tongue, cool with an earthy undertone of peach. He dabbed my chin with a hand towel.

"Where am I?" Pain lanced up from my groin to my swollen cheek. I was lying in a room with a vaulted ceiling and crisscrossed wood beams.

He straightened on the stool. Behind him, clutching the tail of his checkered work shirt, was a girl, half of her face hidden, her blond hair matted. Her lip curled open to bare a sharp fang.

"Among friends," he said.

Billy placed damp hand towels on my forehead. He supported me when I stumbled to the restroom. He nursed me back to health without pressing for answers. He was, in other words, inherently suspicious.

At least the feral five-year-old did her best to make me feel unwelcome. Stacked near the wood-burning stove were art materials—sketch paper, crayons, watercolors—which she ignored in favor of ballpoint pens and rectangular pads emblazoned with photographs of local real estate agents. One of her creative works found its way to my pillow. Beneath the smiling faces of a husband-and-wife sales team—defaced by mustaches and blacked-out teeth—was a truck running over a stick figure, blood and guts spilling out in red ballpoint ink.

"I've seen your friend around Mr. Frog's," Billy said over breakfast. I could stomach nothing stronger than toast and chamomile tea, but he and May ate buttermilk pancakes. Billy paused to tell May, for the third time, to use her fork instead of her hands. "He's a good-looking man and nice enough, but there's something off about him. Rumor has it he's the bar owner's son. He barks orders at Barney and pokes around the sound equipment and inventory."

"He's not my friend," I said. He was a hoodlum, a toady for Megumi's fiancé.

Billy stroked his mustache. "You remember much from the night? After your non-friend kissed you, I mean."

Billy's voice had an even, reassuring quality about it, and made the events of the night sound like a bass-fishing trip. He left the bar shortly after the Culture Club cued up. May's mother, Lizzie, had passed out in a pool of vomit near the ladies' room. He was loading her into his truck when the back door opened and a crowd spilled into the parking lot.

"It looked like a celebration, everybody hooting and hollering and jumping up and down. Then I noticed they weren't dancing; they were stomping. On you. If it hadn't been for the bar stool, I never would have reached you."

"You threatened them with a bar stool?" I said.

Billy shook his head. "No, someone meant to break open your head with a bar stool. But he missed. It splintered and the mob was going to use its legs to skewer you. A gunshot caused the entire congregation to freeze.

"It was Barney, holding a smoking shotgun in his hand, his apron still wrapped around his waist. 'Who's the bastard who broke that barstool?' he said. 'You can't run around busting up personal property! Every single one of you sons-of-bitches is going to pay for that.'"

May watched me with an idiotic smirk on her face, her little monkey brain reveling, no doubt, in the account of my suffering. Billy poured more hot water into my cup.

"Out here, brother, you've got to be more discreet," he said. "Seattle this ain't."

I coughed, which sent spasms through my rib cage. I didn't have the energy to contradict him. What did it matter what a stranger presumed? Billy didn't push me any further. He cleared the table. I dozed off to the rumble of the dishwasher. When I awoke, Billy was sitting on the stool next to my cot, tractor cap pulled low over his eyes. May stood near the door, a backpack slung over her shoulders.

"I've got some appointments at the boat shop I couldn't cancel," Billy said. "I'll drop May off with her mother on the way out. Spare house keys are on the kitchen table, though there's not much within walking distance. Tuna fish sandwich and a salad in the fridge. Drink plenty of juice."

I dragged myself into the restroom. Billy had set out a towel and a change of clothing for me: an oversized Harley Davidson T-shirt and baggy orange sweatpants. They were almost identical to the oversized Harley Davidson T-shirt and baggy black sweats I was already wearing. My own clothes had bloodstains and boot prints that wouldn't wash out.

Dropping my circus-sized clothing to the floor, I gazed at myself in the dressing mirror. My torso was festooned with abrasions, scabs, and bruises. I wouldn't have imagined it possible to look worse than I felt. I stayed in the tub until the bubbles were gone and all that remained were skin flakes suspended in murky water.

Had the progress I'd made since Tanya left been a lie? What if my wounds had never healed but instead lay dormant, had always been on the verge of resurfacing?

Tanya wanted to change my wardrobe. Neither of us made much money as paralegals, yet she gave me "little presents" as if she'd commandeered a Banana Republic boatload of khaki slacks, wool pullovers, and golf shirts. If I didn't wear one of the ensembles at dinner, she'd barely talk until dessert arrived.

Once we moved in together, Tanya woke early to set out my day's clothing. Piece by piece, other things of mine disappeared: first, a pair of jeans torn at the seat; next a sweatshirt with a cranberry juice stain. If I asked, she'd say something dismissive about thievery in the laundry room.

I never made it an issue because, deep down inside, I suspected she was right. My hole-filled socks and grass-stained sweats suggested a disguised internal rot.

Three months after we'd moved in together, I woke parched in the middle of the night. I weighed whether a glass of water was worth the barefoot trek over the kitchen linoleum. Tanya's side of the bed was vacant.

Was she having an affair? The thought popped into my head though she'd given me no reason, at that time, to suspect anything was amiss. It was my unguarded subconscious speaking, the part of me that always knew she was out of my league. When my eyes adjusted to the darkness, I made out a figure hunched over at the dresser.

Tanya extracted T-shirts from the middle drawer, socks and underwear from the top drawer, and dropped them into a trash bag. She left the bedroom with her loot. The garbage chute was outside of the apartment, at the end of the hallway. She returned minutes later and crawled into bed. Puffs of breath tickled my cheek as she examined me for signs of stirring.

The next day, Tanya gave me a new outfit. "Do you *love* it?" she said.

"I think it's great. Very clean and very new."

"But you don't *love* it?" She flattened out the gift boxes and stuffed them, along with the gift wrap and colored tissue, into a garbage bag.

"I'm sure I'll grow to love it," I said.

She shrugged and made off for the recycling bin. She was obsessive about clearing waste. We went through garbage bags the way others go through paper towels.

I picked up a book and stretched out on the couch. She returned and scooched herself with a jolly bounce beneath my feet. She tweaked my big toe playfully.

"Just not the flannel shirt," I said.

She flipped through a magazine. A full thirty seconds later she said, "What are you talking about?"

"I'd like to keep at least one thing. From before."

Tanya didn't respond. A few minutes later, she stood, stretched, and went to the kitchen for a glass of water. Then she disappeared behind the bedroom door.

The next day none of my old clothes remained except for that flannel shirt. We got married the following year. When we returned from our honeymoon, even my flannel shirt was gone.

The Progresso Resort threw my clothes away. What's more, they had the gall to call it a "donation to the under-privileged." My car, its windshield shattered and its tires slashed, had been towed away.

"Please look at it from our perspective," the manager said, a relief map of South America in puffy red pimples spreading across his cheek. "We tried to check you out of the room, but your credit card was denied. We tried to call your residence, but no one answered. Although the Progresso Resort supports charities, we are not one ourselves."

I told him to run my credit card again. Then I had him run the credit card I keep in my wallet for emergencies. I had him run my debit card. Everything was refused. The stares of the well-heeled guests bored into my back.

"Sir," the manager said. "There are a number of organizations that can lend you assistance. If you can hold on one moment, I'll get you their addresses."

Blood rushed to my ears. "Just give me the address of the tow lot. I don't need any other kind of help."

I'd told Billy that he didn't have to wait for me, but there he was when I emerged from the resort's reception building. His oversized Chevy truck, a modified bulbous monstrosity he called "Big Red," was parked in two handicapped spots. As soon as I'd clambered into the passenger seat, he revved up the petroleum-guzzling engine. I handed him the tow lot's address.

Billy nodded. "That's Sebastian's place. Don't worry, we'll be able to work out something that won't lighten your pocketbook too much."

What kind of man has the power to freeze another man's assets? I pondered that question on the thirty-mile drive outside of town, a drive made longer by my intestinal distress. Broad green fields stretched out below the highway, but all I could focus on was the blue Porta Potty in the gully. I descended a steep slope to get there and startled a flock of migrant workers in long sleeves and hats.

It couldn't get any worse than this, hunched over in a plastic outhouse, serenaded in Spanish by people I should never have learned existed. A stellar credit rating had survived the divorce, due in large part to Tanya's profligate spending habits. No matter how rich and powerful Megumi's fiancé was, how could he wave his hand and make my hard-earned 0% interest loans vanish?

Faith Auto Body and Tow looked closed, its corrugated iron doors shut, a mud-splattered tow truck parked out front next to a wood-paneled station wagon and a rusted Datsun 240Z on blocks. As we pulled up, a slender black man in shirt sleeves stepped out of a side door. He took Billy's extended hand and brought him into a bear hug. The man was old, the white fuzz on his head contrasting with motile, liquid eyes.

Billy asked about Sebastian's grandchildren. Years back they'd been part of an interfaith delegation to Washington, DC. Sebastian squinted at my injuries, then clapped me on the shoulder with a strength that belied his scrawny frame.

"Those Presbyterians are always on the lookout for friends in need," he said. "Baptists, we praise the Lord and host barbeques."

Sebastian cranked open a garage door. My CRX looked as if it had been rolled during the WTO protests. The length of the car was scratched and the rear quarter panels were dented. I would have been angry if I weren't so forlorn about my ability to pay for repairs. The cosmetics I could forget about. But the tires and the windshield! There was a jumble of wires where I used to insert my key.

"You're lucky you came by when you did," Sebastian said. "I was going to have the Mexican boys strip it down for parts to sell on eBay. Internet's where the big money is. I don't know why I waste my time fixing things when you can make more tearing them apart. There's a huge market for foreign rice-ers."

Sebastian prattled about new rims and how cheaply he could get me panels that would make my car look "just like those import magazines with the girls on the cover."

I raised my hand. "How much to make it drivable?"

Sebastian looked at me archly. "Where's your pride, man! The only woman who'd climb into a car that looks like this would charge you hourly."

"That's all I want," I said. "That's all I need."

One of Sebastian's eyelids began twitching.

"Guy," Billy said. "Can I talk to you for a second?"

Billy placed his hand on the small of my back and led me a few paces away. Sebastian polished the hood of a vintage Pontiac Firebird and muttered to himself.

"Sebastian's a widower with no mortgage and plenty of time," Billy said. "He'll have your car looking and running as good as new for less than what any other garage would charge just for the repairs. A few Mexican kids work in the garage in exchange for lodging, use of the shop tools, and spare parts."

"How much will it cost?" I said.

"How much can you afford?"

I stared at my sneakers. While I was unconscious, Billy had washed them. The blood stains were now light brown droplets. "I should leave the car here and find another way home."

Billy studied me. "Let me take care of it."

"No," I said. "I can't accept that."

"Can't you pay me back once you straighten things out in Seattle?"

"No," I said. "I mean, yes. But you don't know a thing about me. You might think I need help, but what if I had it coming to me? Helping me makes as much sense as throwing your money at someone who claims to have left his insulin shots inside a locked car that drove away."

"I've fallen for that one." Billy shrugged. "But why don't you let me worry about that?"

Billy and Sebastian talked outside of my earshot. Sebastian kicked at the dirt and gestured in my direction. He didn't return to say goodbye. He reentered the office through the side door, not bothering to shut the garage door.

"How much?" I said, feeling the crassness of my question but unable to resist asking.

"A hull repair and repainting," Billy said. "A few odd jobs to be determined. Sebastian won't take my money, but he'll take my labor. It's like an open service order."

We climbed back into Big Red and rolled out of the rutted parking lot.

"But how much do I owe you?" I said.

"Depends. What kind of talents do you have?"

I stared out the window at the passing fields below the highway. I didn't know what crops were grown there, just that they were green. Only by chance did I discover that a community of invisible migrants worked them.

I knew how to arrange legal binders and get documents to the printer in time for the evening mail drop. And I knew how to sing…or at least I did. Since that night, I hadn't felt like myself at all. Or actually, I felt like my old self. I reached into my pocket for the medallion but grasped only lint.

"I don't know," I said.

Billy winked. "I'm sure we'll figure out something."

The dining room was dimly lit by candles and an incandescent lamp in the corner of the living room. I felt queasy,

Harold Taw

drowsy and, having lost the entire contents of my stomach in several painful heaves, empty. Billy sat for several minutes, listening to the clock's pendulum mark time.

Billy looked out the window. "You have a beautiful voice."

I meant to say thank you, but by the time I realized that it might be rude not to respond, the time for saying had passed. A part of me had broken off and drifted away in the current. I followed Billy's gaze. Outside a waning crescent moon was barely visible amongst the stars.

I closed my eyes and opened them again. "I think I've lost something."

Billy blew at his coffee, though it had cooled long ago, and studied the dark surface. "So have we all."

I tucked myself into the layers of comforters on the cot. May's hostile presence would have been welcome. With just the two of us, the silences suffocated. Billy paused at the hallway.

"Do you know what you'd like to do?" Billy's voice sounded like the crackle of fall leaves underfoot. The solitary rigidity of his posture made me feel forlorn.

"I think I need time to think," I said.

"Take all the time you need," he said. I listened as he padded down the hallway and shut his bedroom door.

"Pain has a secret lesson for you." That's what Troy Bobbins would say. But what if I'd already learned all I wanted to from pain? What if pain's secret lesson was that pain was followed by more pain?

59

CHAPTER 5

Through slit eyelids, I watched Billy prepare an elaborate breakfast for two, and then wait for me long past the time he should have left for work. *Go*, I willed him from my cot. *Leave already.* I wanted to click my heels and return to Seattle. No more charity, no more hospitality.

Billy read the paper. He drank two cups of coffee. He cleared his dishes on tiptoe. Finally, he scribbled a note. He creased his face in my direction and sighed. Then he grabbed his work boots and exited the house in his socks.

What would Troy Bobbins do? PATH: *Prioritize, Arrest doubt, Think positively, Hammer away!* Fine, Troy. Just not now. Today let me enjoy the oblivion of the unconscious and the elite who sponsor meditation retreats. My scabs kept me shifting and scratching all morning. When I'd settled down enough to fall asleep, my solitude was interrupted.

Billy forgot to mention that Liz had a key to his house. She headed straight to the table, her daughter May in tow, and scarfed down the cold remnants of the breakfast Billy had left for me. Only after Lizzie and her progeny had also devoured the turkey and avocado club sandwich that had been my intended lunch did she jerk her head in my direction.

"That him?" she asked May.

May smirked. I recalled the girl's line drawings and my body ached in sympathy. I'd found other sketches scattered around Billy's cottage. In one, a stick figure was tied on the bumpers of two vehicles heading in opposite directions. In another, a steamroller was flattening a stick figure's body. May made liberal use of her red ballpoint pen.

I made conspicuous waking noises. Liz started talking at me as if she'd known I'd been pretending to sleep all along.

Where are your clothes, she barked. Torn up, stained, I said, and the rest donated to the Salvation Army. Why are you wearing *that*, she asked. I glanced down at my baggy outfit and shrugged. Comfort, I said. I didn't note their additional advantage of not sticking to my sores.

Liz shouldn't have offered fashion advice. Her blindingly white bikini top highlighted her bulbous breasts, yes, but also the leathery texture of her parchment-paper skin. In her peroxide-blond hair was a plastic daisy, and slung low on her hips was a floral sarong. She was an inland island girl…a sailor's drunken reality. And why would any mother dress a five-year-old in a mesh tank top and orange short-shorts? Why not stick a cigarette between May's lips and send her to the trailer for beer?

How we ended up sunbathing on a deserted stretch of the lakeshore is simple. Lizzie commanded it, and I didn't counter with an excuse quickly enough. Doffing her sarong, Lizzie smeared coconut oil on her body and lay face up in the midday sun. May dragged an empty paint bucket and a metal trowel off toward the lake—I hoped not to bury defenseless frogs alive. Beneath the beach umbrella I wrapped a towel around my shoulders and waved away the horse flies that swarmed my oozing wounds.

"So what's your story? You a 'filmmaker' too?" Lizzie's voice was raspy, Lauren Bacall with bronchitis.

"I'm retired." Retired until I was forced to find another job.

Liz propped herself up on her elbows. "Hah! Billy sure can pick 'em, that's for sure. Retired."

She rolled onto her stomach and, to my dismay, undid the strap on her bikini top. "Put some oil on my back. I can't reach—" she motioned with a contorted arm to her spine, "here." I hesitated. "Come on. You afraid of what Billy might say? I don't got cooties."

The brown bottle, labeled "Tropical Breeze," was slippery; the twist-cap was gummy and hard to pry off. The gunk oozed into my palm, redolent with synthetic coconut musk. I rubbed my palms together, then placed them on Lizzie's back. She exhaled in satisfaction.

Lizzie's back was scrawny, her spine and ribs poking through slackened skin. Rubbing oil on her was like fondling chicken bones in wax paper. This was in contrast to her fleshy breasts that, even pressed beneath her, retained a perfectly globular shape.

"You carry a lot of tension in your back." I kneaded the lumpy sinews beneath her shoulder blades with my thumbs. She gave an "ungh" of assent, so I continued.

"You'll never know if you're meant to be with a woman until you try," she said.

My fingers kept skidding onto her vertebrae. "Mm," I said noncommittally. I retreated to my low-slung beach chair.

Lizzie rolled over and sat up. As she refastened her top, she let it drop for a moment, letting out an "oops!" A single nipple popped out, a pinched plum-colored nub. Then it was behind fabric, a mere protrusion. She smirked. "That's what Karl said, the sweet talker. World traveler. Hah! Billy wasn't the only one he fooled."

Off in the distance, a boat puttered southward, tourists with binoculars hanging over the side railings. The scent of artificial coconut essence was killing me, and I wondered if it would ever wash off my hands. "Who's Karl?"

Liz cupped her hands under her breasts and examined them. She lay back on her towel and stretched. "Who's Karl? What kind of question is that? May's father. You're wearing his clothes, aren't you?"

Liz fell asleep in the sun, leaving me to wonder whether the progress of skin cancer was an observable phenomenon. I slipped into my tennis shoes and hurried to the Porta Potty. Afterward I walked to the lake. I tossed a rock into the water and dark fish darted away.

Far off in the distance, the snow-capped Cascades were visible, while at the lakeshore it was sweltering. Beautiful place this, if it weren't so damned hot all the time. Give me a dreary Seattle November over this any day. That's when I realized, May was nowhere to be found. No paint bucket, no garden trowel, no May.

I circled back to our encampment. No May. I walked fifty yards in one direction, backtracked, and walked fifty yards in the other direction. No May. I hiked a hundred yards to the road, where Lizzie's Yugo hunched on the shoulder, bird crap and tree sap speckling the paint and windshield. No sign of May.

I was hurrying through the woods back to the lakeshore when, in the corner of my eye, I glimpsed an orange and pink speck far off amidst the shadows of the trees. I sped in that direction, slackening my pace only as I came within earshot. May squatted next to her bucket, tears streaming down her face.

"Are you hurt? Did you fall?" I crouched next to her.

The trowel sat atop a shallow indentation. Next to this was a tiny pile of dirt; next to that was the corpse of a sparrow. It had been dead for days, its eyes having been eaten away by insects. Something had gnawed at its neck; its head was attached by a flap of skin.

I reached forward to poke the carcass and my hand was slapped. May bared her teeth and hissed, the points of her vampire incisors showing. She scooped up the decaying thing, cupped it to her breast, and murmured something unintelligible under her breath.

Drop the diseased thing, I wanted to command. But I could tell my comments would mean nothing—her breathing was shallow and labored, her tear-streaked face turning more red by the moment. If I made a move toward her, she'd likely lunge at my face, and damned if I wouldn't hurl the little savage against a tree trunk.

I took a deep breath and placed my palm into the indentation at our feet. The dirt was cool and littered with plant roots and stones. There would be no digging here without a contractor's shovel. Standing up, I tossed the trowel into the bucket.

"Come on, May. You want to bury that bird, we've got to find somewhere else. Ground's too hard here." I waited for her to stand, but she wouldn't budge. So I walked away. Twenty yards away I found her padding silently at my heels, dead bird clutched to her chest.

I walked deep into the forest until I found a basin of sorts that saw water drainage in the spring but was now dry and sprinkled with short grass. I got down on my knees and dug furiously in the soil until I'd created a creditable grave about a foot deep, a foot long, and six inches wide. I set the trowel atop the loose dirt pile and waited.

May whispered to the dead bird. She laid its corpse out gently in the hole. From her pocket, she retrieved a handful of wildflowers and sprinkled them. She used her hands to fill up the hole. Then she pressed her cheek on the mound.

I watched from a distance. I'm no believer in burial, least of all in the burial of animals. Above or below ground, scavengers, insects, and bacteria will eventually eat their flesh, so why bother? When I die I want to be cremated or, if modern technology allows for it, flushed down a gigantic toilet like a goldfish, disappearing into an invisible netherworld—recycled, chemically treated, reintroduced as lawn fertilizer. Death is nothing but a physical process as messy and mundane as moving one's bowels, yet it's constantly dramatized or, even at May's young age, romanticized. What for?

We walked side by side back to the lakeshore. May slipped her hand into mine.

Billy wasn't surprised to arrive home to find May slathering peanut butter on bananas. "I take it Lizzie's got a date," he said to no one in particular. He did, however, raise an eyebrow about my wardrobe selection. I thumbed through his copy of *Gourmet* magazine while wearing my torn golf shirt with a boot print on the chest, and blood-stained khaki pants.

Prioritize. Arrest doubt. Think positively. Hammer away. Troy wouldn't sit around relying on the charity of strangers. He would take action.

"Could you drop me off at Mr. Frog's tomorrow afternoon?" I said. "I want to ask the bartender some questions."

"Barney?" Billy grimaced. "I'd better join you. I've got some early afternoon appointments but can close up shop early. I'll pick you up at 3:30." Billy waved May away. "Leave the dishes be, May. Why don't you go draw?"

May pulled out one blue and one red pen from her backpack and began sketching. She seemed especially focused today, gripping a pen in each fist, marking with authority. I wondered whether the strange child was still using me as her *objet d'art*.

"Were you good friends with May's father, Billy?"

Billy walked to the sink with the dessert cups. "We were lovers."

"His clothes don't fit me very well," I said.

Billy turned on the faucet and steam rose into the air. He whistled a country tune as he scrubbed. He may not have heard me.

CHAPTER 6

When it's 95 degrees on a weekday afternoon, a bar with no air conditioning should be deserted. Mr. Frog's was half-full and the karaoke machine wasn't even turned on. The television monitors broadcast ESPN2. BMX bicyclists rolled up, down, and around the surface of empty swimming pools. The men in the room—and there was only one woman, sharing a greasy brick of onion rings with her boyfriend— sat alone or in twos.

Some of the men nodded at Billy as we crossed the room. Without turning his face away from the screen, Barney filled a mug with dark ale and slid it to Billy.

"I'll have a Coke in an unopened bottle," I said.

Barney dropped ice cubes into a tumbler and filled it with his barman's spigot. The drink was barely carbonated and so light in color it looked like dirty mineral water. Billy swiveled in his seat to watch the BMX competition. Apparently, the proper etiquette was to refrain from talking until a commercial break. At the other end of the bar, a squat, balding fellow with mottled skin was looking at me. My throbbing ribs recalled his porcine features.

The first commercial rolled and Billy spoke. "My friend's got some questions about the other night."

Barney dug around beneath the bar for a clipboard. He scanned the room and began checking things off of a list. Some of the tables had napkin holders and some didn't; some had ketchup bottles and some didn't. What kind of restocking list was he reviewing?

"I don't like questions," Barney said.

"Don't his bruises jog your memory?"

Barney pursed his lips, thick and soft like a horse's. "All I care about is making sure Mr. Frog's is filled. What you all do in parking lots and parks I ain't interested in."

I used a soggy paper napkin to wipe pus from my broken lip. "I just want some info about John," I said.

Barney's eyes flickered from me to the television screen. The BMX competition had started again.

"Don't know him," Barney said.

Billy removed his cap and set it on the bar. "Pretty boy with the false tan, comes in every couple of months, makes a point of chatting with you in a loud voice. Speaks in a strange countrified accent—'How can y'all serve such strong drinks for such low, low prices?'"

Barney pulled a rag from his apron and scrubbed at a gummy ring on the counter. Several flies flew up, hovered, and resettled. "I ain't lying. I don't know him, but I've got to listen to him just the same."

"Is John your boss?" I said.

Barney reached under the counter for a spray bottle filled with pink liquid. The scent of ammonia filled the air. He began scrubbing again. "Who told you that?"

"John talked to me about quality control," I said. "Made it sound as if you've been working together for a long time."

"Well, if he said it then fine. But I won't say no more than that. I don't want to lose my unvested options or pay trouble damages."

If I hadn't been sitting in a karaoke bar, I would have presumed he meant stock options and *treble* damages. But a bartender signed to a company stock option plan and a confidentiality agreement? Ludicrous.

"Are you implying that Mr. Frog's is owned by a publicly traded corporation?" I said.

"I don't know the technicalities, and I think I'm not allowed to answer."

I rocked on my barstool, dislodging the wadded napkin propped under one of the legs. Was Megumi's fiancé a karaoke slum lord? The place was shabby—the concrete floors, the wooden pillars redolent with meat grease, the gouged tables that appeared to have been stolen from a public park—everything except for the karaoke system.

My eyes passed over the surround-sound speakers partially concealed in the roof beams. Wherever a person sat, he could see the stage, the projection screen, and at least one monitor. Whoever owned this place had dumped twenty-thousand dollars into the audio-visual equipment and virtually nothing into anything else.

Billy scoffed. "He's jerking your chain, Guy. Mr. Frog's can't afford air conditioning."

Barney wiped the sweat from the base of his neck. "You think I don't want air con? I—" He stopped. "I'm not answering any more questions."

I pushed my glass aside. "I need a name, an address, anything. There'll be nothing to trace to you."

Barney's chubby face sagged. The television screen was now playing a commercial for Viagra. An elderly couple ran hand in hand along a beach.

"There's no such thing as 'no trace,'" he said.

Barney wouldn't say a word after that, though he continued to refill our drinks. We kept at him for thirty minutes before deciding to leave. I excused myself to the restroom, stomach roiling but improving. The pig-faced man snorted as I passed. I pretended not to notice.

Men's restrooms are a reminder of how little we've progressed as a species. I closed the bathroom stall, kicked the toilet seat down with my foot, and wiped the spattered surface with a balled-up, tissue glove.

I laid down three strips of toilet paper and eased onto the still-warm seat. I waited, strained, and read the graffiti on the walls. There were the typical line drawings of hairy vaginas with labia large enough to swallow wildebeests. There were erect penises spouting fluid like sprinkler heads. Misspelled observations and jokes—"How can you trust somethin that bleads for 7 days and wont die?"; "How can you tell when a niger's well done? Cut'm open and look for the wite meat." Most of the graffiti had to do with sex—"I can suk my own big, wite uncercumsised cock," et cetera. Nothing out of the ordinary.

So Megumi's fiancé was a karaoke club owner. That might mean he belonged to a karaoke business owners' association. When I got back to Seattle, I could ask Mori about him. Maybe he had dragged Megumi into the Lily Pad to size up the competition. If Mori had known the bastard had been scouting the Pad, he wouldn't have shown such obsequious deference.

The restroom door creaked open and closed. The deadbolt clunked into the strike. Two smallish cowboy boots shuffled across the concrete floor and entered the adjacent stall. The toilet seat fell with a clatter, and wide-waisted jeans dropped to the floor.

I perused the graffiti again to take my mind off of my cramping stomach and noticed that, just to the left of the toilet paper dispenser, was a hole the size of a silver dollar. It looked as if it had been punched out with a tool, as if the dispenser used to be set in the wall a few inches over. It was another sign that Mr. Frog's was a rundown establishment. I was contemplating my feet when I noticed something out of the corner of my eye. The snakeskin boots in the stall next to mine weren't facing forward. They were facing me.

Slowly, I extended my right palm to cover the hole. With my left hand, I pulled at the roll of toilet paper and wadded about ten sheets into a ball. Then I swapped hands, stuffing the hole with tissue. There was a grunt of displeasure. Then whimpering.

What was I supposed to do now? My pants and underwear were bunched at my feet and all that stood between me and a masturbating man was a wad of single-ply. I willed him to zip up his fly and leave the restroom. Instead he pawed the metal partition that separated us.

"Now why'd you go and do that, huh? I just want to watch. I'm not going to hurt you. I'm not going to hurt you, my smooth, hairless little China boy."

His words were panted, accompanied by the rhythmic slap of flesh on flesh. I didn't move a muscle. I stared at the tissue blocking his view of my groin.

"Oh yeah, but you like it rough, don't you? If that's what you want, that's what you'll get. Ungh. Unstop that hole and let me beat you black and blue with my big white cock. Rough. You want to be pissed on, beaten. That's what John said."

A shiver spread over my scalp. Had he been eavesdropping, or had he really spoken to John? "How do you know John?"

"I know all about your kind, on your knees in the public parks, waiting for some straight cock to suck on. You want converts. You won't get me. Why don't you unstop that hole and let me see your cute little rice dick."

I held my breath against the smell of piss and shit. "Tell me about John. First. Did you talk to him?"

He gurgled, a sound midway between a titter and a snarl. "Sick little faggot games. He said you liked it rough. If Billy hadn't taken you for himself I would have split that puckered asshole of yours."

Did I remember any of this? No. Anything could have happened while I was unconscious. I was lucky Billy had saved me. Had he saved me? My throat tightened. "John told you about our games? I thought you didn't want to play."

"For a thousand bucks, I'd fuck my own daughter." His rhythmic wanking increased in tempo. "He said he'd pay more if I got my buddies to gang-bang you. But then I wouldn't get you all to myself. I've got to have you all to myself." His voice lowered to a phlegm-filled whisper. "Come on, China boy, unstop the hole. Please. Show Daddy your pee-pee."

The beige metal walls pressed in on me. Silently, I drew out sheets from the toilet paper roll and, making sure not to move my legs or feet, wiped myself clean. I could run now. I'd be out before he could pull up his pants. But.

"How do I know you're telling the truth? John never would have paid and left. He always stays to watch. *Always.* You're a cheapskate looking for a freebie." I paused. "Cheapskate," I hissed.

He snorted, and the rhythmic yanking stopped. "I don't have to pay for faggot sex! He's the one paying. He's the one!"

"Prove it. Prove it to me."

"How can I prove it? He said it, I swear. He said you liked to be fucked until you couldn't walk. Come on! Unstop the hole. I need to see it. *Please.*"

"No proof, no peep. How were you going to collect your money? Show me, and I'll take your prick in my mouth."

He grunted and his wanking began again, hard and fast. "Proof. Proof. Where's my proof? I got his card. I got his card in my wallet. He said to call him."

"Show me the card. Give it to me right now."

Beneath the wall, I saw his hairy hand fumble at the jeans bunched at his ankles. "Where is it, where is it?" he muttered. "Church...Daycare...Karaoke. There. Got it. I got it. Come on now," he panted. "I need it so bad."

I yanked out the toilet paper separating us, but covered the hole with my palm. "Stick the card through. Do it now or you get nothing." The edge of the card immediately prodded my hand. I pulled it back, and replaced the toilet paper wad.

"Hey! What's going on?"

"Hold on, big fella. You'll get yours. I need to make sure you're legit." The card was printed on a fine-grained, off-white card stock. It read, "John Smith, Vice President for North and South America, Karaoke Group International, Ltd." No business address, but there were toll-free phone and fax numbers and an e-mail address. I flipped the card over. The same information was repeated in Spanish, except the name listed was "José (Smith) Gonzales."

"Okay. I guess you're for real. You must have a huge cock. John always gets me big white cocks. I'll pull out the tissue and you just slide it through the hole. I'll give you a Far East surprise you'll never forget."

I stood and pulled up my pants, slipping the card into my pocket, coughing as I zipped. "Mmm...I can't wait to suckee, suckee." I knelt on the sticky concrete floor. With my left hand, I reached for the wad of tissue; with my right, I reached for my car keys. "Ooh yeah. Poke that pork kielbasa right into my mouth."

He may have had small cowboy boots, but he had an enormous penis. But it wasn't white. It was pink. A huge, pink, hard, uncircumcised dick with a girth so large it scraped the sides of the hole. Severed from its owner, sticking through the wall, it didn't look like a penis—it looked like an irradiated larva writhing in pain.

"Ooh yeah," I said, wrapping my left hand around its leathery base. It bulged and strained like a creature trying to pull itself free of a trap. With my right hand, I chose the door key to my apartment building, a ridged brass key with the words "Do Not Duplicate" etched onto its face.

He groaned. "That feels good, China boy. That feels good. Now spit on it. Spit on it and nibble the tip." His voice rose in pitch.

I clenched that fleshy rod with all my might, until the muscles in my forearm strained. I yanked, and his belly snapped into the metal partition with a thud. With my other hand, I stabbed down hard, the key ridges tearing through skin into something stringy beneath. He squealed just like a pig.

"Let's get out of here, Billy," I said, shoving my hands into my pockets. Billy was still plying Barney with questions.

"All right. Let me pay the bill and—"

"Now. Right now."

"Is there something wrong? You look out of sorts." He reached out to clap a hand on my shoulder.

I pulled away. "Don't touch me."

"Are you o—"

"Just don't touch me." I walked halfway to the door and waited.

Billy didn't say another word. He threw cash on the bar and we left.

I took a long, hot bath. I scrubbed my skin raw with a loofa, and sluiced Dr. Bronner's peppermint soap into every crevice. Cool mint tingled my eyelids while the heat and the soap cauterized my wounds. It was my last night in Chelan. Tomorrow I'd depart this carney village for home, for privacy, for solitude.

After an hour in the tub, the water was cold and my limbs were heavy. I wrapped a towel around my waist and stared at myself in the mirror. At least the swelling had gone down on my shiner. My shirt and slacks lay on the bathroom tiles, where I had thrown them in my haste to bathe. The scent of the public restroom assaulted me. On top of the laundry hamper were clean clothes, all several sizes too large. Some choice.

The door creaked open behind me. I pivoted carefully on my heels, crossing my arms defensively. At the door was May, wearing a sundress with tiny butterflies on it. Her thin-lipped grin was thankfully less malicious than before. I sighed in relief.

"May, you're going to have to wait your turn. Go out into the living room and see if you can help Uncle Billy."

She didn't budge. She shifted her weight from one foot to another.

"Okay, if it's an emergency, you can use the restroom. I'll wait in the hallway."

I tried to step past her but she wouldn't let me. A question fluttered and died in my throat. May had hiked up her sundress and was fondling herself awkwardly, as if trying to erase a pencil mark from her skin. She didn't have any panties on.

I shielded my face with my hand. "No, May. Stop that right now! Bad girl! Bad girl!"

I kicked the door open and stumbled out, clenching the front of my knotted bath towel. I nearly knocked over Billy on the way to the living room.

In the restroom, May began to keen. Her wails increased in pitch and decibel level until it seemed the whole house was filled with pain. It was twenty minutes before the crying subsided, and another ten before Billy returned to the living room. I sat at the dining room table, shell-shocked, still wrapped only in a towel.

Billy passed me on the way to the refrigerator. He placed a glass of iced tea in front of me. "She'll be fine. All she wants is affection, but doesn't know there are right and wrong ways to seek it. Like her father that way."

"I didn't touch her, Billy."

"I know."

"I didn't touch her, Billy."

"I know that." Billy studied me. "You don't have children, do you?"

"No." That was a sore point of my ex-marriage. My fear of the "natural" next step.

"All children are sensitive, May even more so. I watch her and feel like my skin's been stripped off my body and I'm stumbling into the jagged corners of world." He paused. "And I realize how calloused I've become. How calloused we've all become."

"You know what she did, don't you? She came into the bathroom and…she's five years old!"

Billy rubbed the bridge of his nose between thumb and index finger. "Lizzie inherited a big house from her parents. Liz and May share a mattress laid out on the carpet in the living room. The rest of the rooms are boarded up." He paused. "Lizzie likes to bring men home. I tell her to bring May over when she's got those intentions, but if she's had a few her track record's not the best. May sees and hears more than any child should."

Billy turned toward the window to stare out at the stars. A breeze blew in and I hugged my bare chest.

"Why do you dress me in your ex-boyfriend's clothes?" I said.

Billy's smile was faint and distracted. He took a sip from his glass before answering. "Somehow you remind me of Karl. Not in appearance: he outweighed you by a hundred pounds. But in an essential way you're the same. Karl was searching for that missing piece, which meant he always had to keep a part of himself vacant in case he found it."

CHAPTER 7

BILLY`S TALE

Billy spoke in a gentle cadence, like the slap of oars against the surface of a lake. I didn't want to listen, but it felt as if an invisible current tugged me along through his memories.

Karl rode into the shop on a Fat Boy Harley, tires kicking up a wake of gravel and dust. Six-foot-five, shaggy beard, cowboy hat, and leather chaps—he looked like an extra from *Easy Rider*. He would have been intimidating, if it weren't for the ironed jeans, the crooked nose…and the accent. His clipped German lilt clashed with his Western drawl, and the drawl disappeared when he was excited.

Karl had a contract with HBO to shoot a documentary called *Eastern Washington: The Unknown Wild West*. He spent most of his time on the road, interviewing old-timers in the dead or dying towns of Okanogan County and the Methow Valley that boomed during the Gold Rush and the heyday of the silver mines. Chelan was his base camp, where he would assemble his masterpiece.

I'd renovated a corner of the shop for an old friend to use as a ceramics studio—it had a separate entrance and windows that opened out onto the lake—but her husband got transferred back east and she went with him. It had lain dormant for a year, too small for more than one person, too far from town for retail sales.

"Perfect! But too bright maybe," Karl said.

He crammed equipment into the room until it looked like a subterranean cavern, the ceiling and walls oozing wires, cables, and LED lights. Karl liked it that way. He worked with the door locked, the lights out, and the blinds drawn over the picture windows. He referred to the view of the lake as a "distraction."

Karl showed up at the close of the regular work day and stayed for who knows how long. If anyone mentioned him, it was as "the big German biker" or "Grizzly Steiner." If pushed, a person might say he "seemed friendly" or "tips good." For two months, I collected his rent, ignored his creative eccentricities, and that was that. Late one May night, he showed up on my doorstep.

"You'll drink a beer with me, yes?" he said.

I'd never given him my home address, yet there he was. An honest man would have been preparing for bed. But the expression on his face gave me pause, his generous lips rounded into a tiny "O" of supplication. I invited him inside. That was the beginning of a series of drinks, late-night snacks, and finally dinners.

I'd only read about the places Karl had explored. He'd ridden elephants with opium drug lords in Myanmar. He'd nearly lost an eye to a Colombian guerilla's rifle butt. And yet, despite the hardships he'd suffered—or maybe because of them—he had to be darned near the most finicky eater in the world. At the only Persian restaurant in Chelan County, he sent back his Koresht-e-Gheimah, complaining that "it's obvious you think I'm a greenhorn who can't tell when you use the wrong spices." And for all the love he professed for the American West, he couldn't stand American food— "Why must you people Super Size everything, all of it bad?" In other words, he was, in equal parts, charming and a pain in the ass.

I fell for him anyway. The way he approached life disarmed me. It was all or nothing; he didn't care, didn't even register, how anybody else viewed him. For most of us, there's a chasm between thinking and doing, imagination and reality. Not so for Karl.

At two in the morning, after drinking too much wine, Karl wanted to jump on the Harley and blast full-throttle through Main Street. We were both drunk; what if we crashed? What if the cops stopped us? What if someone recognized me on the backseat?

He lifted me bodily out to the garage, plopped me down on his bike, and we roared off into the night. I was scared shitless. But after we passed the main strip, rattling the store windows, a clenched-up knot in my chest—one I didn't know was there—began to unravel. Karl turned the bike onto the highway and we rode for an hour in silence.

Arms wrapped around his waist, wind rushing warm over my face, in the moonlight the countryside looked different. Does that make any sense to you?

I'm a forty-seven-year-old closeted gay man. Hiding relationships, pretending to be someone else, isn't second-nature; it's who I am.

"Who's going to be the lucky girl to tame Uncle Billy?" My family sets me up on blind dates with divorcée and widows. I've become who they presume me to be, an unreformed bachelor. If you feign friendship in public for long enough you'll begin to feign intimacy when no one's watching. I've woken in the middle of the night, stared at the person sleeping next to me, and thought, "What if he ruins my life?" I still did that with Karl, but how seriously could I take myself? For Christ's sake, Karl complained to Barney, of all people, about not putting a proper one-inch head on his beer.

When Karl's advance ran out before he'd completed his video project, I invited him to stay with me. No one had to suspect a thing. I was making extra money by converting my commercial tenant into a residential one.

Late July I brought him to a family barbeque. Karl picked at his food but captivated the kids with stories about a canoe trip down the Amazon, where he caught fish larger than they were. But more than once, Karl reached over to brush the bangs away from my forehead or place a hand on my forearm. He got up from his chair and tried to give me a neck massage, which I quickly shrugged off.

It's his German heritage, I explained to Dad. At the end of the afternoon, Mom accompanied me to the door while

Karl pulled the Fat Boy out of the garage. I leaned over to kiss her goodbye and found her crying.

"Don't ever bring that man to this house again," Mom said.

Karl hadn't noticed anything was wrong. On the ride home, he gushed about how "refreshingly pastoral" my family was. He dropped me off because he was eager to get back to the editing room and use his new insights about the "real America" in his film. He worked feverishly through the night while I lay alone in bed, staring at the ceiling.

I replayed the events of the day, of the previous weeks. Dad's only pronouncement about gay men was "I know one when I see one." All afternoon, he'd been quiet, pressed his fist into his gut. I thought it was his ulcers; I should have known it was because he "saw one," and probably two. If my parents suspected, who else did? Friends? Customers? Cashiers? What did they say about me when I left the room?

That night I hated who I was and where I was from. It would have been easier to have been born in Seattle, San Francisco, or New York, where my parents would join charity marches for AIDS. If I had been younger, I could have run away to the city to live in a loft with a partner and a cat. Karl was everything I wasn't: free from responsibility. I coach Little League baseball on Tuesdays, Thursdays, and Saturdays. I pay into an educational trust fund for my nieces and nephews. I'm in the class of elders for our church. If I left, there would be consequences. If I left, how could I return?

I was still awake when Karl returned at 4 a.m. whistling a classical tune. He took a leisurely bath and didn't climb into bed until an hour later, smelling of lavender soap and lotion. I could feel his face over mine for at least a minute before he sighed, kissed my forehead, and lay down. Almost immediately, he was snoring. I watched him in the gathering light of dawn, chest rolling gently up and down. I formulated a plan.

In thirty-five days he would be on a flight to Germany, and from there, off to another exotic locale. Home could be our haven. No more restaurants, cafés, bars, pubs. We could stay in all the time; I'd cook anything he craved. Outside of work, we wouldn't have to see anyone.

Karl was puzzled, but flattered, by my sudden interest in cooking world cuisines. He withheld his caustic critiques of all things culinary, settling on comments like "a worthy effort" or "it takes time to develop one's palate, if I'm not mistaken." But by the fourth day, he grimaced when he found me in the kitchen. On the fifth day, he blurted out, "Why do you suddenly want to stay in all the time? I'm no homebody."

Intimacy, I answered. He nodded impatiently. *To save on expenses.* Once he completed his film, he'd pay back what he owed me and more. I asked what he wanted for dinner the following evening. On the sixth day he answered anything I cared to cook. On the seventh day, he said I should cook for one.

"Three weeks left and so much to do!" he said. "The night is my most productive time."

He returned home when I was asleep and was asleep when I woke. The last days of our relationship were like the first ones: we had reverted to being landlord and tenant again.

That damned documentary captivated his imagination in a way our relationship never did. I'd tolerated his obsessive discussions about narrative structure, his long, abstract digressions about the inadequacy of using images to expose the "inner world," and his incomprehensible theories about the "nihilistic triumph of evangelical capitalism that simultaneously exploits and represses the human body." But if I asked to see a rough cut of his work, he would, on a good day, say, "Creativity and privacy are synonymous;" on a bad day, he would snap, "This isn't fixing engines, Billy." He could talk for hours about what he *did*—climb the Seven Summits or trek across Cambodia—but ask about what made him who he *was* and he would half nod, half shake his head, and answer cryptically. Parents? "I have them."

Our relationship lasted exactly three months. I date this from when Karl moved in. When you fall into the trap of "living every moment as if it were your last," anniversaries hold an exaggerated significance. We celebrated our one-month anniversary at a B&B in Couer d'Alene. We celebrated our two-month anniversary at a French restaurant in Spokane. We were supposed to spend our three-month anniversary at a picnic on the lake at sunset. I was the only one who remembered.

It was seven days before his departure date, and he spent every waking hour in the editing room. At 5 p.m., I was closing out the books when Karl pulled into the shop garage. He didn't bother coming into my office; he gave a quick wave and made a beeline for his monastic cell. Soon after the door shut behind him, the sound of German opera filled the garage. Karl at work. "Classic" country music—Hank Williams and the like—for leisure time; Wagner and Weill, volume cranked up to ten, for his creative activities.

Not only did he forget our anniversary, he couldn't be bothered to talk to me before shutting himself in for the night. Meanwhile, I'd taken the previous day off to chase down the foods he missed from back home—wurst, champignon cambozola, Augustiner beer; I'd prepared kriek cabbage with dried cherries; all that was left was making the *kasespatzle*.

I was tempted to take the picnic basket to a homeless shelter. But it was a beautiful evening, and as I drove back home along the lake, I cooled off. Karl had lost weight. His jeans sagged, dark rings had developed beneath his eyes, and there were times his eyes were glassy. The film was consuming him because he wanted it to be perfect. I wanted our last days together to be perfect. Neither of us intended to hurt the other, it was just who we were.

It didn't take me long to prepare the *spatzle*. The rest of the basket was already packed. I returned to the shop forty-five minutes before sunset. It was the last week of August, darkness chewing away at the daylight but with the lingering warmth of summer. I knocked hard to make sure Karl would hear me over the music. No answer. I knocked again, this time with my fist. No answer. Was he in the restroom? I couldn't see a thing through the drawn blinds.

I crossed to the garage and pulled open the retractable door. Karl's Fat Boy wasn't inside. His interview footage was all "in the can," and shooting additional footage would have meant lugging his camera, lighting, and sound equipment out for a two-hour round-trip ride. Had he gone out to eat? Maybe he'd remembered our date, rushed home, and we'd crossed paths.

I sorted through some parts orders. Thirty minutes passed, and still no sign of Karl. There was nothing to do but head home. I began lugging the blanket and picnic basket to the truck when I thought, no, I should put the food in the office refrigerator and leave a note. My intent was honorable. But as I stuck a Post-It on Karl's door, I couldn't help but wonder, would it be so bad if I snuck in for an advance peep at his *Meisterwerk?* There was nothing he guarded more fiercely than the sanctity of his workspace. During our very first meeting, he handwrote an extra clause into the rental agreement: "There is <u>one</u> key and <u>one</u> key only to the rental space, and that key resides with tenant Karl May until such time it is surrendered at the termination of the lease."

I lied, of course—I had three extra keys, but the lie was meaningless. What landlord doesn't keep an extra key? I *built* the room; I *own* a repair shop. I could break into the editing room in less than two minutes. Using a key, I didn't have to replace the lock.

The music was achingly loud. Even after I'd found the stop button on his elaborate stereo system, the memory of the music lingered like smoke in the air. I sat down at Karl's editing console, a board filled with dials, levers, and a time counter.

The lights, which I'd replaced months before, didn't work, and the only illumination came from the video monitor's blank blue screen. Not only was the room cluttered with videotapes, cables, spare cameras, editing equipment, and loose-leaf paper covered with Karl's chicken-scrawl handwriting, but also by empty potato chip bags, candy bar wrappers, half-filled Styrofoam coffee cups, and an open peanut butter jar with a knife stuck in it. A Quarter-Pounder wrapper fluttered in a corner, pushed to and fro by the breeze of an oscillating fan.

This space belonged to the same man who raged against the "cancerous spread of fast-food restaurants in the virginal West?" This mess was made by a man who spent an hour in front of the mirror whenever he woke up and went to bed? The room reeked of rotting food and something sticky sweet. The shelves and floor were filled with videotapes piled pell-mell atop one another, but each was meticulously labeled with the name of the subject, date of the interview, and place. There was already a tape loaded in the console. I listened for footsteps, then pressed the "play" button.

It must have been the middle of the tape because the interviewee was mid-sentence. He was an elderly man in a checked shirt standing in front of a burnt-out building. Tears streamed from his rheumy eyes: "—he was never the same again." Karl's large hand reached out from behind the camera to give him a bandanna. The man dabbed at his eyelids and then shook his head in response to an unintelligible query.

Karl allowed the man to recount the bad times—Papa fighting the bottle, how Papa put a pistol into his mouth and pulled the trigger—but kept prodding him into what Karl was really searching for, stories about the heyday of the mining company, when the town was bustling with laborers and prospectors, the glamour of a romantic Wild West replete with gambling dens, brothels, and men who broke the law. Karl had a knack for getting just the right words and images. By the end of the tape, the old man's cheeks were ruddy and the dried tears looked as if they'd been invoked by laughter.

I gazed at the mounds of videotape. Unless Karl began culling his interviews, his program would become a mini-series. Only by chance did my eye catch on a label reading, "Elizabeth Sparkman, Wenatchee, 7/5/01." Elizabeth Sparkman. Lizzie.

That stumped me. Karl's documentary was about the "unexplored" Wild West of eastern Washington. Lizzie's a transplant from southern California. Her parents dragged her here kicking and screaming when she was ten years old. Not only that, she lived in Chelan, not Wenatchee. Was that a mistake or did he drive an hour away to conduct the interview? I inserted Lizzie's tape into the VCR.

The picture was dark, Lizzie's shadowy figure backlit by incandescent lamps. A harsh white light shone on Lizzie's face, causing her hand to shoot up to shield her eyes. "Just a moment," Karl said, and then cursed in German. The lighting became more diffuse and even, illuminating Liz and her surroundings. She sat on the edge of a king-sized bed, the bedspread a drab polyester brown, wearing what she wears all summer, a tank top and cutoff jeans.

"Sorry about that." It was Karl's voice. "You can put your hand down now if you wish. Put your hand down. You're covering your face."

Liz squinted at the camera.

"No, no. Don't do that with your face. Open your eyes wide. That's a good girl."

Lizzie pulled on her fingers. There were more adjustments behind the camera but no speaking for a few minutes.

Karl cleared his throat. "Tell me. What is your name?"

Liz began to speak, then paused. "Destiny," she said.

"Ah, Destiny. A very sexy name." He paused. "Now Destiny, why don't you show me those big, beautiful titties of yours?"

I don't need to describe the tape any further, do I? I hit the stop button and stared at the blank screen. Then I willed myself to watch it, the whole thing. Otherwise I never would have believed it was anything other than a bad dream. I watched Karl's big, hairy ass obscure nearly all of Lizzie except for her drooping eyelids.

After it was done, I watched segments of the other tapes. Some were interviews about Eastern Washington's Wild West days. The rest showed amateur porn, Karl with one woman or two, sometimes instructing them on what to do from off-camera. The room became overwhelmingly stuffy and I had to leave.

By the time I returned home, it was nearly 11 p.m. and there was still no sign of Karl. One minute, I wanted to plunge an awl into his sternum. A moment later, I'd recall an evening we spent together, or his goofy smile, and feel a pang of regret. I rummaged through his things, looking for more. There wasn't much aside from clothes. A plastic baggie filled with Jolly Ranchers, Tootsie Rolls, and Snickers bars. A stack of drink coasters from every bar we'd ever visited. But tucked away at the bottom of his duffel bag was an expanding file. Inside was a jumbled pile of hotel receipts. He had registered under the name "Heinrich Schaefer." His German passport was there too. The picture was dated— in it he was clean-shaven—but again his name wasn't Karl May; it was Heinrich Schaefer. The passport showed tourist entries into the United States but not a single visa for a foreign country.

Trivial eccentricities suddenly made sense—Karl's refusal to let me come to the shoots; his obsession with personal hygiene; the way he bristled when I pointed out incongruities in his travelogues. For more than an hour, I lay curled up on the couch, head cradled in my arms, playing out what this all meant. Was there a documentary or wasn't there? One thing was certain: Karl May didn't exist. I had grown intimate with—developed an intimacy bordering on love with—a figment of Heinrich Schaefer's imagination. Karl May, cosmopolitan yet awkward, epicure and artist, he was a puff of smoke. Who was Heinrich Schaefer? A junk-food consuming pornographer. An immigrant overstaying his tourist visa. What was I to Heinrich Schaefer? An easy lay. Free room and board. A distraction.

People do all sorts of funny stuff with the truth. Throw a tarp over it, stick it in the garage, and pretend it's not there. Bash their heads against it. Drink it down straight, waiting for it to burn from the inside out. Heinrich Schaefer I wanted to stuff into a burlap sack and drown. Karl May I wanted to stay a few weeks longer. The problem was Karl had died and Heinrich lived.

By the time I heard the throaty rumble of his motorcycle pulling up, a calmness had settled over me. Karl, whistling as he opened the front door, faked a double-take. He gave me a peck on the forehead on the way to the refrigerator.

"It's way past your bedtime, little boy. Tonight's a school night, if I'm not mistaken." His hair was tousled and slightly damp. He reached into the freezer for a chilled pint glass, and poured beer into it. He lowered himself into the seat across from me.

"Where have you been?" I said.

"Oh, tonight, Billy, I had a breakthrough! For so long, I had no idea what I was doing. There was this image, there was that image, I couldn't find the right *leitmotif*, everything collapsed into dissonance. But then, aha!, it hit me while watching the interview of a broken-down old man who kept returning over and over to the story of his father. I kept thinking while I filmed him, 'Enough already with your sob story, tell me something that will captivate an audience.' Then I realized, that *was* the story. It's not just the carousing and the gunslinging, but the tragedy, the loss. Without the risk of loss, you have no story. So now, though the film's far from being brooding, the dark undercurrent recurs again and again. Da-DA! Da-DA!" He moved his hands like a conductor's.

"So you were in the editing room all night."

"Of course, Herr Pregerson. Where else would I be? I've been poring over hours and hours of tape, plucking just the right snippets for my piece. I should be exhausted from staring at that damned screen all night, but adrenaline has me flying high."

"I must have missed you."

He drained his pint glass, let out a deep "ah," and wiped his mouth with the back of his hand. "And I've missed you too. I like that you're up right now. You're usually much more of a—what's the word?—'dud.' Ten p.m. and it's lights out."

"You're not understanding me. I went to visit you at the shop. I even brought you dinner. You weren't there."

He scratched his beard and appeared perplexed. "Is that so? Ah! I'm so absentminded. I get lost in my work. I stepped out to clear my mind, to get a bite to eat, if I'm not mistaken."

"I was there for three hours."

"It's so hard to find anything edible in this town. I kept riding and riding. I love to feel the wind on my face." He smiled and leaned back in his chair, relaxed.

"Stop it. Just stop it right now. I saw the tapes. I know what you've really been doing here."

He knit his brows, a perplexed look on his face. "You are talking very strangely now, Billy. Are you telling me that you violated our contract, you broke my trust, by intruding on my workspace?"

How could he be so calm about this? How could he act as if I was the guilty one? "You're a pornographer and a liar. I know there's no 'Unknown Wild West.' Where have you been peddling your trash? Here? Germany?" My hands shook.

He stood up, took a deep breath, and paced the room. "You're the one who broke your promise and you accuse—" He took another deep breath. "I have nothing to hide. You can never know what it's like to be a documentary filmmaker, scraping together your pennies, begging on your hands and knees to funders, just so you can finish a modest project that might make someone think. I'm not proud of what I have to do to support myself. But there it is, Billy. That's life. That's reality. Are you man enough to face up to it?"

I searched his face for a sign he was lying. I reached into my pocket, and tossed the passport onto the table. "Explain that one to me, *Heinrich.* Why don't you tell me again how you stopped those poachers in the Tanzanian wildlife preserve? How do you enter those countries without ever gaining permission?"

Heinrich flipped through the brown booklet disdainfully. "You think it's easy for me to stay in the United States for long enough to complete a video project? Work visa? As an 'independent filmmaker?' Forget about it. Tourist visas last only three months. Why do you think I chose Washington state? I can go back and forth to Canada to get another three months of breathing space. I can do that only so long before the border patrol starts asking me questions. 'So, Mr. Schacter, Schroeder, Schaefer,' whoever it is I am for the year, 'are you sure you're not working? Taking jobs away from hardworking Americans?' You think I'm wrong for doing that? Fine, call the border authorities. Ironic, isn't it? I'm making a film to help people around the world understand America's history, but I can be deported for caring enough to do it right."

"I don't believe you, *Heinrich*."

"Ah, *Richter* Pregerson has declared a judgment against me. He talks all the time about trust, about honesty, about sharing, and yet they are just words to him. Betray my trust and I am to blame. Hear the truth and reject it. You need proof, do you, *Richter*? Hard and fast evidence. You'll have it then." He shoved the passport into the band of his jeans and marched to the door. "How about the *five* passports I travel under? I even have an American one. I have *never* shown anyone a work in progress. But I will show it to you, my skeptical *friend*."

I remained seated. "Where are you going?"

"Back to the editing room, where I keep my truly valuable belongings. Or have you already retrieved them for me?" He yanked the door open and then banged it shut. The Harley's engine roared and he peeled off into the night with a screech of tires. I stared at the closed door, solitude and silence encroaching once again.

"Goodbye, Karl," I said.

If he hurried, Karl could make it to and from the shop in forty minutes. But I knew he would be gone for much longer. Heinrich was persuasive all right. I think the truth and the lie had intertwined so he couldn't distinguish between the two.

What is the truth? The truth is if Karl were to walk back through the door right now—Karl, mind you, not Heinrich—I might take another shot at making it work. I might consider—as I had late at night when I wasn't so intent on protecting myself—running off to Algeria, or Malaysia, or Italy with him. I'm still waiting for Karl to return, though in my heart, I know he's dead.

CHAPTER 8

Billy gazed with a melancholy expression out of the window. I shivered in my towel. I rose, walked into the restroom, and shut the door. Thanks a lot, Billy. Thanks for pretending to be a person I could trust and then using me as a dress-up doll in a gay country-western fantasy.

He had a martyr complex. May and her mother were destined to frequent the same bar, to share drinks and boyfriends. If Billy couldn't come out to his family after forty-seven years, nothing but repressed misery lay ahead for him. Why entangle me in his mess? What was it Troy Bobbins said about happiness? "The happy man avoids unhappy men at all costs. They'll always be there. Why should you be?"

When I returned to the living room, I climbed into the cot immediately. Billy got the hint. He shut off the lights but stood there in the dark.

"Karl wasn't a bad man," he said. "All things to all people and nothing to no one. When I heard your voice, I thought of him: beautiful and lonesome."

Sebastian might be a mean old cuss, but he knew auto body work. He had modified my shabby black CRX into an import speed-ricer: metallic blue paint, air-scoop, ground effects, chromed rims. His voice raised in pitch as he detailed the inspiration for his improvements, but at the end of his itemized list his face clouded over.

"I'm afraid the engine work didn't get done," he said.

Sebastian's specialty was aesthetics. He let the two Mexican boys handle customers' mechanical issues. They were no-shows yesterday. Sebastian found them in a neighboring town's jail, stopped at 2:30 a.m. for rolling through a stop sign. No amount of pleading about their jobs or their characters would budge the sheriff. He was turning them over to the feds for deportation.

"They're good boys," Sebastian said. "Quiet, respectful, send money home to their parents. Idol-worshipping Catholics, but I'll let God deal with that."

Sebastian suggested changing the oil filter, fuel filter, and PCV valves once I returned to Seattle. The driver's side door still didn't lock. He'd cleaned up the jumble of wires but hadn't fixed the ignition. He handed me a steak knife.

"Here's your starter," he said. "Keep it under the floor mat. It doubles as a security system."

I ate lunch with Billy and May before taking to the road. May appeared to have forgotten that she'd assaulted me the night before. She followed our conversation like a tennis match, head turning between Billy and me. Billy and I talked about the weather (fair), road conditions (clear), and water conservation (no progress would be had until regulations on upstream usage were enforced). To preempt Billy from introducing another neutral topic, I rose from my chair and extended a hand. He pulled me into a bear hug.

"Call me if you need help," he said.

I half nodded and half shook my head. "I'll pay you back. I swear."

"Take your time," he said. May tugged at the hem of his jeans, bouncing up and down as if she needed to pee. "Oh yes. May's got something to give you. Go on, May. Go fetch it."

May ran to the bookshelf, ruffled through a plastic folder, and returned with a letter-sized sheet of paper. She held it in both hands, looking down and shifting her weight from one foot to the other.

"Is that for me, May?" I said.

She nodded. It was a crayon drawing in three colors. In the center was a green frog-man wearing a crown. A clenched row of teeth dominated his face and his eyebrows angled sharply downward. His webbed fist held a knife that he used to stab an oily blob whose skin was speckled with a pox of eyes. The two creatures waded knee-deep in a pool of red.

"Thanks, May. I'll frame it and hang it right over my bed." Or perhaps fax a copy to Child Protective Services.

She slapped Billy's knee, and motioned for him to lean down. She whispered into his ear. "No," Billy said. "I'm not going to speak for you." May's face strained.

"Port it," she said.

"Ah," I said. "Port it. Sure, I'll port it wherever I go."

She shook her head and supplicated Billy with her eyes. He didn't say a word. "No," she said. "Port it. Port it!" She grabbed my temples and rattled my head. Ouch.

"Oh!" I said. "Portrait. Portrait!"

She clapped her hands. "Uh huh. Port it!"

I'd always hoped Salvador Dali would paint my portrait. Well, at least in this drawing my internal organs weren't leaking onto the ground. I was about to stand when she demanded, "May wants a hug." Saliva glistened on her fangs.

She threw herself at me, gripping the back of my neck so tightly the circulation of blood to my head stopped. She smelled of baby shampoo and freshly turned soil. Her breath came in quick pants on my earlobe.

"May's scared too," she whispered.

CHAPTER 9

The bills and bank statements went into one pile, the free address labels and coupons went into another. Everything else went into recycling. I hesitated at the manila envelope stamped with the logo of my former firm, Norton, Walters & Eldrich, but finally dropped it into the bin. Tanya could hire a private investigator or contact me through the "Public Announcements" section of the *Seattle Post-Intelligencer* if she needed to reach me.

Troy was right. No matter how small the task, if you attack it with urgency, you're invigorated by its completion. Time for a nap. Now that I was home, there was ample time to untangle the knot Megumi's fiancé had tied in my finances. I awoke at 8 p.m. and lay on the futon listening to the whir of clothes tumbling in the laundry room. My wallet contained $24—$25.27 counting the change. More than enough for an appetizer and drinks at the Lily Pad.

On Fridays it's best to arrive early, right about the time the fixed-income diners are pushing their walkers toward the door. You have your choice of tables and can request five or six songs up front. I smiled as I eased into a parking space at the Pad's front door. Usually that kind of parking karma is reserved for when the police busts up an illegal card room. But tonight, the street was quiet.

There was a faded imprint on the brick wall where the cheap, jade-colored "The Lily Pad" letters should have been. After I rattled and banged on the door, Jimmy finally pulled it open. He wore his Mariners team jersey, shoulders drooping, belly protruding. He looked as if he'd expended all his energy climbing out of the womb so all he could do was stand there and sag.

"Oh, it's you, King," he said. He walked back into the bar.

There was no one in the main room. What's more, there were no tables and no chairs. The neon "Budweiser" and "Miller High Life" signs were unplugged and leaning against the wall. The video strip-poker machine was gone. The glass bar shelves were empty. Jimmy fumbled around in a box for vodka, sour mix, and club soda. He mixed a Vodka Collins and slid it toward me. "No ice, King. Sorry."

I took a sip. Except for temperature, it was perfect. Jimmy shuffled to the kitchen and returned with a half-pint of whole, sweetened milk. I nodded toward the room. "What's going on, Jimmy? Remodel?"

Jimmy curled forward like a pill bug. "A man came in here with a gun. It was hidden in his—" Jimmy patted his left breast. His lazy eye pointed skyward, his other eye gazed past me. "The back of his pants."

"Who came in here, Jimmy? A robber?"

"No. Middle management." He sucked at his straw. At the corners of his lips, the viscous white fluid was coalescing into a gummy film.

"Where's Josie and the kitchen staff?"

He gazed at the empty stage, where the projection screen once stood. He let out a whole body sigh. "The new karaoke machines don't use a DJ. You say the name of a song, and it automatically plays." He shook his head. "Technology."

The vodka seeped through my stomach lining. "Talk to me straight, Jimmy. Mori'd never close the Pad. He loves this place."

Jimmy shrugged. "Everything changes, King." He slid off his stool, went behind the bar, and began shoving more knickknacks—a hula girl toothpick holder, a Space Needle lighter, a flying saucer ashtray—into a half-filled box.

The building was to be taken down in a "soft demolition," which meant the structural supports would be removed so the walls could collapse in on themselves. Jimmy and I packed boxes side by side for two hours. I peppered him with questions, but Jimmy had a habit of talking about whatever crossed his mind. His wandering attention was exacerbated by a sullenness that had befallen him since I had won the karaoke competition. Jimmy had stopped using my real name altogether and, as often happens at a karaoke bar, when the person requesting a song had left the bar by the time it cued up, Jimmy would mutter, "Maybe we should get the King to sing it, he's so popular."

Mori had left his wife of fifty years for Irma. They ran off to open a karaoke bar on an island "in the South Pacific… or maybe the North Atlantic." Decades of karaoke history were to be torn down in a matter of weeks, and in the place of the Lily Pad would rise a modernized, karaoke multiplex, replete with private rooms and "girls who sit on your lap while you sing." It was no surprise that the new owner was the Karaoke Group International. But why hadn't anyone complained? The employees took their two-week severance payouts and shuffled off into a nebulous future. Josie was working the late-night, drive-thru window at Jack in the Box. Ricardo and Jaime moved to LA to help at a cousin's Subway franchise. The others were working part-time in local Chinese restaurants for sub-minimum wage. And Jimmy?

"Jimmy doesn't like to think of the future," he said.

You and me both, Jimmy. As I waited for him to lock up, I drummed my fingers on the steering wheel. In the alley, a dog barked at two winos pulling at the same blanket. Once Megumi's fiancé owned the Lily Pad, he'd probably have all three of them exterminated like lice.

Jimmy slid into the passenger seat. He smiled to himself and patted his jacket pocket. "Nice ride, King. Babes must love your wheels. Just like oh-oh-seven."

At Jimmy's place—a converted shed in the back lot of an abandoned warehouse—he hopped out nearly before I stopped. I watched him avoid my eyes, sling his backpack over his shoulders, and scurry away. Halfway to the front door he stopped. He appeared to be arguing aloud to himself. He stomped his foot and scored the debate by jabbing his finger into his palm. He returned and opened the car door.

"Here, King." Jimmy shoved a crumpled letter at me. "Fan mail."

I tilted the envelope toward the streetlamp's yellow light. The addressee was "Guy Watanabe, Karaoke King c/o

The Lily Pad." There was no return address. Inside was a neatly folded paper placemat. On it was a map of the United States overlaid with a colorful maze. A figure wearing prison stripes clutched a sack to his chest. Above his head, it read, "Kids! Help the Hamburgler find his way home!"

I flipped the placemat over and found a letter written in pencil in the neat, even script third-graders learn in school.

Dear Guy,

I don't have much time. He will suspect if I don't come out of the restroom soon. I wish I could have heard you sing one last time, but I have no control over where I go and what I do.

We'll probably never see each other again. That's too bad, isn't it? I would like a life as simple as yours. Nothing to do but sing karaoke and drink beer (though women shouldn't drink beer—it makes them fat). I wanted to take a plane but he wanted to drive his convertible car. What a bore! He says some people look at the desert and see only sand. He looks at the desert and sees entertainment complexes linked by ribbons of asphalt opportunity.

He sings too but only in private, in the bath, in the car. He watches my reaction. Of course I must hide it. He is smart, rich, and handsome, but he cannot move me the way you do. You sing and I think, "Yes, this is who I am." Am I wrong to believe that deep down inside we are the same? Maybe we knew each other in a past life. Maybe we'll meet again in a future one. In this one I'm afraid we are lost to one another forever.

I am happy to have a souvenir of our time together. I'll wear it close to my heart (unless he makes me throw it away). I hope you will think of me and maybe even miss me a little.

Yours,
Megumi

I turned the placemat over in my hands and found only grease stains. The postmark on the envelope read "Leaven-worth, WA."

Leavenworth. Tanya's mother loved the town so much we made sure never to go there. At some point in time, the town had decided to take advantage of its location at the base of the Cascade mountain range by transforming itself into a fake Bavarian town. The townspeople celebrated Oktober-fest, made Christmas ornaments, and generally behaved as if they were marketing-savvy Germans. Tanya's mom said the town looked "like something out of the *Sound of Music*," but better because it wasn't filled with smelly Europeans.

Megumi hadn't explained herself. She hadn't apologized. What was it with the women in my life? I stabbed the steak knife into the ignition and twisted. The car roared to life.

I drove over the bridge, past Redmond, and into Sammamish to clear my head. I wasn't being fair. Her fiancé had arranged for me to be beaten for my transgressions. He had so terrorized Megumi that she hid in a McDonald's restroom to scribble me a surreptitious note.

"I have no control over what I do or where I go." She sounded less like a fiancée than she did a prisoner. If I read between the lines, wasn't her letter really a cry for help? If she didn't care for me, she never would have risked being caught with proof of her lingering affection.

Also, she still had my medallion.

What was I going to do about it?

John Smith's business card listed a phone number, a fax number, and an e-mail address. The 1-800 number connected me to a voicemail box. Franchisees were to press 1; distributors were to press 2; all others were to press 3 or stay on the line to leave a message. I pushed 1. John reminded me that orders could be placed, and most common questions could be answered, online at the franchisee Web site. I wrote down the Web address.

I had two other leads: my frozen assets and the Lily Pad land deal. The bank's 24-hour customer service representative informed me that a "municipal court order" was blocking access to my funds. Obviously, Megumi's fiancé had filed a sham legal action against me. It was unlikely he used his real name in the suit, but I would be able, at very least, to locate an associated law firm. The more promising lead was the Karaoke Group's purchase of the Lily Pad. By law, all purchases and sales of land are publicly recorded. He may have signed the transfer documents himself.

At 8:30 a.m., the Recorder's Office was waking up, the front desk people blinking over mugs of coffee as I tapped away at a public computer terminal. Mori had been steadily selling off his Seattle properties over the past year. The sale of the Lily Pad to the Karaoke Group International had been finalized a month ago. A search for "The Karaoke Group" returned records for the purchase of other properties on the same block. A click on the hyperlinks to the scanned documents showed that none of them had been signed by Megumi's fiancé or his henchman John Smith. Jay Weed, the Karaoke Group's legal representative, had signed on the company's behalf. That is, Jay Weed, Real Estate & Land Use partner at Norton, Walters & Eldrich.

Any developer with money to burn hired Jay—he wouldn't rest until the City Council, neighboring businesses, and neighborhood groups were singing the project's praises. The new karaoke complex had Jay's fingerprints all over it. Public parking meant a tax break; "affordable housing" meant city support and, of course, another tax break. Jay was a fundraiser for the state Democratic Party, and reaped benefits for his support of the governor and mayor. With Jay behind your project, you could build a brothel for chronically inebriated HIV-positive leather bikers with leprosy and not face a single regulatory obstacle. The mystery of Jay Weed was how a person so well-connected could so lack in social grace.

Jay slammed doors for no reason. He ordered associates to get his coffee and paralegals to pick up his dry-cleaning. He handed out "urgent" assignments on Friday at 5:30 p.m.

Regardless of how much work he generated for NWE, I made it a point never to work with him, which, given my gender, was easy. The best-kept, best-known NWE secret was that Jay worked only with young women. No sexual harassment suit had ever been pressed against him, but I knew his leering and drooling would eventually get him Packwooded. Tanya disagreed, of course, and worked with him frequently.

"You're so callous," she said. "Jay drools because he had a stroke."

Well, okay, but that didn't explain his inability to work with men or the abuse he heaped on women. Tanya didn't have an answer for that. "He's very complex," she said. Why is Bubba at the football game a jerk while the rich Democratic Party fundraiser is "complex?"

I crossed the street and took the elevator to the Municipal Court Clerk's Office. What were my options? Jay was a dead end because, as Gracie put it, with Jay it was "no tits, no talk." Good old Gracie. Only she could be offended by his failure to harass a chubby Asian woman. Would Gracie copy notes from the file for me? That would entail telling her why I wanted the file. What were the chances Tanya knew something about the deal? Pretty good. She was a senior paralegal and one of the few who could stand working with Jay.

Hi, Tanya. I'm sure you're upset I never returned your calls, letters, or legal documents during the divorce proceedings. Or ever. I was wondering if you might jeopardize your job by telling me a little bit about a real estate deal Jay's working on. Even better, would you photocopy the entire client file for me?

The Municipal Court Clerk's Office was crowded. A bearded man wearing an American flag bandanna appeared to be using the computer terminal to search for the names of anyone who had wronged him since the end of the Vietnam War. I typed my name into the "Defendant" search field. A single record flashed onscreen: No. 06-030169, *Watanabe v. Watanabe.* I blinked my dry, scratchy eyes several times before I recovered. Megumi's fiancé hadn't frozen my assets. Tanya had.

Why hadn't Tanya reclaimed her maiden name after our divorce? I wish it was a way of signifying that our years together had meant something. No chance. She kept my surname because she detested her own. On the surface, "Dullard" isn't that bad and is far better than "Swallows." But distaste for her own name was driven by the undeniable fact that every member of the Dullard family—mother, father, brother, cousins, uncles, aunts, nieces, nephews, pets—was tremendously dull.

Spending a holiday with the Dullards was like traversing a vast, windswept wasteland without the invigoration of being outdoors. Dinner conversation, the little there was of it, focused on television docudramas. Not sitcoms, not talk shows, but current-events-driven docudramas like "Mother May I Sleep with Danger" and "She Woke Up Pregnant." Tanya's baby brother, a pudgy, permanent adolescent in his twenties with greased-back hair, was obsessed with all things mafia. His favorite phrase, uttered every ten minutes: "That guy deserves to get whacked."

A week before the wedding, I dreamt we were standing at the altar, reciting our vows. When I leaned over to kiss Tanya, her face was pixelated. I looked at the pastor, and his robes flickered. The entire congregation was sitting on overstuffed couches, faces bathed in a ghostly glow, digging into bowls of Cheetos.

The dream, when I told her about it, nearly sent Tanya into tremors. She feared that her name foretold her fate, that the Dullard blood coursing sluggishly through her veins would eventually coagulate into a life exactly like that of her parents, or her brother, or any other relative who could still press the buttons on a remote control. She battled valiantly, restricting our television viewing to 8 p.m. to 10 p.m. on weeknights and 7 p.m. to 11 p.m. on weekends, but if she was drunk or agitated, she would slink out of bed to get a television fix. At 5 a.m., she would shake me awake.

"Do you think I'm dull?" she'd whisper.

I tried calling Tanya from a payphone in the courthouse foyer. Carolyn, the firm's perky receptionist said, "Sorry, Guy. She left a note that says she won't talk to you unless you come in person." Our first meeting since she left wasn't supposed to be on her terms. But what choice did I have?

Norton, Walters & Eldrich occupied the top ten floors of Bank of America Tower, seventy-six stories of black glass, corners smoothed into curves to maximize the views. For a decade, I'd lived a third of my life in its temperature-controlled environs. Besides the NWE cafeteria, the building housed a food court, a Burger King, a post office, a gym, gift stores, a dry cleaner, a Starbucks, and a Tully's Coffee. The only thing missing was a mortuary.

NWE's receptionist extraordinaire Carolyn reminded me of air hostesses before discrimination suits empowered them to become shriveled and surly. She wore smart outfits that clung to her trim figure, and evinced the steely equanimity it takes to shove a passenger down an inflatable slide into the ocean.

"Why, Guy Watanabe!" she said. "You sounded the same over the phone, but I barely recognize you behind those facial bruises. You look a bit bedraggled."

"Good word, Carolyn. I feel a bit bedraggled. How are things? Still salsa every night of the week?"

"Only Wednesday through Monday. Tuesday's tango. Here to see Tanya?"

I nodded. "Is she in the Paralegal Grotto?"

"She's in, but not in the Grotto. She's in Paul Sanderson's office. He's scuba diving in Cozumel."

Paul Sanderson was a live-hard, play-hard associate who could be found at midnight wandering the halls with a gym bag slung over his shoulder. "What's she doing in an attorney office? Space problems?"

Carolyn flicked her head like a finch. "You haven't heard?"

"The attorneys have traded their view offices for carpeted cubicles."

"No, silly. Tanya's starting law school in the fall, and NWE is footing the bill. The firm's trying to butter her up now that she's going to be an overlord. She's joining the Dark Side, Guy."

Paul Sanderson's office was on the west side of the building, facing the Puget Sound. As I wended my way through the
familiar maze of offices and cubicles, I suppressed my annoy-
ance. I had no problem with Tanya going to law school. She
had the perfect temperament for the law. Due to a flaw in
her character, Tanya enjoyed minutiae, like making sure the
same brand of plastic tab was used in every exhibit binder.
But she had always harbored a working-class resentment of
the lawyers we served. Her father was a retired, union Boeing mechanic. Her only jobs before joining the firm were
waiting tables. She called NWE attorneys "hired guns for the
rich." Now she was joining their ranks.

I swept by the familiar faces before they could recover
and stop me. Everyone knew why I'd walked out of the firm
in the middle of a work day never to return. Why spend awkward moments avoiding the topic?

The office door was open. Tanya's profile was to me.
She cradled the phone receiver against her shoulder as she
typed. "Uh huh," she said. "Uh huh. Uh *huh*. Uh huh."

Tanya is the fastest hunt-and-peck typist on the planet.
Index fingers extended, she poked the keys with fury. Tanya
could type or she could listen, but if she was doing both
at the same time, she was liable to come unglued. While I
watched, she jammed her fingernail on the keyboard. She
shook her hand in pain and looked up. Her face froze, and
instead of "uh huh," she choked out a guttural "ungh."

Tanya looked different. Her hair was shorter, cut so that
it curved inward at her neck. And the strange thing was, I
could see her neck. Tanya was never overweight; she had
baby fat that had lasted into her thirties. She imagined herself to have a double-chin and disguised this not-double-

chin by wearing color-coordinated scarves. Now the scarf was gone, leaving a naked expanse of white flesh. She had lost ten or fifteen pounds, so her face had a determined look about it. I had hoped there'd be bags under her eyes and needle tracks on her arms. Instead, she looked beautiful.

"I need to call you right back, Jay." She blew the wispy bangs away from her eyes. "No, I understand the importance. No, no, no. I understand the importance. Yes, it'll be done by the end of the day." Tanya grimaced. "Look—I have a feminine problem I need to take care of. Uh huh. Bye." She folded her arms.

"Hi," I said.

"Hello," she said.

"Nice office."

"It's temporary. Why don't you sit down?" Her eyes glanced down at my ratty tennis shoes and then back up to my face. She touched her cheekbones and her eyelids fluttered. "Does it hurt, Guy? I mean, do you need a painkiller, or hydrogen peroxide or something?"

I sat down across from her. Paul Sanderson was a business attorney and had all sorts of deal toys—corporate thingamajigs that commemorate the close of a deal—littering his desk. There were paperweights shaped like cubes, pyramids, and dodecahedrons, in the center of which were miniature reproductions of the closing contracts.

"I'm fine. Just got into a little accident."

"Are you sure? You don't take care of yourself when I'm not around." She rifled through her cavernous purse. "I've got Bayer Tablets, Advil Caplets, and Tylenol Extra Strength Liqui-Gels. Oh. I also have some recently expired

113

Neosporin. It should still work." Some kids ate Pez; Tanya had been raised on orange-flavored Johnson & Johnson baby aspirin. The first time we French kissed, my tongue went numb.

"I said I was fine." If I sounded annoyed, it was because I was.

She dropped the bottles with a clatter into her purse. She wore her professional expression: tight at the lips, blank in the eyes.

"I'm sure you know why I'm here," I said. "We've got to talk about our finances."

Tanya pulled a ballpoint pen from the football-helmet pencil holder and started clicking it. "It's about time, isn't it, Guy? I mean it should have been time during the dissolution proceedings, but you never showed. And it should have been time when I filed the garnishment action, but you never accepted service."

"I've had a lot on my mind."

"And the apartment. You could have told the landlord you were leaving. Everything we owned got dumped in the street! And work. Do you realize *I* got you that severance package? You didn't even tell anyone you were leaving. They were going to fire you! And why don't you have an answering machine? You could have at least taken ours. It was a wedding present. It had a digital chip, three mailboxes, and ninety minutes of recording time. It must have cost $200!"

"I went back for the car."

Tanya shoved herself away from the desk, her chair striking with a thunk against the keyboard shelf. She rubbed her elbow and looked over at her purse, wondering, I'm sure, whether to extract an Excedrin Geltab. "That's the one thing you should have left! I can't believe it's still running. That was the most impractical car. Our friends had to lie down in the hatchback space. What if we'd gotten rear-ended? What if we'd had children?"

"It looks a lot better now. Got some ground effects."

"Well I'm glad. It wouldn't have looked so bad if you'd washed it once in a while." She rolled her chair forward.

"Tanya."

"Uh huh?"

"My bank account is frozen."

"I know it's frozen. I was the one who had it frozen, or didn't you know? That's what happens when you don't show up for court and your ex-wife refuses to pay off your debts."

"The Settlement Agreement specified that I kept the cash in the joint account, which was basically everything, and you kept our investments, which were basically nothing. What happened?"

"You read the Settlement Agreement but never sent it back? How could you, Guy? I was trying to make this painless for both of us." She folded her arms. Tanya wore loose clothing and slouched to deemphasize her ample breasts. It never worked. But they appeared smaller now. Probably the weight loss. Seeing her bare neck outside of the bedroom was positively obscene.

"You may find this hard to believe, Tanya, but I didn't find the fact that you walked out on me to be particularly painless."

Her eyes grew round and for a moment I thought she was going to cry. But she set her mouth and rallied. "Why do you have to put it that way?"

"In what way?"

"In such a hurtful way."

I sighed and grabbed a deal toy. This one was a Pyrex carrot. In the center was a floating cigarette with the words, "Phillip-Morris and Vegan Express: Jan. 25, 2002."

"I'm not trying to hurt you, Tanya. I need you to unfreeze my checking account. Look—we can talk. We are talking. There's no reason to involve the courts in our personal business. Right now, I can't even go for a carton of milk at the corner market."

"You're lactose intolerant."

"I know that. It was a hypothetical."

"I don't like that carrot thing." She crinkled her nose. "Could you stop waving it around?"

I hadn't realized that I'd been gesturing. I turned the carrot over in my hand. It had ridges and the leafy top was suspiciously globular. I set it down. "Too phallic?"

"No. It has a cigarette inside." Tanya rubbed her nose. Her favorite aunt, a chain-smoker, had worn a nicotine patch for twenty years and died of emphysema. If a smoker was within twenty yards, Tanya held her scarf to her nose. I once asked her if tobacco made her sick. She said it was the exact opposite. As a child, she curled up with her aunt in front of the television just to inhale the nicotine emitting from her pores. "What happened to your face, Guy?"

"It's nothing really." I stood and looked out the window. A ferry was making its way across the Puget Sound to Bainbridge Island. To the south, scores of orange shipping cranes congregated along the coastline, methodically plucking boxes from cargo ships and depositing them onshore. "Car accident. I hit a deer." True, all true. I turned around. "I don't get the point of this lawsuit."

"It brought you here, didn't it?"

Why was she so pragmatic? So long as we both drank coffee, we would have run into each other in a café eventually. In fact, that's how I'd imagined it, Tanya begging for forgiveness over a latte. I'd also pictured her standing sopping wet on my doorstep, throwing her arms around my neck and telling me to take her back. Instead here we were, at the firm, in someone else's office, picking up where we'd left off: talking to each other and saying nothing.

Tanya's upper teeth scraped at her lower lip. *Go on, apologize,* I willed her, *because* I *don't have anything to apologize for.* Where did she get that tan? Tanya was fair-skinned and any exposure to the sun caused her to break out in a rash. Plus, she wasn't one to take vacations. She liked regular, predictable schedules. Even if she took Friday off, she'd say throughout the day, "Isn't it strange not to be at work?"

"I've been doing a lot of thinking, Guy."

"Mm hm?"

"And I don't know if you'll understand this, but—" She hesitated.

"Go ahead. Try me."

She click-clacked her ballpoint pen. "Over the phone, you know, *that* time, I said a lot of things. Like how we'd grown apart, needed to go our separate ways. Breaking up stuff."

"Yup. I recall that pretty well."

"And, you know, I *meant* it at the time. But I didn't really understand it. And I think I do now. Or at least a little better. I mean, it's not like I went to the conference intending to leave you. It's just that—" She paused. "Do you believe in 'dates with destiny'?"

Her phrasing was all-too-familiar. Was it possible that… no, not Tanya. "I'm not sure where this is leading."

She leaned forward. "You've got to promise you won't make fun of me. You've got to promise, promise, promise. You won't right? I mean, this is the kind of stuff I usually make fun of. The kind of thing I picture fat people in the Midwest buying into. Do you promise not to make fun of me?"

"I promise." Go ahead. Say it. It's really not that hard. Okay, fine, I didn't like telling people about him either.

"I bought the Troy Bobbins *Personal Path* audio series," she said. "I know what you're going to say. He's an infomercial swindler. But before you say that, you've got to listen to him. What he said went straight to the heart of what I was feeling but couldn't express. One lesson in particular— *'Cry Freedom': The Inner Apartheid of the Spirit*—helped me to understand our relationship. In my mind, I was Stephen Biko, and you were the oppressive South African regime squelching individual human potential. Does that make sense?"

She was talking about the second-to-last lesson in the series. Troy's tone was hushed and introspective. "There is a dark night of the soul, my friends. And in order to take that long night's journey into the day, we must identify our captors. We each have a 'date with destiny'—an essential image of what our lives should be, deprived of which we will die, or worse, become the spiritually crippled, wandering the desolate plains of our souls, hands outstretched for public subsidies. Who is threatening you with a cattle prod? Who is flaying you with a rubber hose? It may be the person you refuse to suspect. Ask whose needs you've placed before your own. An oppressive regime cannot exist without the consent of the dispossessed. Remember, 'Biko. Because. Biko.'"

Tanya's lips parted as she waited for me to answer. A dark lip pencil outlined the curves and held the maroon shade within a neat boundary. It was so different from her usually smeared, mismatched lipstick. I shook my head to clear it. Tanya had cast *me* as P.W. Botha. Screw her. She was Winnie to my Nelson Mandela.

"I can't believe you bought into that television mass hypnotism," I said. "I expected more from you."

Tanya blushed, the kind of full-body blush that caused her to scratch at her forearms. "That's just like you, Guy Watanabe—rejecting something you can't understand. I've spent the last year improving myself. I lost the twenty pounds I'd always wanted to lose. I start law school in the fall. Meanwhile, what have you been doing? You're not invisible. I've heard about your wanderings from bar to bar. You've even started singing *karaoke* again." She said "karaoke" as if she were crushing a bug. Meanwhile, Tanya was rubbing her nose. When she was upset, she could rub it raw. But she suddenly stopped, spread her fingers on the desktop, and counted to five under her breath. Aha! A Troy Bobbins "habit-buster" move. She had learned his lessons well.

"What do you want, Tanya? If I apologize, will you drop the garnishment action? Fine. I'm sorry I blamed you for leaving me. I never meant to banish your soul to a shantytown with exposed public sewage."

"There you go again, using sarcasm as a shield." She was in full control again, eyes flashing with fluorescent brilliance. "But sarcasm just means 'I refuse to think out of the box.'"

Damn that Troy Bobbins. He had a comeback for everything. "Tell me what you want, Tanya, and I'll do it. Drop the suit."

"I don't want a *thing*, Guy. I want us to talk. I need emotional closure. Maybe we both do. I know I did the right thing, but I feel guilty. I don't want to continue feeling that way."

I studied her face for an indication that she recognized her proposition to be emotional extortion. She was 100 percent earnest. "Fine. You want talk, you've got it. Talk is easy. Talk is cheap."

Tanya pulled two documents from an expanding file. The first was a motion to dismiss the garnishment action without prejudice. It contained a stipulation that a motion to reopen would be filed in the event "Defendant does not satisfy the terms of the confidential Settlement Agreement." The Settlement Agreement stated that "Mr. Watanabe shall call Ms. Watanabe no fewer than one (1) time per two (2) calendar weeks and engage in active conversation for no fewer than thirty (30) minutes. This Agreement shall terminate six (6) months after its execution unless the parties mutually agree in writing to an extension of the terms." A bicycle courier would file the motion later in the afternoon. As soon as the judge signed the proposed order, Tanya would walk a copy to the bank herself.

I circled the desk and leaned close to sign the Settlement Agreement. Her hair smelled of Head & Shoulders, the soapy blue Milk of Magnesia her entire family swore by: clean, bland and, nevertheless, familiar and comforting. She smiled and placed her left hand on a binder labeled "Karaoke Grp. Int'l: Leases/Subcontractors."

Tanya rubbed at her nose. "You think I'm selfish, don't you? Forcing you to help me get over a hurdle to my self-development..." She waited for me to respond.

"Not at all," I lied. "If our positions were reversed, I'd be doing the same thing."

Tanya exhaled. "It means so much to hear you say that. I—" She paused. "I mean, I know I didn't make a mistake. I didn't. I had a date with destiny."

"Of course you did."

"I did, didn't I?"

"Of course you did."

Tanya's face brightened. "It's amazing what the three Ds—Discipline, Desire, and Dedication—can do." She ran her hands lightly over her hip bones. She caught herself and smiled sheepishly. She extended her hand. "I hope things are going to work out better for you, Guy. Maybe you should try listening to—oh, never mind."

"No offense, but all that Troy Bobbins stuff is just not my thing." I released her hand and nodded toward the stack of work. "Working on anything interesting?"

She blew her bangs upward with a puff of air. "They give me a lot more responsibility now that I'm going to become a lawyer. I'm staffing this real estate development project all alone with Jay Weed. Can you believe it, just a partner and a paralegal? I mean, it's just due diligence and I can't sign anything, but it feels good to be trusted on an important deal."

All alone with Jay the Hairy Satyr? "Awesome. What's the subject matter?"

"Neighborhood revitalization in the International District. Public parking, affordable housing, and private business. A synergistic public-private partnership that will bring much needed investment into the lowest-income neighborhood in Seattle."

Did she memorize that from a press release? "Fantastic. Can't get enough of those win-win, private-public partnerships, can we? What's the business?"

"It's, um, karaoke." She hesitated. "You know how I feel about karaoke. But this is upscale karaoke. The kind of luxury club they have in Asia. This company has it down to a science. Any song, any key, if you can't sing it, the microphone will automatically tune your voice up or down to match the music. You never need to feel embarrassed in front of your business associates."

"That's very, um, new millennium." It also wasn't karaoke. It was lipsynching.

"I know you think I'm being hypocritical, but there's a big difference between being a karaoke *producer* and a karaoke *consumer*. It's the difference between being the CEO of McDonald's and, say, being an obese man who eats Quarter Pounders every day. One creates jobs and provides services in the community, and the other makes minimum wage and eats junk food because he doesn't know how to cook."

"That's a pretty tangible difference."

"It is." Tanya folded her arms.

"Has Jay let you meet the CEO? Have you sat in on any meetings?"

"No. He was in Seattle but never came to the firm. Jay said Asian businessmen prefer to talk over drinks and food late at night. He's a big philanthropist. Jay said *he* was the one to suggest affordable housing."

I rubbed my eye and stared at the binder, repeating the case number over and over in my head. 12306-98118. 12306-98118. "I think I might have heard something in the paper about his project. He's a big Hong Kong entrepreneur. What's his name?"

"It wouldn't have been in the paper. Jay's very hush-hush until every piece of a deal's in place. That way, only *The Stranger* can complain. And who believes anarchists?" Tanya picked up the binder and flipped through the contents. "That's funny. It's not listed anywhere. He doesn't like to attract a lot of attention. It's Horatio...Horatio Koh-something. Loh-something? Jay's been signing the papers on his behalf. He's very well-respected in the Asian American community. He was the anonymous donor who founded Entrepreneurs for Hungry Children."

Not so anonymously, I see. "So why not sign for himself?"

"He's out of town. Jay says he's got a fascination for the American West. For the next few months, he's driving from prospective investment to prospective investment in a vintage Mustang convertible. He told Jay his childhood dream was to drive through the desert, wind blowing in his hair, singing, 'We Are the World.'"

What a fruitcake. "So he's investing in more than Seattle?"

"Oh yeah. Seattle's just his first stop. He's buying up real estate throughout the western states in rural and distressed communities. Jay's handling his Washington deals. I'm not staffing the biggie—a monster project near Leavenworth. There must be three associates and five or six paralegals on that one."

"Sounds like Jay tells you a lot."

Tanya put the binder down and adjusted her skirt. "It's not like that, Guy. He's been very supportive of my choice to enter law school."

"I'm sure he's just drooling over the opportunity to add another female associate to Real Estate and Land Use."

She sat down and glowered. "Don't ruin it, Guy. I almost believed you cared about what I've been doing with my life."

Tanya didn't escort me to the elevator. I was almost bowled over by Jay Weed, who was charging along with his head down, his post-stroke limp moving him forward fast through gyroscopic action. He entered Tanya's office and shut the door.

I made a final stop at the Paralegal Grotto. No matter how many fluorescent lights were on, the brown walls absorbed all illumination. Gracie wasn't in her cubicle. Women's magazines were strewn all over her desktop, three of which were open, so I considered waiting. But Lance—a wormy paralegal with noise-cancelling headphones grafted to his head—said she'd gone on a singles kayaking trip in the San Juan Islands. Gracie, kayaking? She called walking the block from the bus stop to work "hiking." What was the world coming to?

I stuck a Post-It on her phone. It wasn't until I was in the elevator that I realized she would have no way of contacting me. I would soon be back on the road.

CHAPTER 10

Or so I thought. It wasn't as easy to disentangle my financial affairs as Tanya had suggested. Short on cash and long on time, I marinated at the metallic, cubist hatbox we call the Seattle Public Library, vying for forty-five minute blocks of Internet time with homeless men and migrant day laborers.

My searches for "Horatio" and "karaoke," or "Horatio" and "philanthropy" returned nothing but self-help tales, British naval exploits, and meditations on the nature of friendship and truth. His charity Entrepreneurs for Hungry Children had done nothing during its existence except hold fundraising dinners for corpulent businesspeople. Like the number of the beast, his name was never mentioned, but his sulfurous presence suffused the proceedings. In a "Society" column for the *Seattle Asian Herald*, Norene Wong referred to "a prince among men," the "leader of a new generation of pan-Asian entrepreneurs who does good and does well."

Without a password, the Karaoke Group International's Web site was a dead end. A Web search for "Karaoke Group

International" returned the names of restaurants, bars, and equipment manufacturers...and the minutes of a Leavenworth City Council meeting. "Milton Schwarzer again protested KGI proj., &c. Was again informed of win-win situation. Stormed out of mtg."

All tires rolled through Leavenworth. I typed "Milton Schwarzer" into Google and got two results. The first link was entitled, HOTRAWSEXRAUNCHYCUMASIANSMIDG-ETS-FETISH," and the description listed, along with other words expurgated from collegiate dictionaries, "milton schwarzer." Was "milton schwarzer" sexual slang like "Dirty Sanchez?" I clicked on the link and was greeted with pop-ups of women in concourse with garden vegetables, hirsute men practicing animal husbandry, and Orbitz advertisements.

The other link led to the correspondence section of a Leavenworth newspaper.

Dear Editor:

As the letter by Stephen Olsen shows, our citizenry is brainwashed by the City Council's simple formula: all storefronts must look "Bavarian." But what's Bavarian? It can't mean miles of stenciled overhangs. The Dachau McDonald's is modern and thoroughly Bavarian at the same time. The old and the new exist side by side. What we have in Leavenworth is a caricature. We should focus on internal changes—how we think and feel. Only that will allow our true cultural character to express itself.

Milton Schwarzer
President, Nouveau German Heritage Association

Leavenworth was meant to *look* Bavarian, not *be* Bavarian. If McDonald's could become intrinsically Bavarian, why couldn't a karaoke complex? Or did KGI refuse to adhere to the Bavarian storefront regulations? What kind of German nationalist would use a French word meaning "new" to describe a "heritage" association?

Milton Schwarzer sounded like a letter-writing zealot I would avoid on Metro buses. But if he opposed KGI's project or its CEO, he must have redeeming qualities. The enemy of my enemy must be a friend.

What's there to dislike about gingerbread storefronts and hanging flower baskets? A faux-Bavarian town like Leavenworth hardly differs from a Barnes & Noble town square. Impoverished communities would have to adapt or die. Sure, Poulsbo had already staked claim to Little Norway, but there were dozens of quaint cultures to adopt as one's own. A public housing project could be rechristened "New Moscow." The possibilities were limitless.

None of the McDonald's employees remembered Megumi. How could they after serving scores of Asian tourists filing off luxury tour buses en route to Indian casinos and other natural wonders? I needed to find Milton Schwarzer. I'd presumed it would be easy to find a gadfly, but City Hall was closed in honor of the International Accordion Celebration.

Tourists clustered every fifty yards around an accordionist. One played patriotic marches and another played tango. At the gazebo five Native American men in ponchos played a familiar, haunting tune. Two squeezed accordions, and the others blew into wooden flutes. It was the Inca jazz band from Pike Place Market. As if to verify that fact, a sad-faced, dark-complexioned girl in pigtails—the ten-year-old who accompanied the band rain or shine, weekday or weekend—held up a compact disc entitled "Inca Jazz-Polka Infusion." Inca jazz and polka, melancholy and effervescence, yang and ying. The fusion recalled a sunny day spent alone indoors.

Sprinkled amidst the tourists were natives of Leavenworth, or at least the workers of Leavenworth. The women looked like extras from 1970s Swedish erotica videos in their red skirts, white blouses, and black satin bodices. The men wore *lederhosen,* suspenders, and hats with animal hair combs, prepared at any moment to put their hands on their hips and yodel.

A rotund, ruddy-faced native swayed to the music with his eyelids shut. His *lederhosen* were forest-green suede, finely detailed with flowers and vines along the seams. At the end of the song, he clapped wildly. "Wasn't that great?" he said to no one in particular. The band took a break. I introduced myself.

"*Willkomen, Willkomen.* Where you from, stranger?" He pumped my hand vigorously.

"Seattle."

"Good. Good. *Willkomen.* People from all over the world are here this weekend. Wenatchee. Longview. Portland."

Frank Johnson was just the kind of person I had hoped to encounter. Member of the Leavenworth Historical Society, owner of *Klaus's Wursthaus and Chocoteria*, he was filled with civic pride, local trivia, and palpable loneliness. He had been responsible for booking the Inca jazz-polka band and hoped someday to organize the entire festival ("Betty's territorial, but at least I've moved on from *Anniversary of the Autobahn*."). I interrupted at Year 50 of his Leavenworth narrative history.

"Isn't Milton Schwarzer involved in these German heritage events?"

Frank's smile disappeared. "How is it you know Schwarzer?"

"I don't really," I said. "I've heard of him. We've all heard of him, even if we don't agree with his views, right?"

Frank nodded. "I suppose that's true. He's a loud little fellow when he gets a full head of steam. Not like what he says is *all* bad, it's just too radical. All kids need to know is the difference between *Guten Tag* and *Guten Morgen*. Little touches keep tourists coming back, not reeducation programs."

"Right. This isn't a Bavarian town. It's a simulated Bavarian town."

"My sentiments exactly," Frank said. "It's probably Schwarzer's German blood. My Dad was a WWII vet. He always said, 'Never trust Krauts or Japs. They're fanatics.' Let the Euros keep their high taxes and democratic socialism. We're Americans. We adopt the best of every culture, like beer, sausage, and leather shorts." Frank scratched at his thinning hair. "By the way, what was your last name again?"

"Watanabe."

"You're not Japanese, are you?"

"Not exactly."

Frank patted his brow with a handkerchief. "Good. Don't want to offend, you know. We get lots of Jap tourists. Jerry too, since they get that long European vacation of theirs. Two months, can you believe it?"

"Two months is a long time."

"That's why those European economies are swirling down the toilet. They don't know how to put in an honest day's work. As if we all have time to eat with our families." Frank pulled the *lederhosen* higher on his belly.

"So Schwarzer's a fanatic."

"You got that right. There's something shady about him. First of all, he won't drive a car. Rides a bicycle with a bell on it on the freaking highway. And he won't talk about his past. Doesn't say he won't neither. Just glares until you pretend you never asked."

"So no one knows anything about him?"

Frank lowered his voice. "There's some who say he's an illegal who ran away from the Cirque du Soleil. That explains his physique but not his lack of an accent." He cleared his throat. "My biggest beef with Schwarzer," he said in a normal tone, "is that for all his complaints, he never lifts a finger to plan the German-heritage celebrations. Locks himself up in his log cabin and fires off missives to the City Council. How civic-minded is that?"

The Inca jazz-polka band tuned up with flute runs and pulls of the accordion. Frank cocked his head.

"Do you know how I can meet Schwarzer?" I said.

The band began to play. "You want to meet Schwarzer? What in the world for?"

"I always wanted to meet a Cirque du Soleil performer. They're so flexible."

His brow furrowed. "Don't tell him you heard it from me." He pointed over my left shoulder. "Over there, in *Das Puppenhaus*."

A crowd was clustered around an entrance, where the front case displayed an elaborate, multi-storied dollhouse. I turned to ask how I'd recognize Schwarzer, but Frank was already gone, eyes closed, adrift upon the melodic flow of the Inca jazz-polka infusion.

Das Puppenhaus was so popular I had to slither my way through the customers who stopped to gawk in the foyer. Along the walls, in locked glass cabinets, was an array of the valuable miniatures—porcelain dolls dressed in lace, Javanese shadow puppets, tiny sets of bone china and jewelry. But the crowd-pleasers were the mechanized panoramic displays. In one case, chain-mailed knights laid siege to a walled city while defenders tipped thimble-sized vats of boiling oil onto their heads. In another, a father in front of a tract home used a garden hose to wash a Lexus.

Was Schwarzer the *puppen*master of this extravagant showcase for all things small? I looked for him, but no men in *lederhosen* patrolled the exhibits. There were only strapping teenaged girls in scarlet skirts. I was resigned to joining the long queue at the info booth until I spied a skinny young *fräulein* dusting a display case in the corner. A Marlboro box was stuffed into the back hem of her skirt. She slouched and her skin was so pale the branches of her veins shimmered on her forearms. I said "excuse me" three times before she turned around.

"Welcome to the *Puppen*-house." She frowned. "I'm about to go on break. Can you get someone else to help you?"

"I'm looking for Milton Schwarzer."

She rolled her eyes. "Oh, the *Führer.*"

I waited for her to elaborate, but she didn't. "Where can I find him?"

"I dunno. He's here. He's there. Little fucker's everywhere."

"Would you mind helping me out? It's important."

She tucked the feather duster beneath an armpit. "I might if I didn't hate this goddamned place. I can't believe I work with these idiots."

"Sheila," as the girl's nametag read, didn't fit the mold of the other *Das Puppenhaus fräulein.* The others were blonde, top-heavy, and born to serve steins of beer in an alpine village. Sheila had dyed-black hair and the chest of a ten-year-old boy.

Sheila shrugged. "Fine. I've got nothing better to do."

Sheila clomped away in her Doc Martens. I meandered from exhibit to exhibit. In the center of the room, beneath plexiglass, was a replica of Leavenworth's Front Street. The color of every storefront sign, every window and lamppost, had been rendered with meticulous care. It was like hovering over the town in a helicopter. A cluster of figurines stood before the gazebo, where two of five figures in ponchos played accordions. A pudgy onlooker in Bavarian garb had his eyes closed. I located the façade of the miniaturized *Das Puppenhaus* and looked inside. Too many figurines were crowded together to distinguish anyone in particular.

There was a clearance section near the cash register where *Das Puppenhaus* relegated the miniatures that had failed—sides of beef, replica Greenpeace ships, et cetera. At the end of the table were two wicker baskets filled with finger-sized plastic babies. The first basket was a quarter full of white babies. Leaned against it was a note card reading, "Special! $5 each." The second bin was filled to the brim with black babies, but the sign read, "Special! $5 $2.50 each." Curious, I grabbed one of each. Except for skin tone, they were identical.

The largest crowd stood transfixed by a West Virginia strip-mining display, where a high-pressure stream of water tore the top off of a mountain. I glanced back at the signs: "$5" and "$5 $2.50." What would be the harm? I scanned the room, then swapped the signs. Thrusting my hands into my pockets, I walked away, whistling a happy tune. Halfway to the strip-mining display, my knees crashed against a solid, muscular wall.

"Why did you do that?" The voice was a low rumble. The speaker was a midget in a green wool hat, suspenders, and *lederhosen*. He scowled at me, his skin taut like a boy's, the wrinkles on his face hairline cracks in glass. On his neck was a waxy scar—the perfect double-arc of a human mouth. I stared, realized that staring at another person's scar was wrong, and looked away.

"I'm sorry," I said. "But except for the color, they're the same item. They should be selling for the same price."

His torso was a barrel and his limbs were stout and hairy. "You want to price those plastic babies differently, sell them yourself. Inside *Das Puppenhaus* only one law exists, the natural law of supply and demand. I've got no patience for National Palestinian Radio idealism."

He remained standing there, arms crossed. Aside from his scar, his most impressive features were his tree-trunk legs.

"I haven't got all day," he said. "I'm running a business here. Say something."

This was my introduction to Milton Schwarzer.

CHAPTER 11

"Watanabe, huh?" Milton Schwarzer's fingertips traced the upper arc of the scar on his neck. "Sounds familiar."

"It's a common name."

"Not in Leavenworth." Milton surveyed his grazing customers. "All right, Watanabe. You've got my attention. We can talk karaoke. But not here."

We descended the spiral staircase. Schwarzer's hypertrophied legs—his calves bulging and breathing with each footfall—churned with deceptive speed. On the tiered shelving, cardboard shrouded cities and bubble wrap entombed entire peoples. At the end of a hallway stood a polished chrome door reinforced by three deadbolts and a widow's clasp.

Schwarzer's windowless office smelled like a recently defrosted freezer. With a hydraulic hiss, his high-backed office chair rose until he glowered down at me. Sunken deep into burgundy leather, dressed in Bavarian finery, he was fairy tale royalty, a troll king.

"Watanabe." Schwarzer tapped his fountain pen like a truncheon on his palm. "I've heard that name before."

"It's as common in Japan as Smith is here."

"Smith, huh?" He licked his lips. "Did you really drive here to talk about a new karaoke bar?"

The graying hair at his temples and the folds on his neck suggested an old man, but his physique didn't. He clenched and unclenched his fountain pen, knotting the midget muscle of his forearm. A little voice inside warned that it was hazardous to lie, but an equally compelling little voice said that Schwarzer could not be trusted. Best to stick with the script.

"In Seattle, we too are fighting the good fight against the multinational conglomerate Karaoke Group International."

I hadn't expected Schwarzer to embrace me, but I hadn't expected him to receive me so coolly either. I repeated my best lines: "Small business is the vanguard of a free society," and "Some may say we'll be destroyed by the tsunami of corporate greed, but someone must set forth in the dinghy of integrity."

Schwarzer's scar, ropy pink and white, undulated on his neck. It was definitely the imprint of human teeth. A bite that severe should have involved gnashing, should have left a blurred, messy lump of scar tissue. These teeth had sunken into him and held.

"We need your help," I said. "KGI's karaoke complex doesn't belong in Seattle's International District, and it doesn't belong in Leavenworth. KGI will dilute the Bavarian goodwill that you and your faux-German forebears worked so hard to cultivate."

Schwarzer frowned. "That's the point I've been trying to make to the imbeciles on the city council. KGI's karaoke complex hurts our bottom line. Period. They can fantasize all they want about creating a United Nations of faux-countries in the Cascades, each reinforcing the profits of the other. But the last thing we need is KGI bringing Outer Mongolia here along with cut-rate, Third World labor. There are limited tourist dollars. To remain a First World power in control of our resources, we've got to stay on the offensive, whether or not we've got 'jurisdiction' over KGI's land or not."

"Then we're on the same side. Fight them on every front. If Seattle falls, Leavenworth falls. It's the domino effect."

Schwarzer squinted. "I don't give a flying fuck what happens to Seattle. KGI could open ten bars on the same Seattle block and I wouldn't care. You don't have a faux-Bavarian culture to protect."

"But if we share information, we can help each other."

"Maybe. But it seems to me that you're the one looking for information and I'm the one holding it." Schwarzer placed his hands on the desk's edge. "What's in it for you, Watanabe? How do you win if KGI loses? What's wrong with a top-flight karaoke bar in Seattle? Big screens everywhere, the ability to sing any song ever recorded via broadband access."

My stomach fluttered. Any song ever recorded? It had a decadent allure, like free online gaming on an Xbox 360. Stay strong. "Neighborhood businesses serve the community. Corporations could care less about people so long as their profits grow."

Schwarzer's seat lowered with a hydraulic hiss. He hopped off.

"I'll show you out," he said.

"But we're comrades in the same struggle! Won't you help us?"

Milton grabbed my elbow. "I distrust altruists. They shit on you and say it's for your own good."

A cascade of accordion notes greeted my departure from *Das Puppenhaus,* but I was in no mood to appreciate folk music. Schwarzer wouldn't help me unless I had something to offer *him.* All I knew was that Megumi and her fiancé were on a road trip through the southwest. The rest was hidden in the carefully guarded files of Norton, Walters & Eldrich.

I browsed novelty hats at *Der Hut* Hut. I watched teenagers spin saltwater taffy. I rarely drink beer but got a hankering for the sour taste to reflect my sour mood. A merchant selling paintings directed me to Klaus's Wursthaus and Chocoteria.

Passing an alley, I paused. A *fraulein* squatted there, enjoying a smoke, untroubled that her skirt and petticoat sagged onto the concrete. It was Sheila, scrawny *Das Puppenhaus* employee: elbows, knees, and dyed-black hair. She squinted up at me.

"Hey," she said.

"Hey," I said.

"So'd you get your audience with the little big man?"

"I did. He blew me off."

"Well, don't take it personally. He blows everyone off."
Plumes of smoke curled out of her nostrils. "So are you a
fan or what?"

A fan of miniatures? A fan of midgets? "I had a few questions, but he wouldn't answer them. I said that people in
Seattle admired him."

"You said that?" Sheila stood. With her habitual slouch,
she was almost my height; if she straightened, she'd be an
inch taller. "I wish I could've seen his face. He thinks he's
got it so good here in Mayberry. But somebody was bound
to recognize him. He better not blame me because I didn't
say anything."

"About what?"

"About his past. About—" Sheila scowled. "You don't
know, do you?"

I shrugged, hoping to convey the sense that maybe I did.

"Hmm…" She tugged at a hairpin. "Buy me a beer."

"I was on my way to Klaus's Wursthaus. Why don't you
join me?"

"In *Germany*, I'd be able to drink. But not in the good
old hypocritical U.S. of A." She extracted a second pin and
shook her hair loose. It didn't quite reach her shoulders
and was ragged at the ends, as if she'd cut it herself with
paper scissors. "Let's get a six-pack and drink it in your car.
If I'm liquored up, you can pump me for information."

If you look up the word "loser" in Webster's New Collegiate Dictionary, you might find a definition reading, "older
man who purchases cheap beer for teenaged girls." For that
reason, I sprung for the good stuff: chilled Redhook ESB
in a bottle. The mini-mart clerk gave me stink-eye over her

glasses. She could see Sheila standing at the window mouthing "hurry up."

Sheila didn't see a need to drive anywhere. She settled into the passenger seat and guzzled the fluid as if it were ambrosia. The parking lot wasn't crowded, but an elderly couple passed by, the wife tsk-tsking me with her eyes. Sheila flipped her off.

Pleasure licked Sheila's face and her cheeks lost their pallor. Close up, she was not unattractive, though too emaciated for my tastes. I looked for needle tracks but any that used to exist had long since closed. After the second bottle, she wriggled into a more comfortable position and closed her eyes. She scratched a rash at the nape of her neck, one caused, she said, by "Milt's" requirement that all *Das Puppenhaus* employees heavily starch their blouses. Her drinking pace slackened on the fourth beer, so I slipped in a question.

"You suggested that Schwarzer, I mean Milt, might have a past he's running away from—"

"As fast as his short legs will carry him." She giggled, a childish laugh. "Can you believe I'm buzzed? It used to take an entire twelve-pack."

"Well, when you hit your mid-thirties, you can't really drink that much beer." I patted my paunch. "But about Milt. Is there a reason why he's so suspicious?"

"Like a hundred. Like a hundred and fifty." She giggled again then belched. "But first things first. Milt's a big, big, big, big, big, big, big—" She paused for effect. "Big. Porn star." She held her hands out before her, palms facing one another a foot apart. "And I mean big."

Sheila should have said that Milt *was* a porn star, as in *used to be*, as in *past tense*. According to Sheila, Milt's last film was made around 1979, before the videotape revolution (and, I might add, years before her birth). After that, "he sort of disappeared" for a decade. He resurfaced at this or that party in the San Fernando Valley—strung out every time, not interested in meeting the new starlets—then he'd vanish. Rumor had it that he'd hooked up with some heavies in Mexico and Guatemala, running drugs and "carrying out contracts" to keep supplied. "And then in the 1990s, he had a spiritual awakening or something. Bruce said he ran into a lama in the Himalayas. He'd quit heroin cold turkey by tying himself to a post inside of a tee-pee, a piece of leather in his mouth so he didn't bite off his tongue. When he made it back to the Valley, he was on some crazy macrobiotic diet. He ate organic vegetables and no meat. Bruce floated him for a while on his return to civilization. They've got a history together. Milt gave Bruce his first break as a director and Bruce helped drum up funding for *Das Puppenhaus* when Milt didn't have enough capital. And that's what Milt's been doing ever since. Living in this backwater shithole, riding his bicycle to work every day rain or shine, 'growing' his business."

Sheila twisted the cap off of her fifth bottle. I'd taken only a few sips of my first. "I didn't realize midgets could be porn stars. There's a market for that?"

"Are you for real? There's a market for *everything*. Fat, black, Oriental, hairy, whatever. Midgets are a fetish, but Milt had crossover appeal."

"What does that mean?"

"Usually only perverts watch midget skin flicks. Who wants to watch dwarves in rented warehouses doing each other or girls too ugly to get work in other films? Milt's films were different. Edgy, high-concept. There was a special chemistry between Milt and Luba. They were a hot item, onscreen and off. The Brangelina of underground porn."

"So Luba was a midget porn star too?"

Sheila shook her head. "Hah! Milt with a midget? Never!" She stretched her arms and yawned. "Anyway, Bruce says the breakup pushed Milt over the edge."

A distant chord of sympathy vibrated within me. "She left him?"

"Luba left the business. Moved somewhere else and laid low. She's dead now."

"Dead?"

Sheila closed her eyes. "She got 'pneumonia.' Back then, everybody rode bareback. It's a professional hazard."

At the root of all tragedies there is a woman, from Helen of Troy to Yoko Ono. Every man should be afforded a year to medicate his brain into jelly at the end of a failed relationship, but then he had to "wake up and smell the coffee," as Troy Bobbins so aptly put it. What had taken Milt ten years in Latin America and the Himalayas to discover I'd learned from a $299.95 personal empowerment series.

"Has Milt ever talked to you about his crusade against Karaoke Group International?" I said.

Sheila yawned. "He's always bitching about one thing or another."

"They're building a complex in the hills outside of town."

She curled into herself, scratching the rash on her neck. "Take me home, will you, Guy? I'm not feeling well."

I sighed. Sheila was a dead end, good for nothing but salacious gossip. Well, at least she hadn't asked for dinner at Ruth's Chris Steakhouse. I drove off to her mumbled instructions, hoping she wouldn't hurl in my car.

We headed east on the main highway before turning onto a dirt road. We passed a few houses and then nothing but trees for another mile. "Turn here," she said. The tires crunched the gravel of a driveway that led to a log cabin. There were no cars parked out front, but the carport fifty yards away contained several bicycles. As soon as I stopped, Sheila rushed into the cabin.

Time to go home. Milt knew *something*, but I couldn't force him to help me. I just had to accept that I'd struck out. If Sheila passed out while lying on her back, choked on her own vomit and never woke up, it wasn't my fault. All I did was buy her beer; she chose to drink beyond her capacity. I should have shifted into reverse but instead shut off the engine.

The furnishings inside the cabin were monastic. A wood-burning stove, a table with two chairs, a loveseat, a rocker, an antique writing desk, a double bed.

"Sheila," I called out. "I've got to get going."

I heard a flush. Sheila pulled aside a curtain and emerged from the restroom, a partially enclosed area in the otherwise open floor plan. A particle of food was stuck to her upper lip.

"You okay?" I said.

"I'm fine." Her voice was husky. "I just had to pee really, really bad."

"I figured. Well, it's time for me to get back home."

"What's the hurry? Got a hot date?"

"No, nothing like that. I've got house plants. Laundry."

Sheila walked past me to the kitchen. From the refrigerator, she pulled a pitcher filled with amber fluid. "They can wait. Try this iced tea. It's an organic Kuan Yin mixed with fresh mint from the yard. It totally kicks ass."

I've got a soft spot for good iced tea. Not Snapple, which tastes like it's been flavored with chewing gum, but the fresh brewed kind that leaves a trace of soil on the tongue. One glass and I'd leave. It'd be good to wash the sweaty taste of beer from my mouth.

The first sip sent a cold current straight to my head. The fresh mint was subtly spicy, accenting rather than overwhelming the heft of the tea leaves.

"That's some good tea," I said.

"Let me change out of this get-up into something more comfortable." She disappeared into the restroom.

I clenched the glass. *Leave now*, said left brain. *Relax*, said right brain, *you're sharing iced tea, not crack.*

I sipped the cool fluid and looked around. Rural living was the way to go. The cabin was twice the size of my studio and she probably paid half the rent. She might look like a slacker, but she kept her cabin tidy. There were no dust bunnies on the hardwood floor, no *High Life* magazines strewn around. First impressions are wrong more frequently than they're right.

When Sheila returned, I swallowed any further musings. Those threadbare denim shorts! That bikini top! She wasn't beautiful—angles and muscle instead of mounds. But her skin was a uniform color and texture, pale and soft like the

144

flesh on the inner thigh. And beneath her bikini top was a tattoo swirling in red, green, and black. The flank of an animal crouched on the bony shelf of her sternum, but plant tendrils flicked their tongues at her armpits. Its secret was concealed beneath a millimeter of dime-store fabric.

Sheila pulled up a chair. Her face was scrubbed pink. She smelled like peppermint toothpaste. Our knees touched.

"Have you got a girlfriend, Guy?" she said.

The correct answer was no. But was "no" the equivalent of *wink-wink let me see your tattoo?*

"I've been seeing someone off and on." I casually moved my knee away from hers. "That's the real reason I came to Leavenworth."

"I thought you came to talk to Milt about the karaoke company moving into the hills."

"That too. They're related."

"You met your girlfriend at a karaoke bar?"

"I met her and her fiancé in a local karaoke bar. But his company is tearing it down and replacing it with a fancier place."

Sheila's sleepy eyes twinkled. "You're not as mild-mannered as you look! You had something going with Mr. Big's girl and...I get it." She gestured toward my face. "Do those bruises hurt?"

I'd nearly forgotten that purple sworls marked me the way a tattoo or scar would. The blunt pain had become commonplace. "Less than they did before."

"Can I...can I touch them?"

"I guess so."

Sheila's head tilted and I could sense rather than see her hand approaching my face. "Wait. One second," she said. She reached for her glass, still half-full, dripping with condensation. With her fingertips, she caressed the smooth surface. As her hand drew close to my skin, I closed my eyes.

Her touch was light but firm. She didn't skim the surface but pressed into the bruised flesh, transmitting an ache that echoed in my limbs. Her fingertips were living creatures, wet and cold but with hidden warmth, pulsating with blood and ice. Longing washed over me and receded. Images flickered in the vacuum tube of my mind. The exposed flesh of Tanya's neck; a dead deer, a dead bird; Megumi's cone-shaped nipple.

"She took something from you," Sheila said. Her words splintered the images, sending them back into the darkness from which they came. She pulled away and rubbed her forearms. "You want revenge, don't you?"

"I want—" I took a deep breath. "I want an explanation. From her."

"Same thing, isn't it?"

I looked at my wristwatch. Though the sky was bright, it was nearly 5 p.m. "I better get going. I want to make it back to Seattle for dinner."

"Stay for dinner."

"I can't." I glanced down at her tattoo. It might be a—no, the curved lines were vaguely Celtic. "It wouldn't be right."

"Wouldn't be right?" She laughed. "I'm not hitting on you. Besides, even if I was, we wouldn't be alone."

"What do you mean?"

Sheila yawned, a long slow gape that showed the caps and fillings on her molars. "You think I could afford this place on minimum wage? This is Milt's cabin."

How was I to know that the sixty-something proprietor of *Das Puppenhaus*, former midget porn star, and present vegetarian cycling fanatic, would share his plush but firm mattress with an emaciated, teenaged, recovering drug addict with a penchant for black hair dye? A cozy existence, I would say, though Sheila called it "B-O-R-I-N-G." We talked while plucking red lettuce leaves and trellised Roma tomatoes. "The more I get of the straight life," she said, "the more I prefer being bent."

It was an easy conversation, the kind that men and women have once sex is out of the question. I told her my whole sorry story, about my divorce and my "contract" to call Tanya on a bi-weekly basis; about Megumi, her disappearance with my medallion, and the beating I incurred. Her responses—"that's fucked up," and "what a ho-bag"—were somehow soothing. She said little about Milt except that he was a stickler for rules. No smoking in the cabin. No alcohol and certainly no harder drugs. When I asked if the two of them were together, she said, "It's complicated."

When Milt returned, still perspiring from his long ride, he treated my sudden appearance with a coolness usually reserved for missionaries bearing copies of *The Watchtower*. Sheila vacated her chair and set down a glass of iced tea. He didn't say a word until he'd drained it.

"Your car's dripping oil in my yard," he said. He didn't mean for me to answer; he meant for me to leave.

"I wanted to tell you," I said. "That I wasn't entirely candid before. I have other reasons for wanting to learn more about KGI."

Sheila pulled up a chair. "He was fucking Kolling's girlfriend. Kolling found out about it and then fucked *him* even harder."

That was one way of describing it. Sheila launched into an embellished account of my recent travails. Sheila made it sound as if Megumi had lured me into an elaborate trap; as if Megumi was, in effect, the bored possession of a rich man toying with me for sport. I had explained to her the mysterious connection that Megumi and I shared and how I wanted to explore whether Megumi might be, given the right timing and circumstances, "the one." Sheila chose to tell Milt that I "wanted to catch that bitch and cut her." When I moved to interrupt, Sheila cautioned me off with her eyes.

Sheila described how I'd lost control while recounting my tale and squeezed her wrist too hard. To my surprise, there were faint purple marks on Sheila's skin, the origin of which I couldn't begin to imagine (had she, like a magician, used misdirection to cut off the blood supply to her hand while her lips moved?). Milt nodded with satisfaction, and showed no concern about her injury. And regardless of how neutrally Milt attempted to keep his expression, he visibly started when Sheila mentioned that my former law firm served as KGI's attorneys.

"And get this," she said. "His needy ex-wife, who demands that he call her every week, is a lawyer for KGI's business deals. She knows everything there is to know about their Leavenworth project."

Paralegal, I thought, *not a lawyer. And the requirement is bi-weekly*. Milt kneaded his scar between a thumb and forefinger. It appeared to be more swollen than before, as if infected. Sheila excused herself to cook dinner.

"Do you hate her, Watanabe?" he said. In the background was the steady thwack of Sheila chopping onions for pasta primavera. "What's her name? The Japanese girl."

No. Regardless of what Milt (or Sheila) presumed, I didn't want Megumi to get hurt. Was it so hard to believe that I wanted to help her? She was a victim. Was it so wrong to demand an explanation?

I wanted to tell the truth, but I couldn't relinquish the advantage Sheila had handed me. "I'm really pissed off."

Milt's jaw tensed subtly, as if invisible guy-lines in his neck had been pulled taut. He eased himself off the chair.

"Stand up, Watanabe," he said.

"Sheila might need some help with the pasta," I said.

Milt turned one side of his body to me. He set his feet flat on the ground, bent his knees, and looked up. "Never mind the pasta. I want you to push me."

Push him? Still in his cycling shorts, Milt's calves snarled like pit bulls. His grave expression told me this was some kind of test, but of what I had no idea. If it was a test of strength, he didn't need to test me. I'd lose. If it was a test of balance, he'd win because of a lower center of gravity.

"I concede that I'd lose a pushing contest," I said.

Milt squinted. "This isn't a test of strength. It's a test of character. Come on, Watanabe. Push."

I looked at Sheila. She was peeling and mincing garlic. A smirk played at her lips.

We Americans rarely have our misperceptions about the correlation between size and strength challenged. We're a big country with a big army and a big economy; we can out-bomb and out-spend continental unions of sissy European nations. But stripped down to our skivvies, *mano-a-mano*, we're pretty doughy. And I'm pretty close to the typical American. I turned to face the same direction as Milt, and had to squat sumo-style to get leverage.

"What are the rules?" I said.

"Put the side of your foot here," he said, slapping at my ankle. "Against mine. And then put the side of your body flush to mine. No, don't dip your shoulder. Keep it level or you'll lose balance."

Leaning against Milt was like leaning against a cement pylon. He was a human black hole: dense muscle packed into a pinprick of space. But he didn't wield his superior weight-to-body mass ratio against me. Instead, he leaned with the lightest of pressures and, instinctually, I leaned with equivalent force.

"Good, Watanabe. Good. Now close your eyes. And push."

The faint sound of Sheila chopping vegetables floated across the room, like a clock ticking far off in the darkness. My forearm felt the cooled sweat on Milt's skin. He pushed harder and so did I; he eased up, and to keep from toppling over, I relaxed. We stood and swayed, alternately pushing and releasing, my quadriceps feeling the burn of exertion. My eyes rolled up in my head, where I found a flickering white light; at the periphery of the light, shadowy figures gathered.

I pushed with all my might until my thighs screamed and quivered. And still I didn't move. I couldn't move, fixed as I was in place, pressed flush against an immovable object.

"Release now, Watanabe," his voice said. "Slowly, or you'll fall down."

I did as I was told, and only then realized how loose and rubbery my legs were. The sound of Sheila's knife striking the cutting board returned. I opened my eyes and discovered that the pits of my shirt were damp.

"All right, Watanabe," he said nodding. "Maybe I could learn to hate you."

He spoke as if he were paying me a compliment. But I didn't want him to hate me. I didn't want anyone to hate me.

"Are you willing to trade those confidential files for vengeance?" he said.

That was the catch. My only bargaining chips were the KGI client files, and the only way I'd access them was through Tanya. But if she violated client confidentiality, she'd lose her job and her place in law school.

"Any information I secure, I can share."

"Fine," he said. "*Quid pro quo.* The more you share with me, the more I share with you."

Dinner was served. Or rather, Sheila served dinner. She refilled our glasses, served us seconds, and washed the dishes. Milt didn't lift a finger, and didn't allow me to help. Gazing at the bed on the other side of the room, I wondered if the same arrangement held true for conjugal duties. There is a price we all pay for safety and security.

"I have one more requirement." Milt said. He had a *gravitas* that few men twice his size possessed. "But it's non-negotiable."

"Shoot," I said. How to approach Tanya preoccupied me. If I couldn't do that, all the requirements in the world wouldn't matter. When would Gracie return from her singles kayaking trip? She'd picked a bad time to develop a social life.

Milt interlaced his hairy fingers. "I'm going on this cross-country chase of yours."

CHAPTER 12

"Let me get this straight," Gracie said. "You're chasing after an engaged woman and your sidekick is a heavily armed midget porn star."

Gracie relished stating the painfully obvious. After junior high school, most of us develop a trait that inhibits such candor. It's called tact.

I cradled the telephone receiver. Milton snored lightly in the neighboring bed. True to Sheila's word, once asleep, he was impossible to rouse. Not even hours of channel surfing with the volume cranked up had disturbed him.

"*Former* porn star," I said.

It was the third day of our road trip and we were staying at the Westward Ho! Motel in Nampa, Idaho, twenty miles west of Boise. The $19.99 per night double-occupancy room featured a bleached cow's skull atop the dresser but must have once had a seaside motif. A porthole mirror hung over the sink and the soaps were pastel seashells.

Milt had pestered me from Day 1 to contact Tanya, but I'd wanted to talk to Gracie first. She'd finally returned from what I'd thought was a singles kayaking trip. It'd turned out to be a "women in the outdoors excursion" in the San Juan Islands. Either option was out of character for Gracie, who openly envied the firm's quadriplegic interoffice mail carrier because he rode around all day in an electric wheelchair.

"You're sinking pretty low, Guy."

"That's why I need your help. If you can get me enough information from the KGI files, maybe I can ditch him in Utah."

"You want to piss off a man who sleeps with a gun under his pillow?"

I eyed the lumpy mass of synthetic fill supporting Milt's oversized head. During the day, he kept a mirror-plated pistol named "Trudie" tucked into his waistband. He wore a bigger handgun in a shoulder holster and strapped a ten-inch Bowie knife to his calf.

"I can take care of myself," I said.

"You've done a great job so far." Gracie yawned. It was past one o'clock in the morning. She should have been watching *Brady Bunch* reruns on Comedy Central. Gracie could recite the plot line of every episode, not just "Marsha, Marsha, Marsha," and "Mom always said, 'Don't play ball in the house.'" Instead she'd gone to bed early so she could "jog with a friend in the morning." I'd give her a week before Ben and Jerry conquered her fitness resolve. "I can't believe you don't know who Horatio Kolling is. I've never met him, but they take away your Asian Card if you've never *heard* of him. You're way out of your league. That Japanese chick might have been looking for a good time, but she didn't mean to stick around. Are you noticing a pattern yet, Guy? If someone dumps you, you're supposed to move on."

Since when did Gracie become Dr. Phil? I could ask her why she obsessively read women's fashion magazines yet never dated. A true friend accepts and supports your neuroses.

"Are you going to help me or lecture me, Gracie?" What kind of *immigrante flagrante* had a first name like Horatio? What kind of Asian had a last name like Kolling?

"Hold on a sec," she said. There was a toilet flush followed by running tap water. "There might not be anything I can do."

"Jesus Christ, Gracie. It's not like you've never leaked confidential files. Remember when the partners went apeshit because the *Seattle Times* printed the firm's letters that solicited business from owners of sweatshops? Who had your back?"

I heard the fizz of Gracie pouring a Diet Coke. She drank enough aspartame to blind a laboratory rat. "Don't go mad cow on me, Guy. I'd do it if I could, but there's crazy security on the KGI files. Not only do you have to scan your ID, but they're kept in a vault. KGI team members have electronic key fobs. A computer logs access."

What could KGI be doing to justify a separate security system inside the offices of its outside legal counsel? "How about borrowing an ID and key fob from a KGI team member?"

"You know the answer to that, Guy."

I did. KGI was a Jay Weed project, which meant he'd assembled his crack team of sycophants. There was a subculture of attorneys who worshipped his power, stature, wealth, and Ivy League credentials. No self-respecting paralegal could tolerate a group of such self-aggrandizing asses, which meant the only paralegals on the team were cut from the same cloth.

"Talk to Tanya," Gracie said.

I'd have to tell Tanya the truth. She'd have to jeopardize her future for me. She already held my purse strings. I wouldn't hand over my pride.

"You still there, Guy?"

"Yeah."

"You've been divorced for over a year."

"You're wrong. It's been a year since she left me. It's been nine months since the divorce."

"Uh huh. Have you seen her lately?"

"She's lost some weight. So what?"

"It's more than that," Gracie said. "I'm not saying I *like* Miss Analgesic. But she's different somehow. Less wound up. More comfortable in her own skin."

"Tanya's better off without me. Fine. Her life no longer has to do with mine."

"Come on, Guy. You know I think what she did was fucked up. But in the end, maybe it was inevitable. Maybe you're both better off."

Milt was a restless sleeper. He'd twisted and turned until his blanket was wrapped around him, one hairy leg sticking out. Luckily his one-eyed trouser snake (or rather his one-eyed trouser serpent) remained in its den. He should have been courteous enough to ask whether it bothered me if he slept naked.

"Tell me how I'm better off," I said. "Tell me."

There was an uncomfortable silence. Gracie ducked the question, as I knew she would.

"Call Tanya," she said. "She's a freak. But not as big of one as I used to think."

I should have known better than to trust a midget who believed the salvation of Leavenworth lay in Bavarian essentialism. Milton had highlighted the locations of new KGI projects on a map of the western United States. All we had to do to make up the five-day lead Kolling and Megumi had on us was to drive as fast as we could from point to point. Milton had other plans.

"To catch one's prey," Milton said, "one must think like one's prey. Where will they eat? What will they order from the menu? Which tourist attractions will they stop to see and which will they bypass? We creep up behind them to make the kill."

Translation? We traveled to *every* place they could have gone to experience it the same way that they did. At the Swiss Village Cheese Factory, I played Kolling and he played Megumi. He seized my arm and leaned into me, glaring when I showed self-consciousness about the stares we received from other tourists. He peppered me with questions inside the car about the business possibilities I envisioned in the passing landscape. At rest stops, he browsed cheap silver jewelry and souvenir refrigerator magnets.

Have you heard of method acting? Milton browbeat me into playing Sean Penn to his Robert DeNiro. I should have walked away from this farce, especially after he shoplifted a jeweled brooch because "Megumi wanted it." But then, unexpectedly and eerily, our paths began to cross Megumi and Horatio's. The lost-and-found bin at the Basque Museum and Cultural Center contained a pair of pink sunglasses identical to the ones Megumi had been wearing. The guest book at the World Center for Birds of Prey was signed by Horatio Kolling. The Grove Hotel refused to disclose whether Kolling had stayed there, but out front the valet offered to fetch my car. He said I looked just like a man with a cherry-red Mustang convertible who had been traveling with his daughter.

Coincidence? Clearly the fact that we stopped everywhere meant we had to cross their path somewhere. But along the way, during our grueling days of being the most assiduous Asian tourists who'd ever road-tripped across the American west, I began to see through Horatio's eyes. *Here's a community starved for upscale karaoke entertainment. Here's an untapped market of karaoke consumers too dumb and too lazy to create a world-class establishment.* As we wended south, their trail on the asphalt seemed to glisten like snail spittle.

Laugh if you must. This is what happens when you spend your entire day walking, driving, and enduring the heat with a companion who believes he can intuit the thoughts of a girl from a different culture two generations his junior.

"Pull over there," Milton said, pointing to a rundown gas station called Mike's Gas & Smoke.

"I've got a Shell card," I said.

"Am I supposed to play your part *and* mine?" Milton said. "Kolling wouldn't throw away five cents a gallon when all he has to do is cross the street."

The pump was the old manual type with flipping digits. The gas dribbled like honey out of the nozzle. "If he can pay $300 a night for a hotel, he can afford a buck more on gas."

"Don't you understand the difference between what he *can* do and what he *will* do?" Milton said. "Others notice the cut of his suit and the accommodations he chooses. But where he can cut corners, he will. It's in his nature."

I trudged inside to pay. The proprietor was an elderly gentleman in a threadbare tank top and sagging jeans.

"How'd you like Monument Valley?" he said.

"Excuse me?"

He slid three cents across the counter and squinted out at my car. "Never mind."

Kolling was inches taller and much lighter skinned than I was, yet this was the second time I'd been mistaken for him. Still, I told Milton when I returned to the car, there was no way to have *intuited* that Kolling would stop at a particular gas pump in the middle of the desert.

Milton scowled. "The inner world and the outer world are one and the same. Inside is refined outside and outside is unrefined inside. Cause and effect is nothing but an emanation of a man's character. 'Chance' succumbs to 'trajectory.' Like a ball rolling down a hill, a man's strength and discipline determine his course in life. You're the typical American: too complacent to recognize the nature of reality."

I held my tongue. Milton went to work in *lederhosen*. He lived with a teenaged drug-addict/maid/sex-slave. *I* couldn't recognize the nature of reality? I didn't know how he knew what he knew, but he knew more than I did. If I wanted to locate Megumi, his companionship was a necessary evil.

Maybe Milton knew Kolling was a cheapskate because it takes one to know one. Rule number one on a road trip is the equal division of labor and money. If I do the driving, he should pay for gas. If he doesn't get his own room, we should either halve the bill or alternate picking up the tab. The stingy little bastard walked away whenever money changed hands. He owned a thriving business; I hadn't had a job for a year; and I paid for everything.

What else aggravated me? Milton woke up at 5:30 a.m. to practice yoga naked. There are few things more disturbing than watching a nude midget doing downward facing dog a few feet away from your face. By 6:30 a.m. sharp he was dressed, packed, and waiting by the door. He called bathing a "marketing ploy that destroys the immune system." It didn't matter that it was summertime, the car had no air conditioning, and we were heading south into Utah. He smelled so funky it was hard being in the same room let alone in the same car.

He covered his body odor with strong colognes, but what didn't work in the fifteenth century doesn't work today. There was no room for my toothbrush after he spread out his all-natural toothpaste, a gum-massager, hair gel, nostril-hair trimmer, shaver, herbal powders, and vitamin bottles. Could he have kept some of those in his case? Yes. Did he? No.

And for all his healthy habits, I was in better shape. He had an amazing physique for a man in his sixties, but I can walk through a museum without having to sit down. I don't know how he bicycle-commuted twenty miles a day. He took frequent naps, making him a useless navigator. He kept a cup on the side table that he half-filled with phlegm in a single night.

He was an all-around disagreeable person. I called him "Milt" once instead of "Milton," as I'd heard Sheila do. He jabbed his stubby finger in my face and said that I had "permission" to address him as "Milton" or "Mr. Schwarzer." When I touched his forearm to calm him down, he recoiled and said that physical familiarity was a sign of *my* patronizing *him*.

Milton woke from a nap to forage through my glove compartment. Out spilled several Troy Bobbins *Personal Path* CDs—lessons that I'd had particular trouble with, like *Program Yourself for Success: Turn vices into virtues through the power of compulsive ignorance* and *Our Bodies: Divine machines.* Instead of putting them back in place or making a polite inquiry, he ranted that anybody who believed such bullshit had the IQ of a fruit fly. Did he think those lessons had magically appeared in my car? Troy would have been proud of how I responded.

"People ridicule what they don't understand," I said.

Milton scoffed until his chest was racked by spasmodic coughing. I asked him what was so wrong about wanting to improve oneself. Why did *my* becoming a better person provoke such strong feelings in *him?*

"This self-help crap has nothing to do with becoming a better person," Milton said. "It lulls you into believing there's meaning and purpose to life. You can have everything your heart desires: a great job, a great house, a great wife. You can have everything without making a single, goddamned sacrifice. 'Do good and do well.' Balls to that."

"Have you ever listened to Troy Bobbins?" I said. "Have you ever tried to apply his success principles to your life?"

"No. And I never will."

"So you admit you're talking about something you know nothing about?"

Milton glowered. "Don't patronize me, Watanabe. Your generation can't get it through your spoiled little brains that there's no such thing as happiness. There's no such thing as satisfaction. Those sensations are as fleeting as masturbation and with the same effect on the outside world. The focus of your lives is 'me, me, me.' I need more money, more time, more love. The more you get, the more empty you feel. All those self-help lessons do is help you keep running faster and faster on your hamster wheel."

To the right of us, a train moved through the valley amidst mesas and hills. "Is that right? So you know what the meaning of life is?"

"There is no meaning, Watanabe. But there's purity. Not in faith, which is what your self-help guru sells, a drug to help you ease the pain of living. Not in love. That's selfishness, taking from another what you lack. Hate is the one true emotion. Hate is transcendent. Hate is complete. Hate is cleansing."

The clouds above the approaching mountains were layered like stairs. "That's ridiculous," I said. "Hate is a selfish emotion. All you think about is your own feelings, not the feelings of others."

"That's nothing but schoolroom indoctrination," Milton said. "Hate is the only truly *selfless* human emotion that exists. With love, a man might sacrifice himself for others, but his intent remains the same: saving someone or something he values more than himself. Hate makes no distinctions. A man consumed by hatred will do anything to consummate that hatred. Hate doesn't destroy just the hated, it destroys the hater. There's no thought involved; there's no calculation. When a man hates, he becomes nature. He becomes God."

As the days passed, Milton elaborated on his philosophy of hatred, which wasn't "prettified" by "the desire to believe." Nobody *wanted* to hate. It was a force greater than a belief system. Milton's highest compliment was that he hated you. The hater and the hated are consumed together by the dispassionate flame of certainty. In hatred there was purpose without meaning.

It seemed that certain aspects in a normal person—hesitation, doubt, consideration—had been gouged out of Milton's psyche. He didn't wait to be seated by a hostess; he marched to the corner booth and dared anyone to differ. He carried out tedious tasks with equanimity: cleaning his handguns, oiling the blade of his Bowie knife, performing his evening calisthenics, imbibing his many pills and powders, meditating. It wasn't until a week into our trip that I noticed his blistered feet. He hadn't once complained or asked to reduce the amount of walking we did. He was in all things resolute.

Milton fell asleep easily, but his sleep was troubled. I wonder how he would have reacted if I told him that I'd heard him sobbing? Did his eccentric philosophy have anything to do with the scar on his neck, that double-arc of waxy, distended skin that seemed to breathe of its own accord? For what could a scar shaped as a human mouth be but hatred made flesh?

Milton rolled and turned until he'd thrown off his blanket, exposing his fearsome penis to the open air. The appendage was as long and thick as a dildo, but it was unfettered by leather straps or harnesses. It was a bulging, oversized muscle. The rest of his body was stunted to nourish this monstrosity.

It felt like losing to call Tanya from the room's beige rotary phone, an admission that I'd memorized her new number on a cold and lonely night.

"Hello, Guy?" she said.

"Yeah. It's Guy. Well, I guess you knew that."

"Do you know it's 11:57 p.m.?"

Milton's mouth made a sloppy "clop, clop, clop" sound. I cupped the mouthpiece. "I didn't wake you, did I?"

Tanya made her exasperated "unnngh" sound, which always reminded me of a belted Soviet man in leotards lifting a barbell over his head. "You know that's not the point. You didn't want to call, did you? You waited until the last possible moment to call, didn't you?"

"But in the end, I called. Let's focus on that."

"Focus on the present. Focus on the present," she said under her breath. "You're right, Guy. We're here to talk about who we are today. We care about the past only insofar as it gives us a glimpse of what brought us to the present, and how it will affect the future. Every day, the sun rises anew."

That was straight out of Troy Bobbins's *Personal Path* series, *Now and Then: Taking Control of Time and Your Life.* "I couldn't have said it better."

"Things have been so much better since the end of our marriage. I've made so much progress. I look better. I feel better. I have more responsibilities. New relationships." There was an awkward pause. Cold touched the nape of my neck, but she pressed onward. "I wish I could explain how much happier I am now. How soundly I sleep at night and how joyous my days are."

"Yeah. You've made your happiness with our divorce apparent to me."

"Have I? Can you hear it in my voice? How much less it's weighed down by heavy thoughts?" She sighed. "But my progress has hit a plateau. My life was getting better and better and better, then all of a sudden my wheels got caught in the mud. Sometimes, I get sad for no reason. The other night I was alone in the office at midnight putting together press packets for that Leavenworth project, and I began crying. My life couldn't be going better, right? The city looked beautiful way down below, and yet I couldn't appreciate it. I don't know why."

Maybe it was because she was collating paper in an office while other people were spooning their partners. "The Leavenworth project, that's the karaoke complex, right? Sounds interesting."

"It *is* interesting, and Jay's giving me *so* much responsibility on it. But that's the point. I couldn't embrace my opportunities with gratitude. My life is filled with meaningful work, but all I could focus on was the emptiness. If the windows at the firm weren't sealed shut, I could have... you know. I wouldn't actually do *that* because only cowards choose a final solution to a temporary problem. But I could understand why somebody else would."

"I think it's natural to feel sad every now and then, Tanya. Even during our happiest times together, there'd be moments I'd feel down." I settled against the rattling headboard and closed my eyes. "The last day of our honeymoon was amazing. Remember? We rode bicycles through the streets of Santa Barbara half-drunk on wine. At dinner, our waitress had a piece of spinach caught in her teeth. We slept nude in front of the fireplace." Tanya didn't interrupt me, so I forged on. "You were smiling in your sleep, do you know that? And I felt so lucky and tragically sad at the same time. In the morning, we'd check out of our bungalow and return to our normal lives. I wanted us to be like that forever, but I knew we couldn't."

There was silence on the other end of the line, but I heard her breathing. "Tanya?"

"I'm here."

"I didn't mean to get so worked up. All I meant to say was—"

"See, there you go again. It's so typical."

"I'm not sure what you—"

"Of course you don't. It's totally unconscious. You have to look at everything through a negative lens. We couldn't enjoy an expensive meal without you giving away the leftovers to the homeless. 'He's probably sleeping under the freeway,' you'd say, making me feel guilty for wanting to take the food for lunch the next day. Remember when the firm's client sponsored a bowling night? You had to make that joke to the CEO about officer liability for sweatshop conditions overseas."

"I was making small talk."

"It was totally inappropriate." She exhaled. "It's not normal for people to feel depressed when things are going well. You think it's a sign of intelligence or complexity, but it's not. I don't want to feel depressed anymore. It's just an excuse for not moving on with life." She paused. "What was that?"

Milton had made a low, moaning noise, like a cow being ground slowly into chuck. Luckily I covered the receiver before he called out, "No!" He rolled onto his stomach.

"My stomach hurts." I let out a low moan. "Sorry, don't mind me."

"Are you eating Vienna Sausages again? Meat packed in gelatin can't be good for you."

"Never again. I mean it this time."

"Good. Remember, 'A journey of a thousand miles begins with a single step.'" On the other end of the line, I could hear laughter emitting from a television set. I never understood her TV addiction until we broke up. Now I knew all too well how much warmer it was to have electronic *Friends.* "Did you receive my gift, Guy? FedEx said it was delivered two days ago."

Yes or no. "Yes" meant I was still at home, leading a potentially productive life. "No" meant I was chasing an engaged woman cross-country. My apartment manager was probably using the package as a footrest. "That was a really, really thoughtful gift. I love gifts I never would have chosen myself."

"Really?" She drew out the syllables in a disconcerting way. "What did I send you?"

"It's just fantastic."

"I can't believe you, Guy Watanabe. That's just so…so… you! I spend extra to have it delivered overnight and you don't have the courtesy to open it."

It would have been politic to apologize. Milton faced the wall. I rubbed my eyes and stared at his rump. A man in his sixties should not have a butt that firm. Must be the bicycling and organic produce. But I'd never noticed the purple bumps. "I've been really busy, Tanya."

"Doing what?"

"Huh?"

"You heard me. What's got you so busy you can't open a box delivered to your doorstep?"

"It's complicated, Tanya." In the pause that followed, Milton mumbled something and began to snore. It wasn't the freight train roar of the previous night, but it was loud enough just the same. I put a palm over the receiver—not in time.

"What was that?"

"What was what?" I said. Milton called out "looba-loobalooba." He flopped over onto his back again, his sea snake lying languidly on one hairy thigh.

"There's someone in the room with you, isn't there?"

"No there isn't. It's just the TV." I fumbled for the remote control. An arts station: lush, classical music boomed out. "It was one of those indie horror movies. No soundtrack; real minimalist. I've changed the channel now."

Tanya said nothing for a few moments. "In a way, I'm relieved. It means you're moving on. It's not as if I haven't had other lovers too."

I hate the word "lover." "Lover" means something less than a boyfriend and more than a one-night stand; the word has nothing to do with "love." And she had said *lovers*, plural. Megumi had been my first since Tanya, and we'd done nothing more than dry-hump.

I covered my face with a palm. "I'm glad you're moving on, Tanya. I'm glad we're *both* moving on."

"I still care about you, Guy."

Yeah, the way people "care" about global warming, abstractly and in a way that made them feel good about themselves. "I know."

"That's why I sent you the Troy Bobbins *Personal Path* series. Wait! Don't say anything yet." She took a deep breath. "I know there's no way to convince you about Troy's program unless you experience it yourself. There are so many questions about life that I used to have that Troy has answered. Before you write him off, won't you at least *try* listening to him? I can't stand to see you in so much pain."

Pain has a secret lesson to teach you. That was from Troy's very first lesson. Didn't she understand that experiencing pain was the first step toward recovery?

"I'm not a big fan of the self-help industry," I said. "I mean, doesn't having someone tell you the answers to life's mysteries defeat the whole idea of helping oneself?"

"You know what, Guy Watanabe? So does closing yourself off to anyone who might just shake up your perspective. You make wisecracks to protect yourself. I can accept that now that we're just friends. But it still enrages me."

She should try Troy's anger-management breathing technique. Breathe in for three counts; hold for seven counts; exhale for seven counts. "I can't follow a trail someone else has blazed. I've got to find my own way."

"Where are you right now, Guy?"

Adventures of the Karaoke King

"Excuse me?"

I heard Tanya take a deep breath, hold, then release. "I've got caller ID. I know you're not in Washington. I was hoping you'd trust me enough to tell me where you are."

Damn technology. It wasn't just Safeway that could track my every movement. Maybe Milton was right to be paranoid. "I'm in Ogden, Utah. It's between Boise and Salt Lake City."

"Really?" Her voice perked up.

"Uh huh. I needed to get away for a little while. You know. Think about things."

"That's funny. Hold on one sec." There was a clatter as she set down the receiver. On the other bed, Milton's eyelids fluttered. Blood had drained from his face and his lips looked waxy. "Sorry. I thought it might be too good to be true and it was. *The Bobbins Monthly Newsletter* says that Troy is touring the west with his three-day seminar, *Leading from Without: Getting what you want from knowing what they fear.* He was in Boise last week and is in Salt Lake City this week. But the last day of the seminar in Salt Lake City was yesterday. I wish you could have gone. It would have been perfect."

Troy Bobbins just left Utah? I knew he traveled to LA to advise Hollywood stars, and to Washington, DC, to advise statesmen, but I thought the Mormon world was Franklin Covey territory. Too bad seeing Troy in real life was beyond my means. Troy's last *Lead from Without* seminar took place in Hawaii for $1,500, excluding airfare. What a coincidence though. Troy Bobbins was following the same route that we were. But I needed to steer the conversation away from Troy and back to KGI. "About that project you're working on with Jay. I was wondering—"

170

"That must be it!" The wonder in her voice was apparent, even hundreds of miles across the telephone grid.

"What must be it?"

"Technically, I can't talk to you about firm business," she said. "And since we're no longer married, neither of us can invoke spousal privilege against testimony if the other is charged in a legal proceeding. I really shouldn't say anything. But this must be what Jay was referring to."

Jay. The very mention of that hoofed creature conjured the smell of brimstone and rancid lamb chops. Anything Jay didn't want me to know, I wanted to hear. "You're talking to me, Tanya. Me. I haven't changed. Besides, it's been a year since I've worked at the firm. Who could I possibly tell and how would it ever get back to you?" Milton was now curled into a fetal ball, sweaty face pressed into the pillow.

The gears and cogs of Tanya's mind whirred and spun. "Well, I don't think it would be an ethical violation to share my *speculation* based on privileged information, especially since I don't know for *sure*, right?"

If she were trading securities, she might go the way of Martha Stewart. But I wasn't one to step in the way of a good rationalization. "Yeah. Right."

"Right." Tanya seemed genuinely excited by bending the firm's rules on client confidentiality. Maybe Gracie was right. She had loosened up. "Jay says that KGI is about to merge with another company that *everyone*'s heard of. And then, out of the blue, KGI's CEO decides to take a road trip through the southwest. Guess which cities he's visiting?"

Like Milton, I felt like curling into a little pill bug ball. "Which ones?"

"The same ones as Troy Bobbins! And on the same schedule. His next stop must be Santa Fe, New Mexico."

We talked for a few minutes more. Tanya raved about the amazing "synergy" of two remarkable businessmen teaming up. She said it was a natural fit: "Can you imagine how much Troy Bobbins can help the losers who frequent karaoke bars?" On the flip side, the Karaoke Group International's presence overseas would bring self-empowerment to every nation in the world. "What will happen," she said, "when oppressed people in developing nations discover their Personal Paths? I can't see how the Taliban can survive."

How could you do this to me, Troy? How could you team up with the only man in the world whom I could honestly say I despised?

CHAPTER 13

Milton barely touched his oatmeal. His face looked as if it had been bleached instead of tanned by the desert sun. That didn't prevent him from acting like an asshole.

"A merger between KGI and Bobbins is impossible," Milton said. "KGI is focusing its might on karaoke. It's becoming vertically integrated, purchasing everything along the karaoke production chain from video production companies to alcohol suppliers. Self-help conflicts with that strategy. KGI isn't diversifying investments, it's consolidating them."

We'd clashed long enough for me to have finished my Grand Slam breakfast and drained three cups of coffee. I'd provided real, tangible intelligence and he rejected it.

"I may disagree with Horatio Kolling's expansion into Leavenworth," he said. "That doesn't mean he's an imbecile. If Kolling wanted to sell false hope to Yuppies, he'd build his own company from the ground up. Show me your documentation. You promised me KGI's confidential files."

"Do you have any idea how much paper is involved in a business development deal?" I said. "Those files are under lock and key twenty-four hours a day. Should I ask Tanya to fax twenty reams to the Thunderbird Motel business center? Oh yeah. There is no Thunderbird Motel business center. I've given you exactly what you asked for. It's on you if you won't listen."

"I know bullshit when I hear it. I've spent a decade studying KGI's market behavior. Kolling's using your ex-wife to feed us false information."

Only my repressed Asian upbringing kept me from braining Milton with a ketchup bottle. I didn't care what he thought about me, but now he was assailing Tanya's integrity. She'd never betray me. At least, not in that way.

Milton said that altering our strategy would play into Kolling's hands. We should visit the completion point of the transcontinental railroad, where Megumi would have purchased or purloined a souvenir golden spike. We should investigate the large watermelon statue, which neither of them could have resisted.

In his linen blazer and slacks, Milton looked neat and sane. No one could have guessed he was toting concealed weapons. No one would have suspected that he'd spout psychobabble as fact. In my desperation to find Megumi, I'd been taken in by parlor tricks: cashiers who remembered "a cute little Asian girl;" guest book entries in which Kolling had added, along with his name, the appellation "Karaoke King." But I couldn't disregard what was right before my eyes in favor of rank speculation.

I offered Milton an ultimatum. Troy was holding a seminar in New Mexico as we spoke. Either we drove the thirteen hours to Santa Fe today or we parted ways. He could hitchhike, or pedal, or walk his ass back to eastern Washington.

We stared at each other over the check (which I knew he'd never pick up).

"Have it your way, Watanabe." He shoved his bowl of oatmeal away. "Give me an hour to shop for groceries. There won't be vegetarian options between this wasteland and that one."

"We'll exit in Salt Lake City," I said. "They'll have better markets, maybe even a farmer's market. And the prices will be cheaper."

"What's a few cents compared to your valuable time?" Milton said. "I can find everything I need right here."

"I'll drive you."

"Don't move the car." Milton insisted that we never park in front of our room for fear that Kolling or his henchman Smith would discover us. We had parked behind the dumpster at a neighboring cured-meat shop. Two days before, we'd hiked a half-mile to ensure a concealed spot. "If we're going to be in that little metal box all day, I want to stretch my legs."

"Suit yourself," I said. He groused about American car culture and our dependence on foreign oil, but what alternative did he offer? A tandem bicycle? "Since no one helps me drive, I could use the rest."

On the road again amidst the windswept seas of dirt and towering glaciers of pink sandstone. Repaving work and mid-morning traffic had slowed us to a crawl. The minivan in front of us had a bumper sticker that at first glance I took to be a handicapped placard, but on closer examination was a figurine kneeling in prayer.

"It's wrong to bypass Salt Lake City," Milton said. "We'll be missing valuable clues to their intentions."

"That's why we should have stopped there for groceries. But we can't drive all day *and* tour all day."

"Stop there for lunch."

"It's too early for lunch," I said. "We just had breakfast."

"You had breakfast. I had a spoonful of sludge."

And whose fault was that? Milton had gone out for groceries but returned with fruit juice. Fine, I thought, anything to shut him up. I switched lanes and exited at a highway sign reading "Salt Lake City." I was going to make him rush through his meal the way he made me rush to shower and dress in the morning.

The exit led to an arterial street with several lanes of traffic. Small shops were interspersed with car dealerships and planned housing communities. I drove for ten minutes, wondering if all of Salt Lake City was a low-level suburban sprawl. Then I saw a sign for the city of Bountiful.

"If you're trying to get downtown," he said. "You chose the worst way of getting there."

Now he wanted to be a navigator. The map was unfolded on his lap—for the first time, I might add—and I was considering whether I could bear asking for his assistance when the car lost all power. Pressing the gas pedal felt like sinking my foot into mush. I turned on the hazard lights and swerved into the parking lot of a health food store.

A cursory look under the hood confirmed what I already knew: whatever was wrong, I couldn't fix it. The health food store's proprietress invited us inside. Margaret allowed me to use her phone to call a tow truck. She served us ginger cookies and green tea cola.

"Are you LDS?" Margaret asked Milton. He lacked the social grace to acknowledge she'd spoken. She looked at him quizzically, then turned to me for an answer.

LDS. LDS. It didn't stand for Attention Deficit Disorder or Multiple Sclerosis. Ah. Latter-day Saints.

"No, ma'am," I said. "Neither of us is. I hope you won't hold it against us."

"Oh no, dear. Just checking. Saints from all over the world converge on Salt Lake City. Since you'll be stopping here longer than you planned, you can't miss Temple Square."

"I wouldn't dream of it," I said.

Margaret wrote a suggested itinerary on a napkin. Eat lunch at the Pantry of Lion House, the historic home of Brigham Young. Take the Temple Square tour, which left every quarter hour from the flagpole in front of the temple. Explore the two visitor centers. ("Isn't one enough?" I asked. "Oh, dear, no," she said. "Don't worry. They're only a hundred yards apart.") View the ninety-minute movie about the Mormon faith in the Joseph Smith Memorial Building. (Zzzz.) Visit the two world-class malls located across the street. ("What's special there?" I asked. "An enormous Baby Gap," she replied.)

The car was towed to a shop a mile away. We waited an hour for the diagnosis. "Your water pump is shot," the mechanic said. "And your timing belt has snapped."

"I told you we didn't conceal the car well enough," Milton said. "You should have listened to me."

"Is there any sign of sabotage?" The sentence was out before I realized how ludicrous my question must sound.

"There's no way of verifying that one way or another. This is a pretty good-looking car on the outside, and somebody recently steam-cleaned the engine compartment, but cleaning something won't stop the seals from deteriorating and the moving parts from wearing down."

Seven-hundred bucks for car repairs. An extra night in a hotel that cost four times what we'd paid at the Thunderbird. Milton wore a self-satisfied expression as he laid out plans for touring Temple Square and its environs. Did he not understand what kind of financial planning it takes to juggle balance transfers between credit cards, minimize transaction fees, and remain unemployed? Soon I'd have to ask Gracie to rummage through my accumulated mail in search of credit-card offers.

We boarded the bus to downtown.

"Now that they've discovered us, it's more important than ever you listen to what I say," Milton said. "You got that, Watanabe? Without me, you're a babe in the woods."

How could Kolling's henchman Smith have recognized my car? It had gone from being a dumpy, black CRX to a lowered, metallic blue roadster. There were three people who knew our whereabouts: Sheila, Gracie, and Tanya. I knew whom Milton suspected of betrayal, but I had other ideas.

We were doing exactly what Milton wanted to do all along. There was one person with the motive and opportunity to have vandalized my car, if indeed it had been vandalized. That person was sitting next to me on the bus, legs dangling above the floor, panting like a bulldog in the heat.

I was impressed by the vast, multi-media celebration of faith in the South Visitor Center. Push-button interactive displays discussed the role of religion in the family and computer terminals allowed users to conduct genealogical research. Milton wandered from display to display in the disinterested manner that he imagined Megumi would, but he didn't seem up to the exertion. He plopped down on a sofa in the sunlit atrium and closed his eyes. As cool as it was inside the visitor center, he perspired.

Without Milton to goad me, I felt too silly to act the part of Kolling. I stopped at a series of television screens and pressed the button labeled, "What happens to families after death?" A video of an Asian American teen wearing a V-neck sweater rolled on the topmost video monitor.

"I think everyone's scared of death," she said. "But I take great comfort in knowing that our entire family will be reunited for eternity. That reassurance is one of the things that the Book of Mormon provides. I don't suffer from the depression that drives my classmates to drugs and promiscuity."

If Mormonism meant my family being reunited for eternity, I would run as fast as I could away from it. According to the informational displays, Latter-day Saints could save their dead ancestors by proxy. That is, a certified Mormon can purchase a ticket to Heaven for dearly departed non-Mormon family members. That's why there were so many genealogical terminals. If a convert found, for example, that he was descended from Mohammed, the Prophet might find himself wearing a starched white shirt in a new neighborhood in Paradise.

It was time for the tour. I found Milton asleep in the same sofa chair in which I'd left him. It was hard to believe a man so distasteful and surly while awake could look so vulnerable while asleep. His thinning hair was plastered by perspiration to his head.

"But how do you know it's really him, Brother Johnson?"

Two young missionary men in their tidy white shirts stood a few paces away, both staring at Milton. One—presumably Brother Johnson—responded.

"It was part of President Stevenson's crusade against pornography. He had me cataloguing and cross-referencing the actors and actresses. That's 'Milt the Stilt.' There are at least thirty of his films in the vault."

"You've watched them?"

"I didn't want to, I had to. There was always someone else present. No one except President Stevenson is allowed to watch those dirty movies alone."

Milton's eyes flicked open, the brittle blue-green stare fixing on the young men. They took half-steps backward. In limbo between fight and flight, they finally scurried away. I approached.

"They were talking about you, Milton."

Milton wiped yellowish film from the corner of his eye. "Fucking Mormons. Probably watch more porn than the rest of the world combined."

"You're the one who wanted to come to Salt Lake City."

He scowled. "Is it time for the tour yet?" He tried to stand but had to sit down again immediately.

"Whoa, whoa, whoa," I said. "Why don't you take this one off. I get the feeling Megumi isn't the religious type. While Kolling is touring, she'd read a magazine in an air-conditioned café. Why don't I report back to you what I hear."

Several missionaries congregated around a desk, talking in low tones. The two young men were there too, but they stood in the back, avoiding eye contact. Milton absently patted his lower pant leg, where his knife was strapped.

"Fine." His face was wan. "But stay in Temple Square. You don't know where they might be lurking. Meet me here at five. Don't be late."

I walked away without looking back. It didn't matter whether we were in peril or not. It was in Milton's nature to give orders. If I couldn't endure his company for a week, how had Sheila lived and worked with him for months?

A female missionary greeted the family standing next to me with a hearty "*Gutentag*," and they begin chattering in German. I'd presumed the family to be American but I should have recognized that the son's tight shorts marked him as a European. If Milton had been here, perhaps he could have regaled them in his *nouveau* adopted tongue.

A young woman with a walkie-talkie informed us that the English language tour was about to get under way. We shuffled into the sunlight to be greeted by two female missionaries wearing the obligatory uniform—white blouses and simple, earth-toned skirts. The tall, full-figured one spoke first.

"I am Sister Rosselli, a missionary from Italy," she said. "My companion and I will be in the United States for one year and one half. We spent three months in the Mission

Training Center studying scripture and language. Our English is not perfect, so please be patient with us. We will not be offended if you ask us to repeat." The two women exchanged nods.

The shorter, slender missionary spoke. "Welcome. My name is Sister Dos Passos and I am from Brazil. Like you, we are newcomers to the Salt Lake Temple, though we have heard about it our entire lives. In 1847, Brigham Young arrived here with the Latter-day Saint pioneers to establish a temple that took forty years to complete. It took great dedication and persev— " she smiled as she stumbled over her memorized script, "per-SEV-erance. This tour is an opportunity to share with you the history and beliefs of the Church of Jesus Christ of Latter-day Saints."

No strapping milkmaid from Wisconsin was she. Beneath her sleepy lids, Sister Dos Passos's eyes were the color of fine, dark ash. Her hair and skin suggested that her Portuguese ancestors snuck into the Afro-Indian quarter of town. And her voice! A raspy molasses from which tropical steam rose.

We learned how the Angel Moroni, his gilded figurine blowing a trumpet atop the highest spire of the temple, directed Joseph Smith to unearth the account of Jesus's arrival in America. We stopped at the Seagull Monument to learn how the birds saved the crops from ravaging crickets, an early miracle in the Salt Lake Valley. We sat in the Mormon Tabernacle which, absent the choir, looked like a high school gymnasium. My ears pricked up every time Sister Dos Passos spoke. My eyes lingered on the zipper running down the back of her skirt. Missionaries should wear burlap bags, not form-fitting fabrics. Exiting the Tabernacle, I tore myself away from the fixation on her swaying hips to pull even with her.

"What part of Brazil are you from?" I said.

"From a poor northeastern town called Timbauba."

I nodded. "Ah."

She half-smiled, a languid upturning of her lips. "You've heard of it?"

I wanted to say yes. "No. I meant, 'ah, northeastern Brazil.' Not many Mormons in Brazil, eh?"

"Oh, about 700,000. Where are you from? China?"

"Close. Seattle." She shook her head, so I continued. "It's in the northwest corner of the United States. Coffee? Kurt Cobain?"

"Saints don't drink coffee or sniff cocaine. I've heard of Los Angeles and New York. And Salt Lake City, of course."

"How about San Francisco?

Her nose wrinkled. "Earthquake? A big red bridge?"

"That's it. How about Sao Paulo, Nebraska?"

"There's a Sao Paolo in Nebraska?"

"Nah. I'm just joshing you. It's a joke."

Her sleepy eyes smiled, and inwardly so did I.

The North Visitor Center had upper and lower display galleries filled with framed paintings. They depicted critical moments in Christ's life, including his visit to America to teach the Native Americans (before they forgot his teachings and liquidated their white brethren).

A female missionary with a walkie-talkie on her hip guarded a spiral ramp leading to the second floor. She informed Sister Rosselli that our party could ascend in five minutes. While Sister Rosselli fielded questions, I drifted back toward Sister Dos Passos. She stood apart, quietly contemplating the paintings. The artistic style reminded me of a detailed Saturday morning cartoon: each figure looked as if he'd showered after a spin class at 24 Hour Fitness. I concealed my grimace.

"You're moved, no?" she said.

"They're certainly big." I shouldn't have been so critical. No one knew for sure whether Biblical figures wore highlights and body waves in their hair.

"Wait until you see what comes next," Sister Dos Passos said.

The guard unfastened the velvet rope and we ascended the ramp to a domed room. On a pedestal, a towering white marble statue of Jesus Christ looked down upon us. His bearded, VW-van-driving face was serene, and his hands were open in an "I'd like to teach the world to sing" pose. But it wasn't the Jesus statue that inspired, it was what surrounded him. On the surface of the wall curving above, below, and all around was a vast mural of the cosmos. The inky blackness of space teemed with planets, moons, clouds, and milky constellations. This wasn't solitary Jesus suffering privations in the desert. This was Cosmic Jesus, Master of the Universe, floating weightless in His divine grace.

Sunlight streamed through the windows at my back. So fixated was I on Him, I stumbled on my way to a bench. Sister Rosselli cued up the tape recording. Cosmic Jesus spoke.

Behold, I am Jesus Christ, whom the prophets testified shall come into the world. And behold, I am the light and the life of the world; and I have drunk out of that bitter cup which the Father hath given me, and have glorified the Father in taking

upon me the sins of the world, in which I have
suffered the will of the Father in all things from the
beginning.

In Latin markets, I have seen Jesus wall portraits in which his heart pulsed to the power of AA batteries. Cosmic Jesus beat those curios by a mile. Closing my eyes, I pictured the actor playing Jesus in the sound recording: a chubby church father who coached Pop Warner football on the weekends. I imagined the effort it took to coordinate the display—the artist on a scaffold painting craters on the moon, volunteers carting Jesus up the ramp on a moving dolly. I was so enraptured, it took me moments to realize that Sister Dos Passos's knee was resting against mine. Her eyes were closed and a secret smile tinted her lips.

The tour ended in a private screening room, where we watched a video about Jesus's arrival in the New World. We were handed tour evaluation cards. Overall impression of the tour? Clearly a 5. Guide presentation. Clearly a 5+. Would I like a missionary to visit my home to present a free Book of Mormon and explain its teachings? If I could request a particular missionary, then yes. I gazed at Sister Dos Passos like a dog watching a passing airplane. I sighed and marked no.

I sidestepped Sister Rosselli to give my evaluation card to Sister Dos Passos. Our hands touched for a brief, precious moment.

"I hope you enjoy the rest of your time in Salt Lake City," she said. "Are you traveling alone?"

"No," I said regretfully. "I'm traveling with a friend. A male friend. He doesn't like tours."

She glanced at my card. "Are you sure you don't want a missionary to visit you? I thought you were...what's the word?...aroused."

"Oh, yes." I sighed again. "But I'm going to be on the road, and when I'm not I'm usually not home at the times someone might visit." That is, I tiptoed to the door and stared out of the peephole until the missionaries gave up and walked away.

She made a moue, then brightened. "Do you have some time now? I could answer your questions, and maybe practice my English."

More time with Sister Dos Passos? Alone? This was a winning proposition even if she talked about the Book of Mormon the entire time. But Sister Rosselli was listening.

"Sister Dos Passos, I can't accompany you today," Sister Rosselli said. "I volunteered to supervise an extra shift at the cannery. Maybe you can refer him to some Elders?"

Elders? I pictured two geriatrics with canes and reading glasses mumbling about the resurrection. But Sister Dos Passos leapt to my rescue. "The rest of my afternoon is free. I can handle discussing scripture on my own."

"But you know the rules—"

Sister Dos Passos put a finger to her lips. She glanced around, but the other visitors were gone. "This is on my free time, and there are no rules against me going out with a friend on my free time, are there? If we talk about the Book of Mormon too, there's nothing wrong with that."

Sister Rosselli examined me from head to foot. "Brazilians are headstrong," she confided to me. "Okay, Sister, I'll say you went off with a friend. But remember, God is watching."

Until you date a Mormon, you don't realize how much social life revolves around ingesting mood-altering chemicals. No coffee, no tea, no alcoholic beverages. We settled on the Jamba Juice stand in the food court of the ZCMI Mall. No stimulants or inhibition depressants: just the natural high of blended fruit, ice, and Sister Dos Passos's company. I felt a twinge of guilt as we left Temple Square, but the mall was, after all, just across the street. What Mullah Milton didn't know wouldn't hurt him.

She ordered a Caribbean Passion with a femme boost; I ordered a Protein Berry Pizzazz with a fiber boost. We sat at a sticky table in front of a video arcade. At the arcade entrance was a game called Dance Dance Revolution. Set in front of a video screen was a dance floor. Arrows and computer graphics flew by while two teens stomped frantically to the tempo of techno music. Who needed drugs? These kids were high on electronics.

Sister Dos Passos held the Styrofoam cup in her slender hands and sipped contentedly. Through her thin cotton blouse, I discerned the outline of a bra. Mormons wear consecrated undergarments, and that knowledge kept my eyes bobbing involuntarily from her face to her chest. She watched me with her languid half-smile. I had sincere hopes that Mormon missionaries away from the temple acted like Catholic schoolgirls away from home.

"Tell me," I said, "what made you come on a mission to the United States instead of, say, Botswana. I'd say the Mormon Church is doing pretty well in Salt Lake City."

"Many, many reasons." She rested her hand absently on a leather-bound Book of Mormon. "The Angel Moroni revealed Another Testament of Jesus Christ to Joseph Smith in the United States. When Jesus Christ returns to rule over the Kingdom of God, it will be here in the United States. Finally, the best shopping in the world is here in the United States."

I jabbed my straw into the cup to break up a fruit fragment. "That's not quite true. The best electronics in the world are in Tokyo. They've got cell phones the size of pens and MP3 players that hold ten times the number of songs that ours do. And China has new-release DVDs for a buck each. They're all pirated, of course, but who can tell the difference?"

"Oh, I can get pirated DVDs for that price in Sao Paulo!"

"Really?"

"Really. They even have words on the bottom of the screen. What do you call that?"

"You mean subtitles?"

"Subtitles? Yes. In Portuguese."

We slurped our smoothies and marveled over the miracle of transnational commerce. Sister Dos Passos's presence was soothing. There was no rush or pressure about her. Listening to her was like swinging in a hammock on a summer afternoon.

"What is it that brought you to Temple Square?" she said.

"My car broke down. I wasn't sure what else to do in Salt Lake City."

"Don't you think it might be a sign?"

A sign that someone had vandalized my car? A sign that my car needed new parts after 250,000 miles? A sign that Salt Lake City had few entertainment options? "Do you mean—"

"I was watching you while you listened to Jesus."

"Maybe I should explain—"

She held up her palm. "Though we'd just met, I felt an instant connection to you. A charge filled my body. Electricity ran from you, through me, and out into the Heavens. It was— oh, my English, it is terrible—joy. No, more painful than joy."

Bliss. That was what I felt when I met Megumi, and how she felt about me. Why was I thinking about Megumi? Sister Dos Passos took my hand and I felt the charge of her soft, warm fingers. Her eyes were no longer half-closed but fully open. They had a fuzzy quality about them that made me lose focus.

"What," I said carefully, "do you think that means?"

She smiled, and her expression of repose returned. She continued to hold my hand. "It reminded me of the first time I received a revelation from God."

"You receive revelations directly from God?"

"We all receive communications from God, but few have the talent to hear Him clearly. Usually, it's just—what do you call it?—intuition. But the first time I heard His voice, there could be no mistake."

"What did He say?"

"B."

I nodded. "That's one of the primary tenets of Zen Buddhism. An instruction to let go of all your preconceptions and 'be one with the world.' Just be. It's remarkable how that message has significance in every great religion."

"No, silly. B, the letter B. I was taking my college entrance exam and I couldn't answer the final multiple choice question. I'd spent all my time fooling around instead of studying. The test was like reading nonsense. B, He said. The answer is B."

"What was the question?"

"I can't remember the question. All that matters is that if I'd missed that question, I couldn't have gone to university in Brazil. My parents would have sent me to the United States to study at USC."

Yuck. "Didn't you say you were from a poor town in northeastern Brazil?"

"Yes, the town is very poor, but my parents are very rich. They own a sugar plantation and many investment properties."

I licked my lips. The smoothie may not have had any additives, but it was too sweet. A hip-hop Mormon kid—rosy cheeks, baggy clothes, and backward baseball cap—was on Dance Dance Revolution. His feet were a blur.

"Did God speak to you today?" I said.

"Yes." She clenched my hands and looked into my eyes.

"What did he say?"

"*Ele será achado.*"

"Excuse me?"

"Sorry. 'He will be found.'"

"'He' meaning me, right?"

She giggled. "You know, I never thought of that. I assumed it was you. But it could have been anyone. The fat man sitting next to you, or his son with the skin problem. God could have meant 'He' himself, or 'He' the son. But at the time, I thought 'He' meant you."

It is a strange but true fact that in an unbroken line from the Oracle of Delphi to Madame Cleo, the future can be foretold only in fortune cookie form. "Well, let's presume for the moment that 'He' meant me. Who exactly is 'finding' me? Is it God?" I squeezed her hands. "Is it you?"

We leaned forward, forearms sticking to the dried remnants of old smoothies. We were so close I could smell Irish Spring soap mingled with a warm, spicy scent. She laughed.

"I don't know. All He said was 'He will be found.' I will never be mistaken for a prophet. That's what makes Joseph Smith's achievement so incredible. He barely needed to look at the golden plates in order to translate the Book of Mormon. Most of it was finished within three months."

This was her segue into a discussion of the Mormon faith. When I asked her why the Angel Moroni conveniently ran off with the gold plates shortly after Joseph Smith translated them from "reformed Egyptian," she said he brought them in the first place so of course he could remove them. When I asked her about the schism over polygamy, she said that a later prophet revealed that polygamy should no longer be practiced. Pressed about this revelation—synchronized with the federal government's legal prosecution of Mormons—she shrugged. "Why would someone believe a long-dead prophet's words when another has clarified what God commands today?" There wasn't an ironic bone in her body.

Sister Dos Passos's faith was so firm and pure, she thought nothing of grasping the hands of a heathen who harbored the fantasy of a desert thunderstorm drenching her white blouse and holy undergarments into translucence. She didn't attempt to persuade me through argumentation. She told me to read the Book of Mormon with an open mind, meditate upon its teachings, and allow my heart to decide.

The conversation moved on to other topics. She wondered why Americans were so fat. She cared little for *futebol*, and less for politics, but felt great pride that Brazil dominated the World Cup. Her favorite American actor was

Harvey Keitel. The longer we talked, the less her wet torso shimmied in my head. Holding her hands was a chaste, sensual pleasure—a hug held a second longer than necessary, the shared warmth of a single blanket.

Sister Dos Passos and I shouldn't have gotten along. She was a rich religious fundamentalist whose family exploited peasants so they could possess a Rolls Royce, two Mercedes-Benz sedans, an SUV, a vacation home in Rio de Janeiro, and an exalted place in Heaven. She had a fascination for jewelry, "the larger the gems the better." She could distinguish between the Backstreet Boys and 'N Sync. And yet, it was easy for us to talk. She said outlandish things—for example, "I don't think *everyone* should vote, do you?"—with a simplicity that drained the comments of malice. It would be heavenly to come home to her, a sprawling ranch house, and a family as large as John Stockton's.

Before I knew it, it was 5:30 p.m., a half-hour past the time I was supposed to meet Milton at the South Visitor Center. My hours with Sister Dos Passos were all the more sweet given days of Milton's arid, sullen company. I didn't tell Sister Dos Passos I had to leave until six.

"Will you walk me to the bus stop?" she said.

"Of course."

It felt perfectly natural to walk arm in arm out of the mall. The sky was the color of a burnt orange peel, and the tumescent air chased the nine-to-fivers home. The woman who was panhandling at the crosswalk had moved to a grassy patch where she laid her head on her knees. We turned the corner onto State Street and a man's voice called out to us from behind.

"Excuse me, Sister. I was wondering if you might direct me to the South Visitor Center."

We turned to find ourselves face to face with a tall, well-built man in a suit. His deep tan contrasted with his pearly white smile, and he bore more than a passing resemblance to Robert Redford. Though there was no glare, I squinted at him. My body reacted before my mind, ribs aching and the stench of a Chelan bar roiling my stomach. His black plastic nametag read "Bishop Smith." I pulled Sister Dos Passos toward me, but her arm slithered from mine like a fish escaping into the open water. She clasped her hands behind her back.

"I'm sorry to disturb you two little lovebirds," he said, "but you see I'm from an out-of-state ward, and seem to have misplaced my map."

"What a coincidence," she said. "Mr. Watanabe was going to meet a friend there. Perhaps you can walk there together."

"Ah, Brother Watanabe. I feel as if we've met before. You don't happen to belong to a ward in the state of Washington, do you?"

"I'm not your brother, Smith."

"Is that so?" His brows arched and he gazed at Sister Dos Passos in a parental fashion. "He's not a Latter-day Saint? Are you undertaking a solo proselytizing mission, Sister?"

"Mr. Watanabe was interested in finding out more about the Church. I answered his questions."

"Interested, yes." His eyes surveyed Sister Dos Passos's body. "I can see why."

"Don't go, Sister," I said. "We still haven't resolved the issues of racism, patriarchy, and homophobia in the Church."

"I think Bishop Smith can answer your other questions, Mr. Watanabe." Her fuzzy dark eyes urged me to follow her lead. Even through her dark complexion, a blush was surfacing. "He has more knowledge than I do. And his English won't make you laugh."

John Smith nodded serenely. "Ah, the arguments of skeptics. I've heard them all. Really, Sister. You should return to your dormitory as soon as possible. I'll take it from here."

The street was crowded with rush-hour traffic and Mormons waiting for buses. As soon as she left, he'd bring me to an alley, knock me off, and melt into the crowd. Smith had mentioned the South Visitor Center. Did that mean he'd dispatched Milton, or was that simply a cover story?

"Goodbye, Mr. Watanabe," Sister Dos Passos said, soft lips painted into a frown. Her bus stop was across the street. She turned away, then hesitated. "I almost forgot. I promised you a free Book of Mormon."

She reached into her shoulder bag and removed a dog-eared edition. "I'll give you mine. I have marked my favorite passages. Perhaps you will find it useful on your journey." She pulled out a pen and began scribbling. "I'll write my e-mail address in case you have any more questions about scripture." Her handwriting was tiny but fluid. She wrote more than her e-mail address. She included two phone numbers, one of which was international. She drew a heart and signed it, "Teresa."

When she handed me the Book of Mormon, her fingertips lingered on my wrists. "You talk in ways that make my head spin." A smile played on her lips. "But remember: faith is about thinking with the heart, not the mind. Focus on your feelings."

CHAPTER 14

I was alone and unarmed, at the mercy of a violent corporate drone who was impersonating a Mormon. Smith must have monitored me since that fateful night in Chelan. How else could he have known that my car had broken down in Salt Lake City?

Sister Dos Passos crossed the street as if it were a market square in Timbauba, blithely unconcerned with the oncoming traffic, which veered and braked. Her narrow hips swiveled to an oceanic rhythm that American women no longer hear. Smith gave an appreciative nod.

"I'm dying for a cappuccino," he said. "How about you?"

What had Milton's instructions been? *Stay in public places. If he tries to get you into a car or an alley, fight him in the street. Stomp on his instep, put an elbow in his windpipe, gouge his eyes. But better than all that, don't get separated from me.*

"Let's talk at the South Visitor Center," I said.

Smith shook his head. "I'd rather we had a little more privacy. Come on. There's a Starbucks nearby frequented by the Gentiles. I bring my laptop there when I'm in town.

Wireless access isn't free, but I'm guaranteed a good connection worldwide."

"What if I refuse to go?"

Smith pulled back his lapel to reveal a holstered pistol. "Loosen up, Guy. I'll treat you to an iced coffee. That'll take the edge off of this dreadful heat."

Three blocks away was the familiar green logo of the mermaid with the covered breasts. Few non-Seattleites realized that the original logo shows a bare-breasted siren spreading her split fish tail over her head in a pose that would excite Larry Flynt. Smith removed the plastic nametag identifying him as a member of the Mormon Church.

"It's probably a sin to impersonate a bishop," I said.

"And what do you call hitting on a Mormon missionary?"

The rush-hour commuters had already come and gone with their caffeine fix. Aside from us, there were two baristas, a bespectacled man typing at his notebook computer, and a mother sipping hot coffee precariously close to the head of an infant slung to her chest. She used her free hand to sample CDs at a music listening station.

After my smoothie, what I really wanted was a glass of water. But since Smith was paying, I ordered the most expensive drink on the menu, a venti soy Caramel Frappuccino. He directed us to a purple, imitation-velvet loveseat in the back corner of the café. It was, in fact, the same purple, imitation-velvet loveseat found at the Starbucks around the corner from my apartment. Furniture that's unique in its ubiquity: the key to style.

Smith sipped the foam on his cappuccino. "Have you noticed that the smallest size you can purchase is a tall? Tall, grande, and venti. Big, bigger, and biggest—there's no short size at all! No matter what the consumer chooses, he need not feel inadequate."

I slid myself away from him into a corner of the sofa. Smith had a problem with encroaching upon personal space. "Starbucks coffee tastes burnt."

He wagged a finger. "You, my friend, are an elitist. An unemployed elitist. Only in America!"

There was something odious about Smith—the faint aroma of grass, wool vests, and mid-morning tee times. His posture was perfect and he carried himself with the ease of someone comfortable with his privilege.

"Let's cut to the chase," I said. "What do you want from me?"

"What do *I* want?" Smith chuckled. "What do *you* want? That car of yours is hardly the cross-country cruiser. Why repair it? The parts and labor cost more than its worth."

"What am I supposed to do? Leave it on the side of the road and buy another car I'll eventually abandon on the side of the road? Haven't you heard of global warming? How about recycling?"

"If you can't afford a new car, just say so." He rolled his eyes. "You've got a problem with clinging to things you should let go. Case in point: the girl. I can guarantee you she's moved on to other conquests. For goodness' sake, *you've* moved on to new conquests. She's nothing but skin and bones, and she's hardly the conversationalist. Me, I prefer a woman who looks like a woman, but then again I'm a happily married man in my forties. You, on the other hand, are entering the mid-thirties, the most treacherous age for a man, when his *joie de vivre* is in urgent need of resuscitation. Some men train for triathlons, others purchase sports cars. Isn't it painfully obvious why young women seek out men your age? Nice dinners, expensive vacations, green cards. If you'd like, I can refer you to a number of reputable agencies who arrange mail-order relationships for men like you. Choose your country and you'll receive nude photos of young ladies twice as attractive as Megumi and many times more complaisant. Thailand is reliable. Brazil if you favor a spicier mélange."

"Are you attempting to insult me or your boss?" I said. "I doubt he'd be pleased to hear what you're implying about his fiancée."

Smith's arched his eyebrows. His tan appeared to have been applied with a brush. Beneath his eyes, under his ears, and around his collar, his skin was pale. "All the more reason to heed my advice, Guy. This conversation is a strictly off-the-record courtesy. As the immortal Miss Austen noted, 'It is a truth universally acknowledged, that a single man in possession of a good fortune must be in want of a wife.' How does such a man avoid gold-diggers? Quite simply. Follow Mr. Crawford's example and never marry.

"There is confusion in your eyes, but there need not be. Like any flesh-and-blood man, Horatio Kolling has physical needs that have been dutifully satisfied by Miss Megumi. I will admit that Mr. Kolling has a curious attachment to her, but hers is the plight of Scheherazade, telling stories with her body, desperately delaying the day on which she too will be discarded. I don't begrudge her attempts to create an exit strategy, but I do resent the way her antics take me away from my primary duties. Think of me as Mr. Kolling's personal human resources department. I don't create the conditions of employment. I penalize the breaking of rules."

The sweet, icy sludge in my cup sent a shiver of pain into my brain. He was calling Megumi a glorified concubine. Would that explain her nonchalant manner in bed? Stop. How could I even think of believing her fiancé's servant, a man who'd arranged to have me gang-raped? Megumi never would have written that letter if she didn't feel the same connection between us that I did. *That's* what threatened Kolling. Why else would Smith follow me?

"Are you saying you serve as Kolling's pimp?" I said.

Smith's cup quavered, enough to indicate I'd struck a nerve. "My relationship with Mr. Kolling runs deeper than employer-employee. When KGI operated out of a one-room office in Hong Kong, I served as salesman, receptionist, secretary, office manager, and janitor. Mr. Kolling entrusted me with developing the Neighborhood Karaoke Strategy, which has expanded to include nearly twelve thousand franchisees worldwide. While Starbucks and McDonald's draw the ire of WTO protestors, KGI is the most profitable company nobody's ever heard of. In Japan, we've quietly taken over hostess bars catering to PMs and Yakuza alike. In America, our customers see the Coors Light banners and the Monday Night Football giveaways and they think 'one of us' not 'one of them.'"

Smith spoke with the zeal of a missionary. And like any religious adherent, he was making huge leaps in logic. "How," I said, "does a flashy karaoke complex in Leavenworth named Xanadu fit in with this Neighborhood Karaoke Strategy? It seems to me that Mongolian hordes and Oktoberfest are incompatible."

Smith sipped his cappuccino. "I am not at liberty to discuss the internal decision-making structure at KGI.

Mr. Kolling surrounds himself with talented, intelligent people and then allows them to do their jobs. He has final say, however, and when he makes up his mind, our job is to fall in line. I have learned and continue to learn a great deal from his business acumen."

One of the baristas was changing the filter on the coffee-maker, and the other was wiping down the tabletops. They were cleaning a spotless café even though there were hardly any patrons. This was corporate culture at its best. Where was Milton? When I failed to show at the visitor center, he must have gone looking for me.

"Then it wasn't your idea to merge with the Troy Bob-bins Corporation?" I said.

For the briefest moment psychosis flashed in his eyes. "I thought you were estranged from your ex-wife. I hope she hasn't violated the attorney-client privilege. It extends to all employees of the firm, I believe, not just to the attorneys."

A simple phone call and Tanya would be removed from the case and fired from the firm. Gone would be her law school tuition. She'd be blackballed from working at any Seattle law firm. But. Smith knew Tanya was working on the KGI project. And he knew our relationship. What if she'd been assigned to the KGI project *because* of our relationship? That would mean…no. I wouldn't believe Milton. Or Smith. Where did someone like Smith come from? It was impossible to picture him as a child or with children of his own. Was he threatening me or Tanya? Both of us? He sensed my uneasiness and it invigorated him.

"You followed me for a reason," I said. "Last time you incited a mob to beat me for singing Boy George. What are you going to do this time? Force me to admonish customers about their paper cups littering landfills until someone brains me with a travel mug?"

Smith lifted his hands up in mock surrender. "We're just talking, Guy. If I'd wanted to hurt you, there are easier ways. Do you have any idea how hazardous it is to drive an eighties-era economy car without airbags amongst three-ton sports-utility vehicles? You drive long enough and you'll kill yourself without my intervention.

"And then there's your traveling companion." Smith frowned. "Have you any idea with whom you've taken to the road? A drug-addled porn star!"

"*Former* porn star," I corrected. Was Milton stigmatized forever for a job he once held? It was like calling me a "waiter" because I worked in a restaurant during college. "And he's kicked his drug habit. Milton doesn't eat meat, for Christ's sake."

Smith flicked his wrist dismissively. "Once a junkie, always a junkie. Surely you know his past? What he did to his girlfriend?"

"I know enough." That is, I knew all I wanted to know. Sheila said his girlfriend had died of AIDS, which meant a painful, debilitating death, not a violent one. (But then again, Sheila had instructed me never to ask about the scar on his neck.) "He knows a lot more about KGI than you'd like him to."

"Perhaps. But the question you should be asking is *why* does he know so much? Is it for his health?" Smith sipped his drink. "By the way, Starbucks coffee isn't burnt. Only high-quality coffee beans can withstand a dark roast."

"There's no reason I should trust you."

"Trust me, no. Believe me, yes. Think about it, Guy. I may have had you beaten to a pulp, but have I ever lied to you? 'Milt the Stilt' is a time bomb waiting to explode. Tick, tick, tick, tick. The only one he's fooling is you."

*Don't think, feel...*isn't that what Sister Dos Passos told me? At the gut level, John Smith was the stomach flu, food poisoning, and colitis. He would do anything to keep me away from Megumi. He meant to play on my suspicions. Milton might be socially retarded. He was less than forthcoming about his past and parsimonious in sharing his knowledge about KGI. But his acrimony toward KGI emanated from his body like heat from an engine. *Why did Milton Schwarzer hate KGI?* For the same reasons Smith protected KGI's interests: his livelihood. *How does karaoke affect a miniatures store?* I couldn't explain the intricacies of nouveau German nationalism. The important thing was that Milton was on my side and Smith was not. As Milton said, nothing is more trustworthy than hatred.

"You've got questions, Guy. Ask away and Scout's honor," he raised two fingers in the air, "I'll answer truthfully. I made Eagle Scouts, you know. Had I not wound up with two daughters and a rigorous travel schedule, I would have led a Cub Scout troop."

Smith was an Eagle Scout? That made me trust him less. It's inherently suspicious for grown men to wear shorts and kerchiefs.

The glass door swung open with a sharp crack. We looked up; the barista scalded her hand at the milk steamer. Milton stood framed in the doorway, a three-and-a-half foot mass of muscle. His face was livid with fever. The T-shirt beneath his blazer was drenched in sweat. Before anyone could move, he stood before us. His eyes fixed on Smith.

"Thought you could cut me out of the equation, didn't you, Smith?" Milton made no attempt to conceal his holstered pistol. Behind the counter, the baristas looked frightened.

Smith sighed. "Just a friendly conversation, Milton. Multi-party negotiations are so…complicated."

"You've got no authority to cut deals. If Kolling wants to talk, he makes an appearance himself. Got that?"

Smith pursed his lips. "I'll check his schedule. But don't hold your breath."

The scar on Milton's neck was engorged with blood, a living creature clinging to his throat.

"Let's go, Watanabe," he ordered.

The mother with the baby slunk out, and the other customer hurriedly packed away his laptop computer. A barista whispered into a telephone receiver. Smith placed his hands, spread-fingered, on the table.

I picked up my half-filled plastic cup. Milton and I left together.

CHAPTER 15

Is there a difference between southern Utah and northern New Mexico? It felt as if we were plunging deeper into an arid, desert sea. Time was measured by the empty plastic water bottles collecting at Milton's feet.

"How did your ex-wife communicate our whereabouts to Kolling so quickly?" Milton said. "What is she, screwing the lead counsel?"

I kept my eyes on the asphalt disappearing into the gullet of a vacuous sky. Jay had written her a recommendation letter. He'd lobbied to have the firm pay for her legal education. These were platonic favors for the only female who volunteered to work with him.

Faith is about thinking with the heart, not the mind. Please, Sister Dos Passos, tell me that was the truth and not a Mormon marketing jingle.

"*Quid pro quo.*" Milton said. "That's the only relationship to trust."

We lucked out. Rakesh, the 24-hour customer service representative for the Troy Bobbins Corporation, squeezed us into the final afternoon of the *Leading from Without* seminar for a special, prorated fee.

"This is an extraordinary deal," he said in a lilting, Indian accent. "Tip top. I don't know how you twist my arm."

Troy Bobbins, personal advisor to presidents, leaders of commerce, and movie stars would meet with each and every seminar participant for five minutes. But whereas everyone else had shelled out $2,999.99 for the three-day seminar, we would pay only $799.99 per person and receive the same personal audience. Why couldn't Milton accept that Troy's time was worth at least three hundred times that of an elementary school teacher's? He agreed to go only after I persuaded him that we couldn't get past Troy's phalanx of bodyguards otherwise. Once Troy understood how shady KGI was, he would put the kibosh on the impending merger.

I'd driven for thirteen hours straight yet could barely sleep that night. So what if I couldn't afford the seminar? What's another eight hundred bucks when your credit debt exceeds 20K? Some things are more valuable than food and shelter. If we helped Troy to avoid business disaster, he was sure to volunteer advice on more personal matters. If I could ask Troy just one question, what would it be?

The *Leading from Without* seminar took place in a circus tent on Troy's expansive estate in the Santa Fe foothills. No, it wasn't really a circus tent; it was more like a temporary sports arena, replete with skylights and sliding electric doors.

Milton groused about being split up, but I was pleased. The other attendees were as giddy as I was about meeting Troy, and their positive energy was an antidote to Milton's permanent sulk. My cohort of sixty was led into a screening room that contained stadium seating.

"How will I know when it's time to meet Troy?" I asked the usher.

She held up the headphones. "When you receive your auditory cue, please exit to your left."

The others reviewed their notes. I pulled the printed material out of the seat-back in front of me. The workbook was entitled "*Leading from Without, Day 3: Personal Fortitude.*" The cover showed a photograph of Troy. He stood in the middle of the desert, looking up at a looming mesa. In his hand was a walking staff. I turned to the first page.

Effective Leadership

A **leader** does not wait for consensus to be reached, he imposes his will on others. This takes **fortitude**.

Fortitude = *the strength of mind that allows one to endure pain or adversity with courage*

It's lonely at the top. When attacked on all sides, remember to hunker down in your **FORT**.

Façade. 'It is only shallow people who do not judge by appearances.' Project an image of control at all times.

Opportunism. Create a sense of urgency for even the smallest, most inconsequential activities.

Remuneration. Pay equals respect.

Terror. Fear is a more powerful motivator than pleasure is. Your competition should fear your every move; your employees should fear for their jobs.

Today's presentation is made possible by a strategic partnership between the **Troy Bobbins Corporation** and the special effects wizards at **Industrial Light and Magic.** Please enjoy the show.

The workbook contained wide-ruled, blank lines headed by questions. Question 1: "Name three instances in which it would have been more beneficial for you to have held up a *Façade* instead of being yourself." Question 5: "Visualize the *Terror* of losing your job and the respect of your peers. List three ways to create a work environment characterized by motivational terror." For only $20 extra I could take the printed material home.

I pulled on the padded headphones and the murmurs in the room disappeared, replaced by the gentle patter of a piano and the whisper of a stream. Moments later, the room darkened. Three ascending xylophone notes played and a woman's voice spoke:

"The following copyrighted presentation of Troy Bobbins *Leading from Without, Day 3: Personal Fortitude,* may not be rebroadcast or retransmitted without the express written consent of the Troy Bobbins Corporation. Out of courtesy to your fellow travelers on this Personal Path, please turn off all cellular phones and beepers. Now get ready to 'Climb the Leadership Mountain' with Mr. Troy Bobbins."

The curtain rose, filling the room with sunlight so bright my eyes watered. Scarlet earth, tangerine cliff walls, sagebrush. The picture was so sharp I could see a lizard run from one bush to another.

Troy walked onscreen from stage right. His unbuttoned denim shirt revealed his broad chest straining against a form-fitting orange T-shirt. He wore khaki expedition pants with zip-off legs. What he lacked was sunglasses. He shielded his eyes with one hand while gesturing to the stone glacier behind him.

"Let's conquer that mesa," Troy said.

His gait was measured but rapid, and soon the sound of his slightly labored breathing was in my ears. Meanwhile, the camera moved from an overhead position to one just over his left shoulder. I expected him to stop, turn around, and address us, but he didn't. He just plodded along. Occasionally he cleared his throat and stopped to take a swig from his Nalgene bottle.

There was no soundtrack. When Troy stopped to rest, the camera pulled back to show his sweat-stained shirt and his progress on the mesa. Other than that, it was as if we were watching raw footage from an outdoor adventure show. Where were his pragmatic insights on life? Where were his action plans?

Troy looked smaller-than-life against a natural back-drop. The path was filled with broken rock and tenuous handholds carved into the cliff face. At one point he lost his balance and fell to one knee. A close-up showed a nasty scrape.

Didn't we just climb this same switchback a few minutes ago? There—the same squiggly red mark was on the cliff next to the bottom step. Absent these repetitive loops, Troy would have been standing on the top already. I paid $800 for this? I wasn't sure whether to fall asleep or cry.

The ushers were lined up at the back wall of the theater. One stepped forward to lead a participant out of the room. Moments later, another arrived to escort someone back to her seat. I wondered whether to flag one down for a restroom break. But as I considered this, I noticed that Troy had reached the final ascent—a treacherous, fifty-foot cliff. Above was our destination and below was loose scrabble. Losing balance here meant sliding, or falling, all the way down to the valley floor.

Troy would make it to the top, of course. Troy never failed...I just wished the video wasn't so boring. I chided myself for these negative thoughts. Today's video presentation had to be engaging, but not so engaging as to make anyone regret leaving to meet with Troy. If I stopped obsessing about my displeasure, I could start focusing on what questions to ask Troy.

The first rock jolted me out of my reverie. The rock gashed Troy's forehead, sending a trickle of blood into his eyes. Rocks rained down him, striking chest and shoulders, arms, cheek, drawing more blood. Troy twisted out of the way, lost his grip on a crevice, and slid. He scrambled into an alcove.

Shadowy figures scurried along the ridge. If Troy climbed upward, he would expose himself to the projectiles for another fifty yards. If he beat a retreat, he could turn the corner and run to safety. The camera closed in on Troy's tanned face. There was only one option for a man like Troy Bobbins. He took a deep breath and made his assault on the summit.

His decisiveness took his assailants by surprise. For twenty yards, his ascent was uninterrupted. Then what looked like an adobe brick struck Troy on the sunburned crown of his head. His fingers went slack, and he began a rapid slide downward, his head bouncing along the cliff face like a rag doll's. He slid over the ledge and then fell like a sack of potatoes down, down, down to the valley below.

It happened too fast for me to register anything other than shock. Troy should have been standing victorious atop the mesa. Instead he was lying broken on the valley floor. It wasn't a majestic or poetic fall; it wasn't accompanied by a cloud of dust or a clattering thud. One moment he was climbing, the next he was falling. Raucous screeches emitted from the creatures up above. They were cheering. They were jeering.

My breathing had become labored. I looked around the theater at the others. A woman sobbed. We couldn't hear one another, but our thoughts were the same. The video could not end this way. And yet Troy didn't move. Crows alighted nearby. Hopped closer. Waited.

"Guy Watanabe." The female voice in the headphones cut into my thoughts. "Please exit to your left. It is time for your personal audience with Mr. Troy Bobbins."

On my way out, I peeked back at the screen. Troy's leg remained twisted backward unnaturally.

The usher led me down a flight of stairs into a catacomb of meticulously maintained hallways leading past wood-grained doors. Underground office space beneath a circus tent?

I entered a waiting room. Other seminar participants sat in chairs and thumbed through entertainment magazines. A bespectacled receptionist in a powder-blue Troy Bobbins golf shirt smiled from behind the counter.

"Mr. Bobbins would like to get to know you a little better before you meet," she said. She handed me a clipboard with a No. 2 pencil and what looked to be a multiple-choice exam. "Please return this to me and I will call you when it's your turn."

In the upper left corner of my questionnaire was my personal information: name, address, telephone number. At the bottom was a shaded area marked "Official Use Only." In this section, there was a checkmark next to the word: "prorated." I looked up at the other participants. I was the only one with a red nametag.

The questions on the first sheet were general and demographic. Age, race, gender, estimated annual income, number of Troy Bobbins products purchased within the past year, number of Troy Bobbins products to be purchased in the upcoming year, et cetera. The questions that followed were more challenging.

> 9. Which of the following animals would you choose to be?
>
> a. Lion b. Elephant c. Eagle d. Dolphin

I chewed the pencil eraser. The best answer for a leadership seminar would be *a. Lion.* Leo, leader, fire sign, predator, take-charge animal. But was I supposed to select what I knew to be "right," or the one that best reflected my character? My pencil lead hovered over *b. Elephant*—slow to make changes, long memory. No, the operative word was *choose.*

I was tempted by *c. Eagle* but knew this to be a trap-door selection. *Everyone* wanted to soar like a bird. It was a cliché. Caught in a quandary, I filled in the bubble next to the most value-neutral selection: *d. Dolphin.* Happy go-lucky, altruistic, intelligent (though if they were so smart, why did they always get caught in tuna nets?).

The remainder of the questions followed a similar pattern. 11. *If you found a wallet with $5,000 in the street, which of the following would you do?* 13. *Given the traits of the following people, which would you choose to be your life partner?* 17. *If you could describe the world using one of the following adjectives, what would it be?* I eliminated the selections that provided an obvious descriptor of the kind of person I was or was supposed to be, and then chose what remained. When in doubt, in homage to Sister Dos Passos, I chose B.

The final question stumped me.

20. Faced with violent adversaries, broken and bruised on the valley floor, which of the following best describes your response?
a. Wait for death;
b. Pray for a miracle;
c. Ignore the pain and drag yourself up to the top of the mesa again; or
d. Call for reinforcements and, when the time is right, assault the mesa and wreak vengeance on the evildoers.

There was no option to "climb an uninhabited mesa" or "call it a day and find a less perilous activity." I suppose the operative cue was what "best" described my response.

The "closest" response to mine would be *a. Wait for death*, but I couldn't face Troy with an answer like that. Praying for a miracle, *B*, didn't do a whole lot for Sir Thomas More. Answer *C* was a noble (albeit painful and prolonged) suicide. The only rational answer was *D*. Troy's assailants were armed with nothing more than rocks. A small, private force with body armor and rifles could take that plateau and make those jeering monkeys pay.

I filled in *D* and erased it. I filled it in again and then erased it. Why was I so indecisive? Was it a coincidence that answer *B* was the way of faith? I filled in *B* and erased it. I couldn't kid myself. I filled in *D* and handed in my questionnaire before I could change my mind.

That must be the way the leadership video ended, I thought as I paged through a *Vanity Fair* article about the sex lives of JFK and Jackie Kennedy. *Troy led a personal assault on the mesa, punishing those who, for no good reason, attempted to kill him.* There was no reason to feel queasy about that ending. It was an instructional video, moviemaking magic meant to illustrate the principles Troy taught. A leader motivates others to join his cause. FORT, short for fortitude. Façade. Opportunism. Remuneration. Terror.

I organized my thoughts. I could ask Troy about KGI then move on to more important questions. I would ask whether it was the right time for me to wade back into the working world. Would it make sense to ask about my romantic entanglements during a leadership seminar?

It was 4:30 p.m. The waiting room was nearly empty. Those who preceded me must have exited a different way; only two others entered the room after me, both of whom wore red "prorated" tags. I would be one of the last participants to see Troy. What if I missed the video's finale? My last image of Troy would be of him broken, bleeding, and helpless.

An usher led me down a hallway to an audience chamber. The room was far smaller than I'd imagined it to be, hardly more than a utility closet. A dim canister light shone down on a chair, leaving the rest of the tiny space in shadows. The chair faced a double-paned glass window shuttered on the opposite side. Inset in the wall was a tissue-paper dispenser. At the foot of the chair was a wastepaper basket, half-filled with tissues.

"This is supposed to be a personal audience with Troy," I said. "This is so…so…isolating."

The usher smiled. "Mr. Bobbins has to be cautious about his personal security. Don't worry, you won't be able to tell the difference once it starts." She shut the door behind me and locked it. I took my seat and, as soon as I did, the shutter rose with a mechanical buzz.

Troy was not sitting directly across from me. His room was not, like mine, a booth. It was a spacious parlor. Covering the hardwood floor was a burgundy Oriental rug with undertones of blue and white. He sat twenty feet away in a plush, wing-backed armchair, next to a roaring fire. A bottle of Perrier perched on a side table. But what stunned me was the sight of Troy himself.

Troy's walking staff was propped in a corner, and he looked as if he had walked directly out of the video into this room. His khaki expedition pants were torn, exposing a nasty wound on his knee and dried blood on his calf. His orange T-shirt was mucked up with dirt, blood, and perspiration. His face was bruised and cut, though the gash on his forehead had been stitched. The main difference between his appearance here and in the video was, however, his sunglasses. In the desert, he wore none; here, he wore wire-rimmed glasses with lenses dark as coal.

"Welcome to *Leading from Without*, Mr. Watanabe. I'm sorry that you missed most of the seminar. Did you know that if you reenroll in the program within thirty days, you pay only the difference between the prorated rate and full price?" His voice was slightly hoarse.

"Yes. Your customer service representative told me that. And the person at the registration booth. And the receptionist. Thank you. I'd really like to, if I can afford it."

Troy smiled his familiar horsy grin. "If you're here now, you can afford it. We are contradictory creatures, frittering away our money and time on frivolities. AAA estimates that the average American spends 56.2 cents per mile, or $8,431 per year on his car. What do you think a more fulfilling life is worth?"

"Troy," I said, touching my cheek. "Are you really hurt?"

Troy lifted his arm and examined what looked to be a suppurating wound on the white flesh of his forearm. He shook his head and chuckled. "Mere flesh wounds. The director says I shouldn't do my own stunts, but nothing makes a person feel more alive than simulated peril. But enough about me, let's talk about you. We're on the clock, Mr. Watanabe."

There was, I noticed, a digital timer right below the window, next to the tissue paper dispenser, and time was ticking away in lighted green numerals. Two minutes gone already. Ask a question about the meaning of life. Or about my professional future. Stop wondering how an underground fireplace, lit beneath a circus tent, could be vented outdoors.

"Are you selling your company to the Karaoke Group International?" Damn. I couldn't believe that Milton had guilted me into losing precious time.

Troy tilted his head. Because of the sunglasses, I couldn't read the expression on his face. "Selling my company to the what?"

"To the Karaoke Group International. It's also known as KGI."

"Say that first word again," he said.

"You mean Karaoke?"

"Aha!" he said. "You mean kareyokey. But I like the way you pronounce it. It sounds more authentic. Say it again, this time slowly."

"Karaoke. I mean ka-ra-o-ke."

"Ka-ra-okey," he said. "Karey-o-ke. Darn. I'll get it."

"It's a multinational corporation bent on dominating the entertainment industry," I said. "A reliable source told me that you're selling your company to KGI. Is that true?"

Troy shrugged. "I have no idea what you're talking about."

"Really?" I said.

"Really." He was too far away for me to discern whether the question had surprised him, and there were, of course, those sunglasses. But he hadn't hesitated.

Tanya's hunch was wrong. We had no leads. My disappointment was tempered by my relief that Troy was not selling out to the likes of Kolling. Did this mean, as Milton had suggested, that Tanya had intentionally steered us into a trap? The timer showed a minute and fifty seconds. Worry about that later. Move on to more important questions.

"I listened to your *Personal Path* series," I said. "It changed my life. And I'm trying to implement your lessons. But I've had this problem ever since, well, ever since my wife left me. I can't work up the energy to care. Everything used to make sense and now it doesn't."

"Mm hmm. I see."

"It's like I've been walking in a dream for the last year. No matter what I do, none of it means anything." The timer hit the one-minute mark and flashed, emitting a low beep-beep-beep. "I want to know. How do I wake up?" I leaned forward in my seat, the balls of my feet pressing into the floor.

Troy sipped his mineral water, swishing it around in his mouth before swallowing. "Do you subscribe to the Bobbins Monthly Newsletter?"

"No. Not yet."

"Well, that's a start. Have you signed up with a Bobbins Personal Coach?"

Bobbins Personal Coaches called twice per week, each time for a half-hour session. They charged $200 per month. "I haven't."

"Well, there you go.'"

The timer reached zero and flashed. With a metallic rumble, the metal screen began to roll down over the window.

"But Troy," I said, leaning sideways to keep eye contact beneath the lowering blind. "What should I be doing differently?"

Troy waved. "Invest more in your personal development."

The usher led me back to the main floor. I should have fired off my questions one after the other. I should have written them down on a piece of paper and then checked them off as I went. That was the reason I couldn't move on with my life: I frittered away my opportunities.

"Have a good day, Mr. Watanabe," the usher said. We were in the lobby, where a handful of people, most of them wearing red tags, browsed the Troy Bobbins product booths.

"I'd like to see the end of the video," I said.

"There's only five minutes left. The finale shouldn't be viewed out of context."

"Please. It's important that I find out what happens."

I stood in the rear with the ushers. Without headphones, the scene was eerily silent. We were on top of the mesa at last: Troy and a large band of men armed with rifles and torches. The entire pueblo was on fire. The flames were pale, almost invisible, in the sunlight. It was the smoke— great, dark clouds of it streaming from the windows—that menaced. Dark people in threadbare clothes lay in rows on the plateau. I couldn't tell whether they were dead or not. The camera pulled away until the mesa was nothing more than a sandstone matchstick. The screen went black and the credits rolled.

Milton had received the same answer that I had: Troy wasn't selling his business. "But get this. They wouldn't let me piss without an escort. And why the sunglasses indoors?"

"What's the big deal?" I was still disappointed by the questions I'd left unasked. "Who knows what some wacko might do if he got an opportunity to spend time alone with Troy."

"It's not that." Milton fingered his scar contemplatively. "I don't know whether either of us met with Troy Bobbins today. At best only one of us did."

We pulled into the back parking lot of a rubber stamp store a block away from the motel. Milton's safety precautions had by now become second nature. "You're not making sense," I said. "Troy's not involved with KGI. That's all that matters."

"Think, Watanabe. You met Bobbins at 4:45 p.m. I met him at 4:50 p.m. We should have crossed paths in the waiting room. We didn't. And we saw others waiting to meet with him after us. There must have been more than one waiting room."

Troy couldn't have been in two places at once unless Troy was more than one person. Had I been pouring out my heart to a Troy look-alike? Had I been seeking direction in my life from an actor playing Troy Bobbins?

I felt as if someone had kicked me in the gut. Milton, on the other hand, was impressed by the multiplied profits this setup created for the Troy Bobbins Corporation. It was minutes before I noticed that a note had been slipped under the door while we were away at the seminar. The note was signed by Horatio Kolling.

CHAPTER 16

"Jugs" squatted across the four-lane highway from a multiplex movie theater, between a Kentucky Fried Chicken and a Mobil gas station. Black paint coated the shoebox structure's walls and windows like soot. The neon sign—pendulous breasts restrained by a pink bikini—flickered and rotated.

Milton had offered me an assortment of armaments from his locked, multi-level case: a butterfly knife, spiked brass knuckles, his spare pistol. I had turned him down as a matter of principle. Now, faced with an imminent confrontation, I realized the folly of depending on someone else to keep me safe. I slipped the steak knife/car starter out from beneath the floor mat, wadded it in Kleenex, and thrust the weapon into my pocket.

"There, there, and there, behind the dumpster," Milton said, pointing to a back door, a side door, and a window propped open by a block of wood. "When we get inside, take note of the exits. If we get split up, circle back with the car to pick me up at KFC at 5 a.m. Safest place to be is right here. No one expects you to stay put."

Music pounded the chilled air and a redheaded stripper twirled on a pole. The customers' faces soaked up the show like rays from the sun. A thick woman tended bar, where off-duty dancers in bikini bottoms and sweat tops chatted. A muscular eunuch in a tight black T-shirt guarded a purple door emblazoned with the words "Fantasy Labyrinth."

"Why did he sign the note, 'Horatio Kolling, Karaoke King,'" I said.

"He's trying to crawl inside your head," Milton said. "So what if it's a stupid award. It's yours. Don't let him rob you with ridicule. Fall for cheap mind-fucks like that and you'll play right into his hands."

Strippers approached, soliciting private dances. Milton waved them away with a flick of his wrist. I was apologetic, moved by their sad, aggressive eyes. I downed three Sprites in my anxiousness and air-conditioning-induced dehydration. Kolling had said to meet him here at 10 p.m. An hour later there was no sign of a trap, a message, or anything else. Milton sat like a gargoyle and scanned the faces of every patron who entered. Around 11:45 I ordered my first real drink and began watching the show more earnestly than I watched the entrances.

Ebony, Lolita, and Madonna; Conchita, Desiree, and My Lai; Lucinda and LaShawn—the stage was a multicultural cart overflowing with flesh of all textures, sizes, and flavors. Melons and strawberries; eggplants and cherries; if the present dancer didn't catch your fancy, wait three songs and the next one would. The musical selections swung from rock to bluegrass to salsa; the dances ranged from striptease to simulated sex; yet throughout there was a reassuring predictability. Song one: rubbing over the thin fabric of the bikini. Song two, two-minute mark: removal of the top. Song three: topless physical feats ranging from sliding down the pole upside down to vigorous tugging at taut nipples. It was against house rules to remove bottoms. And yet, the DJ reminded us, "Anything is possible in the Fantasy Labyrinth. Only twenty dollars per song!"

"Let's go," I said an hour after midnight. "No one's going to show." The anticipation without release had knotted my neck, and vodka barely took the edge off of the ache. If I didn't leave, I'd vomit, fall asleep, or begin stuffing small bills into the dancers' G-strings.

"They'll show." Milton didn't look up.

"Miss Manners says that three hours late is the absolute limit for kneecapping your victims."

"Keep drinking, funny man. It's happening tonight. The longer we stay, the surer I am. All the energy is flowing through this place right now."

"Look, Milton. Maybe he sent us the note so they could toss our room. Maybe he's just screwing with us. I don't know. But at least I don't pretend to know." I tried to hold his eyes but finally gazed down at my soggy napkin.

"This isn't a hunch," he said coldly. "I *know* something's going to happen. The energy flow auras dictate it. You could make yourself more useful by watching doors instead of titties."

"Fine. I'll just order another drink while we're waiting." I flagged the waitress down and fixed my eyes onstage, where a curvaceous Latina beauty shook her gelatinous mammaries. Energy flow auras. If I believed that, I'd be clasping

222

hands with New Age hippies on an *ashram*, not waiting to be ambushed in a strip club with a former porn star. I should let him walk his short ass back to the motel.

The Latina was followed by Bamboo, a long, thin Asian American with a tattoo on her shoulder. The DJ announced a pricing special good for the next hour: buy three songs in the Fantasy Labyrinth and get one free. His voice was warm and neighborly. "Next on stage is Luba. Luba, don't be late for school, sweetie. You're up."

Luba. The name sounded familiar. It took a moment for the tumblers in my mind to click into place. Luba was the name of Milton's long-lost love: his costar in blue movies. The paleness of her skin contrasted with her plain black bikini and dyed-black hair. Her walk was a languid, feral slouch. She reminded me of the girls who hung out behind the back fence of our high school smoking clove cigarettes, which meant that she reminded me of Sheila. And from the looks of her, if she hadn't dropped out, she'd only recently graduated.

The electric guitar whine of "Sweet Child O' Mine" filled the air. She touched her neck and belly as she gyrated her hips. As the tempo increased, she threw her head from side to side. She clawed at the bikini top as if it were a scab she needed to tear away. The sheer material shifted and lifted but her nipples remained obscured by her cupped hands. I felt myself becoming aroused. Or maybe it was just a full bladder.

"Is this what we've been waiting for?" I said.

"Yes."

I pushed myself up. "Well, don't take her down before I return from the restroom."

Milton didn't answer. He stared at Luba with a reptilian intensity, all the while fingering the scar tissue on his neck.

Contemplating the dirty grout between the tiles as I relieved myself at the urinal, I realized I felt no panic. So what if a stripper who looked like Milton's old girlfriend happened to use the same porn star moniker? He had hired the rail-thin, slouching Sheila at *Das Puppenhaus*. He sought out Luba clones. Here, at the Baskin-Robbins of strip joints, there was bound to be a stripper who looked like "his" Luba. What was she going to do, squeeze us to death with her thighs? A better explanation: Milton was paranoid.

By the time I'd returned, Luba was humping the floor to a second glam-rock ballad. Then, like a puppet pulled upward by strings, she rose on her knees until she was ramrod straight. She tore away her bikini top and clenched it like a smothered insect in her fist. The tiny mounds of her breasts were almost entirely subsumed by burgundy nipples. They glistened in the pulsing light, as moist and vulnerable as open sores. My jeans tightened. Milton muttered under his breath.

"What? I can't hear you over the music." I leaned toward him.

"He's mocking me."

During her third song, a stream of admirers marched one by one to the stage—a kid in a UNM sweatshirt, a New Mexican cowboy with a saucer-sized belt buckle, a pink-faced man with a loosened tie. The businessman held out a fat wad of bills. Luba looped her finger beneath the crotch of her bikini bottom and motioned for him to slide the bills like a green-and-white maxi-pad into the space between. When he tremulously did so, she pulled his palm against her pelvic bone, and licked her lips as the money rubbed into her.

At the end of her set, the air in the room began circulating again. Luba gathered the scattered bills, stuffed them into a gray macramé bag, and disappeared through the backstage door. It wasn't until the end of the next stripper's set that she reappeared, bikini top back in place. She ignored the other customers and strode straight for us. Onstage, the heavy eye shadow had accentuated her allure. Up close, it made her look like a raccoon. Her expression was grave.

"I thought you'd never arrive," she said.

"Here I am," Milton answered.

"I'll never have to face the world alone again." She held his gaze for a moment. Then her hand shot up to her mouth. "I've always wanted to say those lines. This is like a dream come true, Mr. Schwarzer."

Milton's expression was unreadable. "Why don't you have a seat?"

She sat, nodding in my direction. She fumbled in her bag for a crumpled pack of Camels. She lit her cigarette with trembling hands, took a long drag, and blew the smoke out of the side of her mouth. "I have, like, every one of your movies."

"It shows." Milton sipped his soda water. "You must have a midget fetish."

She shook her head amiably. "No. Maybe my father did, but he liked everything. Transvestites. Children. Thank God he had your entire collection. Your movies saved me."

"You've watched them all?"

"More than once."

"And the last three?"

Her brows knit. "They're dark. I can't say I understand them. But you and Luba together, that was—"

"A long time ago."

"I know, but if I could only explain how much they meant to me. I used to fantasize that—"

"Who's paying you?"

Luba looked confused. "The girls are independent contractors. We dance onstage for free but keep the tips. We split the table dances and the private dances fifty-fifty and keep tips for 'extra services.' If customers order us drinks, we get fifty percent of the drink cost. But I'm not trying to get you to buy me a drink."

"You know what I'm talking about. Who put you up to approaching us?"

"I'm an independent contractor. I mean, the club wants me to keep circulating so it can collect fees. But I don't care about that now. I wanted…I needed to meet you. I knew it would happen some day. Don't ask me how, but I did."

"You're lying."

"No, really, I don't care about the money. I mean, sure I care about money. But it's like—" She hesitated.

"What do you want?"

Luba clutched and unclutched her macramé bag. "You mean, like anything?"

"What do you want from me?"

"I've imagined sitting here with you just like this. And you say you'd like to get a little closer. So I take you back to the Fantasy Labyrinth, and—" Luba looked in my direction, suddenly self-conscious. "I'm good. I mean, that's what my customers say. I bring in 10 percent more than the next best girl. And when I'm in there, I think about—" She hesitated. "You know, snippets from the movies. I feel the scenes so vividly, it's like we've been together before." Her eyes closed. "In the dark, I'm not pretending to be Luba. I am her."

Milton didn't say a word, until the hope on Luba's face receded into apprehension. She stubbed out her half-smoked cigarette and lit a new one. Milton sneered. "You disgust me. You're nothing but a cheap imitation humping lowlife hicks for a living."

The music coalesced into a throbbing white haze and I noticed, for the first time, the goose bumps on Luba's bare shoulders. Bruises like finger paint smudges dappled the soft flesh of her forearms. The words didn't register; her face was a blank sheet. Then she blinked and a tiny dewdrop, colored inky black, traced its way down her face. "Damn contact lenses. The air conditioning just dries them out. I'd better...I'd better get back to work."

"Wait a second," I said. "I've never been to the Fantasy Labyrinth." I fumbled for my wallet and pulled out sixty dollars. "I want the buy three songs, get one free special."

She looked at Milton as she spoke. "I'm sorry, a few regulars have reserved me. I'm not sure if I'll have the space tonight."

"What the hell are you doing?" Milton growled to me.

"You were just saying she was the best-looking dancer you'd seen all night and I agreed. We came all the way out here, I want a private dance."

"I said—" Milton looked prepared to tear my neck open. "You're a fool."

"I'd be a fool to pass up this opportunity." I smiled at Luba. "He always acts this way. Tries to uphold that tough-guy persona. Just like in his movies."

She searched my face for an answer. "I think I'd better go now. Joel will wonder why I've spent so long at one table."

Milton put his hand over hers. "No, wait. He's right. You look so much like my Luba I lost myself in my role. He wants a private dance, give him a private dance. So long as right after that, you'll give me a private dance too."

"You want a private dance too?" A child's hopefulness.

"Yeah. I do. But only if my friend leaves satisfied, if you know what I mean."

"What are you talking about?" I said.

"I thought you'd never arrive," she said, scanning Milton's face eagerly.

"Here I am," Milton answered.

Luba seized my hand and led me into the Fantasy Labyrinth.

It was impossible to tell how big or small the Fantasy Labyrinth was. In the illumination from the black-light bulbs, I saw only the lint on Luba's hair. We turned left, then right, then right again, music as loud in the Labyrinth as onstage. Two figures, a floral-scented woman and a heavily breathing man, squeezed past us in the narrow passageway. I rammed into Luba when she stopped. A draft of warm air touched me as she fumbled with the doorknob. A sliver of electric light sliced through a partially open window at the end of the hall. The momentary breeze, scented with fried chicken and gasoline, disappeared when we entered her private room.

Not even the mirror paneling could make the five-by-five room appear spacious. Black paint on the ceiling dangled in thin curlicues, and the solitary furnishing, a purple velvet loveseat, was blotchy and stained. The dim mixture of incandescent and black light that should have hidden these imperfections highlighted them. But Luba's skin glowed with a pale luminescence. She latched the plywood door and we sat down on the sofa. Her small, dry hand held my sweaty palm.

"Are we supposed to do something now?" I said.

There were sparkles on her eyelids and lips. "I'm waiting for the next song to begin. You deserve four full songs, not three-and-a-half."

Pressed against her warm flank, I stared at the perfect bow of her upper lip. She had fake eyelashes like the arms of spiders and eye shadow as thick as a Zorro mask, but that curve of raised flesh covered in lipstick, filmed with cheap silver flecks, was incredibly alluring.

"Um. Is Luba your real name?"

"No dancer uses her real name."

"What's your real name?"

She smiled. Lipstick smudged her front two teeth. "If I told you, I'd have to kill you." She kneaded a knot in my neck. "You look relaxed but you're really tense."

A new song began, a slow jam by an overproduced whiteboy band. "Okay, it's time," she said. Luba unhooked her top and set it to one side. When she stood to face me, her oversized nipples like dark eyes surveyed my expression. One was larger than the other and appeared to be flat along the top.

"Because you're a friend of Milton Schwarzer's, I'm going to go completely nude, which usually costs $50 extra. And I'm going to let you touch me, which is usually $80 on top of that. The rules are simple: you can touch my boobs, my butt, and my pubic hair. No fingers up my anus or vagina. No tongue." She balanced on one leg, slipped her bikini bottom over first one and then the other high heel, and threw the scrap onto the sofa cushion. Her pubic hair was shaved into a neat rectangular strip. "Do you want to take off your shirt?"

"Why would I take off my shirt?"

"Some guys like the skin-to-skin contact. Some guys are embarrassed of their potbellies. But you're not that heavy."

"I think I'd like to keep my shirt on."

"Suit yourself. Why don't you put the stuff in your pocket up here." She patted the alcove behind my head. "I can't tell you how much it hurts to take car keys in the wrong place."

"Um, okay." Wallet, keys, wadded knife—this last item I covered with the others.

With a swift, feline spring, she leapt onto the couch, a knee on either side of my legs, one hand on the back of my neck for balance. The hollow of her neck was inches from my nose. I shut my eyes and smelled talcum powder. She undulated her hips on my jeans, bouncing and rubbing in equal parts. Next to my ear, she let out a soft moan. I felt a stirring within my jeans and, in her position, no doubt she felt it too.

"You can touch my tits, you know."

"Thank you."

"I noticed you staring at them. It's okay. I get into it. I pretend it's, you know, him." She leaned back to give me a better view, then grabbed my wrists and guided my palms directly onto them. Her breasts were so small, I felt the striations of ligaments over her breastplate. Her pelvis scraped my groin in time to the slow jam beat, and hypnotically I rotated my hands over those lumps of flesh.

Luba slithered onto the ground, her back toward me. She grabbed her ankles and thrust her rear in my face so that I came face to hole with her orifices—fragrant folds and a dark, puckered star. They smelled of rose water and dirt. "Remember, rubbing the cheeks yes, probing no."

I caressed her butt cheeks, a study in tactile contrasts. Hard muscle and smooth, flawless skin, filmed with what looked like powdered sugar. "Your skin is incredibly soft," I said lamely. It's impossible to gaze into a woman's birth canal and speak coherently.

"That's sweet of you to notice. I moisturize."

Luba turned around and placed her face onto my thighs. She ascended my body, sliding her nose and mouth across my fly, my chest, my ear. She arched her back as if diving into a pool backward, dropped her hands to the ground and elevated her pelvis to my mouth. If I had puckered, I would have kissed her labia. How much more could I take? Minutes? Seconds?

"Do you like dancing?" I pulled my lips into my face.

Luba dropped her hips, secured her feet behind my back, and sat up so she was perched on my lap. We sat like lovers at a picnic. Except that instead of embracing in a park, she was grinding me in a five-by-five mirrored cell. "Do I like dancing? I don't know. I'm proud of my body and I like the money, so I guess so."

"It pays well?"

"Better than Mickey D's." She twisted her long hair in her hand and threw it over a shoulder. "I started dancing for gift money."

"I'm sorry. I don't know what gift money is."

"Some people work at Nordstrom for discounts on clothes. I started working here. On a good night, I can make a thousand bucks. That's a lot of presents. But when you make that kind of money, it's hard to give up. I'm going to school again and need a new car, a place to stay, stuff like that. Really, you can touch me as much as you want."

She rippled and billowed and swayed; I pulsated and stifled and stayed. My eyes, they dazzled at her flowing knees, her hips quivering near my mobile nose. A beacon flashed and drew near. I wanted to shove her away.

"What is it you see in Milton?" My vehemence startled me.

She paused, a softness in her gray eyes. She stroked my hair. "You've seen his movies, haven't you?"

"No. Never."

"My sister can't stand them. Reminds her too much of—oh, never mind. They're not for everyone. They're… violent. But in the end, everything comes out all right. Milt is like this avenging angel. And in the final scene he always arrives to save Luba. She's been beaten and bruised and raped, but their scenes together are so tender. That's been important for me. He's on my side and doesn't care what happened before."

Without her steady friction, my reason returned. "What happened before, Luba?"

"Let's not talk about that." She began grinding my groin again distractedly. Against my will, my body continued to react.

"And his last three movies are different?" I said. It was almost a gasp.

Luba frowned. "In his later movies, Milt arrives too late to save the girl. It's no longer Luba. It's a look-alike."

There was a lull before the fourth song played. The air-conditioning vent rattled in the ceiling. If she weren't pressed against me, I would have shivered. "Last song," she said. "I'm not going to leave you hanging. Let's finish."

Luba mounted me, gripping the back of my neck with both hands, pelvis pressed with all of her weight against my crotch. She placed her warm cheek against mine and began her rhythmic scraping again. "Come on, baby," she said. "Come on, baby. I know you're close."

It wasn't erotic. I was trapped beneath a fleshy machine bent on extracting my fluids. My penis burned, the skin was raw, and yet my muscles clenched against my will, my back arched, my fingers splayed. I clutched at her bony rib cage and stifled a sob. "Come on, baby," she said. One, three, five convulsions. The thick, hot wetness cooled into clammy embarrassment. She held me against her breast until my breathing returned to normal.

Seconds of ecstasy followed by the lingering sensation that everything in the world was utterly wrong. The story of my life. Luba hummed something under her breath as she pulled on her bikini bottom. She extracted a tube of lipstick from her ugly macramé bag and drew her small nipples into the large disks I'd remembered from the stage show.

"Is there some place I can clean up?" I said.

"Outside. Next to the entrance."

"I really need to go now."

"Okay," she said, checking herself in a pocket mirror. "I'm ready to go."

Milton didn't catch my eye when we emerged from the Labyrinth. He was glowering at Luba. She squeezed my hand. "I never caught your name, sweetie."

"I'm Guy."

"My name's Chandra. But don't tell anyone, or—" She drew her finger across her throat. "You're different, you know? Gentle."

And then she was gone, striding with excited limbs across the room toward her short, surly prize, while the gentle boy slunk off to the restroom.

Four songs is an interminable period to wait when you're sitting in semen-encrusted underwear. Ostensibly, nothing had changed while I was in the Fantasy Labyrinth. The same redhead who was onstage when we arrived at the club was onstage again; again, she was pinning her ankles behind her head while licking a nipple. But unlike before, I could recognize the freak show for what it was, a gleaming pornographic machine churning lust, sex, and shame into a syrupy, mass-produced confection. I avoided the mirrors around me but saw myself reflected in the vacant eyes and rapt expressions of the other patrons.

Four songs with the same bass-line beat, and then six songs on top of that—dancers weaving and darting between the tables soliciting private dances—and still Milton didn't return. Her scent—talcum powder, rose water, and earth—clung to my clothes, and hands, and face. I didn't want to imagine her astride Milton, her eyes closed and lips parted, running her hand along the scar tissue on his neck. But the images came anyway. Bile filled my gut.

It wasn't until the twelve-song mark that I got it through my benumbed head that something was amiss. Soon after, the police burst into the club. Three officers entered the Fantasy Labyrinth. Three others surrounded me, guns drawn.

CHAPTER 17

Four songs. At three minutes per song, that was twelve minutes. Long enough to have explored every crevice of Luba's—no, Chandra's—body. Long enough to have dreamt of sinking my teeth into her warm flank. Long enough to have been utterly humiliated. Twelve minutes is a lifetime inside of a plush mirrored cell. How could anyone outside of the Fantasy Labyrinth understand?

Detective Ramirez played the good cop. He appealed to my sense of justice, of sympathy, of honor. My fingerprints, along with Milton's, were on the steak knife that had been plunged into Chandra's neck. She'd been slit from pelvis to chin with a hunting knife that the police had yet to recover. Her breasts had been sliced right off her body.

"She might be just a stripper to you," Detective Ramirez said. "But she was somebody's daughter."

Officer Johnson played the bad cop. He laid out the crime scene photographs like tarot cards. "A dozen strippers working the floor, but you and your buddy shared the same one. Were her tits your trophies? If the coroner finds your semen in the corpse, we're going to nail you right to the cross, you sick fuck."

Chandra curled in on herself in death as if she could conceal her wounds from the camera's flash. A dark gash ran from her jaw to her womb. In place of the nipples she'd drawn in with lipstick were large, blind eyes dripping blood. This wasn't the girl who told me she'd started stripping for "gift money," whose warm, powdered skin had slid across mine. This was a carcass.

If only we'd left before she came onstage. If only I'd refused to allow her to give Milton a private dance. But I'd wanted Milton to admit that he'd been wrong to think Kolling would show up three hours late. I'd wanted Chandra to discover that her prince was a toad. I'd wanted them both to share my misery that there are no answers and there's no one who can save you. I got what I'd asked for.

If I were a better man, I would have helped the police. As 5 a.m. passed in the windowless interrogation room, I pictured Milton huddled near the KFC drive-thru window, waiting for me with dried blood on his hands. He would have demanded my gratitude for having saved us from the danger posed by an unarmed girl who'd grown up watching porn films in which he starred.

But I'm not a better man. Nothing would bring Chandra back. Not finding Milton or Megumi, not punishing his or my sins. I didn't want to relive what had happened minutes after I'd left her. I didn't want to think about how Chandra had died alone and unloved inside a mirrored cell. I wanted to slip back into the barren scrub brush of my life.

It took thirty-six hours for the public defender to arrange for my release. I'd never, in fact, been charged with a crime, a point my ponytailed lawyer emphasized to the judge. Witnesses had seen me exit the Fantasy Labyrinth with Chandra. I'd spent the remainder of the night in the same chair. The seminal fluids inside "the victim" were not mine. The "perpetrator" had exited through an open window. I had provided information about his identity and regular place of business. I was, my attorney told the court, "in the wrong place at the wrong time." I washed the blood off my keys, discarded my wallet, and carried my personal effects in a ziplock bag.

I would have driven from jail straight back to Seattle if the judge hadn't ordered me to remain within the state. I checked into the Frontiersman, a motel featuring HBO and a sixty-foot cowboy out front, while my attorney attempted to overturn the "unprecedented restriction on a bystander's freedom of movement."

It was unreasonably hot. I cranked up the dripping, wall-unit air conditioner and slept in my clothes from 2 p.m. to 10 p.m. I ordered Dominos pizza and a Pepsi. I relived the day's baseball highlights on back-to-back viewings of ESPN SportsCenter. Could a person watch reruns of the same thing, slightly altered, day after day, until his heart stopped? How would that life differ in any material way from the one I was already living?

At midnight, I rummaged through the ziplock bag for a scrap of paper. Billy picked up after the sixth ring.

"Hello?"

"Hi. Is this Billy?"

"That's me. Isn't this—"

"It's Guy. Guy Watanabe. You let me stay at your place for a couple nights when I was having that problem—"

"I know who you are, Guy. The late hour threw me."

"I'm sorry about that. I should let you get back to bed."

"No, no, I didn't mean it that way. Good thing you called. The cat nearly tore up the screen door trying to get outside. We didn't have the kitty when you were here, did we? That was a pretty surprise, May showing up with a pregnant cat. She calls her Rex. I told her it's a boy's name but she sticks to it."

There was a long pause. "I'd better let you go."

"Now hold on, Guy. It's been—what—two, no, three weeks. What's going on?" Billy's voice was the looped pile of a terry-cloth blanket.

"I've been okay, I guess."

There was another long pause. "I'm just going to put on some water for tea. I've got plenty of time to talk, and don't mind listening."

The brown shag carpet swirled around my ankles. Years of cigarette butts, Doritos, and spilled coffee resided in its depths. Billy said Lizzie had dropped by the shop with the pronouncement that she was visiting a cousin in Iowa "for a little while," so May had been with him for the last two weeks. I said I'd straightened out my finances but had forgotten to send him a check. He told me to take my time.

I opened the mini-fridge and examined the assortment of soda pop, string cheese, and pepperoni sticks. I popped the top of a Coke and sipped the cool liquid aluminum.

"Have you ever woken up from a dream," I said, "and wished you could have stayed asleep a little longer?"

"Mm hm. Of course."

"It's been like that for days, weeks. So long that I don't know whether the person I used to be was a part of that dream too."

"When you wake up, what's missing?"

"The sense that everything is all right with the world. The world's brutal, Billy. Empty. Cold."

"That's how it feels sometimes."

"It's not a feeling. It is. We mistake our feelings or our dreams or hopes for reality, but that just makes it worse when we see through to what's really there."

A kettle whistled in the background and then ceased. "What about love?"

"Love!" I kicked at the covers and sat up. "That train is gone, man. I'm talking about reality, not hormones or lone-liness. Love is selfish. It exists to make us feel better. Once you rub the sleep out of your eyes, you can't see love, only your own distorted reflection."

Billy took a sip from his tea. "I don't buy it."

"What do you mean you don't buy it? Reality isn't an argument. People die every day unloved." I focused on the blurry creases of my palms. Don't think about the symmetri-cal wounds on her chest. Stay right here. "We haven't the capacity to love without self-interest. We don't give a damn about a million people hacked up with machetes in Rwanda or a stripper bleeding to death in a back room. We only care about our friends, family, and people who look like us."

"You have it backward, Guy. It's not our callousness that makes us turn away. It's our recognition of what it takes to feel. Sure, love brings joy. But it also means pain that no reasonable person would invite. We fear being drowned in love, being drowned in our concern for every living thing."

I picked up the remote control without turning on the TV. *Every living thing.* I was talking about concrete concepts, and Billy was leading me down a treacherous, Christian path. I would have shot down his simplistic, spiritual optimism if nausea hadn't afflicted me. I couldn't breathe. And while I was gasping for air, I began to sob. Snot ran down my face and my breath came in heaves. On the other end of the line, Billy murmured platitudes—"It's okay to cry," and "Let it all out." I wanted to shout "shut up," but couldn't regain control over my body; it was like vomiting sea water. When the deluge subsided, I was too drained to argue.

"I'm still here," Billy said. "We can talk for as long as you want."

"I don't want to talk anymore. It doesn't make me feel any better."

"All right then," he said. "We can not talk for as long as you want."

I contemplated the water spots spreading like chemical clouds across the ceiling. I felt worse than I had in the police station, when what I saw and what I remembered couldn't be reconciled. But maybe feeling better wasn't the point.

"Thanks, Billy," I mumbled.

CHAPTER 18

I shut off the lights, drew the curtains, disconnected the clock-radio, and drank straight from the spigot of boxed wine. I fell in and out of blissful unconsciousness and learned to accept the stomach cramps. All living things, from single-celled organisms to the largest mammals, suffer through spasms before dissolving into the chemical soup of our collective destiny. Why fight it? *Knock, knock.* What did the maid not understand about the "Do Not Disturb" sign? My emergency credit card had prepaid for three weeks of privacy. *Knock, knock, knock.*

"Leave me alone!" I said.

The sunlight shone so brightly I couldn't make out the figure framed in the doorway, a slim silhouette. My eyes didn't recover until Megumi pulled the door closed behind her. She wore a pink sundress and matching pink sandals and carried no bags. She sat on my unmade bed, eyeing, without a change in expression, the detritus of my exist-ence—empty chip bags, aluminum cans, an overturned ice bucket. In the artificial dimness, the bedside lamp was our moon and sun. The incandescent glow accentuated her angular collarbones. Her hair was damp. She patted the mattress.

Megumi kissed me. A chaste kiss at first, but soon her tongue pushed past my clenched teeth. It was a deep, tangled kiss, from which my tongue couldn't withdraw, and yet it was almost entirely dry. Her kiss tasted like dust. Her skin was redolent with a scented crème, an over-ripe fruit. After what I'd been through—what she'd put me through—my body shouldn't have reacted. But it did. While I clutched the bed sheets, she mounted me. My penis slipped into her in frictionless silence. Her vagina clenched and released, clenched and released like a fist. Unable to pull out, I ejaculated inside of her, my body convulsing.

She slid off me and entered the bathroom. I heard the trickle of her pee, and then the tub's faucet. She returned with a hand towel and wiped our fluids from my groin. Still nude, she stretched out and fell asleep. Nothing fluttered across her eyelids, no expression of joy or fear marred her perfect face. She slept as if she were dead.

Megumi was still there when I awoke. She ate Flaming Hot Cheetos and paged through a tourist brochure. Her fingertips were coated with a crimson paste.

She'd found me because my car was parked out front. But she didn't share my alarm that Kolling or Smith might find us in the same way. She wanted to buy new clothes and eat, in that order. She didn't question why I'd followed her. She didn't talk about what had happened since we'd last seen each other. "You're going to protect me, aren't you?" she said. *Was it really that simple? Forget the past and start again?*

We shopped in the Walmart children's section. None of the women's styles—designed to flatter the ever-expanding American waistline—fit her tiny frame. She'd chosen me over Kolling, but I'd never thought beyond that to charging $300 worth of children's clothing and flip-flops to my only credit card that hadn't been maxed out. I didn't know what it would take to make her happy. I'd never thought through what it would take to keep her safe.

We should have jumped onto the freeway but instead backtracked to the city center. Megumi was insistent. She was sick of New Mexican food, which she found "too cheesy." She wanted me to take her to a "nice place near the Indian jewelry they sell on the sidewalk." We ate lunch in an upstairs bar and grill. She ordered fried calamari, a Niçoise salad, and a sausage sandwich. All I could stomach was soup, but the nourishment helped to clear my head.

"We should go to the police," I said. "There's something called a temporary restraining order we can get to stop your fiancé from bothering you."

"You don't understand," she said. "They'll deport me."

"What's most important is your safety. I'll visit you in Japan. I'll help you to apply for a visa. We'll spend that time getting to know each other better."

She averted her eyes. "You don't want me."

I waited for the waiter to grind pepper on her salad and depart. *I don't want to pressure you. We've got a powerful, unspoken connection. On the surface we're different, but deep down we're the same. It's best to develop our relationship gradually. Megumi… please, no, don't cry. Yes, I realize you risked your life. No, no, I never meant to take advantage of you. No, I wasn't lying when I said I came for you. It's just…Don't you think it's weird that we're almost strangers? I'm sorry. I didn't mean that. Yes, I came for you. Whatever you want, we'll do. Let's return to Seattle, and I'll find you an apartment. I mean, we'll find an apartment together. He's buying a house there? The police will protect us. Okay, no police. No, I would never allow them to deport you. Okay, no Seattle.*

Megumi didn't want to leave the country. She didn't want to return to Seattle. What was the alternative?

"Take me somewhere you've never been," she said.

They were the same words she'd used when we met. We were running away from something and running toward nothing. It was an all-too-familiar path.

We drove east into the panhandles of Texas and Oklahoma, looking for that special nowhere beyond the reach of the law and the Karaoke Group International. But Megumi wasn't interested in limestone rocks, or twisted mesquite trees, or prickly pear cacti. Her idea of hiking was stepping out of the car at a viewpoint. She asked to stop at every marked tourist spot, even in the midst of flatland desert, yet once we arrived she was eager to leave. She lauded Dallas for its cleanliness, expansiveness, and "newness," but despised BBQ and any variant of Tex-Mex cuisine. She wanted fancy Italian food or McDonald's, Japanese or Thai, and never Chinese.

She didn't complain about my car's lack of air conditioning, but she fanned herself with a map and picked at her sweaty T-shirt. She raided the convenience store for

Pop Rocks, Kit Kats, and sugary drinks, then waited impatiently near the car. She didn't disparage our cheap motel rooms, but her nose wrinkled every time she walked into the restroom. What else could I afford? By my rough calculation, I had $5,000 in savings and $25,000 in credit card debt, the compounding interest rising invisibly beneath my feet like an ocean swell.

Where we went wasn't as important as the proof we'd been there. She wanted a Piggly Wiggly keychain and a palmetto lapel pin. She wanted a rhinestone Elvis pin for her baseball cap from the Civil Rights Monument…then stuffed them both unworn into the glove compartment. Inside her purse was a West Virginia coalminer's hardhat pencil sharpener, a placemat from a New York pizzeria, a lobster bib from Acadia, Maine. What I didn't buy she took: toiletries, shaving kits, hand towels, bathroom slippers, pens, playing cards, necklace charms from enclosed glass cases.

Every day was the same, whether in Fort Wayne, Indiana, or Springfield, Missouri. We selected our destinations over cups of coffee and shrink-wrapped Danishes. We drove for six to ten hours a day, stopping at viewpoints and museums, gas stations and malls and restaurants. We pulled into a roadside motel at sunset. And at 11:30 p.m., Megumi would crawl on top of me. Intercourse was short in duration, as reflexive as blinking or sneezing.

What did I learn about her? Megumi liked entertainment magazines but not discussing books, music, or movies. She liked comic books but not American ones "filled with musclemen and swimsuit models." She admired the long hair and dark skin of Native American women because they looked *khom*, which she translated as "sharp." She described her own fair complexion as passable but plain. She could be wildly affectionate one moment—pressing her head into my chest while we waited in line for a burger, holding my hand throughout the day—and shrink from my touch the next. She asked no questions about my friends, family, or childhood. If I asked her questions she didn't want to answer, she initiated sex or ignored me.

Days became weeks; summer became fall; our long sojourn that had moved north and east looped south and west, until we returned like migratory birds to New Mexico. It was October. I'd somehow persuaded Megumi to take a short walk through the shifting salt dunes at White Sands National Monument, but during the drive to the trailhead her interest had flagged.

Once we stepped onto the sugary sand, I felt overcome by the feeling that I was being smothered. On this broad expanse of white, the sky a periwinkle blue, I couldn't breathe. I was suffocating in the overabundance of oxygen. I fell to my knees atop a sand dune, and began a long slide downward. I slid headfirst, and remained prostrate in the warm granules. I lay there on my belly for minutes before Megumi gave up the notion I would dust myself off and return to the trail. She peered down at me through her sunglasses.

"I can't go on like this," I said. "I feel lost. I don't know who I am anymore."

Megumi sat down Indian-style. She swept her hair into a ponytail.

"You have no choice," she said. "Like me, your soul has been eaten."

CHAPTER 19

MEGUMI`S MISTAKE

Megumi normally went to sleep after cleaning me up, but this night she cradled my head in her lap. She stroked my hair absently and spoke.

I was not born Japanese. I'm from a northern Thai village where there are farms but no crops. In the center of town is a Bangkok Bank and many houses have satellite dishes. Families pray for daughters. The girls in our village are known to be beautiful. We have light skin.

I knew I'd become a working girl. Father is a cripple; mother is weak in the head. I just didn't know it would be so soon. A month after I graduated from sixth grade, my aunt arrived in a big black car to take me away. She left me at a roadside brothel an hour from Bangkok. The customers were truck drivers, dark-skinned men stinking of whiskey and the road.

Smart girls didn't cross mama-san. Shortly after I arrived, Plaey, an older girl in the neighboring room, ran away. Two days later, the retired boxer dragged her back. Her eye was swollen shut. She was locked in her room for a week, surviving on rice and water, not allowed to relieve herself down the hall. I could smell her waste. In the quiet space after customers rolled off of me, I could hear her fingernails scratching the wall between us.

I was mama-san's favorite. My beauty and my age meant she could charge twice as much for my services. She showered me with gifts—makeup, comic books, even a Walkman. She never made me work when I had infections. She visited with tea and rice porridge, fluffed my pillow and told me I was "too pretty for this place." She sold me for a large commission to gangsters with international connections.

"You deserve a better life," she said.

At the age of thirteen, I left my homeland on a fake passport. Gone were bedsores from the springs of the cot, a light bulb swaying over the customer's head to the breeze of an electric fan. Tokyo is a clean, gleaming machine. I serviced businessmen and their *farang* clients on king-sized beds with satin sheets. I rinsed away their odors in deep, whirlpool baths. There were no bars on the windows. Where would I run? It was a kind of death to live illegal amongst the Japanese. They don't talk to you once they discover you're not one of them. There are many working girls in Tokyo. We created our own world in shared apartments and Thai-only bars.

At the age of fifteen, I was the most popular girl at the membership club. Japanese businessmen fantasize about tearing off the uniforms and knee-high socks of the schoolgirls who rub against them in the subway cars. The other girls masked their wrinkles with foundation, wore their hair in pigtails, and shaved their pubic hair. I had the opposite problem. Without makeup, I looked years younger than my age. I caked on mascara, rouge, and lipstick to look like an older girl pretending to be a pre-teen. The men who suspected the truth were my most loyal customers. They were docile and quick to finish.

I have serviced Japanese and I have serviced *farang*. Horatio was the first man I serviced who looked Japanese but spoke like a *farang*. He was the youngest man in a group of old Japanese men, regulars at the club, the ones the younger men usually flattered. Yet the old bent ones flattered *him*. They tortured him with broken English and leaned forward when he spoke. They pushed me on him and he accepted, allowing me to lead him to the backroom.

He sat with his back straight on the edge of the bed as I kneeled to unbuckle his belt. His stomach and chest startled me; all muscle and no fat, it was like caressing a reptile. His penis hung downward, long and thick and, like a *farang*'s, circumcised. I had already begun when he spoke.

"Can't you wash that crap off your face?"

"Sir?"

"You're smearing that gunk all over me. Go to the restroom and wash it off. While you're at it, comb out your hair and strip naked."

"Your friends have paid for a 'full fantasy package.' Don't you want to tear off my panties?"

He pointed to the restroom. "Go."

I was used to taking off my clothes. I was not used to taking off my makeup. I scrubbed to remove it. The reflection in the mirror showed a stranger—a pale, wet mouse with pimples on her forehead. I tiptoed into the bedroom. His full concentration was bent on jacking himself into an erection. He didn't look up until I kneeled. He stared for a long time.

"How old are you?" he said.

"How old do you want me to be?"

His penis became engorged in my mouth. He shoved me onto the floor and mounted me. Two or three thrusts and he was done.

I wiped him down with a wet towel then went to rinse myself in the tub and pee. When I returned, he was looking through my purse. He saw me watching but kept on going, placing everything on the bedside table: tubes of lipstick, a compact, eyeliner, eye shadow, a pack of 555's, a lighter, condoms, chewing gum, a wad of yen notes, a plastic bag filled with cotton swabs, birth control pills, and a government-issued ID.

"Ponthip Ratanakul. Someone else's identity card or have they changed the birth date?"

"My nickname is Pon."

He cast the empty purse onto the floor. "Ugly name."

He pulled on his briefs and trousers. I reached for my skirt, which was at the foot of the bed, but he kicked it across the carpeting. "I'm not through yet," he said.

The air conditioning chilled my bare skin. During sex, the customers didn't notice; after, the temperature encouraged them to dress, pay, and leave. Horatio buttoned his navy-blue shirt, the collar still starched and unwrinkled. He propped his feet up on the bed and considered me.

"What if I wanted to choke you?" he said.

I looked at the manicured nails on his long fingers. We were a "full service" club. Contract girls were required to submit to anything that wouldn't cause scarring. The best-groomed customers asked for the most perverse things.

"It's an extra charge."

He nodded. "I'll try her for a few days," he said to himself. "Then we'll see."

That's how our arrangement began.

No girl at a membership club likes a man who shows up just for sex. Our commissions also come from selling appetizers and alcohol; the more time we spend feeding them, the less time we spend rubbing their potbellies. But if a man is there just for the sex, it's best if he is quick and conventional, like Horatio. He never choked, beat, or peed on me. He arrived when the club opened for six straight days. He tipped poorly but was done before the late-night rush showed up. On his last night, he said to expect "being contacted" soon. A week later, the house manager called me into his office.

The house manager held our passports and working papers; he doled out our commissions and made sure we met our monthly quotas. He poured tea for a *farang* I'd never seen before—tall, blond, and tan, like an American movie star. The foreigner let out a long, low whistle as I took my seat.

"She's a looker, that's for sure. Not my type, but it takes all kinds, doesn't it?"

"She is popular." The house manager struggled for the right English words. "Expensive. Young. Nasty, nasty."

"I don't know about the rest of it, but expensive and young she sure is. My employer could find hundreds prettier and younger in southern China, but he seems to be set on this one. We'll just have to pay the price."

"Good value," the house manager said. He addressed me in Japanese. "A rich man has bought out your contract. I'm sorry to see you leave because you are a very good employee. Good luck. You're free."

John Smith saluted me with a finger to his forehead.

John drove me from the club in a tiny, boxy car. It was odd to see him crammed behind the wheel, head scraping the roof, but he seemed at ease.

"There are a few simple rules to be followed," he said. "The boss will be in Tokyo once a month for five to seven days. He expects to be serviced twice a day, once in the morning and once before bed. While he's in town, he expects you to wait by the telephone in the event he wants company for a meal. While he's out of town, I'll call you at 8:00 a.m. and 5:30 p.m., every day, to ask for your daily productivity report."

"I don't understand. What is a daily productivity report?"

"The daily productivity report is your opportunity to justify the expenses for supporting you. You tell me what you've done, how you've spent your money, and anything unusual he should know about."

"What if there is nothing to report?"

He honked the horn. "Little lady, there's always something to report. Let me make a suggestion. Anything you're
tempted to hide, report. He doesn't like surprises."

The first stop was a medical clinic, a neat, three-story
building at the end of a tree-lined street. With bored eyes,
the guard in the booth of the neighboring African embassy
watched our car pass. We were escorted to an exam room.
John didn't leave the room while my blood was drawn; he
didn't leave the room while the doctor spread my legs and
examined me.

I was accustomed to such tests. The membership club
required an HIV test monthly and a pap smear every three
months. I never got used to the emptiness I felt after the
metal instrument was inserted and removed. I reached for
my clothing but the nurse said to wait for the surgical procedure.

John glanced up from the Japanese fashion magazine
on his lap. "You're getting spayed, sweetie. Far more eco-
nomical in the long run than birth control pills. Procedure
takes only thirty minutes; faster than changing the oil on a
car. Modern medicine is a marvel."

I was awake the entire time. A bottle dripped fluid into
my arm and my fears became blurry figures waving and calling from behind thick glass. There was a sharp pain in my
lower back followed by numbness. The doctor leaned over
my stomach and tugged. It felt as he were pulling a thread
from my sweater. John seemed to smile from behind his surgical mask.

John had told the club to give away my belongings.
I was allowed only the contents of my purse, from which
John removed the snapshots I had stashed. We stopped at

a department store. John chose clothing he knew Horatio would like—simply cut dresses and high heels for more formal occasions. The last stop was a high-rise apartment building. Across the street was a SOGO department store; the sidewalks were full of shoppers and cheerful window displays. The doorman—a heavy man with pockmarks on his face—saluted John with a finger to his forehead. I felt the doorman's eyes follow me onto the elevator.

We stopped on the fifty-fifth floor and walked down a long hallway to the corner apartment. John motioned to the room with a flourish.

"Voila! What do you think?"

I shielded my eyes from the late afternoon sunlight slanting in through the floor-to-ceiling windows. In the center of the room was a glass-topped dining table surrounded by white, wire chairs. On the left side of the room was a beige leather couch and a matching recliner. There wasn't a single painting on the blank, white walls, but there were framed mirrors of different sizes and shapes. Wherever you went, you faced your own reflection.

"It's very big," I said.

"It better be, it costs a pretty penny. One hundred square meters. I don't know what that works out to in square feet, but it's a lot. He must really like you. Unless he plans to spend a lot more time in Tokyo."

I felt a sharp pain in my stomach and took a seat. The sutures rubbed against my cotton dress.

"Your stipend is the same as your previous take-home pay. That's more than generous given you're doing one-tenth of the work *and* receiving free lodging. Keep the thermostat no higher than 65 degrees. Dammit. Whatever the equivalent is in Celsius. He pays utilities and resents needless waste." John held up a plastic card with my photo on it. "Your new identity. You'll get a passport only when you travel. Enjoy your new life."

I took the card and read the name. Megumi Tanita. Me-gu-mi. A clean, carved name. My stomach felt bruised, but the doctor had promised that in a week, after the stitches dissolved, there would be no scar. Long after John left, I sat staring at the city, the cars jerking and turning on the street far below, like toys pulled along by an invisible magnet.

"How can you complain? It's the perfect arrangement," the other girls said. "Not having children is a blessing. You already support your parents." They were right, of course. If Horatio was not in town, I could do anything so long as I answered John's phone calls at 8 a.m. and 5:30 p.m. There were household chores: vacuuming three times a week, cleaning the restroom and kitchen twice a week, disinfecting the toilet and tub weekly, listening to English-language tapes two hours a day. But that still left me with time to wander the shopping malls and video arcades, watch television, and read Japanese comic books translated into Thai.

When Horatio was in town, the work was lighter than at the club. He liked sex in one position and only near the end of the week was his endurance high enough to put my legs to sleep. He didn't speak while he ate and shoveled food into his mouth until finished. He sometimes paid the bill and stood to leave before I was half-finished.

I must have had too much idle time. How else can I explain my unhappiness? Why should I care that the Japanese wives in the complex—married to the same kind of company men who visited the club—ignored me as they chatted in front of their strollers? The girls expected me to pay for everything now that I was the mistress to a rich man. How could I explain that I watched expenses more than ever because I reported them daily. Some days I didn't get out of bed until noon, answering John's 8 a.m. call with my head still resting on pillows. That too was my fault. I couldn't get used to daylight hours.

Since the age of twelve, dawn meant sleep and dusk meant work. Working girls wake in the afternoon for breakfast. At the end of a long shift, we went to the Thai bars to drink, smoke, and forget. The bars don't open until the subways close; the customers are working girls in search of Thai boys—thin-hipped and soft-spoken—who would do whatever we wanted. Trapped in the apartment at night, I found myself sitting wide awake by the windows watching the neon lights blink in the mirrors. I couldn't get Nui off of my mind.

Although dark-skinned, skinny, and short, Nui was popular. I couldn't see him more than twice a week. But at the end of the night, he would take me to his room free of charge. We would lie together and talk about home, falling asleep in each other's arms. If I'd been smart, I would have never visited Nui again. But three months after my arrangement with Horatio began, I found myself slipping out the service entrance and taking a taxi to Thai Street nearly every night.

"I don't understand," Nui said. "If he looks Japanese but speaks like a *farang*, where's he from?"

Nui's room was lit by a single, dim lamp, so it was a strain to focus on any one thing. The ceiling sagged and contained a long, jagged crack. The mattress, stuffed with straw, was pushed up against the false window. If the curtains were pushed aside, there was nothing but exposed brick. But the room was dark and warm. I curled into his back, placed my nose on the nape of his neck, and inhaled. His skin was moist with the spice of his sweat.

"How should I know? He doesn't answer questions like that. You look Cambodian and speak Thai. I look Japanese and out pops Thai. Maybe he's Chinese from America. Or Korean from Australia."

"He sounds like a prick," Nui said. I'd told him how I sent Horatio receipts for the clothing I bought with my own money.

"He's rich. That's how rich people are. That's how they got that way. They don't spend their money on cookbooks and pop music."

Nui laughed, and took that as a signal to change the CD. He skipped forward to a sappy old love song by Thongchai McIntyre. Nui worked two cooking jobs besides freelancing at the bar. His dream was to be a chef at his own restaurant.

"I don't know how you can stand it," he said.

"Shut up. You sleep with fat cows like Uan." I tickled his stomach and he wriggled away. "Besides, he looks more like a man. Not all skin and bones like you."

He pinched the skin at his rib cage. "It's true," he said. "I need to gain weight. Who trusts a skinny chef?"

Nui laid his head on my breast. He was hardly older than I was and his head weighed next to nothing. The two of us, intertwined, could be blown away by the slightest breeze.

"Have you ever thought about what comes next?" he said.

I wrapped my arms around his waist and pressed his belly button with my palms. His hips were so narrow they felt as if they would crack. "There's no such thing as next, *Nai* Nui. There's only now. Right now."

CHAPTER 20

MEGUMI`S MISTAKE (continued)

I suggested another day in the dunes, losing ourselves, and then returning at dusk for a ranger-led talk about the desert ecosystem. Megumi fixed me with a look of untrammeled boredom. She wouldn't continue her story on the road, at lunch, or at dinner. In Albuquerque, to make up for the lack of a recognized tourist attraction, I splurged on a room at a DoubleTree. I suggested a dip in the pool, but she didn't know how to swim. We watched cable TV. At the appointed time, she reached for my belt.

"Let's not tonight," I said. "I want to hear more about you."

She rubbed and kneaded me. "You're very tense."

I grabbed her hand and held it still. "I don't think I can."

"Yes, you can."

My body couldn't resist the force of habit. After Megumi had washed up and wiped me down, she sat on the bed and began speaking again.

The Thai Street manager told me that Nui wasn't seeing customers, but I snuck back to his bedroom. He was sweating and shivering. I fed him painkillers and wiped his brow with a damp towel. I cradled his head, dozing when he did, waking when he started. Could I take him to the membership club's clinic? No, they wouldn't take in strangers. I couldn't bring him to an emergency room. That's where Anchalee was taken after a car accident. Once she'd recovered, she was deported.

I shut off the alarm clock at 6 a.m. "I'll return with noodle soup and juice."

A white film had collected at the corner of his chapped lips. I dabbed it away with a hand cloth. "Don't go," he murmured. "I'm so cold."

"It'll just be a few hours. Don't throw off the blankets. It's good to sweat."

His eyes were bright with fever. "You're going to leave me for him. I know that. Please stay."

"You're delirious." There was no sense in missing my morning phone call for a simple fever. How could I explain it? Could I say I overslept?

A steady drizzle that soaked the bones had fallen for days. In the apartment, the floors would be cold and the windows would let in the unforgiving winter light. Nui's room was warm and dark. If I missed a single call, just one, how could he complain? I peeled off my clothes and crawled under the covers.

Nui's fever broke in the early afternoon. I stacked boxes of juice next to his mattress and rushed home. There were no voicemail messages. At 5:30 p.m., John called.

"And how was your day, Mistress Megumi?" John sounded cheerful any time of the day. Since he usually called from another country, I never knew what time it was for him.

"Fine."

"Expenses?"

I clicked my fingernails on the glass tabletop. I had only three or four things I reported over and over. It was good to appear frugal. "I window-shopped but didn't buy anything. A filter in the refrigerator needs to be replaced. It is expensive."

"That falls into the category of reimbursable equipment maintenance. Circle the total and put the receipt in with the rest of them. Anything else?"

I coughed. "I have the flu. The medicine made me sleepy. I slept all morning."

"Clinic visits are covered. Have you seen the doctor?"

"No. I just need to rest."

There was a pause. "Why did you go shopping?"

I walked to the window. The street grid far below looked like the inside of a radio. "I needed food. And juice. I also need warmer clothes or I'll get more sick."

"I see." There was another long pause. "Anything else you'd like to report?"

"Nothing."

"I'll tell him what you said."

I fell sick with the flu a few days later. No one nursed me. Nui had three jobs and, besides, I never allowed Nui to visit me. I didn't trust the doorman who scribbled notes. I didn't trust the maintenance people who entered the apartment without asking. I didn't trust the housewives who gossiped in front of their open doors.

I shivered beneath the blankets for three long, gray days. In my fever dreams, Nui lay all night with other girls. He flattered them the way he flattered me. He told them they were different and special. The dreams were more real than the time we'd spent together. He never seemed real when I was in the apartment alone, high above the city.

I still felt weak when Horatio's driver delivered his suitcase to the apartment. He was to arrive after dinner. He wanted to work for several hours and then be serviced at his usual time. I spent the evening making sure the apartment was in perfect condition.

He didn't say hello when I opened the door. He removed papers from his attaché case and began working at the dining table. I poured Sapporo into a frosted mug.

Horatio took a long sip. "That was a long flight. Especially long since we sat out on the tarmac for an extra hour. Bomb threat. But I'm here and that's all that matters. Any flight that leaves the ground and touches down again is a good flight."

I sat down. "Mm hmm."

"Some people complain about things they can't control. It's more important to take control of what you can. There's always something to do and more to be done."

"Mm hmm."

He made notes in the margin of a document. I sat waiting for him to say something. "Excuse me," I said.

"Yes? What is it?" He didn't look up.

"I would like to read a magazine on the couch."

"Fine. Go, go read your comic books. Just don't turn on the television."

He didn't approve of my buying comic books, but I bought them anyway—one per month. My favorite was an illegal version of *Candy Candy* translated into Thai, a nine-volume set. In volume one, Candy's best friend is adopted from the orphanage and writes to say she must have no further contact with Candy. I'd reached the scene in which Albert comforts Candy when I noticed it was 9:40 p.m. Time to prepare the bath and bed.

In Tokyo, most deluxe baths are automatic. You program them and the tub is filled at the right time for the right temperature. *Automated?* Okay, automated. Horatio refused to pay for this. Instead, there was a thermometer, so I had to check the water every few minutes.

At 10 p.m., I turned back the sheets, removed my dress and panties, and waited by the edge of the bed. He entered the room and stripped. I slid to my knees and took his penis into my mouth. It took longer than usual for his penis to get hard. As I rose to take my position on the bed, his hands pressed down on my shoulders.

"I'm not going to stick myself inside you until you're tested."

"I...don't understand."

"Yes you do. I pay you good money. But some people don't appreciate the opportunities extended to them." He yanked on the back of my head. I gagged and coughed. He struck me across the temple. The air sparkled and the room tilted. I closed my eyes and opened my mouth. He thrust his penis down my throat.

It may have been ten or thirty minutes before he ejaculated—tepid, salty, and bitter, like blood spurting from a wound. I swallowed everything. I wiped him off with a towel and followed him into the restroom. He lounged in the tub as I lathered his stomach, chest, and shoulders. I massaged shampoo into his scalp. The hot water stung the chafed skin on my neck.

I dried his body and held open the robe for him. I then rinsed the soap scum off my body. In bed, he read through a newsletter. I pulled the covers to my chin.

"I would never put your health in danger," I said. "I'm very clean."

He didn't look up. "You're not a stupid girl. You think about what you've done. I shouldn't have to waste my time warning you."

Horatio demanded oral sex every morning and evening that week. Condoms were not an option. My jaw ached and sores stung my gums. I ate little more than ramen noodles. I wrapped myself in blankets and watched the rain fall outside and in the mirrors all around me.

There was so much he'd given me. I didn't have to share a single room with girls who left their clothing on the chairs and dirty dishes on the table. I didn't have to feign excitement when old men used my panties to masturbate. Outside of one week per month, I could do anything I wanted. If I gave up Nui, my life would be perfect.

I tried to stay away. I walked from newsstand to newsstand and lingered in food courts. I lost myself in the rolling silver balls of the pachinko machines. I turned on the television, the radio, and all the lights. If it was dark and quiet, my thoughts wandered to the memory of Nui's warm body next to mine.

I should have been stronger. But what if Horatio decided to punish Nui for my mistake? My mind was playing tricks, inventing excuses to see him again. Nui'd forgotten all about me, lain down with different girls every night. But what if he disappeared? We were already invisible. Who would look for us?

I pulled the covers over my head but couldn't sleep. So I huddled near the living room window to let the neon light of the advertising signs wash across my face. The traffic rippled in colored ribbons below. There was no real darkness in this place. There was no place to hide.

I pulled on an overcoat and slipped out of the apartment. The clank of the service elevator doors sounded harsh in the silent hallway. I caught a taxi three blocks away.

The girls at the bar were waiting for friends who remained in the backrooms. On the dance floor, a girl hung on Yai, a pudgy boy with gentle eyes.

Nui didn't emerge for another half-hour. A girl I'd never seen before clung to his elbow. She was old—at least twenty-five—and her breasts were so large they fell out of the backless vest so many girls were wearing that year. Nui saw me in the back booth. He nodded, but mostly with his eyes so she wouldn't notice. Ten minutes later he escorted her to the door and hurried over with a broad smile on his face.

"It's good to see you missed me," I said.

"I missed you a lot." He slid into the booth and slipped his arm around my shoulders. "Did the rich man's visit last longer than you expected?"

I shrugged his arm away. "No. I decided we shouldn't see each other so much. I don't have to tell you everything, do I?"

"Did something happen?" He combed his bangs from his eyes. The old hag's perfume lingered in his hair.

"No. It's the same every month, isn't it?"

"Then why are you so serious?" He tapped a cigarette out of a carton. He lit it and took a long drag. He looked silly smoking, arm extended like a woman wearing long gloves. "Let's go to my room. I have a lot to tell you."

He didn't know how much I'd risked by coming to see him this last time. He was a stupid, selfish child. "I don't have the money to pay you."

"You haven't had the money to pay me for a long time. Come on. Let's go to my room."

"I don't want to."

"Yes, you do."

Nui's room was at the end of a narrow hallway. Loud music came from behind one door, while a girl's horsy laugh came from behind another. I would tell him that it was time for me to experiment with other boys. No matter how much he pleaded with me, I'd push him away and leave. He had no right to protest. I paid him, not the other way around. But his stupid grin pushed me off balance. He filled wine glasses with pink guava juice then dragged a crate over so he could sit across from me.

"I found a place, and a landlord who'll sign the papers as long as he's paid in cash."

"You're making no sense," I said. "Say something I understand."

He laughed. "A restaurant to own and run. You and me. I have it all figured out. You'll be the hostess, I'll be the chef. One day, we'll hire our own staff. It'll be perfect."

Words spewed out of him like soda from a shaken can. A Japanese businessman was forced to close down a gambling den and was looking to rent out the space. His wife, a Thai homesick for good food, wrote to Nui's cousin to ask if anyone from the village would be interested in relocating. The space might be run-down, but it was located only blocks away from the water in a seaside town. Nui couldn't wait to quit his jobs, remove the boards from the windows, and scour the junkyards for furniture.

"What's wrong, Pon? You're too quiet." His eyes flickered over me. "Have you lost weight?"

"I don't know anything about restaurants."

He shrugged. "Nobody does at first. My boss is already giving me advice. 'Start slow,' he says, 'Make your mistakes when no one's watching. Word of mouth is the best advertising.'"

I looked past him at the room. To cover the peeling paint, Nui had plastered the walls with posters of Thai movie and music stars holding bottles of Coca Cola. Mobiles of colored fish hung from the rotting ceiling beams. His dresser was nothing but a stack of fruit crates with folded clothes inserted into them. He wanted me to leave everything I had for this.

"I don't *want* to know anything about restaurants."

Nui opened his mouth then closed it again. He fumbled in his stack of CDs, couldn't find the right one, and gave up. "You look tense. Why don't you think it over?"

"You thought you'd get free labor, didn't you? You thought I'd be stupid enough to stand on my feet all day serving customers and get paid nothing, didn't you?"

"I never thought that. It's work, but it's not so serious like that. I thought together, we'd—"

"Together we'd what? Together we'd starve. I'd rather go back to the hostess bar than work for you."

Nui stood and began pacing. "It's not like that. We'd be working with each other. For each other. You understand what I mean, don't you?"

"I know you've got nothing to lose and I've got nothing to gain. Who cares if you fail? You'll just get another job cooking. But what would I do? You think he'd let me run away after all the money he's spent? You're stupid. I hate you."

Nui sat down on the mattress and tried to put his arms around me. I struck his chest. I struck him again and again, hoping to break something. He pulled me close and held me until I stopped struggling. Against my will, tears streamed down my face.

"It's an excuse," I said. "You want to leave me." I could feel his spine beneath his shirt. I hated how skinny he was.

"I want you to leave with me."

"He'll find us. He'll kill us."

"Then we'll keep running."

"I can't."

"What do you want me to do? Tell me, and I'll do it." His voice was soft like a girl's.

"I want things to stay like this forever," I said. "Nothing has to change. I'll be more careful and he'll never suspect. Just don't leave. You can't ever leave me."

The world returned to normal. The next time Horatio came to Tokyo, we had intercourse like before. When he was gone, I was careful. I never missed a telephone call. No one saw me enter or leave the apartment building, and I entered and left Thai Street through the kitchen. Nui was sad for the first week and distant for two more, but he came around. "I'll save enough money for a restaurant in Tokyo," he declared. "Just wait. You'll see."

Three months later, Nui disappeared. Nothing in his room had been disturbed. His clothes were folded in the fruit crates; his CDs were stacked next to his portable stereo. The manager, the other boys, the girls, no one knew where he was.

Horatio arrived a week later. A large deal in America had just closed so he was in good spirits. He described how he'd increased revenue for his associated companies by 150 percent. He began working but I remained seated at the table, waiting. He looked up from time to time, wondering why I didn't leave him alone. After a half-hour, he pushed the binder away from him. In the bright light of the chandelier, his hair glowed blue-black, thick and lustrous.

"Do you know how much I've given you?" His voice was stern and weary at the same time. "Don't you realize how fortunate you are?"

"It was my fault. Not his."

"What really irks me is your ingratitude. People should know the meaning of loyalty and service. I thought a girl of your background would understand that."

"What did you do to him?"

"He got what he deserved." Horatio stretched, twisting one way and then the next, spine cracking. He looked at his wristwatch. "I've had a long day of traveling. Go prepare my bath."

CHAPTER 21

Once my information about *Das Puppenhaus* had been proven to be reliable, my public defender reached an agreement with the government. Sign a declaration promising to serve as a prosecution witness and I was free never to return. We drove in and out of Santa Fe in a single morning. Neither the city nor Jugs looked as ominous as I'd remembered. In the clear fall sunlight, the strip club looked like an auto parts warehouse.

Is that what trauma does? Transform the mundane into a phantasm, sear ugliness into one's retinas until it's impossible to see anything else? Chandra, Milton, and the Fantasy Labyrinth were banished to a locked chest in my past, but when Megumi fell asleep and I lay alone with my thoughts, the lockbox rattled. How long before memories scar over, become insensate?

What was I to Megumi? A green card. A way to exchange a miserable life for one slightly less so. A docile lover who held onto her with something like relief. What was she to me? No demands. No children. We could drift like this forever, developing no roots and no home. We were back in New Mexico and it was as if we'd never left; no matter where we went, we stayed in the same place.

"I'm happy," she said.

"Me too," I said.

She curled into herself and faced the wall. Megumi was affectionate while awake. Asleep she couldn't bear the lightest brush against her skin. We kept to our own sides of the bed. We shared our solitude.

The phone booth stood in the corner of an all-night gas station, next to a bus stop that, even at this late hour, sheltered two men. They were young and wiry, dressed in black slacks and white dress shirts, tails untucked. The gas station attendant, a South Asian man with a graying mustache, was locked within a sealed cage, surrounded by bottles of motor oil, chewing gum, and soda pop. He slipped the phone card into the tray along with my change.

"Guy?" Tanya said. "It's you, isn't it? Do you know what time it is?"

I touched the pale band of flesh on my wrist. My watch was on the side-table, sleeping with Megumi. "Pretty late."

"You haven't called for months and then all of a sudden it's urgent. I thought for sure it was a hospital or morgue." Her words were rapid-fire but hushed.

The phone receiver smelled like spit and beer. "I'm sorry."

"You could have called to say you couldn't call. I deserve that much at least, don't I?" She sighed heavily. "Where are you calling from? It's so noisy."

The bus had pulled up. Young men peered out vacantly from the windows. Bus boys, bellhops, cashiers—laborers of the non-criminal underworld. The doors hissed closed and the bus departed.

"I'm in the southwest," I said. "Just outside of Albuquerque, New Mexico."

"Still? You haven't moved very far."

"Yes, 'still.'" Why did she have to say it that way? "I don't just pass through a place. I like to really see it." The rock. The sage brush. The gas stations and tribal casinos.

There was a rustling at the other end of the line. "Can you hold on one sec, Guy?" she said. The sound cut out.

Tanya had an affinity for phones. She changed her outgoing voicemail message daily, at work, on her cell, and at home. She had hit the mute button before I could hear what she didn't want me to hear.

"I'm just saying," she said, as if there had been no interruption at all, "that vacations can last only for so long. The longer you're away from Seattle, the further behind you are."

Further behind what? Further behind who? She was paraphrasing Troy's introduction about the "will to succeed." *If you're not busy striving, you're busy dying.*

"I called to talk, not to receive a Troy Bobbins lecture."

"There you go again, putting him down without giving him a chance." She continued to speak in a hushed tone. "I wish you'd give his *Personal Path* series a chance. It's exactly what you need to find direction in your life."

I know that damn series by heart, and look where I am now. Fuck. Now I was blaming Troy for my problems. Troy: the only person who'd been on my side since the divorce. I tried to rub the odor of oil and dust from my nose.

"Why'd you call, Guy?" she said.

A Chevy Impala pulled up to a gas pump and stopped. No one got out and the engine remained running. The driver was slumped over the steering wheel.

Should I ask? No. Should I ask? "Things weren't always bad when we were together, were they?"

Far off in the desert night, a motorcycle howled.

"Have you been drinking?" she said.

"What? No. Look, Tanya. You're the one who said we should talk about feelings. So there, I'm talking about them."

"You sound drunk."

"I'm not drunk!" The louder I spoke, the more drunk I sounded. "Never mind. Forget I even called. Let's talk again in two weeks. That's the contract obligation, right?"

"Wait, Guy. I'm sorry." She took a deep breath. "You caught me off guard. It's the middle of the night and I'm waking up early tomorrow. I want to be your friend. I want to listen."

Translation: you're a desperate freak. I shouldn't have called. Megumi was waiting for me in bed. She didn't ask for explanations. "We can talk about this some other time."

"No. You're right. Let's talk. I want you to know that there's nothing—"

A murmur of a voice. A male voice. Just a snippet of sound before she hit the mute button.

"—you need to hide from me," she continued. "If you're ready to be honest with your feelings, I'm ready to be honest with mine."

It was like an aural hiccup. Why make an issue of it?

"Who was that, Tanya?"

"Who was what, Guy?"

"Just now. Who was that?" The Chevy Impala's engine was still running. Would the driver wake before he ran out of gas? Maybe he'd expended so much energy getting here he no longer had the strength to fill up. "I heard a man's voice just a second ago."

"I don't want to cut into your time by talking about me, Guy." She was offering me another chance to save face. "Are you still traveling with the same woman?"

It was strange that her presumption, wrong before, was now right. Before I was traveling with Milton. Milton the murderer. Milton, who'd suggested that Tanya was banging her boss to get ahead. He'd suspected her of feeding information to Kolling and Smith, and I hadn't believed him. But how else had they found us in Salt Lake City and Santa Fe?

"Who was that?" I said.

"I've resolved to do less talking and more listening. You first, Guy."

"God dammit, Tanya! Just tell me!"

Don't let it be Jay. Anyone but that cloven-hoofed hobbit. Anyone but that drooling, bipedal rodent. God hear my prayer.

"You sure you're done?" she said. "Yes? Well, I've been meaning to tell you for a while, but it never seemed like the right time. But then, 'Time itself isn't good or bad, it's what we make of it.' I'll have you know I'm not ashamed, so there's no reason to waste time with long explanations. He's helped me to become the person I'm meant to be."

I crouched down and stared at a dirty wad of chewing gum. Damn you, Milton. I hope you rot in Hell.

"It's Jay," she said. "Jay Weed. You and your friends have never given him a chance. He's so much more than what you make him out to be."

I slammed the receiver down before I realized what I'd done. At the gas pump, the Chevy Impala's engine had cut out, the driver still hunched over the wheel. The gas station attendant and I each wordlessly dared the other to examine whether the driver was unconscious or dead. I would say my phone card ran out of time. I would say I was happy for her. But not now. For now, an old man and I shared solitude and suspicion over the hood of a stalled car.

"Are we going to stop at the casino?" Megumi said.

"I told you already. No."

We'd agreed on the itinerary. We would stop at Acoma Sky City, the oldest continuously occupied pueblo in America, perched atop a 400-foot mesa. After that it was a straight shot to the Grand Canyon. We didn't have time for her to watch me lose at blackjack. I don't know what it is with Asians and gambling. A casino planted in the dried-up desert sea of Mars would be teeming with Asian tourists.

The Acoma Visitor Center was newly built in the New Mexican pueblo-meets-suburban-tract-home architectural style. There wasn't much to the valley floor: the historic village was atop the mesa, and the new settlement was miles away, closer to the highway and casino. An elderly couple asked me to take their photograph. I declined their offer to do the same for Megumi and me. Besides the elderly couple, a bespectacled man thumbed through a worn Peterson

Field Guide, and two parents tried to stop their children from smacking each other. The weather had turned too chilly for there to be too many other visitors. We filed into the shuttle bus and spread out to different corners.

"You don't care how much I've given up for you," Megumi said. "You wish you'd found that medal of yours instead of me."

"I never said that."

Sure, I'd asked her about it once or twice, maybe three times, and always in an offhand way. How could she "not remember" what she'd done with it? She collected freaking drink coasters. How could she have left behind a medallion engraved with my name?

Our tour guide was a short, pan-faced Acoma man in his mid-twenties, a caterpillar of hair crawling across his upper lip. As the bus climbed the mesa, "Mark" recited a litany of facts and figures in a rapid, well-rehearsed stream of words. Megumi stared out the window.

What did Megumi give up to be with me? By her own admission, she was a domestic slave. She sexually serviced a penny-pinching, sadistic corporate executive. He never planned to marry her. Why was she trying to make *me* feel guilty for not proposing on bended knee?

Every Asian family has an ugly male relative who returns to the homeland for a bride, even if that homeland is five generations removed from the present. In my family, that relative was my borderline-retarded cousin Alec, a forty-five-year-old usher at a local cinema. On a fourteen-day trip to China, his parents arranged for him to marry a Chinese woman. I was following in the footsteps of a man who still wore corduroy shorts. At least he had a steady income and had married a former nurse. I was jobless and was supporting a former prostitute.

Our first stop on top of the mesa was a spot between the church and the cemetery. Mark smiled, his eyes becoming horizontal slits. "When the Spanish burnt down our places of worship, they forced us to build this beautiful 21,000 square-foot church and convent. My people hauled every material used in its construction—clay, stone, wood, nails, everything—up the 367-foot mesa. Worst were the timbers used for the 35-foot-long *vigas*, which come from Mount Taylor, thirty miles away. If the timbers touched the ground, we were lashed mercilessly and the logs abandoned. Those who died during the construction of San Esteban del Rey were buried within its walls, which in some places measure seven feet in width."

Mark gestured to the twin bell towers which pierced the heavens. "The bells were imported from Mexico. The price? Two Acoma boys and two Acoma girls. These children became the slaves of Spanish colonists. We leave a gap in the cemetery wall so their spirits can one day return to their ancestral home."

It was impossible to remain irritated at Megumi during Mark's recitation of Spanish atrocities. What did our problems amount to when compared to the attempted extermination of a culture and a people?

The interior of the church felt as if it were underwater, the sound and light muted, the vaulted ceiling shrouded in darkness. There were no pews, just an expanse of packed dirt. Paintings depicted the stations of the cross: Roman soldiers piercing Christ's side with spears; Christ being led to the crucifixion. Mark bowed his head and crossed himself. The others shuffled about, exchanging whispers. The adobe walls were cool to the touch. In the silence, a person could sense the long-dead Acoma around us, swimming in their earthen crypt.

"Do you think," I said in a low tone, "that some of them were buried standing up? That suspended in these walls, some of them are reaching out to us?"

Megumi yawned. "I'm hungry," she said.

Mark was as giddy as a schoolgirl while he described how his people pitched the missionaries off the cliffs. He wore a rueful smile when he narrated the Spanish retribution: they cut off the left feet of the men, enslaved the women, and sent the children to be raised by Christian families.

By the time we reached the plaza, I wasn't the only one benumbed by our guide's gleeful accounts of brutality. The elderly couple, so spry and sparkling at the beginning of the tour, leaned wearily against one another. The others had ceased to ask questions for fear of what Mark might say. Only Megumi was unaffected. She wolfed down two orders of fry bread and then zeroed in on the jewelry. A number of Acoma families had set out tables in front of their ancestral homes.

"Do you like this one?" Megumi dangled the charm between her narrow collarbones. It was turquoise on silver. It looked like a "female" symbol, except the circle was elongated and the arms and leg were flared.

"It looks nice on you." Nearly anything looked good on Megumi. Even my medallion. She'd probably worn it for a day or two, then relegated it to the bottom of her suitcase, where it rattled around with her spare change.

"That one's 33 percent off for today only." The owner of the stand was a heavy woman with a braid that reached down to her ample bottom. "A pretty charm for a pretty woman. Are you two newlyweds?"

"No," I said too quickly. Was that a look of disappointment on Megumi's face? I avoided her eyes. The sign on the tray read, "~~$89.99~~ $59.99." Anywhere else, this junk would cost ten bucks. Couldn't she trade-in some of the crap she kept buying? Did she think I was made of consumer credit? I grimaced and reached for my wallet. Then I stopped. I'd seen that symbol before. "Didn't you say that all of these were authentic Acoma crafts?"

"Of course."

"But this is an ankh."

"A what?" Her expression changed from sunshine to heavy clouds.

"An ankh," I said. The spark of recognition didn't light in the woman's or in Megumi's eyes. "The Egyptian symbol for eternal life. *Egyptian.*"

"So?" the woman said. "It was made by an Acoma living on the res. It's authentic Acoma jewelry."

"You don't like it?" Megumi said.

"It's not matter of like or dislike. It's a question of authenticity. Of false advertising. Who's to say the necklace wasn't imported from Taiwan?"

The woman balled her fist against a meaty hip. "You calling me a liar, mister?"

"It doesn't say 'Made in Taiwan,'" Megumi said.

"Can we talk about this alone?" I said.

Reluctantly, Megumi put the charm back into the tray. The vendor rolled her eyes. Taking Megumi's elbow, I led her out of earshot to a storefront offering a postcard rack that shielded us from the wind.

"Look, Megumi. I'm not saying, 'Don't get it.' And it's not the price. I swear it's not the price. But we're on the Acoma reservation. Why not get some Acoma pottery, an artistic representation of a community's spirit?"

"I can't wear pottery," she said.

"Well then, maybe not an ankh. How about a Kokopelli?" Kokopelli was a hunchbacked Native American spirit with wild hair who played the flute. His figure was everywhere in the southwest: on cliff petroglyphs, pottery, hair salon signs. A Kokopelli necklace would at least be geographically authentic.

"It's not important," she said.

"Are you sure? Because I'm not trying to stop you."

Megumi shook her head.

I gave her hand a light squeeze, which she didn't return. Over her shoulder, I noticed the Acoma vendor talking in an animated fashion to our tour guide. Why was it unreasonable to want to purchase Acoma art in an Acoma pueblo?

Mark called our group toward the bus to give his parting remarks. The driver waited for us with the door open, playing on a Nintendo DS.

"I'd like to thank you all for visiting our ancient city," Mark said, "a source of pride and a site of tragedy. In answer to a question raised by Mrs. Reynolds a few minutes ago," he nodded at the elderly woman, "I would like to say, no, we feel no bitterness toward the Spanish for the atrocities they committed, or toward the Americans, who stole thousands of acres of Acoma land. If our positions were reversed, perhaps we too would have obliterated your history and enslaved your children."

I should have bought the necklace. Ford manufactured engines in India; Toyota assembled cars in Kentucky. If an ankh was made by an Acoma, it was an Acoma craft. Maybe one day the Acoma would compete with the Afghans and Pakistanis in the rug-making business. I was buying into the same logic that supported Milton's crusade for an authentic nouveau German identity.

Mark nodded toward the obese boy. "In answer to Joseph's question, yes, he did see Michael Jordan leaping from Sky City to the Enchanted Mesa in a Nike commercial." There were appropriate expressions of awe. "You might have seen an SUV skidding to a halt at the same cliff wall from which we threw the Catholic missionaries during the Pueblo Revolt. And, most recently, self-help guru Troy Bobbins filmed an instructional video here."

I straightened. My sensation of déjà vu had not been due to the casino or the adobe structures. The Troy Bobbins video had featured the trail that led down the cliff face only paces away from Mark. Troy's destination had been the very place we were standing. The city he'd turned into a bonfire had been Sky City. The people who lay face down in the dirt had been the Acoma.

"And now, I'd like to offer you a choice," Mark said. "You can return to the Visitor Center aboard the bus. Or you can join me on a descent down the traditional trail, where the sweat, blood, and tears of my people have become part of the earth."

En masse, the group surged toward the bus. Megumi stepped in that direction too, but I tugged her back gently.

"I'd like to walk back to the Visitor Center," I said.

She frowned. "But only poor people walk."

"This is important to me."

We proceeded single-file, Megumi first, then me, then Mark. Megumi was as sure-footed as a mountain goat—it must have been her lower center of gravity—and soon opened a sizable distance between us.

Though there were handholds in the cliff walls during a steep section, the path down was remarkably anti-climactic. It would have been a different story, of course, had I been leading pack mules, or carrying a log that was not supposed to touch the ground. But in my tennis shoes on a dry, clear day, it was hardly a hike at all. It was an example of movie-making magic by the Troy Bobbins Corporation. In addition to tilting the cameras, the director probably used computer-generated imagery to elongate the walls and make them appear to be more slick. New Zealand became Middle Earth; Acoma Sky City became Troy's "Mountain of Success."

Mark told me he was an extra in the Troy Bobbins video, along with the younger men in the tribe. It was his brother-in-law who had earned a $500 cash bonus for bopping Troy on the head with a Styrofoam brick. Mark described Troy Bobbins, the international celebrity, "as a real, down-to-earth guy. He did whatever the director asked him to do. He disappeared into his trailer between takes."

We paused at a switchback. "Did it bother you to lay face down in the dirt while Sky City burned?"

He shrugged, the fuzzy patch beneath his nose twitching like a mouse's whiskers. If I ran into Mark on the street, I never would have guessed he was Native American. With his bowl cut and dark complexion, I would have thought him to be a Filipino gardener.

"When you're lying in front of blue screens, you can't take any of that too seriously. Besides, our people have been through worse without getting paid for it."

The bus passed us on the way down. They'd arrive at the Visitor Center only minutes before we did. If Megumi had exerted herself, she might have beaten the bus. Mark watched her pink hat flopping at a quick but steady pace below us. He winked.

"You're in good there, bro. She's a real looker. A man feels like a million bucks with a woman like that."

"Thanks, man," I said.

Megumi rolled her window down during our drive off the reservation. She took off her hat and let the cool wind blow through her hair. Mark was right. I should feel lucky to be with a woman like Megumi. She was beautiful and grateful and she wanted to be with me. Why question her motives? She didn't ask for furs…just overpriced, cheap kitsch. She let me sleep as late as I wanted and never pressed me about career plans. I would always compare favorably to deportation and sexual slavery.

Maybe Milton had been right all along, the only relationship a person could trust was *quid pro quo*. No one needed to know about her past, and I could forget my own. We could start a new life together in the perpetual present. We might learn to love one another. And if we didn't, a shared solitude was still better than being alone.

CHAPTER 22

The Grand Canyon defied my expectations, which had been shaped by faded postcards and refrigerator magnets. Water, soft and ubiquitous, had carved implacable rock, exposing its mineral sinews—a reminder that the weak can overcome the strong, that every living creature is insignificant and impermanent in geological time. I could have traced for hours the sinuous curves of the river that had rent this vast gash in the earth.

I squeezed Megumi's hand. "What are you thinking about?"

"The river looks dirty," she said.

We stayed for thirty minutes. Megumi stopped sulking over a hot-fudge sundae at Dairy Queen.

"Why don't you like civilization?" she said.

How wrong she was! I missed low-fat dressing and organic greens, Copper River salmon season, same-sex couples walking hand-in-hand on the sidewalks. In short, I longed to return home to Seattle. But the bottom line was this: in the cities, Megumi longed for desolation; in outposts, she longed for the anonymity of the throngs. Every place was better than the last until we got there. My job was to travel infinite space on dwindling resources. Not once had she noticed that I'd stopped buying snacks for myself, asked for tap water, filled up on bread or chips. Days on the coasts meant weeks of living in the spaces in-between. I loved civilization, but we couldn't afford it.

Or maybe we couldn't afford it on the weekends. There is no better bargain than Sunday through Thursday during the off-season at a Las Vegas Strip hotel. In the city of dreams, a poor man can live like royalty armed with a credit card, a coupon book, and a willingness to sit through time-share presentations. That night, in our bed at the MGM Grand, the sex was better than it had ever been. We were beginning to understand one another.

Barnes & Noble suburban strip malls are transforming America into Vegas, but nothing can beat the original. How could Milton's faux-Bavarian town compete with the pyramids of Luxor, the canals of the Venetian, and the cobblestone avenues of Paris, Las Vegas? The city teems with the beautiful and the obese; millionaires and Latino sex club touts; and, best of all for Megumi, all-you-can-eat buffets.

In Vegas I could, for a short time, treat her to first-class accommodations, poolside cabanas, and extravagant shows. Four hundred dollars for a slip of fabric? I swallowed my panic. How the sales assistant fawned over us was worth every penny of the money I didn't have. Tanya had harped on my inadequacies but never inspired me to fix them.

With Megumi by my side, my reservations about securing mindless employment were being squeezed like droplets of poison out of my system. I wanted to become a better man for her. I didn't need to be as rich as Kolling to make her happy. A touch of class every now and then—a night out, an expensive dinner, a pair of glittering earrings—and we would thrive in middle-class paradise.

The waiter couldn't keep his eyes off Megumi. How could I blame him? At the boutique she'd modeled the dress wearing her undergarments, but now she wore nothing underneath. Her nipples seeped forward like twin bloodstains through the sheer, red material. The plunging back revealed the flutter of her sparrow muscles, the curve and cleft of her ass. We tore through two bottles of wine and I tried to rush her back to the room. She shook her head.

"I want to watch you win," she said.

The lowest minimums of $15 were at the blackjack tables lined three-deep and enveloped in clouds of smoke. Feeling Megumi's impatience, I took a seat at a $25 table. The other players, all men, appreciated her arrival. Megumi placed her hand on my shoulder and my doubts about having maxed out my ATM withdrawal limit evaporated.

The first card shoe fell the way any shoe might—sometimes good, sometimes bad. I was up $50, then down $75. I prefer to stretch the game out with small bets. I'd intended to bet more daringly for Megumi's sake, but the erratic play of the others checked me. Our table was a United Nations of hues and playing styles. At the first position was a short

Asian man with thick, almost opaque eyeglasses. He bet either $25 or $1,000, and never an amount in-between. He split when he should have stayed; he doubled-down when he should have stayed or hit. And yet, in the aggregate, he was somehow breaking even. I sat in the second position. To my left, a fellow in a cowboy hat and a bolo tie followed the strategic norms but laid down any amount for his initial bet with seemingly no rhyme or reason. Next to him was an olive-skinned young man with too much gel in his hair. He threw down high bets every time, sometimes playing smart and sometimes with pure bravado. In his velvet-like, burnt-tangerine shirt, he was more interested in looking good than in playing well.

"Where are you and your young lady from, Slim?" It was the cowboy speaking. "Slim" was a better nickname for him than for me. Though older, he was in fine physical condition. That might have contributed to the smug look on his face. No one reeks of superiority more than an older, accomplished man.

"I'm from…we're from Seattle."

"Rains a lot out there," he said. "Doesn't it?"

"I would find it quite depressing," the flashy dresser said. He had a prep school accent with undertones I didn't recognize. His eyes lingered a second too long on Megumi. "It's enough to make anyone put a shotgun in his mouth, not just fabulously wealthy singer-songwriters." He motioned for another card. "Busted again. *C'est la vie.*"

There was a change in dealers. Dolores was replaced by Romeo. Only Filipinos choose names with flair like Romeo, Bong Bong, and Caramel. He put the cards in the automatic shuffler and nodded at me. Funny thing about Filipinos, even when they found out I wasn't the same ethnicity, they treated me well for resembling one.

"Pardon me, young lady." The cowboy addressed Megumi. "Isn't this a school night? What's a young thing like you doing in a casino?" He gave me a wink.

"I have identification." Megumi began to open her purse. I put my hand on hers.

I needed to get used to men ogling Megumi. It was, after all, a compliment paid to me as much as to her. Tanya was attractive but resided within spitting distance of the median. Megumi, especially in that red dress, indicated my status at the top of the social food chain.

"Has your boyfriend taken you to any shows yet?" Mr. Faux-Velvet Shirt said. He must have been in his early twenties.

"We went to see Sheena Easton," Megumi said.

"The free show?" He stifled a laugh. "You couldn't pay me to see that. There's nothing more hideous than an old maid inviting you inside her *Sugar Walls.*"

"You said the show was very expensive," Megumi said to me. "You said she was very popular."

"We couldn't let those tickets go to waste," I said. "And we both enjoy music."

"Expensive?" the cowboy said. "Little lady, if you want expensive, you should go see the water show at the Bellagio. I bring every one of my friends and family to see it at $150 a person. They've got thousands of my hard-earned dollars by now."

"I was disappointed by *O,*" the young man said. "The water tank is an engineering marvel, but I think it's missing that *je ne sais quoi* of the other Cirque shows. I keep going back in the hopes that I'll be proven wrong, but I never am."

The attitude at the table had shifted. My only ally was Romeo, the dealer, who shook his head in commiseration. I pushed forward $100.

"Hey, hey, big spender!" The cowboy clapped me on the back. "That's showing some stones. I was wondering if you'd ever bet more than the minimum. I'll see your $100 and raise you another $900. I think this little lady's going to bring me more luck than she's brought you."

The others laughed. Hair Gel bet the maximum too. Only the Asian man wasn't joining in on the hilarity, though he appeared to be ogling Megumi through his rectangular eyeglasses.

"*O* is really good," said a black man with a broad nose and an African accent.

"I would like to see it," Megumi said. "Can we afford it?"

"Of course we can afford it," I said. I hadn't meant to bark a response. Two tickets at $150 a piece; that was $300, or six weekday nights of accommodation. Why would someone who couldn't swim enjoy a water show?

I lost my $100. Then I lost another $100. Then I lost $75. And then $25. The cowboy and Hair Gel commented every time. I won a few minimum-bet hands and then lost my gains. I mumbled that it might be time to cut our losses. Young Master Hair Gel said the opposite held true.

"What you should really be doing, uncle, is doubling your bet after every loss," he said. "That makes it mathematically impossible for you to lose. The longer and colder your losing streak, the more prodigious your single win."

Double or nothing: the twisted logic of a boy gambling with his daddy's money. What if I lost $10,000 and didn't have the $20,000 to change my fortunes? Table limits laid waste to that strategy. The only way to win was to know when to walk away. I looked at Megumi for affirmation, but she was looking at Hair Gel, who was looking at her. I pushed forward my last $100.

I won. I let it ride and hit a blackjack. I let it ride and won again. I'd been down $300 and had moved to up $600 in the course of three hands. It was time to leave.

"There we go, Slim," the cowboy said. "You might be able to take her to dinner *and* a show now."

"The question, old man," Hair Gel said, "is whether you're playing to be a winner or to avoid being a loser." He winked at Megumi.

I left my $1,000 on the table. That was two months of rent plus the approximate value of my car. Megumi caressed my neck.

Romeo's delicate brown hands flicked the cards around the table. My first card was a 6. The dealer's up-card was a 7. Romeo turned my disappointment into elation by dropping a 5 next to my 6. My cards tallied 11, which was the textbook doubling opportunity. I could make $2,000 on my hot hand instead of $1,000.

"Hot damn, Slim," the cowboy said. "Luck be a lady for sure."

Megumi's hand slid down to the small of my back. Until she did so, I hadn't noticed it was damp with perspiration. Romeo had dealt the cards quickly, but the hand was being held up by the bespectacled Asian man at position one. He had a $1,000 initial bet on the table and his cards were a 7 and a 2. Obviously he should hit or double and win a bundle of money. Instead he put another $1,000 on the table beneath the 2.

"Sir," Romeo said. "Are you sure you want to split that instead of doubling?" He kept his fingertips on the dealing shoe, reluctant to draw a card out. The stubby man grunted in assent.

"Are you crazy, Charlie?" the cowboy said. "You're going to blow yourself up and screw everyone else at the table. Don't do that unless you're an idiot. You're betting yourself into a corner."

I hoped the Asian man's name really was "Charlie." Logic told me that what he did had no bearing on my hand. But superstition told me that by drawing out extra cards he would deny me what I really needed.

On the 7, "Charlie" drew a 6 for a total of 13, hit again for a 3 to total 16, then hit *again* to get a 5. His hand was 21. If the dealer had 21, he would push; otherwise, he would win.

"Lucky son-of-a-bitch," the cowboy said.

On the 2, he drew a 5, then an 8, then another 5 for a total of 20. Another almost-sure winner. Even then Charlie's fingertips itched to take another hit. He resisted.

"That's how a winner plays it." The youth ran his fingers through his rigid hair. "He turned the law of probabilities on its head."

Romeo looked at me. "Sir?"

I looked at my eleven again. "I should double, right?"

"You're damn right you should double," the cowboy said. "Hirohito just busted the bank without cards as good as yours."

"The chart says you should double," Romeo confirmed.

My heart sunk. "I don't have enough to cover that. Do you take credit cards?"

"I'm afraid you would have had to establish a line of credit beforehand," Romeo said. "Would you like to double for less?"

The additional $9 in my wallet would hardly help. Megumi stepped forward. She counted $1,000 in $100 bills onto the felt and then paused. "Can you double for more?"

Romeo smiled. "I'm afraid not, ma'am." He ran a pen over the bills to make sure they were legit. He placed two purple chips next to my stacks of green ones.

Several chairs down the African gentleman cleared his throat. "If I may comment, Mr. Slim. We're near the end of the shoe and it appears that your neighbor has played out a number of low cards. That's good for you because it suggests you will receive a good hand and the house will receive something approximating 17. But the shoe is cut three decks deep and there are still a large number of low cards unaccounted for. It might be more prudent, especially given your financial situation, *not* to double. The pain of losing everything would be far greater than the pleasure of realizing this substantial gain. And it is always better not to be indebted to our dearest friends."

That made perfect sense. How would I feel about losing Megumi's money? That's exactly how the old Guy Watanabe would have played it.

"Nuts to that," the cowboy said. "If it turns out to be wrong then, hell, be wrong at full speed. There's a reason why the dark continent is mired in poverty. But, by all means, follow his advice if you like."

I knew what Megumi wanted of me, what she expected of me. She'd never mentioned that she had her own money.

I'd paid for everything, from motel rooms to Slurpees. She allowed me to pay because that was my role as a man. Her man.

"I'm doubling," I said.

The next card to fall was an ace. On my doubled wager of $2,000, the total of my cards was 12. I blinked rapidly. "Can I split those?"

Romeo frowned. It was hard for him to see another Filipino suffer. "I'm afraid not."

I couldn't tear myself away from staring at my 6, 5, and ace. I didn't look up when the cowboy slapped my back in commiseration. Or to glare at the sniggering young man who was now openly leering at Megumi. Her hand was no longer on my back and I felt damp fabric clinging to my skin. The others stood pat with good hands.

The dealer's turn. His up-card was a 7 and his down-card turned out to be a 4. The next card was a...5. I sat up straight. The next card was a queen of spades. 26. The dealer had busted. I was $2,000 richer; or actually $1,000 richer since half of that total was Megumi's. I kissed her hard on the mouth.

"Yes!" I pumped my fist. "Yes! Yes! Yes!"

Hair Gel frowned. "You didn't really win. It was the dealer who lost."

He was wrong. I'd won the money. I had the girl.

"Don't hate the player," I said. "Hate the game."

It felt good to be an asshole. Romeo colored me up to four orange chips. Megumi and I floated across the floor to the cashier. As we waited in line, we leaned into each other. Tomorrow we'd purchase front-row tickets for *O*. Tonight we'd ascend to the top of Stratosphere Tower for a decadent chocolate dessert, then retire to our room for a bubble bath and more.

A cheer went up from the roulette wheel. The croupier pushed forward a pile of chips.

"I don't even want to think about how much that person just won," I said. "I'm ecstatic with our $2,000."

Megumi made a moue. "Is $2,000 so little to win?"

"It might not be much in the grand scheme of things, but winning 2,000 bucks gambling is like finding money in a pair of washed jeans."

"Roulette looks fun," she said.

We'd reached the front of the line. "Let's not press our luck. The key to winning is knowing when to leave."

"But I'm just starting to have fun," she said.

The cashier tapped her fingers on the counter. Seconds ago, Megumi had shared my elation but now her eyes lingered on the casino floor. My rationality wrinkled its nose, but the liberated, wild part of me that had withered away during my adult years, *that* part of me wailed for more. *More, more, more, more, more.* I was on a hot streak. Why shouldn't I ride it, and Megumi, all night long?

Ring a bell and a dog salivates. That same, Pavlovian response describes the thrill that runs through your body at the sound of silver dollars ringing into a slot machine tray. It doesn't have to be silver dollars—it can be nickels or tokens. There is something deep and instinctual about the linkage between money and chance. It's a sensual rush to hear the roulette wheel spinning, the ball rolling on the hardwood until it reaches repose on the number of your fortune.

I'd wanted to exchange our money for smaller chips and then bet on red or black. Betting colors on roulette makes its odds approximate those of blackjack, i.e., slightly worse than betting on a coin flip. Megumi would have none of that.

One bet with all our money, she said. One bet on a single number. She didn't want to win another $2,000. She wanted the 1 in 38 chance to win 35 times our $4,000 stake. Those were better odds than winning the lottery, she pointed out... the difference being, of course, that a person paid $1 for a Lotto ticket. I asked her to choose the number. She refused.

"The good luck is part of you. It's your karma. We've got to use it now before it turns sour. You must choose your special number."

"I don't have a special number."

She looked surprised. "Then what did you dream about last night? Was it fire or water, earth or air? Or were you falling?"

"I can't remember."

Megumi considered that silently. The bustle around the roulette wheel continued. "What was the happiest day of your life?"

The day I won the karaoke competition. No, that was a pitiful answer. There had to have been better days in over thirty years of being alive. It wasn't when I met Tanya: I had a flu that day and my first impression was that she looked clumsy. Our honeymoon? That wasn't a day, that was an entire week, an entire period of life. Maybe Megumi wasn't asking me for a lucky number at all. Maybe she was testing me.

"Today is the happiest day of my life. Right now. Being here with you."

"Don't lie." She examined me with cool, almost hostile, eyes. "When did you win your karaoke medal?"

I couldn't remember my anniversary or my parents' birthdays, but I knew that date. Countless times I'd fingered the numbers etched on the cool metal surface of my long lost medallion.

"Good," she said. "Add those numbers together and what do you get?"

It took me a moment to realize that she wanted me to add the single digits together to get the magic number. It was 22.

"Good," she said. "Now you must put all our money on 22."

I acted before reason could bludgeon sense back into me, reaching between two seated players to place our orange chips on 22 black. The croupier shook his head. He asked which color I wanted and in what denomination. I said the highest denomination, since I was going to be putting it all on 22 black. That attracted a murmur of approval from the crowd and a smile from the croupier. He pushed forward four $1,000 red chips "to match the lady's dress." The pit boss, a well-dressed man with a thick neck, paid us a visit.

"That is the table maximum, sir," he said in an ominous Eastern European accent. "Are you sure you would like to wager so much money on a single number?"

I nodded toward Megumi. She pressed her cheek against my shoulder. "Whatever the lady commands," I said in my best James Bond voice.

The pit boss nodded at the croupier. "Yes. It is always best not to argue with a beautiful woman."

The croupier spun the wheel and tossed the tiny, white ball. It rolled round and round the wooden rim for an eternity before it descended into the colored wheel, hopping once, twice, thrice, tap dancing toward our destiny. Had I chosen wrong? Megumi's dress was red, my chips were red. Should I have chosen a red number?

"Twenty-two black," the croupier said. "Twenty-two black."

A cheer like I hadn't heard since the karaoke competition burst from the spectators. Megumi squealed as if she'd been crushed beneath a metal girder. Thirty-five times $4,000 was $140,000. In one fell swoop I'd eliminated over $30,000 of credit card debt and had over $100,000 to spare. That was enough for a new car, a new house, a new life. I shoved my tongue into Megumi's mouth and slurped her surprised saliva. I loved Megumi. I loved her with all my heart.

We fucked all night. And it was good. Better than good, more than routine. The third time through Megumi gasped and clenched, bringing me to a violent orgasm in which she extracted the last dregs of fluid left in my body. I was a desiccated husk that could be sucked out the window, caught on a jet stream, and blown to another continent.

I don't think she faked it. Usually her moans were faint, detached, and rhythmic. This time she let out sharp, guttural shrieks. She didn't jump up afterward to clean herself but allowed me to stay inside until my penis went limp.

"I still don't understand your numerology." I said. "Why wasn't 22 bad luck? I may have won the competition, but I lost the medallion."

She stroked my hair. "It was your destiny to lose your medal to win me."

CHAPTER 23

There's an art to leisure—doing nothing of social value or significance—that few understand. A person can't simply fill the hours with swimming, shopping, dancing, drinking, et cetera, ad nauseam; especially when he hasn't won the lottery but a few years of wages. A man picks his pleasures and then savors them. On this Megumi and I were in agreement.

Megumi loved the seafood buffet at the Rio but our staple was the stringy meat at Coco Palms. I suggested a suite at the Bellagio; she was satisfied with upgrading to a king-sized bed at the MGM Grand. What she adored about Tiffany's weren't the precious stones but the name, the logo, and the powder-blue shopping bags.

"I don't want a diamond," she said. "Let's save for a house."

That was a source of tension: her increased reliance on the pronoun "we." Our relationship wasn't what I'd imagined *the* relationship, that is, the terminal one, would be. I wanted to date someone for a year, move in with her for a few more, and then marry once our possessions had become intimately commingled. I'd hoped that the $140,000, half of which was hers, would promote her independence. What would prove devotion more than the ability to walk away but choosing not to? When I suggested depositing the money in separate bank accounts, Megumi dissolved into tears.

"Don't you trust me?" she said. "Don't you care about me?"

We were sitting across the desk from a bank official. He watched with a strained smile before excusing himself to the restroom.

"Of course I trust you," I said. "I want you to trust *me*. The money is half yours. You can do whatever you want with it and I won't have the right to complain. If you didn't want to be with me, you wouldn't have to repay a cent. We're equals, don't you see?" I tapped her passport. "I'm never going to keep you captive with a visa."

Megumi's identification was her Japanese passport. Her photograph looked like a middle-school portrait, except the birth date suggested she was twenty-four years old.

"Maybe you're like him," she said. "You want me only for one thing."

Of course I deposited the $140,000 into a joint account. Megumi was traumatized by her relationship with Kolling, by her short, tragic life. She slipped into dark funks and asked if I'd miss her if she disappeared, whether I would protect her if Smith arrived to reclaim her. She watched me swim from beneath an umbrella, covered from ankles to neck to keep from tanning. Those minutes underwater were my haven.

You've got to learn to live with what you can't rise above. Bruce Springsteen, "Tunnel of Love." There are moments of perfection in a relationship; there is no perfect relationship. There were times I wanted to drown inside of her. And there were moments when her presence galled me. In a city foreign to us both, we existed in a bubble with only each other for company. I would have appreciated her more with periodic breaks.

I encouraged her to go shopping on her own. We planned her itinerary together, circled the stores on a tourist map, made provisions for what I would do if she didn't return by the end of the afternoon. The first day she returned within fifteen minutes, convinced that she was being followed. She was. The bellhop came to the room with her sunglasses, which she'd left at the concierge desk.

The next day she left for an hour, and the following day for two. Megumi didn't buy much—when it was "her" money to spend, she was alarmingly frugal—but she loved window shopping, an activity that bored me to tears. Every day she gained a little more confidence. One day I found her downstairs playing the nickel slots in an attempt to win a Ford Mustang. It was the first time I'd seen her gamble.

An independent Megumi would be the perfect wife. We already could be together and not intrude on each other's privacy. I wasn't asking her to dissolve her reserve; I wanted her to recognize my own. Self-sufficiency is a necessary condition of shared solitude.

I'm not much of a sports fan, but watching football in Vegas isn't a sporting event: it's communal bonding. Pecuniary interest is a force stronger than race, religion, or creed.

Caught up in the USC-Cal game, I forgot about our dinner date until it was too late. When the game went to overtime, I figured that Megumi couldn't get more upset than she would already be. I returned to our room at 8:30 p.m. She wasn't there.

She'd wanted to see David Copperfield. I'd wanted to wait until Tuesday when there were no football games on television. She hadn't left a message at the front desk. She wasn't at the slots, tables, or restaurants. At midnight I forged through the crowds on the Strip, hoping to find her eating a banana split at Baskin-Robbins or haggling with a vendor. I returned to the room at sunrise, wide-awake but trembling from exhaustion. Her clothes were folded in the dresser, her suitcase was in the closet, and her used bathrobe was thrown over the chair.

But Megumi was gone.

The police officer scrutinized me with a thinly veiled disdain reserved for panhandlers reeking of malt liquor. She capped her ballpoint pen.

"Let me get this straight, Mr. Watanabe," she said. "The missing person is a Thai national traveling with a fake Japanese passport and name. You don't have any photographs of her and don't know any of her friends or family members. You're convinced that her fiancé, or her fiancé's employee, has kidnapped her; except her fiancé isn't really her fiancé, but a corporate CEO who treats her like a possession. *You're* not her fiancé either but intend to marry her. You think."

"We can't waste any more time," I said. "She's probably out of state by now if not out of the country. Should I have gone to the FBI? Wait, they don't have international jurisdiction. It's the CIA. They have prisons in Europe, right?"

"You've had a long night, Mr. Watanabe. I think it's best you go back to your hotel and get some rest."

"Aren't you going to call a sketch artist?" I said. "Or put out an all-points bulletin? She's disappeared without a trace and you won't help me? Where's your heart?"

The officer's hair was cut short and she looked as if she could out-bench-press me, but her expression softened. "You mentioned a joint bank account. Ask the bank employees if they've seen her within the last twenty-four hours."

"It's Sunday," I said. "The bank will be closed."

"Call their twenty-four-hour customer service line. If everything's in order with your checking account, come back and I'll help you file your missing persons report." The officer frowned. "You have a place to stay tonight? Enough to eat?"

"How can you ask me that?"

Milton warned me that Kolling was a master of deception. He'd made it look like I'd been beaten in an eastern Washington bar for singing Erasure and the Culture Club. He'd sent Smith, dressed as a Mormon missionary, to sow the seed of doubt in my mind about Milton. He'd lured us into a strip club to separate me from the one person ruthless enough to protect me.

Maybe Milton hadn't murdered Chandra after all. Smith might have been waiting in a corner of the Fantasy Labyrinth. He might have disarmed Milton and stabbed Chandra. Milton couldn't return because he'd been framed. Kolling had arranged everything, I just didn't know how.

He'd forced Megumi to enter the bank shortly before it closed Saturday afternoon, where she withdrew everything except for twenty-two cents. He'd made it appear as if she'd entered alone, when I knew Smith must have been lingering in the lobby, making sure she didn't let anyone know she was acting under duress.

Megumi wouldn't have left behind her clothes, makeup, shoes, and meticulously hoarded souvenirs from our time on the road. She wouldn't have taken our money and disappeared into the desert alone, leaving me with a hotel bill that maxed out my last credit card and swallowed all but the crumbs in my Seattle checking account earmarked for interest-only payments. She loved me. She must.

CHAPTER 24

The fraulein answered the phone with a cheery "*Guten Morgen!*"

"Mr. Schwarzer is no longer associated with *Das Puppenhaus*," she said. "And we are restricted from discussing anything pertaining to him. *Das Puppenhaus* is under new management that has a renewed commitment to Bavarian excellence."

"Would it be possible to speak with Sheila?" I said.

"May I ask who's calling?"

"Tell her it's Guy. Guy Watanabe."

"Sheila left *Das Puppenhaus* two months ago to spend more time with her family," she said. "But we will honor our commitments regardless of when they were made. Would you please hold, Mr. Watanabe?" There was a rustle of paper.

It couldn't be a coincidence that Sheila quit her job when Milton went on the lam. Milton and Sheila. Megumi and I. We'd vanished together, two-by-two. We were destined to find one another again.

"Guy Watanabe?" she said. "Your Japanese kimekomi doll arrived weeks ago from the Chinese warehouse. We would have called you earlier, but the previous administration failed to collect your phone number. Let me confirm your address and we'll ship it out immediately."

My first nights with Megumi, I'd been plagued by nightmares. In them, I kissed the lipstick circles of Chandra's nipples, which spouted tepid, salty fluid. Those nightmares, redolent with rose water and mud, eventually ceased. That meant I was ready to see Milton again.

At every gas pump along the way to southern California, I inserted my debit card gingerly into the card readers as if tenderness might eke out a few more dollars. What else could I do? Have Billy pick me up? I wasn't about to invite another lecture from Gracie. Milton had disappeared into a suburban community pressed up against the San Bernardino Mountains, its resemblance to everywhere and nowhere lending it the privacy and seclusion of an Indian ashram. My "shipping address" turned out to be a tract mansion on a broad, arterial street.

The doorbell was answered by a massive Pacific Islander in an aloha shirt. Gazing down at me over his neck folds, he asked what the hell I wanted. Once I'd given him my name, he grunted his assent and used a key to lock the front door from the inside.

"Sheila's taking care of the little bugger," he said. "You're going to have to wait."

"Lopeka" led me across white tile floors into the west wing of the mansion. The building was shaped like a horse shoe with the entrance at the bottom of the U. In the center were a courtyard and swimming pool. Another Pacific Islander, ensconced in a soap opera, lounged on the couch. Lopeka poured me a Coca Cola and joined his compatriot. I took a seat at the kitchen counter.

The brushed-steel double oven and Sub-Zero refrigerator were a far cry from the modesty of Milton's cabin. Yet there were telltale signs of his presence: plastic bins of whole grains, fruits with "organic" stickers, garlic and vine-ripened tomatoes piled on the counters. Sheila joined me twenty minutes later. Her hair was cropped into a crew cut and dyed red-lavender, but the tattoo visible between the spaghetti straps of her tank-top was unmistakable.

"What are you doing here, Guy?" she said. "You got what you were looking for. You're supposed to live happily ever after."

How did Sheila know so much? Milton had disappeared before Megumi had found me.

"The last two months were the best in my life," I said. "We were going to buy a house. Then Kolling stole her away from me. He kidnapped her, Sheila."

She rubbed her nose with the heel of her palm. "What comes around, goes around, I guess." Her manner was as cool as the temperature-controlled environs of the mansion.

"I don't know what Milton said about Santa Fe." I paused. "If he hasn't told you the truth I'm not going to be the one to explain. I'm not here to judge him. I need his help to find Megumi. Milton and I still have one thing in common. Our enemy."

"Do you know he lost everything?" Sheila said. "The store. The cabin. All of it. And do you know who took over?

KGI. They rolled everything up in a few weeks. Kolling owns *Das Puppenhaus* and nobody notices the difference."

"You can't blame me for ratting him out, Sheila. I spent all night being interrogated. I bought him time to escape. If I didn't give them *something*, I'd still be in jail." She said nothing. "Christ, Sheila. A girl was murdered. She couldn't have been much older than you. One second she was raving about how exciting it was to meet her idol Milton Schwarzer. The next she was bleeding all over a stained couch."

My vehemence startled me. It was like tearing off a scab. Sheila's expression hardened.

"Milton killed her," I said. "He stabbed her to death with a freaking hunting knife. Setup or not, he nearly decapitated her. Doesn't that matter to you?"

"I didn't know her. I never met her. She could be a starving slave in Sudan for all I care." Sheila rubbed her nose. "I worry about the living, not the dead. All you had to do was run around in circles collecting souvenirs and snapshots. If you stayed out of trouble long enough, Milt could've had everything he'd dreamed about. A decade of sobriety flushed down the toilet by a stripper with a midget fetish. She deserved to suffer."

Though Sheila sounded furious, she looked miserable. She shrugged my hand away. The Pacific Islanders looked over with inquisitive, elephantine eyes. She glared until they turned back to the television.

"I didn't think you had it in you to do what you've done." Sheila wiped her tears away. "You seemed so gentle, so confused. Milton warned me. After you two pushed, he said you were kindred spirits. He meant it as a compliment, but I pitied you."

Sheila reached into her back pocket and pulled out a folded piece of paper. She spread it out on the counter and slid it toward me. It was the printout from the Web site of a Santa Fe newspaper, dated from a month ago.

Grisly Slaying in Upscale Hotel
Remains Unsolved

The lobby of the M Hotel is as swanky as ever. Built before the high-tech bubble burst, it was meant to attract a different clientele—young software tycoons—with its silver walls, purple sofas, and zebra-striped rugs. There are still remnants of that lost generation, flirting over cocktails and BlackBerry devices. They continue with their lives in a way that the employees of the M Hotel cannot: not after a maid found one of the guests stabbed to death in the penthouse suite. Since then, five members of the M Hotel's staff have resigned and others attend trauma counseling.

Little is known about the victim, John Smith, a regional vice president of a multinational karaoke corporation. Even less is known about his companion, a diminutive Asian woman in her teens or twenties. And the more facts are uncovered, the murkier the picture becomes.

Mr. Smith was found nude and horribly mutilated, his genitals having been sawed off and stuffed into his mouth. He was stabbed in the throat so violently that his spinal cord was partially severed. When the autopsy report found traces of his own semen on his severed genitals, the presumption was a crime of passion. The primary suspect was his traveling companion. Detective Ramirez saw it differently.

"My suspicions were raised by the amount of sheer physical force that would have been necessary to subdue Mr. Smith," Detective Ramirez said. "Witnesses say our Jane Doe couldn't have been taller than five feet tall or weigh more than a hundred pounds. Mr. Smith was six-foot-two, around 220 pounds, well-muscled and fit. Could she have done it while he was sleeping? Even then his reflexive reactions should have created evidence of a struggle and there was none."

Detective Ramirez dug deeper. There was no murder weapon. There were traces of Mr. Smith's blood in the bathroom tub, but no other physical evidence. Jane Doe's clothes and luggage were left behind. Only she was missing. A crime of passion or the vengeance of a jealous paramour? A murder and an abduction? Detective Ramirez won't rule out plausible scenarios but is disturbed by Internet rumors.

Bloggers have linked the grisly murder to one that occurred in the Santa Fe strip club Jugs only days before. They've posted leaked crime scene photographs for comparison. The primary suspect in the Jugs murder is Milton Schwarzer, a performer in the adult entertainment industry who has long been connected with organized crime. Detective Ramirez isn't, however, crediting the blogosphere rants.

"The first victim was an adult entertainer killed by an adult entertainer in a strip club," he said. "The second victim was a karaoke executive killed by an unknown assailant in a four-star hotel. We in Santa Fe aren't accustomed to this level of violent crime, which allows imaginations to run wild. I would just like to assure our community that we are doing everything in our power to bring these criminals to justice, and any well-founded leads are appreciated."

Sheila was watching for my reaction. I reread the article. Smith was dead? I'd be lying if I said I hadn't fantasized about killing him for sterilizing Megumi and brutalizing me. He was corporate swine and deserved to die like a pig. But there was a yawning chasm between desire and action, fantasy and reality.

"Would you like to see the photographs?" Sheila said. "Bruce has a color printer here."

"No," I said. No more crime scene photographs. Even the fading memory was too much.

"What do you have to say for yourself?" she said.

I stared at the article, no longer reading the words but reliving Smith's last moments. Smith was Kolling's confidante, his hired gun; it was Smith's job to punish others for what the circumstances suggested he'd done. Megumi should have been traveling with Kolling, not Smith. There was no reason for her to share Smith's hotel room. Yes, her hair had been damp when she arrived at the door of my motel room, but that didn't mean anything more than that she'd recently showered. She showered twice a day. I'd presumed her long silences were due to her nature, or her traumatic childhood. The only violence she'd ever shown was when we made love. She scratched my back with her fingernails; once, she broke the skin on my neck with her teeth. She was pleased when I cried out. But rough sex was a far cry from castrating a man. Megumi couldn't have overpowered Smith. Ennui shouldn't be mistaken for cruelty. There was only one explanation.

"I don't know how Milton was able to sneak up on Smith," I said. "But I owe him a debt of gratitude. He had the fortitude to do what I'd only dreamt of. He freed Megumi. He made it possible for her to come to me. And now he has to help me find her again. We can't let our enemy win."

Sheila glared. "Milton didn't kill Smith. He was already in Nevada when it happened, being hidden by one of Bruce's friends, a member of the 'family.' If he *had* killed Smith, he would have been proud. He would have taken that little Asian bitch as a hostage. No, Guy Watanabe, only one person had the motive, opportunity, and ability to kill Smith. That was you."

I scoffed. It was a nervous reflex. "I killed Smith? *I* killed Smith. Oh yeah, sure. Megumi watched while I stabbed him to death, laughed as I fed him his own genitals. We had sex in the bathtub while he lay dying on the bed."

Sheila hit me. She swung and struck me on the sternum, and only her teetering perch on the stool kept the blow from landing with more force. "What the fuck is wrong with you? You've become just like him."

She hit me again and again until I grabbed her wrists and wrenched them down. Her bird bones flexed; she crumpled to the ground. I would have let her go, but she tried to bite me. Lopeka put me in a headlock. I couldn't breathe, my body enveloped in his prodigious belly. Sheila remained in a heap on the tiled floor, slapping away the other Polynesian's hand when he tried to help her. She kicked at Lopeka until he released me. The two large men shrugged and returned to their television soap opera.

"Milt's been hacking and puking and peeing on himself," she said. "The only thing that raised his spirits was hearing that you'd killed Smith in a way that he deserved."

Bruce Zatz was Milton's childhood friend, the director of Milton's adult films before and after Luba. He owned the middle-class mansion along with several others just like it that he used as the sets for his expansive pornography catalog. Most of the porn industry worked in the San Fernando Valley. Bruce had made a killing on real estate speculation in the nearby, cheaper Inland Empire and passed his savings on to the consumer.

Sheila had acted in Bruce's "gonzo" videos. When her drug habit got the better of her, he gave her an ultimatum: either dry out with Milton or lose her job. It was no coincidence that Sheila, properly made-up and attired, bore a striking resemblance to Luba. Maybe that's why she'd shaved her head for her new role as Milton's nurse and attendant.

Sheila spent twelve hours a day changing his bed pan, giving him sponge baths, and preparing the few meals he could keep down—whole grain cereals and pureed fruit. Milton was the one dying of AIDS, but he and Sheila were both wasting away. She took no breaks. She slept on a chair in his room.

By order of Bruce Zatz, pornography kingpin, I was a prisoner in suburbia, with oversized, overly relaxed Pacific Islanders as my jailers. He transmitted his messages to me through e-mails to Sheila. I was allowed run of the house, use of the pool and the actors' wardrobes left in the closets, but not the freedom to come and go. He didn't want me to finger Milton for Chandra's murder, or him for harboring a fugitive. I could gain my release by helping him with "a few things" that he would explain in person, but he set no firm date for a meeting.

Milton was too weak to see me the first day. I saw him the following morning. He was a monkey paw of his former self. His face was speckled with purple boils. One of his eyes was bloodshot and yellowing. Sheila had recently bathed him, but I could discern the sweet stench of excrement over the disinfectants.

Sheila had stopped hiding the truth and I pieced the rest together. Milton had never meant for me to find Megumi. He and I were supposed to lose ourselves in the desert until he could negotiate a way to purchase KGI's majority interest in *Das Puppenhaus*. But Milton had underestimated Kolling's ability to take what he wanted without giving anything up. Tanya hadn't been feeding Kolling information. Milton had betrayed me.

Here lay dying a man who'd been willing to sell me to Kolling for his own pecuniary advantage. An unremorseful murderer. He'd never been on anyone's side but his own. His suffering should have gratified me. Instead I pitied this gnarled, truncated man. The scar, usually his most prominent feature, blended into the wrinkles on his neck.

"Get out of here," he said to Sheila. "I've got business to discuss with Watanabe."

Sheila grimaced but, after making sure his water glass was filled, did as she was told. It was ten minutes before Milton spoke again. The subject matter had nothing to do with business. At least, it had nothing to do with *our* business together.

CHAPTER 25
MILTON'S LAMENTATION

Luba never bled. There were no tampons to flush, no pills to pick up, no rubbers to wear, no days to count. Bruce and I took it for what it was in our industry: a blessing. I never asked how she'd become barren. Secrets define us. Take them away and all we have left is what we've become.

Mainstream smut peddlers worshipped at the altar of Holmes and Seka, everything bigger and blonder. There was never a sexual "revolution," just a Reformation that flooded the world with saccharine, Playboy fantasies. The freaks—the midgets, the obese, the amputees, and the ugly—remained underground. Luba had the figure of a twelve-year-old boy and brittle hair dyed a tarry black. Her collapsed nasal septum left behind pinprick, monkey nostrils. One eyelid drooped lower than the other. We hadn't hired her for her beauty.

Luba's trademark was her nipples: symmetrical disks as large and thick as a man's clenched fists, the color of bruised cranberries. Those blind eyes protruded—bulbous, smooth, and waxy—from her flat chest. Kneaded between my fingers, gnawed between my teeth, those fleshy knobs were as dense as twine. Her secret, our secret, was that the presence of her nipples was really the absence of them. Criss-crossed with fine lines, her teats were fused masses of scar tissue.

A compass and scalpel couldn't have traced more perfect circles. I never asked how she got them. She never volunteered the information.

I once worked for the city public utilities company. Twice a week I started my rounds early and finished by mid-afternoon. On those days, I visited Simone's apartment, the first customer of her long night. She would answer the door looking like the washed-up whore she was, wearing an oversized T-shirt and no makeup, rubbing sleep from her eyes. This day was different.

Simone wore a satin teddy that revealed the gelatin of her generous ass. Her room—usually littered with unwashed laundry, saturated with the scent of cheap incense—was spotless. She moaned and pleaded while we fucked. That's what tipped me off. Simone rarely spoke and when she did nothing "nice" dribbled from her sore-infested lips. She didn't hide her disdain—that's why I returned. Nothing is more demeaning for a dwarf than being patronized like a child or a retard. Simone's cunt was as wide and watery as the truth. We didn't pretend to like each another. I paid and she performed.

I heard a rustling in the closet. I pushed Simone away and tore the sliding door off of its runners. Standing inside, between a shoe rack and a laundry basket, was a balding man in a dress-shirt and a paisley tie. Slacks bunched around his ankles, he gripped his friction-chafed pencil lead. I punched him until his face collapsed inward like a pulpy anus. I stopped kicking him only because Simone, that dirty mercenary bitch, offered me the money she'd been paid for the show.

It wasn't until I cooled off that I counted the money. The downtown desk jockey had paid $700 to watch me screw Simone. How many more of his type were out there? One in a hundred? One in a thousand? How much would they pay to satisfy their cravings? Weeks later I took out a second mortgage on my townhouse and, with Bruce, founded an adult film studio. If there were suckers willing to pay to watch a circus freak fornicate, I would be my own ringmaster.

It made sense for Luba to move in. She'd become a fixture in our ten-minute loop films and giving her room and board was a way to cut expenses. If she missed a bus or showed up high, the film crew, makeup artist, and janitor still had to be paid. For months, Luba and I were house-mates, sleeping in separate rooms, screwing if we were awake at the same time and there was nothing better to do. Then one night she didn't leave my room.

We started on the living room sofa; we ended up tangled on my bed. Afterward, I lay there watching through the open restroom door as she peed. She hunched over the toilet like an animal, one eye smaller than the other. After she'd wiped and flushed, she should have slunk back to her room. Instead she crawled under the sheets and pulled my head to her mangled breasts.

It was disgustingly maternal. The scent of her sex had turned marshy. I would have pushed her away if I hadn't become so damned tired, my strength ebbing while she stroked my hair. Her scarred aureoles blurred my vision.

"There are times," she whispered, "that if I close my eyes, I almost forget you're a midget."

Our loops had a simple formula. I played a leprechaun, or a genie, or a troll who forced women to trade sex for their release. I dressed in asinine costumes while the girls said, "Oh my, what big cock you have!" "Little people" activists said I portrayed a demeaning stereotype. Worse would be not to profit from those fantasies.

Some adult shops stocked two copies of our short films, ran them simultaneously in the peep show booths. Theaters in Chicago and Washington, DC, screened our loops before their main features. Bruce and I made a name for ourselves in the business, but that reputation wasn't translating into profits. Most Americans saw midget porn as a half-step away from bestiality.

We slashed production costs. We used a single warehouse set by rearranging the pillows, sofas, and drapes.

Bruce forgot to deposit a check and our utilities were shut off; it took twice what we owed to get them turned on again. We hired streetwalkers and coke whores as talent. In the end, we didn't hire anyone but Luba. She wore a different wig for each shoot. Luba had simple needs. She slept twelve to fifteen hours a day. She moved soundlessly around the house in her underwear, eating cereal for every meal. She never called family and had no friends. Her only hobby was playing with her dollhouse.

When Luba moved in, her sole possession, aside from a trash bag filled with clothes, was a Victorian dollhouse. If I'd known anything about miniatures at the time, I would have wondered how she had disassembled, moved, and reassembled the elaborate structure while sleeping in shelters and abandoned buildings. With a patient hand, she repaired blemishes to the faux-brick façade, the shingle roof, and the front steps. Dollhouses struck me as the pastime of spoiled girls whose parents could afford a room dedicated to toys. Yet any money that didn't go up Luba's nose wound up in miniature wing-backed sofas, four-poster beds, baby grand pianos, fireplace tools, and lamps. She spent days poring over catalogues. Once her package arrived, she would disappear for an entire afternoon into her fantasy world.

My first gift to her was a porcelain doll with black hair, pudgy cheeks, and a dress with petticoats. It cost a hundred bucks, and she looked more startled than grateful to receive it. She displayed it in a mirrored, glass box in our entryway. When I asked why she didn't put it in her dollhouse, she said, "It deserves a special place."

I didn't challenge her lie. No matter how much she said she liked the doll, she never put it in with her precious things. The doll's glassy-eyed perfection became a hateful sight.

"That's the Milton Schwarzer I know and love." Bruce slapped his sweaty palm on mine. We'd picked up a black girl on the Sunset Strip to double up. She was lying in a stupor between us. She hadn't made a sound throughout and didn't make a sound now. "I was starting to think that Luba locked up your cock in a little pine box."

Bruce kneaded the girl's quivering haunch. "In the old days you'd pop three times during the day and three times at night. You're Milt the fucking Stilt, man! What's happened to you?"

"Why should I pay for what I get paid for doing?" I said. "If you took care of our finances, we'd be back in the straight world within a month. I mean to stay my own boss."

Bruce held up his hands. "Don't be so serious. I'm just saying I miss the old Milt. Luba's making us good money, but don't forget our priorities. You and me, buddy, friends forever. The dynamic duo. None of this ménage-a-trois shit."

The hooker was breathing in spasmodic hiccups. Her hair was matted and she emitted a god-awful stench.

"Luba's nothing but meat," I said.

Our receptionist had Crohn's disease, which meant she couldn't shit without telling us about it and blamed everyone else for her pain. That's why her greeting me with a smile was suspicious. The shoot had been called off and Bruce wanted to see me in our office. He and Luba were there, drinking champagne, two empty bottles at their feet. She was on the couch while he wriggled in front of her, acting out one of his exaggerated stories.

"Never call off a shoot without my approval," I said.

Bruce saluted me with an open palm. "*Heil*, Milton," he said. Luba giggled. She was a junkie who couldn't hold her liquor. "But please allow this Jew to share the Good News from another very important Jew. Sidney Rosen called this morning. He's going to fund us. Not just our first picture, but the entire trilogy: three fucking feature-length films. We're going legit, my friend. You and Luba are going to be stars."

CHAPTER 26
MILTON`S LAMENTATION (continued)

Milton wouldn't allow Sheila to feed him a slice of grapefruit; he turned away and spit it out on the bed sheet. She blamed me for tiring him out. She wouldn't let me see him again until he demanded it, late the following evening. His eyes were moist and glassy. Within hours he'd aged weeks. He began speaking before I was seated.

Bruce and I had spent years trying to get investors to fund a feature-length film. No one would touch us. "Too disturbing," they said. "Too dark." Bullshit. The Billie Jack movies glorified gang rape. Charles Bronson bankrolled a career on retaliation. Investors steered clear because of me. No one wanted a midget to play the hero instead of the fool. No one except for Sidney Rosen.

Sidney Rosen wasn't one of us. He was born into the daylight world of business, politics, and philanthropy. His family dominated the market in refrigerator parts, appliance patents, and other things that are everywhere but never seen. He endowed chairs at universities, served on the board of the United Way, cared for a sister with Down Syndrome; he'd done everything right and good in the world except marry. He began funding pornography at the age of seventy, when his new hobby could be called, according to him, "an eccentricity instead of a perversion."

Rosen knew our movies better than I did. He spouted lines we'd never scripted and didn't remember. He owned reels that we'd lost after our storeroom was flooded. We hadn't sent him my script. He heard about it through somebody then got a carbon copy from Jaime Menendez, a strip-club owner in New Jersey who'd never bothered to call us back. Rosen promised us everything: three 16mm film cameras, a union crew, on-location shoots, extra talent.

Rosen didn't believe in half-ass measures. He meant to have the same impact on pornography that he'd had in business and society. His goal was to rid the world of glamour pornography, "that invidious, superficial, and dishonest varnishing of human sexuality; adolescence stripped of its life fluids, rinsed and spun-dry until it's a confection." Rosen hated lens filters and soft lighting. He wanted to see every pimple, scab, and scar.

"You realize, Milton, well, of course you do," Rosen said, "no man would trade places with you. No matter how many women you lay, no matter how much money you make, you're like a donkey in a Tijuana bar: the attraction but not the star. Viewers are fascinated by your deformity. Astounded by the girl's degradation. One feels depraved watching you copulate. That's the effect pornography should have."

The four of us—Rosen, Bruce, Luba, and I—sat in Rosen's drawing room. At street level his mansion looked like a sprawling, one-story home behind a gate. In reality it was six floors that cascaded down the hillside like a waterfall of wood and glass.

Bruce clenched his hands, worried that Rosen might have pissed me off by speaking his mind. But I hadn't entered the business to make friends. I was in it to be my own boss, to get paid for sex instead of paying for it. It's best to take money from those you hate.

"I want complete creative control," I said. "Not a scene cut, no changes to the story or the ending. I want to hand-pick every cast member."

Rosen was a dried-up old man with a back as curved as a fetus. "I'm not about to meddle in matters of your expertise. I have but one condition. I have a particular fondness for Miss Luba." He nodded at her. "I am funding you as a pair. She must be the heroine."

Luba looked up from the floor. She'd been silent while we toured the mansion. She was awkward around strangers and fancy furniture made her nervous. When Rosen tried to talk to her, she looked to me to answer.

I'd written the trilogy long before I met Luba. She didn't fit the role of a buxom biker babe whose flowing platinum hair would trail behind as she rode pillion on my motor-cycle. My costar needed to be hungry for sex and punish-ment: she would be beaten and humiliated in every scene. If she didn't suffer, what would be the use of saving her? Luba's meekness was fine for ten-minute loop films, but on the big screen it would come across as reluctance or, worse, endurance. With our increased income, she could go to beauty school for a certificate and work as the makeup artist.

"I'm afraid this is a non-negotiable point." Rosen's face was stern. "I will not consider anyone else in the starring role."

"We agree," Bruce said. "Are you kidding me, Mr. Rosen? Of course Luba will be the star. Milt just thought that with a bigger budget he might get a little more variety in his sexual partners. He wanted Seka, not Luba. Heh, heh, heh. Right, Milt? We're all professionals here."

Luba waited for me to answer. She'd never read the scripts. She didn't know what the part would take out of her.

"It's a deal," I said.

In pornography, sex is a job. No more physical than building houses, no more demeaning than cleaning toilets. Luba got paid a lot of money. On the street, she gave blow-jobs in portable toilet stalls for $20 a pop. With us, she had a trailer, wardrobe, and regular schedule. If you discounted my ownership interest, she was being paid 60 percent more. Don't believe that crap about exploitation. In porn, women get more pay for less work.

If I couldn't get it up, the entire shoot came to a stand-still. Bruce groused about the shifting angle of the sun, the extras muttered about lunch. A man can't fake the "money shot," and without the climax, we had nothing. Luba? Whether she felt pleasure, pain, or nothing, all she needed was a tube of lubricant and no one would be the wiser. The raunchier the scene, the more she was paid. She should have thanked me for the group scenes. They paid four times what a solo scene would have.

Luba was spoiled. We'd shot scenes one-on-one because we couldn't afford anything else. Rosen's infusion of cash paid big, but it was never enough for Luba. No matter the temperature, on the day of a gangbang her body was covered with goose bumps. Spread-eagled on the floor, her arms and legs bound by rope, she sought out my eyes, as if she expected me to end the scene early, pull her away from them, cradle her head against my chest. She was a professional and needed to act like one. This was make-believe rape, as fake as the dollhouse that she outfitted with the money she earned. Every movie, I hunted down and killed her tormentors. In the final scene, Luba and I screwed next to their corpses, the corn-syrup of their stage-blood filming our skin. As I thrust into her, she sobbed uncontrollably.

"I thought you'd never arrive," Luba said.

"Here I am," I said.

Rosen loved the "realism" of our films. He poured money into marketing that he never made back. Our second feature became the first midget skin flick to headline at a New York adult theater. We became an underground sensation, universally respected among the powers-that-be in the adult film world. At parties, producers, directors, and talent would ask me where my "other half" was. No one understood that it was acting, all acting.

Luba hardly left our townhouse. A local high-school kid delivered her stash to the back door. She shot up and played with her dollhouse. I came home to find her staring glassy-eyed into its tiny windows.

I was in prison once, a three-month sentence for a petty drug offense. What I learned is this. Don't fear the muscle-bound faggots who spend all day pumping iron. They work and pose all day. When the lights go out, they sleep like babies. Watch out for the wash-outs who hang around the edge of the exercise yard, alone or in pairs, mumbling to each another. Those are the ones who'll slip an awl into your ribcage.

So it is in the industry. No performer brings home chains, cock rings, and anal beads. If you fuck on asphalt, in the back of vans, or on top of tables, you want to screw on a real bed, like a married couple, when you go home. There are perverts behind the camera who, like Bruce, return home to apartments wallpapered with imported porn. They're our audience; they blow their wads and are satisfied. The sick fucks hover in the background, clutching at the purse strings.

Yeah, I'm talking about Rosen.

I dropped Luba off at Rosen's mansion on Tuesday nights and picked her up on Wednesday mornings. She came back without scrapes, cuts, or marks. She didn't look any different, but something happened during those sixteen hours that changed her. For days after spending time with Rosen, Luba wouldn't leave my side. Not when I ate, slept, or pissed. She sobbed when I left the house without her. When I stood, she looked startled, following me with her eyes. It was oppressive.

"She looks fine to me," Bruce said. "Do you really think Rosen would do anything to hurt our profits? Come on, Milt. She's got you by the balls."

The more she clung to me, the more she drove me away. Rosen paraded me around like a two-headed geek at his parties. He jabbered about what he wanted to see in our next picture. He showed up on set and criticized the scenes while we filmed them. I licked his bunghole without complaining. All I asked of Luba was for her to do the same.

A week before it happened, I convinced Luba to leave the house for once. We walked to Baskin-Robbins right before closing time, shared a banana split, and walked home. We stopped at a bench overlooking the freeway, watching the river of headlights thin into a trickle of glittering points. Luba slouched down, resting her head on mine.

"Milton?" She rubbed at her pinhole nostrils with her palm. "I spoke to God again."

For weeks, she'd been seeing God everywhere: in light bulbs, dish rags, the garbage disposal. She wasn't just spitting out what she heard from a televangelist. She was seeing the actual face of God but lacked the words to describe Him. He never had a message for her. He just listened.

"What did you tell Him?" I said.

"I said I was tired." She closed her eyes and squeezed my arm. "I'm so tired."

The telephone call didn't come from Rosen. It was one of his servants, the same one who met me at the back door. She hadn't been moved. She was curled up on the tiled floor of a cavernous restroom. There was green residue beneath her nostrils and around her mouth. The cabinet doors were open and empty cans were scattered everywhere.

They wouldn't allow me to use the house phone. I drove her to the emergency room. I slept in the waiting room. A nurse brought me to her mid-morning. They'd wiped her face and washed her hair. Eyes closed, she looked like a resting child. When she woke up, that same innocence was in her blank eyes.

She couldn't speak. She understood general things, like how to motion for water, food, and her bedpan, but long sentences got her worked up. She stared at me bluntly, her features softening. A monitor showed her heart rate. If I stroked her hair, her heart rate went down. If I continued my attentions, she fell into a stupor.

Bruce didn't come to the hospital. He hated being around sick people. His first question was, "Does that mean she can't work?" His second question was, "Rosen's not pissed off, is he?" Bruce was the one who found Luba's parents. Luba was the first and last porn star to use her real name. Her parents were nobodies: they wore dull expressions and clothing in shades of beige. They hadn't seen her since she was sixteen years old and weren't happy with the reunion under these circumstances.

"It's better this way," Bruce said. "You're Milt the fucking Stilt, not a retard's nursemaid. I feel bad for her, but let's face it, man. The girl screwed up. Thank God she failed at ending her life the way she failed at living it. Rosen never would have continued funding us if she'd been found dead in his house. Let someone else take care of her. Our lives go on. She's meat, remember? Nothing but meat."

I wonder sometimes if it wasn't her father who'd burned those blind eyes onto her breasts. He didn't look the part with his parted hair and wool trousers, but looks are deceiving. Evildoers don't have brands or tattoos. Only in books and movies can you tell the bad people from the good.

Would he torture her again now that she couldn't fight back? Would she turn him on less because all she did was drool? I don't know. Just like I don't know how she really got her scars. They might have been self-inflicted.

Her parents didn't return my calls and never came for the dollhouse. Sometimes, late at night, I sat in front of that Victorian mansion. I opened its doors and windows. I searched the tiny trunks, credenzas, and medicine cabinets for an answer. But everything was empty.

Only through blind luck did I discover why Luba had never displayed the expensive porcelain doll I'd given to her inside of the dollhouse. I threw the doll's display case against the wall. It shattered into mirrored fragments, but the doll escaped without a scratch. I carried it to the doll-house, intending to drown it in the claw-foot tub.

It didn't fit.

When I bought the doll, I'd violated the first rule of miniature collectibles: scale. The doll's hips were too wide for the chairs; its head scraped the ceilings. In its surroundings, it was freakish and absurd. Just like Luba. Just like me.

CHAPTER 27

What is it about frailty that evokes pity? Milton deserved to die the way Chandra had: alone inside a mirrored cell, his suffering reflected back on him infinitely. Milton's hand was clasped between mine when he died. It was warm. Then it was cold. That was all. A person goes from flesh to meat within a second.

Sheila poured his ashes into a hole between two ice plants yards away from the swimming pool. Lopeka and I, along with the Polynesian brother whose name I couldn't pronounce, watched through the sliding glass doors as she tamped down the earth with a trowel. None of us thought to join her until it was too late.

Time passed in a climate-controlled blur. The Polynesians watched television nonstop. I joined them for football games and SportsCenter. Sheila acted as if neither she nor we existed. She scooped whatever we ordered—Chinese take-out or pizza—onto a paper plate and returned to her room without even nodding an acknowledgement.

One afternoon the garage door rumbled open and Bruce's two soccer-uniform-clad daughters tumbled into the living room. The girls commandeered the television remote control, shrieking and slapping in a way that made a vasectomy sound appealing. Bruce was rotund but not obese, tall but not unusually so. He wore an expression that befitted an older man with young children. Weary.

"We've got some business to discuss, Mr. Watanabe," he said.

The bookshelves in Bruce's office were filled with classics—*Ulysses, Moby Dick, The Canterbury Tales*—all bound in leather with the same metallic foil lettering. Noticing my pursed lips, Bruce bragged about his "Great Books" monthly subscription. He planned on reading the entire western canon once he retired. What kind of man begins reading at the end of his life books he's sure not to comprehend? An ambitious one, I suppose; a man who approaches reading as achievement rather than as pleasure. A man who wouldn't spare the time to visit until his friend's ashes had been buried in a six-inch cat hole.

Lopeka stood at my elbow, close enough to cast a shadow. One false move and I'd be mashed into poi. Bruce rubbed his eyes. "When you were seven years old, did your parents throw you a party with a clown, an inflatable moonwalk, and catered food? If I got a Whopper and a cardboard crown, I was happy. What about you?"

"My birthday's near Christmas," I said. "I got a combined birthday-Christmas gift purchased with the spare change left over after buying gifts for everyone else."

"There you go," he said. "And you're not any worse off because of it. Poor people don't have to worry about what to buy for their kids. Their kids are content with rocks, sticks, and tin cans. My daughters are the reason I keep my nose to the grindstone. I don't want them to have to suffer the way I did."

I didn't respond. He sounded like attorneys at the firm, moaning that their sixteen-year-old daughters had flipped their Audi A6 sedans. Colored kids were safe at school, protected by metal detectors, on-campus officers, and full-body frisks while privileged white kids might be gunned down any minute by disaffected Goths.

"I respect what you did to Smith," Bruce said. "If someone raped one of my daughters, I'd do the same thing: cut off the bastard's pecker and force it down his throat. That was ballsy as hell, and I don't mean that as a pun. It's just the thing that Miltie would have done. Milt the Stilt, not the born-again German vegetarian cyclist pansy who took his place. You're not a vegetarian, are you?"

"I eat meat," I said. "But I'm no killer."

"Of course not," Bruce said. "You never came within a hundred miles of John Smith. I never harbored a fugitive. We've never had the conversation we're having right now. Let me tell you something, Mr. Watanabe. A man without secrets can't be trusted. If I didn't have something to hold over your head, I would have to find another way to ensure your silence."

I was too unschooled in the subtleties of mafia-speak to understand the full import of his statement. Was Bruce expressing the camaraderie of one criminal to another? Or was he telling me I had a choice between being guilty and trusted or innocent and dead? The expression on Lopeka's face provided no clues. He appeared to be contemplating the episode of *Days of Our Lives* he was missing.

"What was masterful about castrating Kolling's hench-man," Bruce said, "was that it was a form of communication. Terror is the weapon of the weak, but no one should under-estimate its force. Nothing is more fearsome than a man who has nothing to lose. I fret about private school tuition, the housing bubble, whether I've invested too aggressively. You've got no wife, no children, few friends. Your death will be commemorated by banks writing off their losses. You're more free than any man I know."

I glanced down at my hands, which had become chapped from the air-conditioned clime. I'd disappeared for months and no one had noticed. If this was freedom, maybe I was better off enslaved. I'd fantasized about living with Megumi in a beach-side hut, but maybe we should have purchased a house we couldn't afford. I could have returned to a job I despised not because I wanted to, but because I *had* too. Responsibility is the glue that binds two people to one shared solitude. Kolling had snatched Megumi away along with my meager dreams.

"That bastard Kolling," I said. "If it had been him instead of Smith in that hotel room, more would have been missing than his nuts."

Bruce combed his fingers through his varnished hair. "That's the spirit, Watanabe. If you'd killed Kolling instead of Smith, what would you have done?"

It seemed forever had passed since I'd seen Kolling sit-ting in the back booth of the Lily Pad, his arm draped over Megumi's shoulders. All I remembered were his too-full lips. Jimmy had announced me as the Karaoke King, and he'd sneered.

"I would have cut the smirk right off his face," I said. "Without lips, he'd have a permanent grin."

"That's fucking awesome." Bruce raised his palm and I slapped it. "After you stuffed his dick into his mouth, you could have put his lips on his crotch and said, 'Who's the bitch now, Kolling!' I fucking love it. That's just the sort of think Milt the Stilt would have thought up. Back in the day, we would have filmed that shit, the FCC be damned."

I felt exhilarated and disgusted. It wasn't good or right to picture myself grinning over Kolling's mutilated body, his mouth and genitals exchanged. But it was thrilling.

"Let me ask you something, Watanabe," Bruce said, wiping tears of mirth from his eyes. "If you got another shot at Kolling, if you could steal back his girl and give him what he had coming all along, would you do it? You know he fucking deserves it for what he did to you and Miltie. Would you *carpe diem*? Or in this case, *carpe testes*."

"Are you kidding me?" I said. "I'd jump at the chance."

"You sure now? You're not just beating your chest because he's not here? You could do it again? One up what you did to Smith?"

I thought of Megumi in Vegas on the night we'd won the $140,000 dollars. I pictured her perfect nipples pressing against the sheer material of her dress. I recalled the envy in the eyes of the other men. She'd been mine once.

"Fuck, yeah," I said. "Hand me the fucking knife!"

Bruce looked at Lopeka and nodded. The big man scratched at his groin; no, he reached into his pocket for something.

"Then have I got a fucking deal for you," Bruce said. "All you've got to do is give up who you are for who you're meant to be."

Bruce drove off in his Escalade with his daughters, who left behind a trail of broken picture frames and candy wrappers. Sheila took care of the details: passports, identity documents, plane tickets, travelers' checks, and credit cards.

Guy Watanabe or *Balthazar Salgado*: what difference did it make what I was called? At least now people wouldn't ask if I was Filipino; they'd presume it. Bruce hoarded identities the way he hoarded literary classics, knowing that one day he would have use for them. Balthazar Salgado was the grip on an adult production who'd suffered a stroke and fallen into the pool during an outdoor orgy scene. No one thought to disentangle him until after the fusillade of money shots. Bruce kept the decedent on his payroll because American travel documents always come in handy. His film company was making inroads into the eastern European talent market.

The only deceased Asian girl Bruce had under contract was named "Jade Sin." Bruce's friends would doctor the passport and related documents once we took a clear photograph of Megumi. Bruce promised us new lives anywhere outside of the United States and an income equal to one and a half times my highest salary at the firm. All I had to do was fly to Shanghai, China, and steal Megumi from Kolling.

"Milt would have wanted him dead," Bruce said. "But I think we can honor his memory without you winding up as shark chum. You get away with the girl and Kolling will get the message: he's not invulnerable. Besides, power vacuums, in politics and karaoke, are dangerous. Knock off one karaoke king, and who knows what kind of despot rises to take his place. Stability at any cost is always better for business."

I told Bruce that my taped confession to the murder of John Smith wouldn't hold up in court. Look at what happened to Jon Benet's confessed killer. Bruce shrugged. "Insurance," he said. "It's as good as destroyed so long as you stay on the right side of the line. We've got the same enemy, which means we're friends."

"You're such a fucking idiot," Sheila said over a Cherry Garcia sundae. A benefit of entering Bruce's employ was that I was no longer under house arrest. I'd lured Sheila out of her hermitage by promising all-you-can-eat ice cream at Ben & Jerry's. "Don't you realize there's no such thing as a free lunch? I thought I'd be out of the business in a year. But here I am, wading deeper and deeper into shit."

"How did Milton get that scar on his neck?" I said. She'd said never to ask Milton but had never volunteered an explanation. "The one that looks like teeth marks."

Sheila stabbed at her sundae with a plastic spoon. "You know what, Guy? Oh, excuse me, *Balthazar*. The wounds you can see are never the ones that matter." She stared into the melting ice cream. "If I were you, I'd be wondering what you're supposed to do if it turns out that what's-her-name ripped you off and ran away."

Did Sheila think I hadn't been turning that question over in my mind every night since Megumi had left me? It didn't matter whether Kolling had snatched her or if she'd run away. The bottom line was that I hadn't been able to protect her. If she knew that, she *should* have taken the money and run. That was the old Guy. I wouldn't make the same mistake again.

More troubling was John Smith's fate…but that too had an explanation. Megumi might have drugged him. She might have waited until he was asleep. Didn't her actions qualify as a reaction to post-traumatic stress? I don't see how what she did was distinguishable from an abused wife setting her husband's bed on fire.

"I love her, Sheila," I said. "And she loves me. Don't make that face just because you don't know what the word means. I take responsibility for my shortcomings. If I fail her again, she can take her new American identity and leave with my blessing. That's how much I care about her. She needs my help. I'm not about to just cut and run."

We finished our sundaes in silence. She shivered while she perspired and her eyes were glassy. It didn't take a forensic investigator to see she was using junk again.

Bruce had told me that killing Kolling wasn't necessary, but he'd also mentioned that my guide in Shanghai could supply me with whatever "accoutrements," legal or otherwise, I might need to complete my mission. The more important question was whether I had the guts to take a pound of Kolling's flesh for all the pain he'd caused me.

"You know what your problem is?" Sheila said as we clambered into my car. "You're traveling halfway around the world for nothing. Wherever you go, there you are."

CHAPTER 28

Does comfort equal enervation? Skylight sunlight, recircu-
lated air, HDTV, and on-demand video—the mansion was
a human terrarium transforming me into a household reptile like Sheila, like the Polynesians. I drove off alone into
Springsteen's America—a full tank of gas and the window
down, ribbons of asphalt leading to the promise of a better
life—but strained to hear the song of the open road. America was once a location; now it's a socio-economic condition.
Megumi and I would live like royalty in a Third World country. Americans at home and abroad watch the same satellite
television channels, purchase the same name-brand clothing, dine at the same fast-food restaurants. There would be
nothing to miss.

Fuck Sheila. I wasn't Bruce's "bitch." I was using him
to achieve my own personal goals. His people had staked
out Megumi's condominium and knew her daily schedule.
I could save Megumi, strike back at Kolling, and start a new
life in one fell swoop. Sheila doubted me because she sub-
consciously wanted me to fail the way she had. As Troy said,

"Never take advice from people who've been drinking the Haterade of mediocrity."

I passed an abandoned gas station and a closed gun shop, drove until I somehow exceeded the boundaries of the suburbs. I turned around in the pitted parking lot of what I took to be an International House of Pancakes in disrepair, its signature blue roof bowed and in need of a pressure wash. It was surrounded by an encampment of pickup trucks and textured plastic teepees that stretched into a field of knee-high grass, glowering in the moonlight like post-apocalyptic ruins.

I squinted at the red neon sign: "Choi's Club: Karaoke/ Friends/Pool." Why not? Balthazar Salgado would have countless opportunities to sing overseas, but this would be Guy Watanabe's farewell performance.

The other patrons, leaning over the billiards felt or chalking cues, watched me as I waited in front of the "Please Wait to be Seated" sign. If I hadn't known better, I would have thought I'd entered a Tijuana bar, except there were no drunk high school kids around, just sun-scorched men who looked as if they'd trudged in from the strawberry fields.

"That sign's just for show," she said. "Sit anywhere you like." She was past me, two pitchers clutched in each hand, before I could respond. Her voice was smoky and lightly accented. Ms. Choi, I presumed. Her short, muscular legs and long torso marked her origins as surely as if she had been draped in a South Korean flag. Korean women are an acquired taste, packing in five-foot frames an expanse of stomach proportionate to six-foot Danish supermodels. Ms. Choi moved with rapid steps, the tight denim skirt shortening her stride like a kimono.

Choi's Club did not employ state-of-the-art audio-visual equipment. A projector beamed a washed-out picture onto a portable movie screen. The song was Wham's "Careless Whisper," but the video showed Korean men dressed in circus colors and headbands banging drums while women in similarly garish dress danced with their arms outstretched, flicking handkerchiefs up and down. The picture shook as if it had been taken with a handheld camcorder.

The singer's voice, despite his Fernando Lamas accent, wasn't half-bad, but the musical accompaniment was putrid—synthesized music that sounded as if it had been regurgitated by a Fisher-Price keyboard. The pool tables were packed but the karaoke section, which included booths, tables, and a dance floor, was deserted. Had Ms. Choi downloaded computerized MIDI files for free? Here was a living illustration of why independent karaoke establishments would survive only in the hinterlands of Horatio Kolling's brave new world.

A man sat alone at the far end of the bar, near the emergency exit. Empty shot glasses stood like abandoned chess pieces on the counter before him. Most drunks hunch over or cradle their heads in their folded arms. This one hinged forward at his waist with a back as straight as that of a Pilates instructor.

I picked up the song binder. A newcomer starts with something upbeat and familiar to gauge the audience's tastes. Never put in more than one or two songs at a time to avoid being labeled a microphone hog. *A Whole New World*–Theme Song from Aladdin; *All Out of Love*–Air Supply; *As Long as You Love Me*–Backstreet Boys. Yuck. I skipped forward. *Glory of Love*–Peter Cetera; *Have You Ever Really Loved a Woman?*–Bryan Adams. What about *Cuts Like a Knife* instead of the song that signified when Bryan jumped the shark, dragging Marlon Brando into the ocean with him? Where were the karaoke standards? *Brown Eyed Girl*, not there. *Someone To Watch Over Me*, not there. *Wind Beneath My Wings* was there, but no way I'd sing that for a straight-male crowd. The entire list had been selected by an overweight Midwestern housewife.

On second glance I realized that the poor sod at the end of the bar wasn't a Latino. Though his complexion resembled a burnt carrot, he was white and well-dressed. His shirt was unbuttoned to his sternum and mud coated his lower pant leg. Why did he look so familiar?

"What are you drinking, stranger?" Ms. Choi said. She'd slid behind the bar without my noticing. I'd have to be more attentive in Shanghai.

"Do you know how to mix a Vodka Collins?" I said.

She arched a thin painted brow. Like all Korean women, her makeup was immaculate, though thankfully not rolled on like dough. "Why wouldn't I be able to mix a Vodka Collins?"

With a flick of the wrist she poured the vodka into a metal tumbler and topped it with a squirt of seltzer. But she didn't add sour mix. She pulled out a bucket of lemons and squeezed a wedge into the tumbler, juice running down her slender hand, and added a pinch of powdered sugar. She licked her fingertips, then pulled the concoction up near her ear and shook it fetchingly, her cleavage jouncing in the upper globes where they were visible in the open V of her blouse. She poured the drink into a tall Collins glass and pushed it forward. I sipped its cool, tart wetness, mesmerized.

"This is wonderful," I said.

She winked, then jabbed a finger at the open binder. "You might sing?"

"I think so. Is there something you haven't heard in awhile?"

"Anything would be a relief from Jorge." She nodded toward the singer at the edge of the dance floor, who was on his feet swaying to Lionel Richie's "Three Times a Lady." His skin was dark teak, his eyes sparkling like a Santa Claus who'd hit the eggnog too hard. "The only English he knows he learned from karaoke. But what can I do? It's either him or me, and I'm too busy to sing when it's this crowded." She paused. "Do I know you?"

"I'm Guy Watanabe," I said.

She squinted. "Yes, I suppose you are. I'm Sunny Choi. I own this place."

"So I'd presumed."

"It's not much, but it suits me. I can't stand waking up early." She brushed a wisp of hair from her face. "Are you really Japanese?"

There was one question I'd never answer again as Balthazar Salgado. "You won't hold it against me, will you?"

She smirked. "My parents might, but they don't like me running a bar either. 'Stupid! Stupid! Your sister's a doctor and look at you! Serving cocktails to low-class people,'" she said in a thick Korean accent. "Truth is, we're part Japanese too, but if they admitted that they'd have to commit ritual suicide."

"At least they're interested in what you're doing. The only thing my parents ask is whether I'll remarry."

I pinched my thigh. Never refer to failed relationships. Makes you look desperate. Sunny politely ignored the reference.

"If you know what you want to sing, I'll bump you to the top of the list," she said.

I gazed at the fat, unappealing binder. How did someone who looked as cool as she did have such bad musical taste? "You've got so many of my favorites, I'm having a hard time choosing."

"Give me a holler whenever you're ready." She'd filled four pitchers of beer while we'd spoken. "I can't wait to hear you. Most of our drop-ins are of the white trash variety." She nodded at the drunk at the end of the bar, not bothering to lower her voice. On cue, he belched and graced us with a horsy grin.

I watched Sunny's low-slung ass flex as she glided across the room. Had she been flirting with me? It had been so long since I'd met someone open and authentic, her cheery irreverence felt like a slap in the face. She must be trilingual in Korean, Spanish, and English. How cool was that when folks like me mangled a single tongue?

"That there's a prime cut of meat, if I ever saw one, mate." The only thing worse than a drunk is a drunk Australian. "How old do you think she is? Oriental girls don't age like the rest of them. They look about sixteen until they turn forty-five, then kapow!, they turn ninety overnight. You with me, mate? You speak English, don't you? Not like this wetback lot."

I should have moved to an empty table. But something about this Australian drunk grabbed my attention. Those bright white teeth; the lustrous, if sweaty, hair; he was the spitting image of…But no. Troy was a teetotaler. He'd spent an entire lesson discussing the evils of mind-altering chemicals, including caffeine.

I moved a few stools closer. He smelled as if he'd slept in his expensive suit for days.

"Excuse me," I said. "I'm sure you get this a lot, but has anyone ever told you that you bear a striking resemblance to—"

"So you going to get in on that action?" he said. His bloodshot eyes were still fixed on Sunny. "Because if you don't, I sure as hell will. I once banged a girl in Bangkok who looked like her. Absolutely unreal what she could do with her pussy. I saw her pull a string of razor blades out of her snatch and I said, 'That's the one for me.'"

Troy Bobbins wouldn't be this crass. He'd held a torch in a "Take Back the Night" march, the only male in attendance. He advised heads of state. He'd been honored by the Dalai Lama.

"You remind me a lot of—"

"It's all a marketing gimmick," he said. "You get drawn in by the rumor that Oriental girls have horizontal slits. But they're as vertical as any other girls'. Those yellow ratbastards are enterprising, I'll give them that. Never go into business with those sneaky cunts. Answer me this riddle: If I'm the goddamned brand, how could *my* job be outsourced?"

Could this be the same Troy Bobbins I'd met in Santa Fe? There was no way to be sure—that Troy had been wearing sunglasses and was separated from me by twenty yards and a plate of glass. Which Troy was the real one and which

was an actor? What if there really was no Troy Bobbins, just a
Troy Bobbins Corporation that hired a stable of look-alikes?
Please God, no.

"I need to know," I said. "Are you Troy Bobbins? Did you
sell your business to the Karaoke Group International?"

"Did you choose your song yet?" Sunny said. I nearly
fell off the barstool. Those short legs propelled her forward
with remarkable stealth.

"I'm still trying to figure it out," I said.

"How about you let me take the mike for a piece?" the
drunk said. "You can shut off the machine. I'll sing the
whole thing *a capella. He had a woman he loved in Saigon. I've
got a picture of him in her arms now. Born in the U.S.A.—I was—
Born in the U-S-A, hey!*"

Sunny didn't look at him. "What do you think about
Rod Stewart? I haven't heard him for a long time, and I've
forbidden Jorge from even trying."

Rod Stewart? He could sing "Happy Birthday" and it
would sound like "Maggie Mae". There was only one Rod
Stewart song I could sing without vomiting in my mouth.
"How about 'You're In My Heart?'"

Sunny clapped her hands. "Perfect! That's absolutely
my favorite Rod Stewart song."

"Is that the way into your panties?" the drunk said. "How
does that go again? Hum a few bars, and I'll stoke your fire."

"Listen, Troy," I said. "I think it'd be better for all of us if
I called you a taxi. Go home and sleep it off."

"You know him?" Sunny looked vaguely disgusted.

Troy stumbled closer and threw his arm over my shoulders. "Of course we know each other. We're best buddies.

Wherever he goes, I go. Whatever he bangs, I bang. What do you say? You want to be the meat in a Troy Bobbins sandwich?"

"Hey, man," I wrenched out of his sloppy grasp. "You've crossed the line. It's time for you to apologize and get the fuck out of here."

"Don't be cross with me, mate," he said. "I was just playing around. Why's everyone got to be so politically correct? Barmaid, get my friend here another of whatever sissy drink he's drinking. I'll have another single-malt whiskey, neat. Put it on my tab."

Sunny shook her head. "You're done for the night. I'm not going to get sued when you plough your car into a lamppost. Pay up and go home."

"You have no idea who you're talking to, do you sugar tits?" He looked at me. "Tell Susie Wong here who I am. Then tell her she doesn't deserve to lick my hairy arse."

"*Mechinom*," Sunny said. "You can suck my *kochu*."

"Troy—" I said. Too late.

In my peripheral vision, I'd noticed the wave of men surging toward us bristling with pool cues. Before Troy could spew another obscenity, he'd been seized by callused hands and lifted overhead like flotsam. The synthesized music sounded a triumphant electronic parade march.

"I'll have you all deported!" Troy screamed. "I own this town! I'm going to spend the rest of my life making sure you and your children never step foot in the United States again!"

Snap. Crackle. Pop. And those were the sounds I heard *after* the emergency door had been shut behind him. It happened so quickly it seemed as if the mob had been hired to move a few crates of vodka. The pool players were racking up new games. Jorge hadn't stopped singing: "*Feelings... whoa, whoa, whoa, feelings.*" Didn't they realize Troy could buy them, sell them, make them disappear? They should have called his agent instead of provoking his wrath. What were we compared to a man of his stature? Please, God, let the drunk be nothing more than a Troy Bobbins wannabe. Otherwise we'd all be in deep trouble once he sobered up.

Sunny swept Troy's empty shot glasses into a bus tub. She touched my forearm.

"I adore Rod Stewart," she said. "I'm going to cue up your song right now."

No stage. No singer's monitor. A single cordless microphone that I took from Jorge's hand. The setup was no more than—it was considerably less than—a home karaoke system. The words on the screen were almost too blurry to read. The speakers crackled from a bad wiring connection. It was a karaoke system that would make good singers sound bad and bad singers sound worse.

The only people watching me, even noticing that there had been a change in singer, were Jorge, who opened and closed his hand as if it still held a microphone, and Sunny, who leaned against the bar with her arms crossed. On-screen the Korean dancers in traditional dress were on again, looking like an East Asian edition of the Cirque du Soleil, the women swaying back and forth, *flick-flick-flicking* their colored kerchiefs in their outstretched hands.

I didn't know what day it was
When you walked into the room
I said hello unnoticed
You said goodbye too soon

It took more than a single verse—maybe two, maybe three—but I could feel that old feeling returning. A pop song lasts three minutes, but within that time you can travel vast distances. For a few moments, there was no Megumi, there was no Milton, there were no murders; Tanya and I were still married, my job had not become as exciting as scooping dung at a zoo; there was no one and nothing I was chasing. The mental sludge tarring the gears of my mind was flushed away, allowing me to exist in a world of sound, light, and the vibrations emanating from my diaphragm. Damn. I sounded good.

I couldn't stop myself from swaying back and forth like a schoolgirl with a lighter at a Mötley Crüe concert. Through my carefully slit eyelids, I watched the bar owner Sunny Choi. And she watched me. Her arms uncrossed and her lips parted. She mouthed the lyrics with me, neither of us needing to look at the screen as a guide.

I won't lie and say that I floored the crowd. Half of them didn't look up from the green felt. But a few of them clapped. Jorge pumped my hand with vigor. And Ms. Choi? She smiled and brought the three of us a round of tequila shots on the house. Not just any tequila. Patrón. And the synthesizer played on.

Jorge and I alternated the rest of the night, with efforts from the enigmatic Sunny Choi sprinkled in for good measure. Her spirits-soaked voice made Christina Aguilera's theme song for *Mulan* sound like a jazz standard performed by Ella Fitzgerald (by way of Wendy Carlos). I doubt she had much of a range—she cheated on the high notes by uttering them like a spoken-word poet—but it didn't matter. Her voice was warm and intimate, drawing us in as if this were a drawing room and we were her guests. Or was the Patrón affecting my karaoke judgment?

I bought drinks for Jorge. He bought drinks for me. Sunny lined up shots for the three of us. I joined Jorge for a duet of "Endless Love" (he sang Diana Ross's part). I stared at the Korean dancers on-screen, wondering why their dresses looked like bed sheets that had been hiked up to their necks. In my own personal ode to Irma Johnson and the demise of the late, great Lily Pad, I sang Whitney's version of Dolly Parton's song "I Will Always Love You." That didn't go over well, but it didn't matter. While Sunny sang "Arirang," Jorge and I danced around the room, flicking Kleenex tissues clutched between our fingertips. We laughed until tears streamed down our cheeks and Jorge had to be carried by his friends to his pickup truck.

At the end of the night, I tried to help Sunny put the chairs on the tables, but each one I put up knocked another one off. She parked me on a stool next to the back door that was thrown open to the warm, night air. She shoved a mug of coffee into my hands. "You just conserve your energy, mister," she said.

She vacuumed, wiped down the counters, washed the dishes, stuck a wad of bills between her cleavage and dropped the rest down a slot in the floorboards. I'm not one for hangovers. No, my headache begins shortly after my peak of intoxication and continues until long after I've fallen asleep. This night was no different. Everything was shrouded in gauze, my entire body raw, almost bruised, to the touch. My bones felt as if they would rattle out of my mouth as Sunny drove us home in a Toyota Tercel that lacked a rear window and shock absorbers.

The green and white light from the 7-Eleven across the street obviated the need to turn on the lights. She led me across a living room littered with odd objects of rubber, plastic, and bone. The dog curled up on her bed, whose tail thumped at our arrival, had to be cajoled in Korean with treats pulled from her pocket (so *that* was the peculiar liver smell) to take his place outside the closed bedroom door. Meanwhile his mistress and I made the beast with two backs in the ambient convenience-store glow, the fur he'd left behind coating our bare skins.

The house smelled like dog, the bed smelled like dog, we smelled like dog. Every part of me, from my hair follicles to my toenails, ached with her every caress. *I shouldn't have drunk so much. I'll never be able to get it up.* I closed my eyes and conjured up the image of Megumi working on my erogenous zones as methodically as a machine, her mosquito-bite titties almost impossible to grasp…and my hands clasped on Sunny's more generous mammaries, which collapsed under the pressure, gave way like half-filled water balloons. *At what age do the suspensory ligaments in a woman's breasts surrender to gravity?* Her headlamps sagged and swayed, pulled downward by a dark nipple, as she rocked her hips on my pubic bone. *Breasts are supposed to be firm.* My body wasn't listening to my mind. It just reacted.

Once, twice, three times a lady.

There were breaks in between, of course. Even if the thirties are the new twenties, a man my age can't survive such an onslaught without regular breaks and plenty of fluids. Every time the pressurized toilet flushed, a suction roar shook the house, setting the dog to barking and then wheezing from exertion. After the second bout, feeling loose (though still pained at the base of my skull), I waxed philosophical.

"In my opinion," I said, "there's no such thing as intimacy, just shared solitude."

Her head disappeared. I felt a hot tongue run along the center of my scrotum, jolting my eye sockets.

"Does that feel like solitude to you?" she said.

Later, much later, I pressed my ear to her belly and listened to the oceanic rumblings of her stomach acid. She hummed a familiar tune. Was it Billie Holiday? No, it was something from the era of skinny ties and pastel slacks. The band? Exposé: no-talent girls in ankle-breaking high heels. The song? "Point of No Return." I hated that synth pop crap. But this night it enchanted me into a deep slumber.

CHAPTER 29

A tongue lapped at my toes. Quick, confidant licks—wet and rough. The moisture cooled deliciously on the webbing between my toes. Did I have the reserves for this?

The dog looked like a stuffed animal that had been mended using scraps from torn dresses and blankets. One ear flopped forward and the other stood straight up, the bell of his hairless inner ear speckled with dew drop scabs. He let out a low, distinct "woof" and trotted out of the room.

My slacks, briefs, and shirt were intermingled with thong underwear, an apron, and a chewed-up nylon bone. Everything was dusted with iridescent strands from *canis familiaris*. It was nearly noon. I'd slept for seven or eight hours straight. True slumber, not that simulacrum of sleep that I'd experienced for weeks. My cell phone showed five text messages.

Along with a Movado watch and a Coach wallet, the Nokia mobile phone was one of Balthazar Salgado's many new accessories. Sheila had spent an hour explaining how to use the Web browser, MP3 player, voicemail, camera, and text messaging before settling on, "Just fucking answer it, okay?" She'd failed to instruct me on how to silence its incessant beeping and vibrating. In my drunken haste I'd wadded it in toilet paper and shoved it beneath the dog's bed.

I scrolled through my messages.

From: Sheila
whr u@?

From: Sheila
u p*d or somit?

From: Sheila
u bonking or w@?

From: Sheila
dnt wear yrslf ot. uv got a plane 2 ctch.

From: Sheila
u K? leev by 2 or d boyz r cmng 2 gt u

Electronic pidgin. I parted the blinds. There were skateboarders in front of the 7-Eleven, but no Polynesians. Had they parked the SUV out back? I thought they'd stopped following me after I was placed on Bruce's payroll.

I didn't get Sheila. One moment she was hinting that I should take Balthazar Salgado's cash and credit cards and run; the next, she was sending thugs to collect me. Did she think I would abandon Megumi? Last night meant nothing. I got drunk and horny, that was all.

I heard music. Not a radio but an electronic keyboard set to "piccolo," the real instrument's breathiness transformed into a fuzzy electrode tone. It would have been a melancholy song if not for the background drum track. Who would create a disco version of "Groovy Kind of Love?" The song hadn't resuscitated Phil Collins's career, and sounded worse in the hands of a no-talent Korean barmaid. Excuse me, bar owner.

Sunny didn't notice when I entered the living room. She was sitting in front of a keyboard and computer monitor, her brow a fist of concentration, tapping her feet in time to the music. Her hair, which had cascaded around her shoulders in bed, was now tied into a practical ponytail. She wore an oversized T-shirt and nothing else. The dog's tail thumped the ground one-two-three. She turned around.

"Hungry?" she said. "I can fry you an egg."

"I think I should leave," I said.

"I make a great cup of java." She rose and walked into the kitchen, her dog padding off behind her.

Sunny's cramped kitchen contained barely enough counter space for her appliances: a rice cooker, a waffle-maker, an oil-spattered deep-fryer, a hot-water carafe, a toaster oven, a kettle the size of a pressure cooker, and a pressure cooker the size of a Shop-Vac. Pots and pans hung from a ceiling rack, a stack of used and carefully unwrinkled Saran Wrap sheets rested on the dish rack, and dishes piled up in the sink.

She fried me an egg, doused it with Maggi sauce, and threw it over rice with a side of kimchi. I hadn't thought I was hungry until I'd shoveled the sloppy mess down my throat. Even better was the coffee, which she served in a mug emblazoned with a photograph of her homely mutt. It tasted like an Indonesian varietal—earthy and without a hint of acid. I complimented her talent for libations.

"The only beer my customers appreciate is cold and cheap," she said. "I served Mac and Jack's African Amber once. They said it tasted like Mountain Dew."

That was, of course, the pitfall of having migrant day workers as one's clientele. If she ran a karaoke bar in north Seattle, where the median household income hovered above $100,000, where peace protestors drove Subaru Outbacks outfitted with bike racks and leather seats, there would be a line to get in. All she needed was someone else to handle the music.

Sunny interlaced her fingers and stretched toward the ceiling. Standing, I was five inches taller than her. But seated, her long, lithe Korean torso made her three inches taller than me. As I'd kissed my way up her body, it had seemed as if her belly would never end. Beneath the threadbare Kirin Beer T-shirt, Sunny's breasts sagged. It was easy to talk to her, but that was because she knew more than any woman should about sports. She laughed too loud. She didn't have Megumi's refinement or beauty.

Sunny held my gaze for a moment too long. "If I tell you a secret, do you promise not to get mad?"

"Why would I get mad?" She better be on the pill. She better not have genital warts. Why hadn't I used a condom?

The dog followed her out of the kitchen. Sunny returned to hand me a yellowing newspaper, an old copy of the *Seattle Asian Herald.* I stared back at myself from the front page, the medallion hanging like a lawn ornament from my neck. The caption read: *"Japanese" American Guy Watanabe won the title, followed by an African American and a Caucasian.* That Norene Wong: she knew how to write copy for our community.

"I didn't know anybody outside of Seattle read this," I said. Or actually, anybody outside of Chinese restaurants, where stacks of the freebie *Seattle Asian Herald* collected dust on the window sills. "Did you know who I was when I walked into the bar?"

"I had my suspicions," she said. "I was sure of it once you began singing. I've never been so moved."

Long ago in Chelan, Megumi said the same thing, but there was a huge difference. Megumi had been moved by my singing regardless of my title; Sunny had been moved *because* of it. Within hours, Guy Watanabe would cease to exist, and so would his allure for a karaoke groupie like Sunny. Megumi wanted me no matter what my name, or her name, really was. We would become nobodies together.

Sunny stacked the dishes in the sink. She pulled on rubber gloves then pulled them right off again. She sat down, posture so perfect she looked down on me from the lofty heights of her elongated torso. "What did you think of the music accompanying the videos? Did you like it? It was different, right?"

I looked down. Her dog was under the table, head between his paws, staring at me with oversized, rheumy eyes, imploring me not to tell the truth.

"I've never heard anything like it," I said.

"Sure, but did you like it? Did it move you the way your singing moved me?" She leaned forward, her braless breasts undulating. She was unusually well-endowed for an Asian woman, which was probably why gravity had found her early. "You're a karaoke expert. You've probably sung in the highest-class karaoke bars. How do my compositions compare?"

"You arrange the music yourself, right?" I said. "With your Casio keyboard and computer."

360

She nodded. "But don't let that influence your judgment. Just tell me if you thought it was any good. Don't worry about hurting my feelings. I'm not sensitive like that."

"Really?"

"The only way I can get better is if someone with real talent gives me his honest opinion. Jorge is tone-deaf, and nobody else at the bar cares."

Like so many Korean women, Sunny's face was as broad and round as a moon. But was it waxing or waning? She teetered on the edge of her seat, waiting for my pronouncement.

The old Guy Watanabe would have praised her effort to reinvent classic love songs, as if it was her intent and not the result that mattered. But the new Guy—excuse me, Balthazar—wanted to state things as they really were. Sunny ran a bar filled with tattooed field workers, all of whom she could drink under the table. She was tough. She could handle the truth.

"Synthesizers work only for a narrow selection of artists," I said. "European bands from the eighties like Flock of Seagulls and Kajagoogoo that disappeared for good reason. They might work for certain ballads, but only if you use a setting like 'piano' instead of 'accordion' or 'electric organ,' which you seem uncommonly fond of. You've gotten so fancy with the reverb, distortion, and echo, it sounds like a Nintendo game."

"Uh huh," she said. "What else? Don't pull any punches."

"There are inherent limitations to a simulated 'electric guitar.' There were solos on certain songs that, though they might be technically correct, sounded absurd when tapped out on a keyboard. Instead of the subtle bend of guitar strings, it's a cat falling into a trash bin."

"Anything else?"

"Um," I said, "You should consider expanding your song selection. There's nothing wrong with having a few sappy love songs, but an entire binder devoted to them? It lulls people to sleep, if it doesn't make them hurl."

"Thanks for being so honest," she said.

"Not a problem. I can't believe you programmed that many songs all by yourself. It must have taken forever."

"Weeks in front of the computer. I developed carpel tunnel." She stood. "Come on, Henry," she said to the dog. "Let's go into the living room and lie down on your favorite rug."

She and her dog exited the kitchen before I could react. I sat there staring at a mountain of stained plates and dirty glasses. She'd asked for an honest opinion and I'd given her one. Was there something I'd missed?

Sunny was seated with her back against the sofa on the hardwood floor next to Henry, who was lying on a fake polar bear rug replete with glass eyes and gaping jaws. I took a seat on a nearby rocking chair. From the creak it gave, I suspected that its rocking days were over.

Sunny was busy stroking Henry's belly. He tilted halfway over, both ears flopping open like Dumbo, his eyes trained on me.

"Don't worry, Henry," she said. "Mama's not upset."

I looked up at the eight-foot-high Ikea bookcase that appeared ready to tumble forward. The thin fiberboard was overflowing with paperbacks—Jacqueline Susann, Stephen King, *Tuesdays with Morrie*, and other things people read on vacation—but these were outnumbered by three-ring binders. *The Very Best of Sade* read one, the title scribbled on with permanent marker. *The 100 Greatest Love Songs of All Time* read another.

"I admire your courage in opening up a karaoke bar," I said. "There's so much competition out there. These days, everything's controlled by conglomerates."

"Uh huh."

Her computer monitor was playing a screensaver: a three-dimensional treble clef spinning and whirling in outer space to synthesized music. The tune was familiar. Something by New Order. Or OMD. Or Dream Academy. I never could distinguish among the three of them. Didn't she understand that musical genre had spawned nothing of lasting value?

"That's a great screensaver," I said.

"I'm sorry," she said, getting to her feet. "Is it bothering you? I'll turn off the speakers."

"Not at all. I like it actually."

Sunny shook the mouse until her desktop reappeared. She closed her music program until all that was left was the screen wallpaper, a photograph of Sunny and Henry standing in front of the ocean. Henry looked younger, his sagging belly not quite as prodigious. She looked younger too, and happier, though she was wearing the kind of floppy Gilligan hat that Asian grandmothers favored.

"I hope you didn't take my comments in the wrong way," I said. "I was trying to give you constructive feedback so you could attract more customers."

"I'm not taking it the wrong way." She plopped herself down next to Henry and rubbed his ear between her thumb and fingers. "My mother says worse things. 'Are you still wasting your time on that keyboard? You have no talent. Stupid! You're stupid!'"

"The production of karaoke videos is big business," I said. "How can anybody compete with professional musicians, videographers, and directors? A ton of money goes into making real karaoke videos."

She stopped petting Henry to fold her arms. "I thought I *was* making real karaoke videos. But who am I? Just a nobody who owns a karaoke bar where nobody ever sings. You're the Karaoke King. You know everything there is about karaoke."

"I didn't say that. I'm just saying that in this day and age, it's impossible to compete in the karaoke arena unless you have state-of-the-art equipment and laser discs with sophisticated music and graphics."

"I can't afford all that."

She cleared the sofa by brushing everything onto the floor. The revealed cushions looked darker than the sun-bleached sofa back. Reluctantly she made room for me but shrugged away the hand I placed on her forearm.

"You're a big karaoke superstar," she said. "You don't know what it's like to be 'common'—no, worse than common, 'bad' at what you love to do most. I pour my heart and soul into those songs: I lower the octaves, slow down the tempos, make sure the music doesn't overpower the vocals. But I've heard the whispers. What? Do they think I don't understand plain Spanish?"

Did she want the truth or a pretty lie? She would never make it in the karaoke world without a business partner. Someone with better musical taste.

"Don't give up," I said. "I'm sure everything will work out."

Sunny scooted six inches away from me.

It was maddening. Ten hours ago we had been fucking like bunny rabbits and my every move had invoked a sigh. Now I tripped over landmines anywhere I stepped. My Asian friends had warned me about Korean women. Avoid dating them: if they aren't psychotic, their parents are. If she didn't want to know the truth, she shouldn't have asked for my opinion.

She laid her head on my lap. Close-up, I could see the imperfections on her face—an overlarge sun freckle, a missing eyebrow drawn in with eyeliner. Men salivated when Megumi walked into a room. Sunny? She was twice Megumi's age and looked a hell of a lot better after a couple of shots of Patrón. How had I been attracted to her? How could her dark, cinnamon scent be arousing me now? I pushed her head off of my lap before she noticed.

"I've got a plane to catch," I said. "I'm sorry, but I've got to leave."

Why should I have regrets? The only time I'd lied was when I'd suggested that her karaoke bar could stay afloat when a single immigration raid would decimate her clientele. Who cared if she thought I was lying about the plane flight? Why had I asked for her phone number when she didn't want to give it to me and I planned never to call? She barely uttered a word on the way back to the bar to pick up my car. She didn't kiss me, hug me, or shake my hand. Even in the realm of one-night stands, her manners were deplorable.

Sheila and the Polynesian brothers accompanied me to the airport. I could tell by the glazed look in Sheila's eyes that she was high. At the security gate, she threw her arms around my neck and pressed her lips to my ear.

"If you decide to make a run for it," Sheila whispered, "remember to ditch the phone."

"Why do you think I'm not going to follow through?" I said.

"Sometimes I think you're not a fucking idiot," she said.

Sorry, Sheila, the old Guy Watanabe might have been tempted by a life of serving beer to illegal immigrants and returning home to a stubby-legged barmaid and a flatulent dog. But nothing and nobody would stop me from saving Megumi now. What was I leaving behind in America? A failed marriage. A teenaged junkie who, along with a psychotic midget, had betrayed my trust. An hours-long tryst with a woman who thought that REO Speedwagon's oeuvre represented the pinnacle of the civilized arts.

"Surround yourself with the winners in life and you too will be a winner," Troy taught. "Surround yourself with the losers, and you will follow in their footsteps."

It didn't matter that Troy used an Australian actor as his body double. How he ran his business didn't alter the salience of his lessons. It's not every day that a person has the opportunity to wipe the slate clean. Today I became a new man.

CHAPTER 30

"There she is, Mr. Salgado." George Weller tapped my forearm. "Just like clockwork."

"Clockwork," according to George, constituted five hours late. We'd been parked since 8 a.m. across the street from her high-rise condominium complex. He tapped me every time the revolving door disgorged another resident. I focused my binoculars in time to glimpse her duck into the back of a Mercedes-Benz sedan.

Her hair was cut short à la Audrey Hepburn in *Roman Holiday*. She wore sunglasses against the sun and a peacoat against the cold. But there was no mistaking Megumi's expression: the absence of tension around her mouth and eyes that I'd once mistaken for ennui.

The boys peeled off on their motorcycle. We waited for them to radio back before following. Megumi's car crossed the river and traveled northwest along the highway out of Shanghai proper. Where could she be headed?

The boys' fluorescent-green crotch-rocket flitted like a motorized dragonfly in and out of the heavy traffic. I wondered aloud whether they were drawing too much attention to themselves. George answered that half the population had received drivers' licenses within the past year, and the other half drove illegally. *Not* driving erratically would have been conspicuous.

It made me feel uneasy to trust armed, illiterate teenagers, but what was my alternative? I had hired them.

I claim a meager percentage of Chinese heritage, which may explain why the soil didn't call out to my bones the way it did with Amy Tan. Confronted by the crowd of tawny faces at the Shanghai airport, I was relieved to be greeted by a balding British expatriate, waving a sign with my adopted name scribbled in permanent marker, his shirt pitted with sweat in the middle of winter. The last thing I wanted in a rich city teeming with poor migrants from the countryside was to identify with the masses.

Shanghai is more capitalist than any other city in the world. Anything can be bought or sold here, from Gucci bags and Rolex watches to human organs and their fleshy containers. "Communism" meant shutting up and getting to work, whether in the backseat of a limousine or on a bicycle seat dragging a trailer of used machine parts. Shanghai is the Wild West, Ayn Rand's Paradise, authoritarian libertarianism at its finest. It's a city where Balthazar Salgado's wealth could make any venture possible.

Allow me to illustrate. I asked George to procure me an unregistered gun. He procured me two armed, unregistered peasants. The first was a cousin to George's housekeeper, a gangly boy with a shriveled paw where his right hand should have been. The second was a short, dark-skinned boy with a nascent mustache and volatile eyes. They wore the same clothes every day and were overjoyed when treated to cellophane-wrapped pastries. If they were arrested or disappeared, no one would come looking for them.

Their unswerving loyalty cost 1/100th the nightly charges for my suite at the Ritz Carlton, where my bathtub commanded a view of the bright lights and big shopping of Nanjing Lu. There is nothing like the stark reality of poverty to make a man appreciate wealth.

We exited the highway in a commercial district. But the restaurants, pharmacies, and sidewalk vendors soon gave way to a suburban community—two-story homes with garages, manicured lawns, window-boxes of flowers—then a guard house, a factory, and scores of identical concrete buildings. We parked in a pitted, gravel area beneath balconies filled with laundry fluttering on lines. Next to us were a few motor scooters and a hundred single-speed bicycles lined up neatly in racks.

Through the binoculars, I could make out the driver leaning against the side of Megumi's car. He had a broad, squat body and a cap pulled low over his eyes. He was smoking a cigarette. Two teenaged girls exited a building, and he angled his body to watch them pass. Megumi had apparently gone inside.

"Where the hell are we, George?" I said.

George stroked his stubbly chin. "Looks to be a factory dormitory, sir. They're quite efficient for the high-tech companies; there's not a hundred yards between the workbench and the bunk. Floor boss can check if the girls are sick or just faking it. Never have to worry about being short-staffed."

The question he couldn't answer was what Megumi was doing at a factory dormitory. Kolling was involved in every stage of the karaoke production process. The factory might be producing karaoke sound systems. Or microphones. Or furniture. What if Megumi had begun to meet surreptitiously with girls from backgrounds as impoverished as her own? What if our Vegas winnings had gone toward helping young women climb out of poverty? The more I cogitated on this, the more it made sense. What I'd mistaken for coolness was a steely determination to help others.

George tapped me. Megumi's bodyguard trailed behind, her peacoat folded over his arm. In the American southwest, she'd worn nothing but tank tops and shorts; now she wore a cream-colored blouse and a beige business jacket. Her gait was forthright and deliberate. Commanding.

Megumi visited two more factory dormitories before the afternoon was out. The routine was the same. Megumi and her bodyguard entered the building and then exited forty minutes later. The final stop was different. No factory and no dormitories, just squat clapboard residences like army barracks scattered across a dirt lot. The Mercedes was parked in front of a residence, the driver leaning against the hood of the car. Three bare-chested boys stood nearby, one clutching a rubber ball. The driver's vigilance kept the boys from approaching the luxury sedan.

We parked in the side-lot of a gas station. Next door was a store that displayed bottles of pickled roots and snakes. Megumi and her bodyguard were trailed out of the house by a girl in a wrap-around skirt and a T-shirt. The girl clutched a baby to her chest and, even through the binoculars, I could make out two damp spots on her shirt. She must have said something because both Megumi and her bodyguard turned around.

Megumi's mouth moved rapidly. Shortly after, the bodyguard said something. Megumi jabbed an index finger. The girl flinched. Megumi pointed in the girl's face once more before walking away. The bodyguard hurried off in her footsteps.

There was a simple explanation for Megumi's behavior. She had dressed down the girl for uttering something of the self-defeatist variety, what Troy Bobbins called "success sappers:" rationalizations invented to justify remaining underprivileged. If Megumi was to help these poor girls, such pessimism had to be stomped out mercilessly. Megumi had clawed her way out of abasement into riches. If I had a tenth of her strength, I never would have lost Tanya to that hairy cretin Jay Weed. Marrying me would legitimize Megumi, but it would also save me. She made me want to be a more industrious man.

"I don't mean to disturb your thoughts, Mr. Salgado," George said. "And I hope you won't think that I'm out of place for asking this. But with your wealth, why wouldn't you choose one of the other bar girls? I mean, why go to the trouble of kidnapping this one?"

George was drunk. He'd been thrilled to gain admittance to the American Club and had quaffed his weight in liquor, taking my suggestion to "knock himself out" literally. He'd already regaled me with his "Tales of the Orient:" how he'd banged a Chinese girl he'd tutored in English; how he'd slept with the wife of a mid-level party official; how Chinese girls found him irresistible due to his "Western respect for women that Chinese men have yet to learn."

"Megumi's not a bar girl," I said, the room pulsating after countless tumblers of single-malt whiskey served neat. "And I don't care about her past."

"But, sir," George said. "She enters a karaoke bar every night dressed to the nines. The bars here aren't the same as in the States. The only customers are men, and a lot more than singing takes place in the backrooms."

"Megumi loves to listen to people sing," I said. "That bastard Kolling sends muscular monkeys to follow her everywhere but there. When she's inside the bar, she's a prisoner. But at least she can pretend she's free. She can pretend she's with me."

George squinted then laughed. He held up his glass. "Well then. Here's to saving the damsel in distress. May the kidnapping be an unparalleled success and she satisfy your every fantasy."

CHAPTER 31

From: Sheila
DdU fnd her yet?

From: Sheila
wuz d wrd? hw cum it's takN u so lng?

From: Sheila
av u givN ^ yet?

From: Sheila
RU ded or jst retardd?

Sheila's text messages were as welcome as bamboo slivers shoved under my fingernails. Did she think I'd given up my life and my name to enjoy the company of an obsequious Brit twelve hours a day in the backseat of an unheated Volvo sedan? My problem wasn't effort, it was opportunity. Megumi was rarely alone.

Some days she visited girls living in dormitories on the outskirts of Shanghai. But she was always accompanied by the Mongolian Ivan Drago, who was never more than two steps away and appeared to be translating on Megumi's behalf. Other days, Megumi didn't leave her condominium at all. Her bodyguard or driver fetched plastic bags of take-out food from a Thai restaurant down the street.

This is what the stakeout entailed, Sheila. Sitting on my ass, drinking boxed iced tea, and eating ramen from a Styrofoam cup. Listening to George recount every sexual encounter he'd had since he lost his cherry at the age of nineteen. I stopped feigning interest. He kept talking.

The one night I decided, fuck it, I'm going to get real food with Balthazar's money was the night Megumi took an unaccompanied stroll to a nearby shopping mall. We were out of walkie-talkie range and George didn't hear his cell phone inside the restaurant. We returned to Megumi's condominium to find the boys arguing with the doorman. They'd decided too late they should seize her inside the lobby, the problem being that no one in his right mind would have allowed those street urchins into a luxury complex. The boys had no idea they'd jeopardized my mission.

"Tell them," I said to George, "if they ever touch Megumi, or act without direct orders from me, they'll have a lot more to worry about than not getting paid."

The tall one hung his head. The short, dark one glowered.

Megumi went only one place unaccompanied. At 9 p.m., seven nights a week, Megumi was dropped off at the Kara-oke Café. The highlight of my dreary day was watching her walk the fifty steps between the curb and the front door. Gone was her office attire and sunglasses. She wore dresses with open backs and spaghetti straps, her pale skin illumi-

Harold Taw

nated by the neon lights. One night her body shimmered in periwinkle blue sequins.

"What do you think would happen," I asked George, "if I waltzed right into the lion's den to extract Megumi?"

George let out a low whistle. "I think, sir, you'd be better off seizing the girl on the street, guns blazing, and take your chances in a Chinese jail. The party makes your family pay for the bullet, but at least it's one bullet. You disappear behind those doors, he's got every right to do what he will. And Kolling's got a reputation as quite a vengeful sod."

The convenience store had become a control center of sorts. We met the boys in its parking lot in the morning and at the end of the surveillance day. It was our rendezvous point for emergencies. George and I were there buying our instant dinners when the walkie-talkie at his hip crackled.

"The young miss is on the move," George said. It was 7:15 p.m.: ninety minutes before Megumi was scheduled to leave for the Karaoke Café.

We didn't move fast enough to see her car pass, but we glimpsed the taillights of boys' motorcycle accelerating hard and changing lanes. We crossed the bridge and followed the contour of the river. Traffic slowed and then stopped. To our left were impressively heavy buildings of a European character, their stone facades illuminated by arc lighting. To our right was a broad walking promenade along the water. Our driver honked and pushed the car's nose into the adjoining lane.

375

"*Hao, hao*," George said into the walkie-talkie. "Her car's pulling over. If she exits, do you want the boys to follow on foot?"

"Keep her in sight," I said. "Got that? Tell them to stay close but not to make contact. I don't want those little fuckers to touch her."

The Bund was lit up like a parade on Disneyland's Main Street. The crowd was a cross-section of everyone living, working, or playing in Shanghai: children in school uniforms, missionaries clutching Bibles, cigarette-smoking day laborers, executives in suits, wide-bodied white tourists.

"The boys say she's left the car without her bodyguard," George said. "She's alone."

"Where?" I said. "Where is she right now?"

George repeated his question several times before getting a response. "They're having a hard time keeping up with her. She's moving fast."

George pointed. The silver Mercedes sedan was parked between tour buses. The driver and the bodyguard looked out at the river, their backs to us.

"Stop the car," I said. "Tell your driver to stop the car right now."

The car lurched to the right, only to be caught half in one lane and half in the other. I slapped the rear of the passenger seat. George held the walkie-talkie to his ear.

"The boys say that they can grab her," he said. "They said they can grab her and hold her until you come."

"No!" I shouted. "They follow and radio back their position. Where are they?"

"They're across the street from a building with a green roof. Near a lamp post. Wait, there are lamp posts everywhere. She's stopped next to an old man who's painting watercolors. She's looking through his work."

We halted a few car lengths past the Mercedes. Our driver honked at a passenger exiting a taxi cab. I flung open the door.

"Shouldn't you take the walkie-talkie?" George said.

"Christ, George. I can't speak Chinese. You're coming with me."

George was panting by the time we'd crossed the sidewalk to join the currents of people.

"Will you hurry up?" I said.

"I'm trying, Mr. Salgado."

George ran with his wrists up and flopping as if his hands were attached directly to his armpits. He bumped into a man photographing his wife. I left him behind and sprinted.

I almost raced past the old man with the watercolor brush. His wrist moved fluidly over a scroll stretched out on a piece of cardboard propped on his lap. A number of bystanders watched him paint, but none of them was Megumi and the boys were nowhere to be found. Press on or wait for George? His lumbering trot befitted a fat man, not a lanky one.

"No luck, what?" he said, panting.

"Ask them where she is," I said.

George spoke into the walkie-talkie. The only response was static. "Perhaps they've shut off their radios so as not to draw attention to themselves."

He continued to babble, but I wasn't there to listen. My eyes scanned the promenade as I ran. There were pieces of her everywhere, the thin lips on other faces, a scent in other women's hair. The tall boy darted toward the curb, his deformed hand curled like a lobster claw. I called after him but he couldn't hear me in the din. Where was his compatriot? The boy waited for an opening in the traffic and then walked straight ahead, the hurtling vehicles somehow missing him.

I was nearly struck by a taxi cab when I tried to follow. I had to wait with a Japanese tour group for the signal to change. A vendor approached pulling a cart displaying colored shoelaces. Men in suits mingled with women in shorts. Was that her slender calf near the purse stand, her oddly square foot with toes of an almost uniform size? No. But she was close. I could feel it.

I caught up to the boy just inside the entrance of a grand hotel. He stood in the lobby, turning round, a confused look on his face.

"Where is she?" I said. "Where's Megumi? Megumi. Do you understand me, you idiot? Where is she?"

His dull eyes showed not a speck of comprehension. I tore the walkie-talkie from his shoulder holster and shoved it in his face.

"Call your friend," I said. "Your *pengyou*. Ask him where she is. You understand?"

He nodded. He pressed the red button and spoke. Nearby, the concierge and doorman watched us. Guests waited in line at the front desk and others flowed in and out of the hotel. In the next room was a lounge and a restaurant. The boy shook his elongated head.

"Is she here?" I said. "Is she in this hotel?"

He shrugged.

"Then what the hell are you doing here? Why are you here?"

He shrugged again. He didn't understand a word.

"Call George," I said. "And stay here. Understand? Call George. Stay here." I pointed to him and to the ground. "You. Here. Understand?"

He nodded.

If I was following the boy and the boy was following no one, where did that leave me? He'd crossed the street for a reason, entered the hotel for a reason, yet was too dimwitted to do anything more than shake his head.

Megumi was here. I could feel her the way the ocean is sensed through the moisture and tang of salt in the air. She was a distant tune. Where was that music coming from? I walked out of the lobby and into the lounge. It was jazz but not bebop; it was mild—a big band sound without the big band.

Five elderly Chinese men blew into their brass instruments with vigor. Their faces were creased, finely wrinkled, sanded into a universal race. It was standing room only, every table occupied. I scanned the room. And found her.

Not a piece of her, not a facsimile of her, but Megumi herself. She was tucked into the rear corner of the bar, near a closed door, a tall glass with an umbrella in her hand. It was the perfect seat to listen to the band unobserved. It was an acoustic enclave, where the music could wash over her, crash against the walls, and recede. Her lips were parted, the way they'd been the night we met in the Lily Pad, when she'd been listening to me sing. The only difference was her dress. Tonight she wore a sleeveless navy-blue number closed at the neck. She was indescribably beautiful, unspoiled, true. How could I ever have compared an aging Korean barmaid to Megumi?

We hadn't bridged our solitudes before, but this time we would succeed. I'd crossed the ocean for this woman, given up everything I'd known for her. If we could recreate that first moment—our rapturous beginning—it wouldn't matter who I was or what I'd failed to achieve. I almost didn't want to proceed, didn't want to burst the bubble of this perfect moment.

An African American couple in eveningwear moved in her direction. I followed behind them. I was halfway across the room when she stiffened. Her eyes darted to the right of the musicians. Behind a waitress was the short, dark boy, staring at Megumi. He was in his leather riding jacket and jeans. He looked woefully out of place, this teenaged peasant in the middle of a jazz bar. How had he avoided hotel security?

Megumi disappeared. I'd taken my eyes off her for the briefest moment and all that remained was a closing door. The boy burst through first and I tried to follow, but a man in a coat and tie stepped into my path. He barked something in Chinese.

"I have no idea what the hell you're saying," I said. "And I don't have time to talk about this. Let me pass."

"Excuse me, sir," he said. "You are a guest?"

"Yes, goddammit. Let me by."

Through the door was a hallway with restrooms on either side. And beyond this was another lounge, this one not crowded, a few people sitting on divans. Two bellhops passed by pulling a luggage cart. The dark-skinned boy stood looking at the numbers above the elevator, but before I called out, he ran through a door leading to the stairwell.

The lift was at floor eight and descending. Did that mean she was on floor eight or one above that? Go to the top and come back down. The boy would ascend; I would descend; we would close in on Megumi like a vise. I stepped into the elevator with three other guests and waited. Floor two. Floor three. Floor seven.

There wasn't anyone on the top floor. The restaurant was being renovated, the entryway criss-crossed with yellow ribbon. Beyond was darkness, the scent of concrete dust, and a breeze from an open window. I ran a circuit around the hallway. All the doors were shut. The entire floor may have been closed for the construction work. I ran downstairs.

There wasn't anyone on the next floor. Nor on the next one. Nor on the next one. But still I descended, hoping to trip over Megumi, expecting to run into the boy. I saw neither of them. Floor five. Floor four. It was important to reach her before the boy did. I couldn't bear the thought of his hands touching her.

It was maddening, my breath coming in rasps, my heart pounding to keep up. They'd both disappeared. Were they in a room? Had she fooled him into heading upstairs and then slipped out the back? She would never go out alone after this. She would curl up to her captors, never realizing that her salvation had been only steps away. She was running away when she should be waiting for me.

Wounded deep in battle, I stand
stuffed like some soldier undaunted
To her Cheshire smile. I'll stand on file,
she's all I ever wanted.

I called out her name. The guests winced, moved away as if I were crazed. Fuck them. She'd been right in front of me. We could have left Shanghai tonight; yes, tonight, on a red-eye flight bound for anywhere. And now she had vanished, could be speeding away in the platinum Mercedes-Benz.

By the time I reached the ground floor, I was an empty gourd. The lobby teemed with strangers, and outside the hotel were twenty million more. No one cared if she was lost to me again.

George and the boy with the deformed hand approached. "Mr. Salgado," George said. "Thank goodness I've caught up with you. Kar Wai radioed. The young lady's holed up in a rooftop restaurant. He doesn't know how much longer she'll stay put. He's awaiting instructions."

How could I have been so stupid? I'd beaten the boy to the top floor. How could I have been deterred from searching the restaurant by yellow tape? Of course she would hide there. I'd run around like a madman for no reason.

"Tell him he's not to make a move without me," I said. "For all she knows, the boy means to rape her."

"Of course, Mr. Salgado," George said. "We'll do anything you say."

We stepped into the elevator. The tall boy stared down at his feet. I noticed for the first time that they were shod with decrepit, mud-covered sandals. His deformed hand was shoved into the pocket of his denim jacket.

I came for you, for you, I came for you, but
you did not need my urgency
I came for you, for you, I came for you, but

your life was one long
Emergency

I moved through the darkened restaurant loudly, clumsily, tripping over chunks of dry wall and empty plastic bottles. I could see nothing except for what was framed in the open window: the Oriental Pearl TV Tower, piercing the sky over the river like a glowing, space-aged hypodermic needle.

"Megumi," I said. "It's me, Guy Watanabe. You can come out. No one's going to hurt you. The boy who was chasing you works for me. Megumi? Come out. It's Guy."

George had radioed the boy but had received no reply. It was possible they'd both moved somewhere else. Why couldn't I remember the boy's name?

"Where are you, kid?" I said. "*Lai, lai, lai*. Come out. No more hiding. Come out and tell me where she is."

No response.

"Megumi? It's Guy. I'm here to help you. I couldn't say it before, but I can now. I love you. And I want us to get married. Did you hear that? I want us to be man and wife. No more running. No more cheap motels. A real house. New lives for both of us."

The only sound was the faint rush of traffic from twelve stories below. But silhouetted in the window was a delicate head and shoulders. It flattened, a petite figure crawling out of the restaurant. Before I could react there were footsteps and a crash. Two figures rolled on the ground. One of them cursed in Chinese.

The one on the bottom was Megumi, her face pale in the ambient light, her throat emitting a gurgling sound. The boy let out a high-pitched yelp. A thin line appeared on his cheek, and that line became smudged with droplets. I kicked him in the chest. And the stomach. And the head. George and the other boy arrived.

"For God's sake, man," George said. "We're on your side!"

Megumi curled up into a ball beneath the window sill. I thought I saw a sliver of silver between the knuckles of her clenched fist, but I blinked and it was gone. The gash on the boy's face was real, however, and bled profusely.

"Megumi." I knelt down. "It's me. Guy Watanabe."

"I don't have the money," she said. "He took it all. He forced me to give it to him."

"I'm not here for the money," I said. "That's nothing compared to finding you. I came for you. For you. I came for you."

Her face was devoid of expression. And then it dissolved into relief. She threw her arms around me and sobbed into my neck. Sitting together on the floor, I told her about the fake passports, the plane tickets, how we would soon become Mr. and Mrs. Salgado and sip tropical drinks at a Third World beach resort.

We reaffirmed our love for one another and laid out an escape plan. It would be too dangerous to leave tonight. Her bodyguard was expecting her back. It would have to be the following night at the Karaoke Café. We parted for the night through tears of joy, though since Megumi's weeks in captivity had dried up her meager emotional reserves, all the tears were my own.

I paid the boys twice what they were owed, which staunched their sulking about the wound to Kar Wai's face. Megumi's razor blade missed his eye by less than a centimeter, but the important thing was that it had missed. Though deep, the cut was clean and thin; nothing a few stitches couldn't patch. It wasn't as if the scar would detract from his good looks.

George and I parted at the entrance to the Ritz. He pumped my hand for a bit too long. "I'm sure you realize Mr. Salgado, well, of course you do, that this plan has the pungent aroma of a setup. Are you sure you wouldn't prefer the boys to accompany you?"

"I'm the one who suggested the location," I said. "The Karaoke Café is the only place we can meet that won't send out warning signals immediately. We'll get five or six hours to escape instead of thirty minutes. Even if Kolling were in Shanghai, he couldn't stop us from leaving the country in time. And I know that son-of-a-bitch. The last thing he expects me to do is waltz right into his karaoke establishment. So that's exactly what I plan to do."

George didn't look convinced but shrugged. "Godspeed, Mr. Salgado."

CHAPTER 32

The maitre d' ushered me to a table, the blue beam of his penlight dancing before us on the floor. The radiant glow of the video screen transformed the club's patrons into shadows shifting in the darkness. They could be sensed rather than seen, fluttering like bats within this electronic cavern. The maitre d' handed me a palm-sized computer with a lighted touch screen.

"Press here," he said, "for English songs. Your companion will bring your microphone. You've chosen a lady already, yes?"

I nodded. The maitre d' took my drink order and disappeared.

The unattached girls were at the bar, the only place, aside from the video screen, that was illuminated. They sat in short skirts on high stools, like canaries in a cage, their makeup and posture impeccable. Their dresses were eerily similar in all ways except for hue, like bridesmaids modeling different colors for the bride. In the darkness, it was impossible for my eyes not to be drawn to them, especially the one who stood out. She was plumper than the others, not hefty but fuller figured. She looked familiar somehow.

"You rang, sir?" the maitre d' said.

"The girl at the bar," I said. "The one in the…is that cyan? Teal? Would it be possible for me to talk to her for a moment."

The maitre d' pointed the penlight at his own face. "That one cannot speak English, sir. You have to choose one of the shades of yellow. Perhaps the young lady in the goldenrod? She is fine, is she not?"

"Would you ask the woman in the seafoam dress to come sit with me for a moment?"

"As you wish, sir." He paused. "There will be an additional charge, of course."

"Of course."

The thin beam of blue light traveled from her face to her feet, barely enough time for me to confirm what I'd seen from a distance. She sat down and pressed against me, the warmth of her thigh seeping through the thin fabric of my trousers.

"You're a friend of Megumi's, aren't you?" I said. "I saw you in front of your home. You were carrying a baby. An infant. Was that you?"

"*Shenma? Dui bu qui, ge ge. Wo bu shuo Yinguen.*"

I squeezed her hand. "It's okay. I'm a friend. A *pengyou.* I'm a *pengyou* of Megumi. Do you understand? Megumi. *Pengyou.*" My tongue slurred the Chinese tones.

She withdrew her hand. Had I accidentally insulted her? Maybe no one was supposed to know that Megumi was helping her to escape from this high-class brothel. Had she mistaken my friendly overture as a threat?

I clutched at the song-list console. "Would you like to sing? *La, la, la*...understand? I would like it if you would sing for me."

Her fingers flew over the lighted keypad, drilling through submenus until she found her song. Then we waited. Only the working girls sang, their dulcet tones filling the darkness like a rising sonic tide. I breathed this musical fluid into my lungs, losing track of whether I was facing up or down, mesmerized by the perfection of their pitch. If their caresses were half what their voices promised, a man would willingly dash himself against the rocks for their attentions.

Megumi lured you here. You have not returned to the womb. You are trapped within a sealed tomb.

The absence of light was playing tricks on my mind. The old Guy might succumb to such doubts and insecurities, but not Balthazar Salgado. My neuroses evaporated when the girl began to sing, the microphone's green LED light illuminating her lips. How could such a young girl produce a sound like heated caramel? I leaned toward her...and discovered, drowned within the amplified music, a strained dissonance. Was she emitting two sounds at once, one assured and the other quavering?

The beam of a red penlight targeted her forehead like the sighting dot of a rifle. She broke the song off mid-verse.

"Get out of here," Megumi said in English. Her tone was peremptory. "Go to your place at the bar."

There was a rustle as the girl left the table. Megumi took her place next to me. The music continued for a few bars then stopped. A new song cued up.

"I was waiting for you," I said. "I thought I recognized her."

"Be quiet," Megumi said. "We haven't any time. Come with me."

Megumi took my hand and led me into another large room with another video screen. And then through another one. We pushed through double-doors into a hallway lit dimly with paper lanterns. After the near-subterranean darkness, it seemed as bright as a Las Vegas casino. We passed private karaoke rooms, their smoked glass doors closed. Next to a riveted steel door was the window to a lighted office occupied by a heavyset man wearing a uniform. He fumbled over the control panel and the heavy door buzzed open.

The hallway beyond resembled the one in the Ritz Carlton, right down to the numbers on the doors. Lotus-bud lamps sprouted within alcoves.

"Where are we?" I said.

Megumi didn't answer. At a corner room, she swiped a magnetic card through a reader and the door swung inward. Inside was a neatly turned-down king-sized bed, a round table with two thin-cushioned chairs, and a restroom. If I had ignored the absence of a window, I would have presumed myself transported to a four-star hotel.

Megumi began kissing me deeply, furiously. Her mouth was honey-sweet and the warmth of her skin made me tremble involuntarily. She was wearing the orange dress with the spaghetti straps she'd worn the first night we'd met, when she'd been on Kolling's arm. Beneath my fingers the sheer material felt strangely rough. Cheap.

"We should wait until we leave the country," I said.

"We are being watched," she whispered. "Keep your voice down and keep moving."

She stopped my head from swiveling in search of the camera. Was it in the overhead dome lamp? Behind the painting of orange koi fish swimming in a stream? She unbuttoned my shirt. How could I focus on peeling her tangerine dress when a man in another room watched our every move on a black-and-white video monitor?

Megumi dropped to her knees and unclasped my fanny pack. She threw it on the chair next to her purse. She unfastened my belt. I clutched her hair and pulled.

"I can't do this knowing we're being watched," I said.

She rubbed my crotch. "If you want to live, you'll do what I say. The guard will watch until we're done and then ignore us. Slip off the left side of the bed and the mattress will obstruct your body. Crawl to the door. I'll prop it open so you won't have to reach for the doorknob."

Megumi pulled my pants and briefs down to my ankles in a single, swift motion. She threw them next to the bed. "I am throwing your clothes there. That way, you'll be able to dress before leaving."

She pulled on my flaccid penis with one hand while the other kneaded my scrotum. It didn't feel like sex but carpentry, sanding with a rough-grade of paper.

"When we are finished," she said, "stay in bed and pretend to fall asleep. This often happens once the client has been satisfied. I will wash up in the restroom and slip out of the room. They will believe you have decided to pay for the full night and I am retrieving my overnight kit. I will wait for you near the emergency exit."

My penis remained limp. She kissed the tip then pressed her lips on the shaft as if blotting off lipstick. "You must wait for thirty minutes—longer is okay but no less than that—

and then follow. Take a right and another right. Right and then right. I will wait for you on the other side of the door. Don't worry about the alarm. I've disarmed it."

Megumi took my penis into her mouth. She held my testicles in an uncomfortably tight grip, fingernails digging into flesh. "What's wrong? Aren't you excited?"

"I can't get excited. I won't get excited until we're out of this place. Out of this damned country."

She looked up at me, her eyes placid. Her complexion was perfect, and looking down the front of her dress, I could see her nipples. My penis glistened with moisture. And I couldn't get hard. I didn't know if I'd ever have another erection.

"Stop thinking so much," she said. "Close your eyes and stop thinking."

During my nighttime imaginings, Megumi's ministrations had been feathery caresses. Now it felt as if she was exfoliating my genitals. The harder she tried to stimulate me, the more pain she induced, until I pushed her forehead away. This was not how I remembered our intimacies, but it was my memory that was at fault.

I fumbled for the strap of her dress. "If you could just take off your dress..."

She pulled the strap back onto her shoulder. "Stop fooling around. Ejaculate and be done."

I closed my eyes and imagined removing her dress. There were her perfect nipples, her flat stomach. Megumi smelled like soap and hot water; she didn't have an identifiable scent of her own. I imagined perspiration on the bed sheets and fumbling in the darkness, tripping into bed, laughing. A long, long torso that never seemed to end and breasts that sagged, that formed into the shape of my hands. Yes. The visualization was working.

What did I smell? Cigarettes. Tequila. Dog hair? I pictured Sunny Choi's moon face, the crow's-feet at the corners of her eyes, the way she swept her hair from her face and knotted it with a single hand. How could I be aroused by a barmaid who'd been so wet I could hardly feel myself inside of her?

Megumi jerked me off onto the carpet. She squeezed until every drop was out.

"I will go the restroom and pretend to clean myself up," she said. "You pretend to sleep. Thirty minutes—no less than that. Remember! Or you'll endanger us both."

"Thirty minutes," I said.

I had to yank at the bed sheets, which were tucked tightly under the mattress, to create a pocket into which I climbed. The sheets were clean and cold. I put my forearm over my face.

During her absence Megumi had become a creature of softness and light, the perfect woman. But the reality was that we didn't share just solitude, we shared isolation. Our relationship was as arid as the sand dunes Megumi had so despised in southeastern New Mexico. We shifted like salt, altering our shapes but not our substance.

I heard Megumi return to the bedroom and pick up her purse. She leaned over me. "We are only thirty minutes from our new lives." She paused. "I love you."

I wanted to respond but my mouth was too dry. I heard her pull the heavy door closed.

It was right to chase her. We would remake ourselves into better people. If I needed more, all I had to do was ask. We would have the rest of our lives to cultivate love.

Twenty minutes. Twenty-five minutes. There was muffled activity in the hallway. There was an electronic double-
beep next door; no, the lock on this door was disengaging.
I opened my eyes to find a group of Chinese men in dark
suits standing at the threshold.

They rushed forward before I could wriggle free of the
bed sheets. An elbow in the windpipe kept my head pressed
deep into the plush pillow until a rag was stuffed into my
mouth and sealed with duct tape. A hood was pulled over
my head and everything went black, speckled with pinpoints
of light. They trussed me up in the blankets and carried me
out of the room.

They said not a word throughout, which, given the
weightlessness of my body suspended by the many hands on
the sheets, lent the sensation of being borne away by ghosts
to my own funeral.

CHAPTER 33

I slept easily. I was thankful for that. While awake, I felt as if I were asleep. I was thankful for that too. What was left for me? What was left of me? Guy Watanabe had been abandoned stateside. Balthazar Salgado had been betrayed in a Shanghai karaoke bar.

Kolling's men treated me like livestock. They unloaded me from the car's trunk somewhere by the sea, the scent of salt water as strong as that of engine oil. They dumped me into a room with broken office equipment: wobbly chairs, computer monitors, desks with moisture rings on their surfaces. I was fed and watered, given enough clothing not to shiver too badly, and otherwise left to my own non-thoughts.

On the morning of the third day I was ushered out of my cluttered cell. I was in an office of some sort, a single-story building with thin walls and small windows. The employees averted their eyes as I passed their cubicles.

A doctor and a nurse were waiting for me in the infirmary, talking to one another through surgical masks as I was strapped down to an examination table. Two of Kolling's thugs, one on each side, remained to restrain my arms, but they needn't have bothered. I was resigned.

Executions are accompanied by rituals: last meals, last words, official pronouncements, witnesses. This was euthanasia. I was being put down like a horse with a broken leg.

The nurse's sole role appeared to be to comfort me. She rested one gloved hand on my cheek and stroked my hair with the other. She spoke in Chinese syllables that were light and encouraging. The doctor wore scratched spectacles. The syringe held an impossibly long needle. I felt a sharp pinch and icy tendrils spread across my throat.

Did my life race before me? No. I was filled with regret. Not with regret about having trusted Megumi, but for having not lied to Sunny. I should have said her electronic compositions were beautiful. I'd spent my entire life lying to myself and others yet felt compelled to tell her the truth about her lack of talent. I wish I hadn't hurt her that way.

I gurgled and then the gurgle receded as if it had been sucked down a mud hole. My throat muscles quavered and collapsed, leaving a dry ache. I tried to speak; I tried to grunt; I tried to scream; nothing emerged. I opened and closed my mouth like a suffocating fish.

But I didn't die.

Kolling's men escorted me to his office. He sat behind a desk that had the clean lines and brushed metal of

German furniture. He didn't look up when I entered, instead holding up a cautionary index finger to indicate that he was not to be interrupted while reading. His men pushed me down into an orange plastic chair that some might have considered chic but reminded me of an elementary school classroom.

Kolling uncapped his fountain pen and signed the page where a Post-It was affixed. He clasped his hands and sighed.

"It is human nature not to appreciate what one has until it is gone," he said. "Mr. Smith is lost to me and now trivial matters consume so much time I can't get more important work done. But I suppose you know very little about work, Mr. Watanabe, having done so precious little of it during your lifetime."

Kolling's British accent startled me. I knew he wasn't American but certain sounds emitting from Asian lips still caught me off guard: British-inflected English, Southern accents, hip-hop idioms.

"Your problem," he said, "the problem with all Americans really, is the blindness occasioned by your privileges. Americans preach hard work and seek leisure. Born into comfort, you've amounted to nothing. Born into poverty, I've purchased more than half of the worldwide karaoke market, and my share is growing every day. A man is measured by what he possesses: wealth, skill, beauty. Everything you have, I have taken from you. And I'm stronger because of it. Life is a competition and you are the loser."

We stared at each other without saying anything, he because he chose not to and I because I lacked a voice. Then Kolling began his tale.

CHAPTER 34
HORATIO'S DEDICATION

I can pinpoint exactly when I began to hate my father. The two of us were celebrating my thirteenth birthday in the space that served as our bedroom, kitchen, and living room. Sheets of plywood separated us from the steam press, the washing machines, the canister clothes dryers, and the conveyor belt. A naked bulb hanging from the ceiling illuminated festive toilet paper strung from nails. Father sang "Happy Birthday" in his thick Chinese accent, unable to get through the song without hacking and spitting into his handkerchief.

He smelled of phlegm and mothballs and the herbal tea we percolated as a humidifier, which meant I smelled that way too, the odor clinging to my hair, my undergarments, the bed sheets. All day we dealt with the stench of middle-class whites in Johannesburg—menopausal secretaries who drenched their blouses in perfume, barristers whose shirts reeked of cigar smoke and red meat. But the night scents were worse. We shared the same bed. I lay down next to father and inhaled the death he exhaled from his lungs.

"Make wish! Make wish!" my father said.

I glared at the candle sticking out of the cupcake, the same stub of wax from last year. What did I want? Not to wake up at 4:30 a.m. to sweep the store and warm up the machinery. Not to spend my day behind the cash register, smiling as housewives complained that they'd handed me a fifty-rand, not a twenty-rand, note.

I gazed into that narrow, weary face that so resembled my own and knew exactly what I wanted. I blew out the candle.

I was born white of a white father in Johannesburg, South Africa. How can this be with two Chinese parents? With my unmistakably Mongoloid features? The answer is that paper can become reality.

The day my parents immigrated to South Africa the weather was unusually hot and exceedingly wet, which resulted in flooded streets and irritable bureaucrats. The immigration officer who interviewed my parents was one such bureaucrat, the discomfort of his soggy socks exacerbated by the sting of having been reprimanded by his superior. In most instances, a man takes out such mundane frustrations on those less fortunate than himself. This anonymous civil servant bit the hand that fed him.

"Name?" he asked.

"Koh Ling," father answered, meaning surname "Koh" and given name "Ling."

"Kolling, huh?" he said. "Plenty of Brits by that name, know a fat chap at the club by that name, or no, that's Kolfax. Those buggers upstairs go on and on about the low birthrate of whites but never do anything about it. I can."

Surname "Kolling," given name "None," my parents were given the same name at the port of entry, each abbreviating it to "N. Kolling" for simplicity's sake. They were issued the same identification number and duplicate identification cards, the photograph of Father (or Mother?) too dimly lit to distinguish between the two. These were the days of manual typewriters and onionskin paper, carbon paper in triplicate. It would have taken physical exertion to correct the error. My parents gained the rights and privileges of whites in the apartheid system without risking their lives or marching in the streets. But there is no blessing without a curse.

Blessing: they could have traveled anywhere without carrying a colored passbook. Curse: they never left a five-block radius for fear they would be stopped and their secret revealed. Blessing: they opened Kolling's Cleaners in the profitable, whites-only financial district. Curse: Chinese business associations ostracized them for refusing to help their brethren secure permits to operate in the same neighborhood. Blessing: they had access to First World medical care in a Third World country. Curse: they feared visiting a white doctor and disdained visiting a colored one.

Mother worked through her pregnancy, setting down her mop when her water broke. And when the water became blood, she waited until I'd been born and swaddled, until the floor had been swabbed and the sheets laundered, before hunching over at the dryer and expiring.

The single act of courage in Father's short life was to call a white ambulance. When the paramedics balked at the sight of Mother, he waved her identification papers in their faces. An argument ensued. If the papers were correct, the proper procedure was to conduct a medical inquest and to file a death certificate. If the papers were incorrect, the proper procedure would be to request a racial reclassification before they disposed of the body. Both resolutions required too much effort. The existence of two N. Kollings provided them with a way out.

The duplicity of names allowed the paramedics to drive away with Mother's corpse and her identification papers never to return. It was easier to make a body disappear than it was to acknowledge the death of someone who'd never officially existed. Father said that everything had turned out for the best. Losing our white privilege wouldn't have brought Mother back to life. There was me to think of. In lieu of a death certificate, Father received a birth certificate.

I was a white child born of a single, white father: immaculately conceived by a man and racially reclassified by the universal human aspiration for administrative convenience.

Father regaled me with stories about my entitlement to a gated mansion, private schooling, a car and driver, tennis lessons, a table overflowing with cured meats. He said this even as he kept me out of colored schools because I was white, and out of white schools because I was Chinese. He said this though I worked the same sixteen-hour days that he did. I never learned how to ride a bicycle, but by the age of seven I operated a four-hundred-pound steam press.

Father was content to live in that void between paper and reality, to subsist on extravagant imaginings. On the walls of our store were sun-faded posters of Durban and Cape Town, white women in bikinis lounging beneath umbrellas on the beach. We paid the white police officers to keep us safe from the black street toughs, and the black street toughs to keep us safe from the white hooligans. But when the front window was shattered, and the walls were spray-painted with racist epithets, we huddled in the backroom with the lights off waiting for the squeak of their sneakers to fade into the night.

That's how it was for years: grandiose timidity. As I grew, Father shrunk. He spent less time behind the cash register and more time in the work room, though the chemicals irritated his lungs. More than once I chased him out of the front room before a customer noticed the red sputum on his lips.

At the age of twelve I took over the accounting, separating what we reported to the government and what we stuffed into our mattress. I found that for all his parsimony, Father had no idea how much cash we'd accumulated. As his health deteriorated, he waved away my reports, though numbers were the reason we slaved away. He babbled about what it would be like to walk along the seashore, even as it was me, always me, who walked six miles roundtrip to the colored district for groceries.

We paid twice what other cleaners did for supplies and charged customers ten percent less. Father wouldn't hire additional help, forcing me to work both the front room and the back. He rejected my idea to provide pickup and delivery service to the neighboring office buildings until other cleaners did the same and it was too late to start. He wanted nothing except to continue as we always had, wasting away our miserable lives in the shadows.

On my thirteenth birthday, I realized that I'd been more a servant than a son, living with less freedom than the poorest blacks. They attended school instead of educating themselves through books borrowed two weeks at a time from the public library. Jobless or hungry or forcibly relocated, they knew more of the world than starch and brighteners. I massaged Father's feet when mine ached worse. I rubbed Tiger Balm on his heaving chest.

Father's condition was a curse. And a blessing.

For years Father had entrusted his health to Uncle Lo, a Chinatown herbalist of some renown. After examining Father, he asked me to return to his shop. Uncle Lo reached haphazardly into a number of jars, extracting twigs and tea and fine powders. He mixed these together in a mortar and pestle, adding as the last ingredient half a bottle of baby aspirin.

Uncle Lo noticed my quizzical expression. He shook his head. "We are all dying. It's best to numb the pain."

I returned every two weeks for Uncle Lo's concoction, which changed every time except for the baby aspirin. He waved away my concerns about Father's deteriorating condition. "Nature is the best remedy," he said.

Mouse got his nickname for his ears, which fanned forward like tree fungi, and not for his eyes, which were horizontal black gashes. His face, his arms, and his belly all had a distended quality about them, as if he were a water balloon on the verge of bursting. If the sun hit him from the right angle, one could imagine tawny undertones beneath his dusky complexion. A low-level bureaucrat must have caught him at just the right time of day because he classified Mouse as colored and his half-brothers as black. It was for him a source of great pride.

From the first time I walked into the colored grocery market, Mouse had taken to monopolizing my time, the only thing that kept him from shirking work or throwing dice with his half-brothers and friends. He claimed that his father was full Chinese—not a poor villager who'd migrated to South Africa as a laborer, but royalty from a northern province (the name of which he couldn't recall). He knew this, he said, because his mother was a witch. She'd flown in through the palace windows on a plate and been captured while trying to exchange it for a golden serving platter. The price of her freedom was to return home impregnated with his seed.

This day we met on a rutted football field at the border between the colored district in which Mouse worked and the black township in which he lived. Trash had become part of the playfield: Styrofoam ground into peat, paper wrappers and plastic bags skimming along like tumbleweeds. Several bare-chested black teens were scuffling over a misshapen ball. A few of the younger ones had begun to puff up and stare at me before Mouse reached my side.

Mouse handed me a green plastic bag. Inside was a peanut butter jar with the label torn off. The jar was three-quarters filled with a brown paste on top of which was a crust of yellowing oil and hardened animal fat. He pulled at his earlobe, scored with what looked to be nibble marks from his namesake.

"Mama says you've got to follow her instructions exact," Mouse said. "The first day one spoonful. The next day two.

Then three. On and on until the whole bottle is finished. He's got to swallow it all or it's not going to work. Most important: Mama said you've got to save the last spoonful for yourself. You've got to eat it too or it's not going to work."

I eyed the concoction more closely. What had appeared to be a brown, smooth sludge was in fact saturated with particles that looked like insect legs and fruit seeds, some dark and others a mealy white.

"Why have I got to eat it?" I said.

"She said the last one is his soul." Mouse looked from side to side nervously, but there was nothing around us except for the corrugated iron rooftops of the nearby shanties. It was a perfect day, sunny and neither too hot nor too cold, though the football players kicked up dust and the trucks expelled black exhaust. "You don't eat his soul it's going to haunt you now and then follow you into your next life. You've got to hold that poison in until it becomes a part of you. At first you're going to get weak, but then you'll feel stronger, stronger than you ever felt before."

"How does she know this?" I said.

Mouse rubbed his broad, flat nose with the back of his hand. "How you think she killed my father?"

Father never resisted taking the medicine. Although during the day he rarely stood still, at night he wanted me to tend to him. He didn't eat much of anything anymore: rice, some vegetables, a sipping soup. He drank Uncle Lo's tea, and the vapors emitting from the tea kettle soothed his throat and lungs. I massaged his back, narrow as a child's, and his feet, riddled with sores and bunions. His relief showed in his closed eyelids and the laxity of his limbs.

I didn't scoop the brown sludge from the peanut butter jar. I'd purchased a hand-blown bottle at the bazaar and poured the concoction into it. He'd shaken his head and muttered "too expensive," but I could tell from how he touched the bottle, as if afraid it might shatter, he was impressed. I waited until he'd almost fallen asleep before I prepared the first spoonful.

After he swallowed it, he let out a low moan. "It is nothing on my tongue but feels like fire in my stomach."

"Give it time, Father," I said. "It is cleansing you from the inside out. Uncle Lo says it soaks up the toxins in your body. It's burning up everything bad inside."

He ground his teeth and sweat broke out on his brow. "It's as you say, son. I am full of poison and the medicine is eating it up. But it is almost more than I can bear."

"Hold on, Father." I squeezed his hand and it closed spasmodically on mine. "Let nature take its course."

Father never turned his head away. He might pause, chest heaving, for a minute, but he opened his mouth for more. His stomach might convulse, but he fought to keep the medicine down. And as the days wore on, his muscle contractions grew less violent. The knots in his neck and back unraveled, lay in lax bundles beneath loose skin.

His coughs and wheezes came fewer and farther between. His breathing reduced to a trickle, an airy rattle so faint I had to press my ear against his chest to detect it. Yet maddeningly he rose each morning to carry out the day's chores.

Father would not stop working. Eyes glazed, hair matted, he reached for the next shirt to be ironed, the next ban-

quet sheet to be laundered. He had no idea I'd been turning away customers, or that the cash I stuffed into the mattress at night was the same I'd withdrawn in the morning,
leaving only enough work to keep him occupied. He moved
between the steam press and the conveyor belt, the washing
machines and the barrel dryers, with plodding steps.

At night, however, he collapsed on our mattress of
money, still comforted by the sound of paper bills shifting
beneath him. In the last days, his only sustenance was the
elixir—now twenty-five, then twenty-six, spoonfuls of gritty,
speckled sludge. He choked it down, not a droplet spilling
from his lips. And at last he lay silent. There was a single
spoonful left, the one for me, flakes of yellow-white coagu-
lated fat and black insect limbs drowned in brown goo. Outside a police siren wailed and I heard the patter of boots
on the sidewalk, the sound of a metal gate clattering shut.
Uncle Lo's herbal tea simmered in the kettle. All was as it
always was except for one thing: I was free.

I was an orphan and that meant an orphanage, but even
that was preferable to the life I'd led. There would be no
meals to prepare, and the only work would be homework.
There would be playfields and other children. Adults would
serve me for a change. And when I turned eighteen, I could
rely upon my secret inheritance, the mattress of money, the
assets from over a decade of toil in this country.

Father's final gift to me wasn't my racial status, which
could and would change over the years based on the pre-
vailing social whims. In an effort to boost tourism, the
Nationalist government eventually classified Taiwanese as
honorary whites but kept local Chinese classified as colored.

No, Father's gift to me wasn't color, unless it was the green, yellow, red, and violet of our national currency. His gift was independence and the means with which to enjoy it.

Father's rasp startled me from my reverie. It was more than the last spasm of an expired body. His breathing was weak, but his chest was moving, almost imperceptibly, in and out. I placed my fingertip beneath his nostrils and his nose twitched. He groaned.

"What is it, Father?" I lowered my ear to his mouth. "What do you want?"

"The machines," he said. "Turn on the machines."

Father tried to rise, but my forearm on his windpipe held him in place. As slender as I was as a boy, I still outweighed this husk of a man. It didn't take much to suffocate him, not even conscious pressure. It was a matter of allowing the weight of my body to do the work. He struggled for a moment and then surrendered, expiring with the sound of crushed leaves.

I'd done nothing more than hasten the processes of nature, as the elixir had done no more than advance a terminal condition. Quantity of life means nothing if there is no quality of life, and Father had ceased living long ago. The last spoonful of medicine, and the witch's instructions, beckoned me.

What does a soul taste like? It is gritty and acidic, coats one's tongue and throat, and burns the bowels. One's teeth grind on twigs and pebbles and legs that were trapped during the mixing process. Eating a soul fills a man up and empties him out again, leaving him with an insatiable hunger. Once a man eats a soul, nothing else will satiate him.

CHAPTER 35
HORATIO'S DEDICATION (continued)

I should have hated Kolling, or feared him, or mustered a nauseous revulsion, but I couldn't. We shared an affinity: a fault in our essential make-ups. The mold had called for platinum or gold or iron, but sawdust, sticks, and mud had fallen in.

Kolling drummed his fingers on a stack of documents and contemplated me in an absent manner, as if I were a vase for which he had no space.

"If I were a vengeful man, I would have had you killed," he said. "If I were a sadistic man, I would have had you tortured. I asked Megumi what should be done with you. She answered, 'Give him what he deserves.'

"What is it that you deserve, Mr. Watanabe? Does the good you've done for me outweigh your bad intentions?"

When a man comes from nothing, he can never accumulate too much. "Poverty" is an absence, a void, a hollow space repugnant to all but clerics, artists, and philosophers. "Wealth" is the opposite. It can be touched and measured; its interest compounds daily. Everything I have, I've earned. I'm grateful for every cent, for every day my fortune grows.

Would I have preferred to be a karaoke star? I've never considered the question. Why should I subject myself to the censure of people who possess inferior tastes? While my peers drank, and sang, and caroused, I founded a company that transformed their frivolity into my fortune. I make their happiness possible. Without the Karaoke Group International, the world would be strumming guitars around campfires, not luxuriating in state-of-the-art karaoke facilities.

What was Mr. Smith before he entered the employ of the Karaoke Group International? A wastrel foreigner, teaching English to spoiled Hong Kong schoolgirls. With a bachelor's degree from a small liberal arts college, he never would have risen to Vice President of KGI if he hadn't started as my secretary. He moved from a shared flat to a high-rise condominium. His daughters attended private school; his wife sunbathed at the American Club pool. Was that enough? No. It's never enough.

It's true that Mr. Smith was the primary architect of the Neighborhood Karaoke Strategy, and that the NKS guided KGI's initial growth. We now control 55 percent of all neighborhood karaoke bars, large or small, upscale or dilapidated. KGI franchisees make up 85 percent of all newly opened karaoke bars. Under the NKS, it didn't matter whether our franchises were located in Icelandic coastal towns or Indian slums. If they were profitable we would back them.

The NKS may have been Mr. Smith's idea, but an idea amounts to nothing if it can't be transformed into bricks and mortar. Mr. Smith bore no risks. He pocketed stock options and annual bonuses. He worked for KGI. I *am* KGI. If I said it was time abandon the Neighborhood Karaoke Strategy, his duty was to bore holes into the hull and ensure that the ship sunk quietly to the ocean floor.

"How can we change course now?" Mr. Smith said once. "Look at the numbers, Mr. Kolling. We are making money hand-over-fist in the very locations that she claims are 'too ugly.' Bombay peasants may not spend as much per night as the elites who crowd our upscale locations, but they spend the same way, bust or boom, and enter the bars 365 days a year. If you want my candid assessment of Megumi's opinions, here it is. Her expertise, as exquisite as it might be, is not in the realm of karaoke. She should stick to what she does best."

I knew resentment when I heard it. We changed the wardrobe of the girls in the Shanghai bar—replacing their plastic number buttons with tailored dresses that varied by hue—on Megumi's suggestion. With a negligible investment, our revenues increased along with employee morale. Subsequently, I handed over wardrobe responsibilities for KGI-operated bars to Megumi. Mr. Smith feared a further erosion of his role.

Mr. Smith was my confidante. He handled sensitive personal business, which included chaperoning Megumi. And Megumi has not always shown adequate propriety. But I make decisions based on results. He, who was no one before meeting me, should have understood that.

The inspiration for our present business strategy came to me on one of the rare occasions I took a vacation. It was a sweltering day in Bangkok, when the exhaust sticks to one's face and refuge must be sought in air-conditioned malls, fast-food restaurants, and cafés. We'd returned from Megumi's village, where her parents own a home, an automobile, a motorcycle, and two televisions. Megumi's relatives sought her advice, and the younger girls hung on her every word. I'd deigned to go with her to give her face, and she'd reciprocated by showering me with affection and a volubility that was inimical to her nature. With hours to kill before boarding our flight, we sipped lattes in a Starbucks café around the corner from our hotel.

"If all your karaoke bars were this clean," Megumi said. "You wouldn't have to pretend not to own them."

"I do not 'pretend' not to own anything," I said. "KGI believes it makes better business sense not to bludgeon local communities over the head with the fact that control of their karaoke resources lies overseas. That way, we will not become an easy political scapegoat for Communists, Islamists, or any other –ists who rabble-rouse against free trade."

She shrugged in the infuriatingly simple way she had. "Why isn't Starbucks afraid? Why doesn't Coca Cola change its name? Thai people like things foreign better than they like things Thai. No one's ever heard of KGI."

How had I unconsciously swallowed the poisonous philosophy of my father, of all overseas Chinese?—that it is better to profit unseen. It's the psychology of the beehive, of drones building catacombs for their queen and never themselves. KGI's success had blinded me. Our only advantage over an independently owned local karaoke bar lay in economies of scale: we could buy and sell our products more cheaply. What would happen if a Starbucks entered the realm of karaoke, offering superior facilities, superior sound, and superior drinks at a marginally more expensive price point? Corner coffee shops and independent bookstores had gone extinct. What about the local karaoke bar?

I outlined the principles of the One Karaoke Establishment vision during our senior staff meeting. KGI would no longer serve as karaoke slumlord. Under OKE, we would repurchase each and every one of the independently operated karaoke franchises and run them ourselves according to a single master plan. It would involve assuming leases, hiring staff worldwide, and shifting investments to increase positive cash flow during the years we ran in the red. But in the end, we would rebrand the bars with the KGI name and logo. We would raise the standard of karaoke to never-before-seen levels of comfort, convenience, and quality.

My senior executives gave me a standing ovation. Mr. Smith chose this time to challenge my authority.

"People don't want big, glitzy karaoke complexes," he said. "In every survey we've taken, in every focus group, the consumer said he wanted a place that was part of his community, a community watering-hole, if you will. Wouldn't a slow transition be more prudent? We could establish test locations and build from there."

Silence ensued. He'd already voiced those concerns in private. He knew better than to make them public. If the specter of doubt is raised among men who contribute the maximum to their retirement accounts, the world could be set on fire and they'd be too paralyzed to reach for a bucket. Mr. Smith exhibited a lack of decorum and common sense.

"KGI is not the right organization for men who lack imagination," I said. "We will never be content with chasing consumer desire when we can shape it."

Mr. Smith's apologies came too late. I fumed about his behavior after my evening bath, the only time in the day when I truly relax. Megumi massaged my feet. I said that I was considering demoting Mr. Smith, or even terminating his employment. To my surprise, she came to his defense.

"He wants to protect you," she said. "You should fear the managers who say nothing."

"I don't fear anyone," I said. "Least of all men who have no sense of gratitude and obligation. Mr. Smith has become a wealthy man implementing my ideas. Once I have made a decision, his job is to adopt it as his own."

Megumi pressed her thumbs into the arch of my foot, her tiny fingers exerting remarkable strength.

"It is easy sometimes to forget one's place," she said.

What am I to do with you, Mr. Watanabe? Were it not for you, I never would have doubted Megumi, emboldening Mr. Smith to pursue his devious plan. Were it not for you, Mr. Smith might have usurped my throne.

I had lost my good opinion of Mr. Smith, but who else would chaperone Megumi during our visit to America? While Megumi's proclivities were well-known to Mr. Smith, they were unknown to my employees. For her to succeed as KGI's Manager of Talent Procurement, her inconstancy could not become public knowledge.

I never suspected Mr. Smith of coveting Megumi. He was, in my mind, the consummate family man. During our business trips, he sent three postcards a day home to Hong Kong, one each for his wife and two daughters. His children wallpapered their room with them. Every spare hour of the hundred days per year he was not traveling for KGI, he attended soccer games, violin recitals, and his wife's charity events.

More persuasive than my trust in Mr. Smith was this simple fact: he was not Megumi's type. What is Megumi's type? A man with no capital, poor earning potential, a shabby appearance, an inflated ego. I will not psychoanalyze her predilections, except to say that she feels comfort in the arms of those to whom she bears a marked superiority. I knew from the moment I saw you lording it over the denizens of the hovel you called a karaoke bar that you were a threat. And true to form, she disappointed me.

So preoccupied was I with Megumi's most recent betrayal that I'd failed to watch Mr. Smith closely. I discovered after his death that he'd been attempting for months to convince KGI's managers that the OKE strategy would destabilize our company. He was surreptitiously requesting financial reports from our banks. He was plotting to establish a competing karaoke network and he meant to take Megumi with him. He meant to break from KGI on the very night you murdered him.

Megumi told me how you succumbed to blood lust. She hid in the restroom while you cut at his flesh and tendons long after his death rattle. Were it not for her detailed description, I would scarcely have believed you capable of such fortitude. But I am a man who has felt life escape from his own father's crushed windpipe. I know the truth when I hear it.

I retrieved Mr. Smith's casket from the airport. Before delivering it to the funeral home, I had my driver pull into a back alley so I could view his corpse for myself. His spinal cord was visible. His genitals, which had been severed from his body, were stuffed into a foil-lined bag that was tucked into his armpit.

I paid for his funeral. It was the least I could do given his years of service to KGI. And I attempted to shield his widow from the unseemly circumstances surrounding his death, that he was naked, had recently ejaculated, and had his own genitals lodged in his throat. This was, of course, impossible in the age of digital information. The story had taken on a life of its own, a local officer having sold the crime-scene photographs to an underground Web site.

Mrs. Smith was drunk during the funeral. She mumbled during her eulogy that maybe he had deserved his fate for never being home when she needed him. She laughed through her tears as she described how her youngest daughter ran from her father because she didn't recognize him. As we left the cemetery, her oldest daughter said, "Mama, I feel as if my heart will burst." How did Mrs. Smith respond? She slapped the child. In front of her parents, in front of his parents, in front of his gathered family and friends.

I delighted in this. Mr. Smith's personal and private lives had been reconciled. I could not have paid a professional to exact more delicious retribution.

Megumi has been a changed woman since her return. Months with you allowed her to understand the folly of following her feelings rather than her reason. She has proven to be a fine manager of talent: recruiting attractive, docile girls and keeping them in line. She may have professed her love to you, but she has proven her devotion to me. What are words compared to actions. Feelings cannot be measured, but fidelity can.

You stole Megumi from me. You have paid for that crime with your voice. You eliminated the one true threat to KGI's long-term financial stability. For that, I am offering you safe passage home. Return to what is left of your life and take care never to cross me again. Only a fool grants clemency twice.

Kolling stood, removed his blazer, and tossed it on the chair. He began unbuttoning his dress shirt, revealing his undershirt and an all-too-familiar red, white, and blue ribbon. When he had unfastened the fourth button I saw it, the circular disk...the golden medallion.

An acidic numbness seeped into my throat. Every ridge on the county seal, every letter of the inscription, was known to my eyes.

"This was her gift to me," Kolling said. "I own a majority of the worldwide karaoke market and my share grows every day. I am the Karaoke King."

CHAPTER 36

FROM GUY WATANABE'S SHIPBOARD JOURNAL

Day 1

Maybe Kolling is right. A man stripped of his possessions is no longer a man, but an animal that knows it will die. I am being shipped home in a sealed container with seven illegals and four pallets of portable DVD machines. It doesn't really matter who I am anymore.

A canister fan agitates the torpid air and a string of Christmas lights provides our only illumination; they're plugged into extension cords that run out through a hole in the wall to a generator of some sort. Clotheslines and bed sheets divide our space into three quadrants: one for the toilet buckets and the DVD machines; one for the only woman in our midst; and one for the men and more DVD machines. The rest of the space is consumed by cases of plastic water bottles, canned food, and personal effects.

The boys aren't particularly interested in me, not even in my inability to speak or understand them. They're preoccupied with impressing the only woman they'll see for weeks. They puff out their chests, wear strained smiles, and look at her longingly while her back is turned.

I've fallen in with the old man, Sha Long (sp.?). Even in the dim lighting, his spine shows through his T-shirt. The boys will wind up as busboys and dishwashers, but what's the old man going to do in America? He won't live long enough to work off the cost of his passage. Sha Long gave me this journal—a leather cover stitched onto handmade paper. He watched me write the first sentence and clapped his hands as if I'd performed a magic trick. I don't know why an illiterate man would carry a journal. And I certainly don't understand why, having carried it for so long, he would give it away to a stranger. But I'm grateful. There is no worse a fate than being left alone with one's own thoughts. If I couldn't write, I might actually have to think.

We have an enormous stash of canned food: bamboo shoots, straw mushrooms, baby corn, and sardines in spicy red sauce. But there's no can opener. Anyone who wants more than the twist-tab sardines has to smash the cans open—a messy project in these cramped confines. The boys are exhilarated by the challenge. A frontrunner for the girl's affections has already come to the fore: a tall, thin youth in a yellow T-shirt. He has a mop top and a slightly crooked smile. He presented her with a can of mushrooms nearly three-quarters full, his hands dripping with juice.

I was going to try my luck at prying open some canned baby corn—my stomach cramps call for something bland—but Sha Long stopped me. He reached into his cavernous backpack and produced a plastic bag filled with a mixture of almonds and dried fruit. What else is in the old man's backpack? Contents more practical than what the boys have brought onboard: entertainment magazines and comic books, playing cards, cigarettes, and scores of pirated CDs and DVDs. A two-week voyage to a new land and all they packed was entertainment and tobacco. They're the reason Kolling dominates the worldwide karaoke market. Say what we will about education, the environment, and human rights. In reality, what we want most is to be distracted.

I should mention something that's disturbing me. I recognize the girl.

This is the third time I've seen her. The first time was in front of the hovel she called a home, a baby on her hip, her shirt damp with breast milk. The second time she sat next to me in Kolling's karaoke bar, singing with an angelic voice. I think I'm the only one here who knows her true profession.

She avoids looking at me. Otherwise she almost appears to be enjoying herself. The boys have lined her sleeping area with blankets and jackets and do everything but balance balls on their noses to hold her attention. They're a far cry from the well-heeled customers to whom she's accustomed. For all I know, they come from villages near hers. Is this the first time she's spent time with boys her own age?

Day 2

When I awoke, it felt as if someone had scoured the inside of my head with hot sand. Sha Long caressed my cheek with his leathery hand and dripped water into my mouth. It's comical to be tended to by a man whose bones are so brittle it's painful to watch him stand. Sha Long gestured to his watch—a baby-blue Swatch Skin designed for a thirteen-year-old girl—spinning his ancient finger around the dial one-and-a-half times. Eighteen hours. No natural light penetrates the crevices of our container. We may, in fact, be buried at the bottom of the stacked metal boxes. Beneath the overpowering odors of excrement, perspiration, and machine oil, there's the hint of brine.

Sha Long prepared a feast for me: prunes and dried figs, pistachios, a fresh apple, and a starch that reminded me of Navajo flatbread. He even persuaded me to take a swig from a bottle filled with a hot-pink fluid with a root floating in it. It was disgusting, and now my mouth tastes like kerosene. But it perked me up. Sha Long is alternately generous and nasty. He responded to a boy's request for food with a spittle-laced tirade. It's not my place to suggest that he share his supplies and, to be quite frank, there's not enough to go around. I'm grateful to be on Sha Long's sunny side.

Three of the boys don't look so good. Motion-sickness, I suspect. It's not that the ship is bucking violently. At its worst, the ship shakes less than a train. But riding atop acres of water throws off a person's equilibrium. The ground undulates, ebbing and flowing along with our stomach acids. The sick boys take turns pressing their mouths to the floor. I nudged Sha Long and he pointed to a quarter-shaped hole. There are quarter-sized holes drilled into the floor every five feet or so. Air vents. I stuck my finger into one and didn't feel even the hint of a draft. I tried to take a gulp of air, and it felt like sucking an ice cube through a straw.

All the boys, even the sick ones, rally whenever the girl emerges from her "room," but there isn't nearly the same amount of playful banter. She looks good, perhaps better than yesterday, her hair pulled back into a neat ponytail. It just goes to show the power of context. Days ago, she was breastfeeding an infant. Her cheeks are swollen from the weight she must have put on during pregnancy, but here it looks like lingering baby fat, not fat for a baby. She's probably not even twenty years old. The flush on her cheeks is a sharp contrast to the pallor of the seasick boys. What do girls do with their babies when they emigrate? Do they leave them with families or give them up to orphanages? Was the father a boyfriend or a customer?

That bastard Kolling. He's got millions in the bank but ships her in a crate to save himself a few bucks. Not only is he charging her for her own transport, he's probably taking a percentage off the top. Vertical business integration at its best.

Day 3

Sha Long has given me his watch. I meant only to borrow it, but there was no way of communicating the difference between borrowing and begging. Time's become an obsession for me—a way of keeping my bearings in this sunless, starless place. It's a little past 7:30 p.m., Shanghai time, which means it must be 3:30 a.m. Seattle time (or is it 4:30 a.m.? Does China observe daylight savings time?). I noticed dried blood on my shirt, sprinkled around my chest like a splattering of chocolate fondue. I thought the hypodermic needle had left no trace, but, of course, I was preoccupied at the time.

Sha Long speaks to me as if I could understand Chinese. When I shake my head, he speaks slowly, as if I were a child. I should refuse his offers of assistance. Sha Long needs all the nutrition he can get. But the truth is, I'm consumed by an overpowering hunger. I must be recovering my strength. It's hard to refrain from raiding Sha Long's backpack for more. That's why I guard his belongings as if they were my own—I can see the way the boys look at the food, with ravenous glances that rival the ones directed at the girl.

The boys continue to bash their cans against the available hard surfaces but seem to have lost all pleasure for the challenge. The sardines are almost gone, and no one has the taste for them. Since we have nothing to do except conserve our energy and air, you might think we wouldn't waste time worrying about variety in our diets. The opposite is true. There is time, time, and more time to think about the food we're missing.

I realize I haven't been fair to the boys. No one has been hostile toward Sha Long and me, though Sha Long's rudeness would justify it. A stocky boy with a bad bowl haircut offered us an opened can of mushrooms. Sha Long wouldn't acknowledge his presence, and snatched from my hand the dried fruit I offered in exchange.

Is it possible to leave behind who you are for what you might become? That's the promise of America. Just because I've failed doesn't mean these boys will. And that kind of pisses me off.

Day 4

I slept poorly. Since my eighteen-hour slumber, I never seem to sleep at all. I hear the others talking or getting up to relieve themselves. The smallest things bother me. The tapping of the canister fan. Coughing. The shuffle of feet on the metal floor.

How did Nelson Mandela endure decades of isolation, imprisonment, and torture only to emerge preaching peace, love, and understanding? If I make it home alive, I'm going to gorge myself on Ben & Jerry's ice cream and let my lactose-intolerant stomach roil while I vegetate in front of the television. If I scrape together enough money, I'll pay someone to break Kolling's legs with a baseball bat. Or maybe I'll buy a new car.

Troy Bobbins taught that we're not the sum of our thoughts or ideals but of our everyday actions. He meant "we are what we do" right here, right now. But doesn't that make the past more relevant rather than less? If you eat Big Macs your entire life, you won't look like Brad Pitt after a salad and a half-hour on the Gravitron. I've spent the last year paddling toward shore only to find myself in the La Brea tar pit of my past, sinking like a triceratops toward anaerobic death.

Troy will get back on his feet. He started his career by selling blenders out of the trunk of his VW Beetle. His was a life of striving, of overcoming any and all obstacles. It doesn't matter if he goes on a bender, or turns out to be a loud-mouthed, racist drunk. The other 95 percent of the time he's a winner. His vices are momentary lapses; success is his "habit."

Some people have pivotal moments; I have trivial ones. There was a three-hour wait to see B.B. King during Summer Nights at the Pier. Ten feet from the gate, a handsome couple—he wore a Hawaiian shirt tucked into Dockers, and she wore a sundress that showed off the tan lines on her shoulders—cut into line right in front of me. One word and the others would have followed me in turning them away. Instead we all shuffled along, trying not to notice their smirks.

It's no surprise that Megumi chose Kolling. If you've got to spend the rest of your life in Purgatory, you might as well choose a room with a view.

I just dozed off. I said I couldn't sleep, and disappointed myself even in this.

The boys, though encamped along the opposite wall from Sha Long and me, are close enough to spit on. They would have to communicate telepathically for me not to hear them. When I opened my eyes, their conversation ceased. It restarted too enthusiastically. The girl disappeared behind the bed sheet leading to her enclosure. Normally, the boys would have protested her disappearance. This time they continued talking in loud tones.

I've got nothing against the girl. Who knows how long she's been working for Kolling, and for how many more years she'll be engaged in sexual servitude. I've neither the capability nor the inclination to reveal her secret. Her social acceptance here (she veritably glows) is the sole bright aspect of this bleak journey. But here's something I never considered: she doesn't trust me.

What does she know about me? I was supposed to be a customer, someone affluent enough to drop cash at Kolling's upscale karaoke establishment. I spoke English, which, given my face, was an oddity. But the important thing was that I could speak. What could explain my silence now? How does an affluent customer wind up in a container with rural Chinese villagers? Why would I have disappeared into the back room with her supervisor? The girl had been frightened of Megumi.

Kolling has set me up. I appear to be one of his henchmen, sent to ensure that his cargo arrives "intact." I'm older than the boys by a decade. The only person with whom I associate serves me hand and foot from a backpack filled with food I won't share with the others. On the way to the makeshift lavatory, one of the boys—the one with a broad flat nose and sloped shoulders—didn't turn as we passed. He bumped me hard.

There would be a simple way for the girl to get rid of me: tell them I was a flunky sent to threaten her. Whoever took me out would be a hero. I couldn't defend myself with words or weapons. Question: if this is true, what's the best way to assure my safety? It would be supercilious to bribe them with Sha Long's stash now. The best course of action is to let them believe I'm dangerous, that I'm connected to people who could make their family members disappear. The more weakness one shows, the more the pack closes in. Deterrence works in personal relations as well as geopolitics.

Day 5

It must be the air that's muddling my thinking. The atmosphere is growing more dense, as if we're underwater, at the same time it's growing thinner. Does that make sense? It makes me wonder whether our container might not be covered by a gigantic tarp, or whether we might be inside the ship's hull. I'd presumed that we were on the ship's deck. But what if I'm wrong?

Thank God we're near the canister fan, that damned canister fan that grows louder by the second, as if the propeller blade will clatter loose. The air is barely agitated here—I can feel the breeze only on the fine hairs of my arm—but that's better than nothing.

Sha Long's chest is laboring. He's lying on his side—asleep, I think, though his eyelids are at a disturbing half-mast. The boys are more subdued than usual. A few of them are motion-sick again. The girl has spent the day in her private area.

Have I become paranoid? The boys aren't particularly friendly to me but, aside from the stocky one, haven't been unfriendly either. Body-aching, oxygen-deprived, I haven't been the most approachable person. Sha Long isn't eating and can't keep down water. But his weakened state doesn't keep him from barking if the boys venture too close to his backpack.

The stocky boy passed out. One moment he was lumbering toward the lavatory, the next he slumped onto the ground like a sack of rice. This all took place in complete silence, so the immediate reaction was to stare at him. The boy in the yellow shirt was the first to act and the others followed. They poked and prodded him and checked his eyelids until someone exclaimed. The stocky boy's hand, jammed into his pocket, was wrapped with torn-up T-shirts. The fabric was wet to the touch with blood. The boy stirred and yanked his hand away. He refused to let them examine it.

This is not a good place to be injured. There are no antibiotics and no doctors. The buckets are filled with excrement and the dampness that used to be relegated to the lavatory area has seeped along the corrugated floor toward us. The heap of crushed cans and empty water bottles grows by the second.

When did the boy cut his hand? A day ago? Two?

Day 6

You know what they say about idle hands? It's doubly true for young men, testosterone coursing through their veins.

426

The boy in the yellow shirt and a light-skinned boy with long bangs—i.e., the two most jovial boys in the group—got into a shoving match a few hours ago that stopped only when the girl screamed at them.

All that's been forgotten now that we have video entertainment.

Sha Long was fast asleep when the boy in the yellow shirt tiptoed toward us. He pointed to Sha Long's backpack and spoke to me in low tones, which of course I couldn't understand. I shook my head. His brows knit and he asked another question. Again I shook my head, this time wearily. The boy held up his finger and went back to the others. When he returned, he held a portable DVD player in his hands, one of the many stacked inside our container. He held up the electrical cord and once again pointed to Sha Long's backpack. I finally understood.

Our encampment is the "power center" of the container. The canister fan is above us, the string of Christmas lights comes down from the ceiling near where Sha Long sleeps. The two extension cords were coiled beneath Sha Long's backpack. The boy wanted permission to plug the DVD player into one of the outlets.

Generally, I'm all for video entertainment. I was a charter member of Netflix, visited our local video store several times a week, and signed up for the Blockbuster thirty-day promotional memberships so frequently they stopped offering them to me. But given the choices amongst (a) air, (b) light, and (c) Korean soap operas dubbed into Chinese, even I have difficulty arguing persuasively for (c).

Would my concerns be any less grave if the boy in the yellow shirt had offered up, say, the first two seasons of

Deadwood and the special boxed set of the *Lord of the Rings* trilogy? Those are considerations that I thankfully have not had to wrangle with. And my caution about straining the generator to which we were hooked with superfluous electronics equipment might have won out if it were not for this: allowing them to replace the Christmas lights with the DVD player made Sha Long and me instantly popular.

Oh, I could grouse at why the boys were lugging around a vending cart's worth of pirated DVDs in lieu of such trivial items as toiletries, a first-aid kit, and supplementary food, but that would be nitpicking. When the DVD player is plugged in, the eight-inch LCD screen gives off so much light there's no need to keep the Christmas lights on. And the truth is that it's quite pleasant that our divided encampments have joined into one.

Sha Long complained about moving but only as a matter of form. He's only half-conscious. I sit with my back against the wall, squinting at the tiny screen when the camera pans out for a wide shot. The beauty of these soap operas is that melodrama transcends language. Two beautiful young people fall in love. The boy gets into a horrible accident. The girl thinks he's dead. He returns years later with amnesia (what would soap operas do without amnesia?). The girl is going to marry someone she doesn't love. The boy recovers his memory just in time.

It's formulaic as hell but leaves me weeping like everyone else. Maybe I've spent too long in the container. Maybe I've spent too long away from home. Maybe these soap operas remind me of a Korean barmaid who probably owns the soundtrack to the damned series. What if I'd stayed another night at Sunny Choi's run-down, two-bedroom house redolent with the scent of geriatric dog? I hadn't thought I was capable of having sex that many times without the use of pharmaceuticals. And more than that, it was comfortable being with her. Her breasts were perfect, warm weights in my hands.

I think the girl and the boy in the yellow shirt make a nice couple. They flirt shamelessly now, each providing a running commentary about what happens onscreen, disagreeing about everything.

I caught the girl looking over at me. We nodded at one another. And then she was debating the others about the soap opera again.

Day 7

How did we survive without our electronic pacifier? Modern man no longer spends all day hunting and preparing food. What do we do with our excess energy, our stray thoughts? We would kill one another without adequate and abundant entertainment resources. That's what will bring down fundamentalist Muslim states. Denial of access to *Baywatch* reruns will lead to revolution.

There's a period drama on right now, the women in the traditional Korean dresses that look like colored potato sacks, the men wearing funny-looking hats with ear covers. Same story though. The hero is a good-looking boy in ragged clothes who is really royalty in disguise. The heroine is a poor but cultured girl from the countryside coveted by a rich, crooked official.

Recycled material is reassuring. When traveling across the ocean in a sealed shipping container, one prefers Bruckheimer over Cronenburg. There's a reason why movie musicals flourish in India. Upper-class Americans and Europeans want their comfortable lives shaken up by painful reminders of *les misérables*. The underclass? They want explosions and sentimental dreck.

Sha Long's condition has gotten worse. His forehead is hot to the touch and the only reason he's not bathed in sweat is he can't keep any fluids down. The girl and I removed his soiled garments and swaddled him in clothing dampened with water. His skin looks like an old grape, his legs are criss-crossed with scars.

The girl is a natural at nursing, better than I am by far. She cradles his head in her lap and swabs his forehead with a T-shirt. She hums a flat, almost atonal air. It seems appropriate for our surroundings, bouncing against the container walls like notes from a bruised accordion. She can sing better than this, I know. But beauty is context: there's no way to express desolation without dissonance.

We don't talk, of course. But more than that we don't attempt to communicate except as it relates to Sha Long's needs. She must be starved for something other than sardines, baby corn, and bamboo shoots but refuses my offers from Sha Long's stash of goodies. She gestures toward him though she and I both know he can't eat any of it.

The boys suffering from nausea are comforted by the endless chatter from the tinny portable DVD player's speakers, but there is far less commentary than when we first plugged in. The stocky boy sits apart from us, hunched over his hand, which remains wrapped in a mitt of fabric. We have soap operas but no soap. We have canned foods but no utensils. I've used the empty plastic bags from Sha Long's goodies as gloves while handling food. But the boys have been scooping out of the cans with their hands. There are too many trips to the lavatory.

The girl, though thinner than at the beginning of the voyage, remains carefully groomed. Before and after she handles Sha Long, she squeezes a clear gel onto her hands from a plastic bottle stashed in her purse. She doesn't offer it to me or to the others.

We are trapped inside of a floating Petri dish. The air that dribbles in through the canister fan is cool but the temperature is rising.

Day 8

Sha Long is worse. He's conscious for no longer than thirty minutes at a time. The soap operas play to an inattentive audience. The boy with the injured hand shoved another boy. Then he curled up against the wall and went silent. Where are we? Will we stop in the Pacific Islands or continue onward? Maybe we've traveled west and are instead heading toward the eastern seaboard. For all I know, we've been circling the Chinese harbor.

Day 9

I thought I was imagining the sound at first: a distant, high-pitched squeal like someone letting air out of a balloon. But the silences are punctuated by labored panting.

The boy with the injured hand crawled into the girl's vacated chamber yesterday and won't allow anyone near him. We ignore the animal-like whimpering. Everyone except the boy in the yellow shirt.

He has been rifling through our possessions in search of something, anything, that might ease the other boy's pain.

He dumped the contents of Sha Long's backpack on the floor: walnuts, a block of fruit paste, a bag of shrimp chips, an empty picture frame, a plastic baggie filled with dried herbs, a Hershey's chocolate bar with almonds, a stack of blank picture postcards of San Francisco.

The girl pulled her purse beneath her knees. She stays with us now, sleeping next to Sha Long, her back against the wall. The boy asked her a question. She shrugged and shook her head. He repeated his question in a stern tone. She looked away. The boy stood there for a moment, almost teetering forward. He frowned and walked away.

His self-righteousness pisses me off. Short of morphine, nothing in the girl's purse would have helped. If the injured boy's hand is infected, dime-store antibacterial gel will make him scream instead of whimper. If our savior isn't willing to amputate the appendage with a sardine-can lid then he should just sit down, shut up, and learn to ignore the sound like the rest of us.

Day 10

I'm writing in the dark. More than darkness, blindness. I can't tell whether my eyelids are open or closed. There are no shapes, only sounds, immediate, abrupt; bodies bump against one another with confused cries and intakes of breath.

Am I scribbling on top of words I've already written? If the journal is right-side up, then I've skipped far enough ahead; if it's upside down, I'm inscribing new experiences atop of old ones, obliterating both. Why did I write on both sides of the page? If I'd chosen only one side, there would have been a way to salvage my writing. Losing sight is like losing a limb, there are phantom optic sensations masquerading as the real thing. Sometimes the darkness seems to spark red and blue.

I was tending to Sha Long. I placed my fingers beneath his nostrils to make sure he was still breathing. I wondered about the fine lines on his face. Were that many wrinkles necessary to express the range of human experience? I brushed my fingertips on his cheek and the world disappeared.

There was a hush for perhaps a second. Then the boys began chattering like a cageful of monkeys. There was fumbling in the darkness, bare feet kicked against my legs, and then...light. The boy in the yellow shirt was on his hands and knees. He replaced the canister fan's cord with the Christmas lights' cord until we got settled and then we were plunged into darkness again. We can live without light but not air. Then the constant whir that represented life ceased too.

The boys banged on the walls. They dumped the trash on the ground and kicked the cans, sending them bouncing off of person and object alike. They tore open cardboard boxes and hurled the DVD players against the walls.

There has been no response from outside. All these days there has been no indication that life beyond rodents exists outside the container. There's the sea and the creak of metal.

There isn't enough air in here for all of us. Someone tore the canister fan out of the wall, but the resulting hole isn't big enough to fit a man's head through. We breathe and it keeps getting hotter and hotter.

The boys have commandeered our encampment. It wasn't planned. They surged upon us. Someone stepped on Sha Long's hand. The muted crunch, like damp twigs snapping, was louder than his almost imperceptible intake of breath.

The girl and I dragged him as far as we could from the group. She pulled him onto her lap like an oversized doll. Her blouse, like my shirt, is wet to the touch with perspiration.

Day ?

When I awoke, there were hands beneath my armpits and a jagged opening pressed against my cheek. We won't make it this way, taking turns at the hole where the canister fan used to be, like scuba divers sharing a tank. It's that damned do-gooder orchestrating these rescue attempts. I can hear him prodding and cajoling, but I feel as if pipe cleaners have been shoved up my nose and my skull's filled with sharp pebbles.

The girl shouldn't be sobbing for Sha Long but for us. Doesn't she understand what a blessing it is to die quickly instead of being smothered? We had to tear Sha Long out of her grasp. He was so light and insubstantial I feared he would pull apart like an overcooked chicken. Her fingernails raked across my face.

We dragged Sha Long into the lavatory, as far from us as possible. After the others trudged off, I sat with him. I wanted to tear apart a cardboard box and bury him under the brown paper leaves, but I found my fingers too clumsy and my muscles too sapped of strength. I returned to the common area and collected discarded clothing. I covered him in T-shirts and denim jeans, rolled him up like a fish.

It's unbearably hot. I've stripped down to nothing and still it's not enough to release the heat or remove the stench.

The girl doesn't take her turns at the hole. She strikes anyone who draws close, saving particular venom for that one particular boy.

I forgot to fold over the page corner. I must be writing on my writing. It doesn't matter does it? Paper, like a person, is disposable.

Day ?

I am still here. We are all, save Sha Long, still here. Maybe I've made it out to be worse than it is; maybe my body has adapted. I've grown accustomed to the aches in my joints and neck. It hurts to think. Hurts to keep breathing. But half-dead means half-alive.

How can that boy keep moaning? When he's silent, I pray he's fallen unconscious. He's just gathering his energy. It starts as a murmur, like a baby's gurgle. It becomes a whine strangled within his belly. It bursts forth in spasmodic sobs tapering into the rhythmic bleating of an electric sheep.

I want him to stop. He must want it to stop too. The pain I mean. He is suffering and he's making us suffer more than we already are.

I'm not thinking straight. He will make it. We will make it. If we've survived this long...has it been hours or days?... we can make it all the way through. Conserve energy. Conserve breath.

The girl is still nearby. She's barely moved since we removed Sha Long. I extend my foot to brush my toes against her calf. Her skin is hot to the touch, hotter even than my own skin. She doesn't shrink from the contact and she doesn't invite it. She takes it for what it is: a gauge to assure me she is still alive.

She is turned away from me, from everyone. She has stopped sobbing and her breathing is shallow but strong. She has retreated to a place far away. She has the gift of absence within presence. It's a quality with which I'm familiar.

Megumi! Was there no way for me to fill that void within you? Have we become so damaged that we think everything we touch will turn to shit? Maybe destiny is nothing but the deep channels of a personal history that we stop struggling against.

Day ?

Someone has stolen Sha Long's backpack. It doesn't matter. I couldn't swallow solid food if I tried. The girl remains curled into herself.

There was a scuffle. Two boys rolled on the floor. A muffled groan and it was over. Like a fire, a fight can't last on limited oxygen.

The stench is getting worse. There are some things that familiarity or force of will cannot conquer. But what is there to do? He is wrapped and shoved as far from us as possible.

The last time in the lavatory, I tried to touch him to reassure myself that he had once existed. He was walled away behind a profusion of cardboard. Someone has more strength than I can muster.

Without food or water, how does the injured boy continue to whimper?

Day ?

It is quiet. So quiet that the ballpoint moving across the page is painfully shrill. Is there even any ink left?

I slid my hand along the girl's soft, bare haunch and she didn't stir. I pressed my nose against her spine but didn't dare press my fingers against the artery on her neck. Is her skin warm because she's alive or because of the tropical temperature within the container? I'd rather not know.

I couldn't bear to move her. I'd rather we disintegrated together like newspaper in a gutter.

Day ?

I ignored the scratching until it became a tap-tap-tap like the branch of a tree against a window. I crawled toward the sound, toward the hole high in the wall of the container. I expected to bump into one of the boys, but my path was clear except for debris—empty tin cans, discarded clothes, the sharp plastic pieces of shattered DVD players. The crown of my head struck the wall. Someone should have been standing there, sipping air, the strong getting stronger. If I could bear the pain of standing, I would have it all to myself. I rested.

The tapping stopped. All I could hear was my own breath. And then...my name. From outside the container. It must have been the settling of contents in a neighboring container. It must have been a rat falling from a perch. It must have been an auditory hallucination—my oxygen-starved mind speaking to itself. I waited.

"Guy," a voice said. "Guy. You must listen to me."

I pressed my cheek against the metal wall. I willed myself to stand though my knees threatened to splinter. I stood as if I were falling, and when I had climbed as high as I could, I couldn't tell if I was standing or lying down, gravity pressing me against the cool surface like a specimen on a glass slide.

I tried to say her name, but the syllables wouldn't pass through my lips, and my lips, chapped, fragile muscles atrophied, beat like a moth's wings against a light bulb.

"I had no choice but to trade your soul for my life," she said. "You will learn to live without it. It is lonesome but not impossible."

I closed my eyes. Or did I open them? In the darkness, it was impossible to tell the difference.

It should be easy to live without one's soul: there is no question of what is right, there is just convenience. But when everything is possible, it is impossible to be satisfied. I came from poverty but live in affluence. There is nothing I need. But I want. I want.

I never cared for John the way I cared for you. He was a way of getting more—more time to myself, more money for shopping, more freedom of movement. He should have understood: he held the keys to my cage. It was an exchange.

"He doesn't deserve you," John said. "He doesn't appreciate you."

John felt guilty at first. He pushed me away afterward, as if I had polluted him. In time he lingered longer in bed. He asked why Horatio asked him to pick up dry-cleaning as if he were still his secretary. He said that he idolized Horatio until he discovered how little Horatio understood about how business ran "on the ground." He bought me small gifts—earrings, pendants, necklaces of the kind I couldn't wear around Horatio without attracting attention.

Then I became involved in the business.

"You don't know the first thing about karaoke," John said. "And neither does he. The karaoke experience isn't about new and better technology. It isn't about sounding better. It's about being accepted for how you sound, good or bad. Our focus should be on small, neighborhood karaoke bars. Period. Not building pleasure domes of ice. Not buying out self-help empires."

As my influence in the company grew, I needed John less. When Horatio eased the restrictions John enforced, John said I couldn't be trusted. He followed me around town when not ordered to do so. John had regained Horatio's trust by retrieving me from the karaoke bar and making sure you learned a lesson. John had me where he wanted, under his control and in his bed. Then came what happened in New Mexico. While Horatio was out of state signing the Troy Bobbins merger papers, John's report arrived by special delivery. John had paid for an outside consultant to write a report on the feasibility of KGI's reorganization. John read the report in bed, refusing, the way farang *men do, even to put on his underpants or cover himself with a blanket. He pointed to charts. He read the conclusions out loud. They vindicated his opinion: the new OKE strategy would fail. Maybe not in the first three years but eventually. There was no way to sustain such investments in a market that would, regardless of facilities, remain the same size.*

"It's not too late," he said. "The land bubble hasn't burst. We can sell what we've acquired at a minimal loss, then move to reestablish our franchisee network. They don't want to fly solo. They don't know the first thing about running businesses themselves."

John was happy; I was angry. The last thing I wanted was for us to return to the way things were, when he reviewed what I bought, told me when I could eat out, ordered me around like his servant.

"If you open a competing business," I said. "Will you take me with you?"

"Are you kidding?" he said. "I'm going to explain this report to Mr. Kolling. It might hurt his pride, but eventually he'll come around."

"You're a liar," I said. "What you really want is what he has. The company. The money. Me. You're a traitor."

"Me, a traitor?" he said. "I'm trying to tell him what everyone in this company is too frightened to say. I've given my life to him. He gave me my first opportunity and has rewarded me prodigiously. It would be disloyal to remain quiet while he drives KGI into the ground."

He paused and looked down at himself, suddenly self-conscious about his nakedness. "This is...this is not something that I planned. I am a human being and I have needs. It's a madness that comes over me. It's a sickness. But you can't lead me to betray him. I would never leave Horatio."

I began crying. And he comforted me. But he didn't understand that I was crying tears of rage.

I seduced him. I drugged him. I killed him.

It was not difficult. I watched my uncles slaughter pigs, and humans are not so different from swine. I expected him to struggle more than he did. John was strong in life but feeble in death. More than anything he looked surprised. He prided himself on being one step ahead, but he never realized I knew the combination to the case where he stashed his drugs and weapons.

I thought you could help me to leave them both behind. Horatio would blame you for John's death, and blame John for his treachery. I thought I could learn to be happy with you. But I haven't any practice at being happy. Horatio would have found us one day. It was only a matter of time. I left you to save you, but you've been stubborn.

I didn't despise John. He was, like most men, simple. And he deserved what he received. Pretty words and gifts don't make up for years of suffering. Pain must be repaid with pain. That's the rule of karma.

Day ?

It couldn't have been her. She wouldn't have boarded a ship bound for the United States. She must be living the same life of gilded confinement that she has always lived. I am blind. I am deaf. I don't know if I am writing in a notebook or dreaming of writing in a notebook. It would be better to be dreaming. Yes. Let this be a dream.

"Open the purse," she said.

I pried the girl's stiff fingers from the purse's handles. I poured my hands inside, fondled a plastic bottle, a leather billfold, compact, a fabric bag filled with wrapped plastic cylinders…and…a cell phone. Its shape was unmistakable—rectangular, metallic, cool to the touch. I flipped open the clamshell. Which button to turn it on? The welcome message that Sheila had programmed, the one I hadn't learned how to change, appeared.

"Good morning, Guy. Don't do anything stupid."

Why had Megumi given the girl my cell phone? Why hadn't the girl told me about it herself? Did I have reception? No. The backlight disappeared. I pressed a button and it lit up again. Once I had a signal, I could send a text message to Sheila. For now, I had to conserve the battery.

Megumi said other things. But I don't want to think about them now. Nothing matters except continuing to breathe, keeping my chest moving up and down. And waiting.

<u>Day ?</u>

No reception.

<u>Day ?</u>

No reception. I can't breathe.

<u>Day ?</u>

I'm not going to make it.

CHAPTER 37

Had Milton smelled bleach when he passed from life to death? Had John Smith, drugged into immobility, felt as if his wrists were cuffed to a handrail? Did Chandra awaken on the other side to find herself attached to an IV drip stand? Heaven might have white walls and a white ceiling. But polished gray floors, a nurse with a bad dye job, and khaki-clad guards? They spoke English, which meant I hadn't been exiled to a foreign afterlife. Noticing my silent exertions, they replaced my hospital gown with red cotton pajamas and carted me off in leg irons and handcuffs to a cell.

A cot, a chrome wash basin, a chrome toilet with no seat. If I closed my eyes, the bright fluorescent lighting turned the world a shade of pink shot through with the leafy veins of my lids. I was served three square meals a day of food that looked as if it had been reconstituted from powder. I was escorted daily to an exercise yard where, through the chain-link fence and past the highways and haze, I could discern Mount Rainier. The guards wore patches on their shirt pockets that read "Northwest Detention Center."

I wasn't dead. I was home.

The poison that John Smith had slipped me, that Megumi had in turn slipped him, was a derivative of the *datura* plant, a Caribbean extract used to create zombies. Odorless and tasteless, at low levels it creates a compliant stupor. At higher levels it stops the heart. That's when these "dead," who may have been conscious all along, were lowered into their graves. Trapped underground for days, deprived of oxygen and light, these poor, brain-damaged souls emerged from the earth with no option except to serve the witchdoctor who dug them out. Imagine that. Everyone saw you die and rise again. You're a zombie. No matter how you protest, no one will believe otherwise.

What might have been easy for a man was impossible for a migrant, the sole conscious survivor of the *MV Meriwether.* The other survivor, a boy whose arm needed to be amputated at the elbow, wasn't likely to awaken from his coma. The Chinese vessel arrived in the Port of Seattle with most of its human cargo freshly dead. They had stripped their clothes in a vain attempt to escape the unbearable heat caused by the build-up of carbon dioxide. Their fingertips were bloody from prying at the air holes.

Someone tipped the authorities to the smuggling operation. The dead girl? She was the only migrant carrying identification papers. Her name was Megumi Tanita, a Japanese citizen, naked limbs entangled with those of a Chinese villager. Or so it appeared. Why would a Chinese villager clutch a Nokia mobile phone subscribed to a U.S.-based calling plan? The handset was untraceable, but a single telephone number was programmed into it. The number belonged to an employee of a known pornography kingpin and tax evader. Bruce Zatz was suspected of trafficking eastern European women. It was no stretch to connect him to trafficking Chinese migrants.

How did I know all of this? The government wanted me to talk, and talking was the one thing I couldn't do. The doctors agreed there was no physical reason for my failure to speak. My silence was hostile, evidence that I was protecting Bruce and the Chinese smugglers. That made me an accessory to murder if not a murderer myself. When the Homeland Security attorney visited for his frequent interrogation sessions, a Chinese interpreter in tow, my wrists were cuffed to a metal band around my waist. The guards made sport out of goading me into speech.

My cell door was thrown open and I was doused with ice water. My bedding was removed and I shivered on the wire netting of the cot. I received nightstick jabs to the ribs. I found a piece of shit underneath my pillow. In the middle of my long, lit nights, music blared through a speaker mounted in the ceiling. Sleep-deprived, I flinched when doors opened or guards called to one another. I cried intermittently during the first weeks of my confinement, but tears without sound are mistaken for pride. Eventually the tears, like my voice, dried up. I went through the motions of living, but it felt as if Guy Watanabe, the real Guy Watanabe, had escaped long ago to a place that was warm and dark instead of cold and bright. All that was left was for this husk to disintegrate.

By week six, I no longer gestured for pens, scratched messages onto the wall, or arranged my food into words. If the guards forced me to the center of the cell, arms forward and legs bowed as if I were riding an imaginary motorcycle, I held the position until my thighs cramped and I fell to the ground. I kneeled and waited to be cuffed before being asked to do so. But for my silence, I was the model detainee. The guards weren't to blame for my treatment. They believed I needed to be broken and broken I was. A man never suffers sufficiently for his sins. If I didn't deserve this, who did?

That is the law of karma: pain for pain. Karma doesn't work on individuals but on a people. Every bad act we commit is repaid by a visitation of misfortune on a stranger. If we keep hurting one another, the suffering will rise like a tide and surge over the land. We will drown in our just deserts.

The absence of sound doesn't clang into one's consciousness the way the presence of sound does. The rare detainee wearing the low-security blue pajamas, he might call out for an attorney or complain about conditions. But for the most part isolation, a well-placed kick, and a bucket of ice water kept the cellblock serene. There is a difference, however, between hushed and extinguished.

The Russian in the neighboring cell was the only detainee who'd been in solitary confinement longer than I had. He was young and ugly, his face a sponge of red acne. He'd bitten off a detainee's ear, and he'd tried to do the same to a guard. He'd never been quelled without exacting retribution. No longer. One morning he was wheeled to the infirmary, his cheeks caved inward like wax crushed by callused thumbs. He hadn't uttered a sound as he was beaten. Neither had any of the other detainees.

The guards spoke to one another about supervising a "pen full of dickless mice." Their jokes grew cruder, their demeanor more abrasive. But the silence took its toll. Their voices became hushed; they turned at the sound of their own footsteps. No more discipline was meted out because none was warranted.

At breakfast, I bit down on aluminum foil in my scrambled eggs. It was a carefully folded gum wrapper. Inside, in small block letters, were these words:

WE ARE WITH YOU BROTHER. STAY STRONG.

Nothing could have disheartened me more. I hadn't sought solidarity with illegal aliens waiting to be deported from our country. I wanted to be recognized for who and what I was: an American citizen, guaranteed full rights and privileges. These hopeless migrants had mistaken my debility for a protest and were now following suit. Not a single detainee would speak out in supplication or in pain. Without knowing who I was or why I remained silent, they shared my solitude. Damn them.

"Is this what you want?" Rajiv Patel said. I'd expected the Homeland Security attorney to be a former football player and fraternity member, a white man who talked about women's asses when they left the room and told ethnic jokes when he was alone with his buddies. Instead he was a young South Asian with a diamond ear stud and a tailored suit. "You've already got blood on your hands. Now you're poisoning the prospects of the other detainees. Some shouldn't be detained in the first place. Some have a real shot at asylum. Some need medical attention. They say nothing and lose out on services, a fighting chance. They're being deported so quickly we can't keep up with the paperwork. All because you're protecting your boss."

Patel had worked every angle on me. He'd described his immigrant background, his mother leaving an abusive husband in India for a mail-order match to a Boeing engineer. He told me my cooperation would save lives. He hinted that under-the-table cash payments would make me a rich man in rural China. He said I'd be locked up in the detention center for the rest of my life. He threatened extradition to China to be tried and executed. In other words, he did his job. Under different circumstances, we might have had beers together. Sunny and I could have double-dated with Patel and his undoubtedly hot South Asian girlfriend. The interpreter was a different story.

In the initial interrogation session, I carefully enunciated every syllable of, "I am an American." The interpreter said I wasn't speaking Mandarin but Hokkian, the dialect of a poverty-stricken province. He translated my Hokkian phrase as *Kan ni na bu chao chee bye*: "Fuck your mother's sweaty pussy." I knew better than to try to make myself understood. I kept my mouth shut and my hands on my thighs.

"This is fucking crazy," Patel said to the interpreter. "Why are they following this bozo? He's a murderer. An extortionist. We can't transfer the troublemakers because the 'silent protest' spreads like a virus to the other facilities. There are no complaints about conditions, no complaints about treatment. No one enters the infirmary unless he's unconscious. The detainees won't stand up for themselves."

The interpreter shrugged. "Doesn't that make your job easier? They're all going to be deported anyway."

Patel scowled. "There's a process. There are rules. I was in a removal proceeding where a twenty-two-year-old mother wouldn't speak to her attorney or the immigration judge. Her children are American citizens. Her husband is an American citizen. She got deported to Mexico and can't return to the U.S. even as a tourist."

"Why was she detained?" the interpreter said.

"She crossed the border as a child. She didn't even know she was illegal until she got a speeding ticket."

The interpreter scratched his neck. "My cousin's been rejected entry because we give amnesty to illegals. Why should the child of a field worker get better treatment than a math professor? She cut in line. I have no sympathy."

Patel shook his head. "There's such a thing as mercy. Without mercy, what are we?"

The interpreter, an old, balding man with halitosis, licked his chapped lips. "We are right."

The detention center had another staff interpreter. He was a young Chinese man who applied so much Dep to his hair that the strands were paralyzed into a varnished, angular block. Jerry was the same age as the boys who'd died in the container. He arrived unexpectedly one morning with two guards. I have no idea what he said in Chinese, but from his conversation with the guards I gleaned that I had a visitor. The "silent protest" had gained attention among Christian activists. A Catholic diocese had somehow gained permission to speak to me.

We were all color-coded: the red being the security risks, the orange having violated the criminal code, and the blue having merely overstayed visas. The guards led me through the low-security dormitories, where the blue-clad detainees were allowed to socialize with one another. No one spoke. It was like gazing into an aquarium, fifty men playing cards or laying on their bunks in underwater silence. Sound resumed in the administrative building but became muted as I passed by.

My restraints weren't removed in the interview room. I was seated at a chrome picnic table, facing a bank of smoked-glass windows. Jerry translated the guards' instructions: I was not to stand during the interview or have any physical contact with my visitor. Jerry stood at my elbow while the guards stepped back a respectful distance. The door opened. Through it shuffled a diminutive nun. Her gown appeared to be too large, and her habit hung loose and low over her forehead. Her eyes alighted on the interpreter.

"What are you doing here?" she said. Her voice was abrupt and familiar.

"I'm Jerry Huang," he said. "Chinese interpreter. I'm here to help you to communicate with the prisoner. Excuse me. Detainee."

The nun smirked. "Interpreter? I don't need you. I studied in China for like five years. I speak Chinese fluently."

"*Shi er?*" the interpreter said. He launched into a stream of pleasantries in Chinese.

She flicked her hand dismissively. "Yeah, yeah, yeah. Go over there. I'm here to talk to him, not you."

Jerry looked wounded but did as he was told, joining the guards to permit us some privacy. Sheila looked me over. Her brow wrinkled for a moment, then returned to its neutral expression.

"You look like shit." she said. "No wonder they mistook you for a Chinese refugee. It's easier to secure an audience with the Pope than it is to visit you."

Sheila belonged to a different world and a different life...one I'd begun to suspect I'd never see again. All she had to do was tell them who I was and I'd be set free. How had she known I was imprisoned? Sheila understood my question before I mouthed it.

"Your phone has a GPS tracking chip. It's kind of like what they put in people's pets but more high tech." She shook her head. "Geez, you must have lost like twenty pounds, though I admit you kind of needed it. That British guy said you'd succeeded. When we saw you were on the ocean, we thought you were on a cruise ship. Funny, huh?

"When the ship turned toward the U.S., Bruce got pissed off. You weren't supposed to reenter the U.S., remember? I mean, you had a Swiss bank account set up for auto-pay. I was texting you warnings, but you never responded. I thought you were too busy getting reacquainted with what's-her-name to answer."

It doesn't matter. Tell them who I am, I said. *Get me out of here.*

Sheila looked down at her sleeves, which were so long they covered her hands. "I left like ten voice mails. Crazy, stupid shit, like 'Smooth sailing, sailor!', 'Don't wear her out, Big Guy,' 'Don't spend your money all in one place,' I don't remember them all; I was loaded. No big deal, right? Except a few weeks ago, the feds burst into Bruce's office like he was harboring Bin Ladin. They've been crawling up Bruce's ass ever since: tax records, employment records, invoices. They even got hold of my real birth certificate. Fucking A. Anyhow, Bruce is not happy, Guy. Not at all."

I stared at her. Sheila wasn't here to spring me. Bruce would have been pleased had another detainee slipped a shiv between my ribs. It was the only reason to be thankful for eight weeks in solitary confinement.

Please, Sheila. I won't say anything about Bruce or Milton.

Sheila squinted to read my lips. "That's the only reason you're not dead yet. The problem is, he needs to make sure there's no way you can be linked to him. The feds have been tracking down everyone from Bruce's nanny to his chiropractor. They've already found nineteen-year-old chicks who are supposed to be fifty-two-year-old secretaries and Czech bodyguards who are supposed to be Mexican gardeners. You can't resurface as a long-dead Filipino camera grip. You can't resurface as Guy Watanabe because your identity's back in circulation. Bruce imported a Malaysian dude with a fourteen-inch cock. Every time I see him, I shake my head and say, 'If Guy could see himself now.' He's scrawny. All his nourishment went to one place."

Sheila pulled back her habit to scratch her cropped hair. She'd allowed it to return to a natural brown. Noticing the others' stares, she pulled the habit back into place.

"Bruce sent me here to tell you he doesn't much like this whole 'silent protest' thing. He's trying to avoid attention, not attract it. He says you should start talking, just not about him. Don't speak English; say something in Chinese.

And stay out of the U.S. Do that and you won't have to look over your shoulder once you're out of prison. But he can't funnel you money. You didn't follow through on your end of the bargain."

I let my chin drop to my chest. A life of silent exile in China. Penniless and alone.

How could you do this to me, Sheila?

"I told you not take his money, didn't I? Who do you think convinced him your silent protest thing was a way to protect his interests? Just because I'm not willing to throw myself in front of the bus doesn't mean I want you to suffer. I didn't make you chase that crazy Japanese bitch. I want to help you, but I can't. Not with the way Bruce is watching me. You've just got to do what he says. It's not much of a life, but it's all you've got left."

I closed my eyes and pressed my cheek against the cool chrome table. Sheila began babbling. She said she was taking a GED course and was considering nursing school. It was hard, however, to give up the money. She could make more shooting two scenes than a nurse made in a month. She said she'd been in and out of rehab, but realized the only way she would quit was on her own, cold turkey, the way Milton had. She said she and her parents were on speaking terms again. They wanted her to move back home. Her stream of patter eventually petered out. We sat in silence until a guard said our time was up.

Sheila's upper lip trembled. "Stop acting all high and mighty. The silent treatment doesn't make people want to help you. It just pisses them off."

My removal hearing was so uncomplicated the immigration judge didn't bother to brave the traffic between Seattle and Tacoma to show up in person. He attended via a live video feed. A television monitor was placed where he should have been sitting. He ate a sandwich during the proceedings and called out for a warm-up on his coffee.

I couldn't blame him. He was nothing more than a rubber stamp once the detainees refused to speak on their own behalves. Samatar Cawl was ordered removed to Nigeria, though members of the Somali community asserted that Mr. Cawl was a Somali. Madihah Baroukel was ordered removed to Algeria but was advised to apply for asylum based upon the brand on her face and the assassination of her two sons by Islamic radicals. She didn't have an interpreter because she hadn't requested one.

The only disruption came from Homeland Security attorney Rajiv Patel. The immigration judge advised him to advocate on behalf of the government instead of on the behalves of the detainees. When Patel brought up the "silent protest," the IJ told him it had done more for the immigration backlog than a hundred new regulations.

"If I were permitted to bestow awards on detainees," the IJ said, "I would award one to our Chinese John Doe. He lubricated the wheels of justice."

I was, of course, ordered removed to China. That didn't surprise me. What did was my cheering section, two senior citizens wearing T-shirts emblazoned with the slogan, "Wage Peace." While I was being led out of the courtroom, they called out to me. "Keep your hopes up...God be with you."

It was ironic that my only supporters were people from whom I would have fled had they approached me at the supermarket. I paused at the exit, turning to look at them with an expression of gratitude. That's when I noticed someone who hadn't been there earlier—a middle-aged Asian woman wearing wire-rimmed glasses and a sharp blue suit. She held a cell phone in front of her face, its tiny camera lens pointed at me. It wasn't until I was back in my cell that I recalled where I'd seen her before. The woman whose suit color matched her purse, shoes, and cell phone was Norene Wong, editor-in-chief of the *Seattle Asian Herald.*

CHAPTER 38

I couldn't eat a meal without being interrupted by a message of solidarity: "YOU ARE NOT ALONE," "WE ARE MANY, THEY ARE FEW," "GOD CARES FOR THE WEAK AND DEFENSELESS," blah, blah, blah. Someone slipped me a gold crucifix inscribed with the words "WE REMEMBER." Custom-engraved, religious iconography shoved into my hash browns is not comforting. No one wants to be a Christian in the Roman Empire. I sympathize with alien detainees I read about in the *New York Times Magazine*. But give me a damn pen and the first thing I would write is *I am not one of them*.

My only visitors were Rajiv Patel and the balding interpreter. They pressed me—the leader of a leaderless rebellion—to stop it "in the name of justice." Somehow I had transmogrified into an idea, an abstraction that inspired the migrants to dash their American dreams against the rocks of impersonal laws. A concept had transformed the detention facility into a warehouse for living ghosts.

"You've accomplished in months what Congress and an army of immigration judges couldn't in decades," Patel said. "You've turned people into broken goods to be sent back to their countries of origin. Why did you survive? You're the least deserving."

Patel was right. Any of the migrants who'd died—even the oldest—would have made more out of half the opportunities I'd had in life. But sometimes survival has nothing to do with merit or tenacity. Sometimes it's just dumb luck. And sometimes, luck is nudged along by community activists.

A newspaper editorial arrived with my dinner tray. A pixelated digital photograph showed a haggard migrant in red detention pajamas. I should have combed my hair.

The MV Meriwether: Why to Oppose a Rogue's Protest

By Norene Wong, Editor-in-Chief

Twelve weeks ago the Coast Guard, acting on an anonymous tip, boarded the MV Meriwether a few miles short of Seattle. Inside a shipping container they discovered eight Chinese migrants, only two still alive. The conditions were decrepit: buckets filled with excrement; a moldering corpse covered in cardboard; the freshly dead stripped naked to alleviate the carbon-dioxide sauna, their fingertips bloody from attempts to scratch through the metal walls. One survivor had his arm amputated and remains unconscious.

The general public has reacted with a mixture of outrage and sympathy: what kind of barbarians could treat their fellow men this way (and, incidentally, what kind of humans would choose to be treated this way)? Our political leaders made hay about the threat of a terrorist attack: What if it had been Al Qaeda shipping biological weapons instead of Chinese gangs shipping illegal aliens? Let me tell you my reaction to the hubbub:

Here we go again.

Do you realize that 40%–60% of all illegal immigrants entered America legally and overstayed their visas? That number included 100,000 Canadians. How many Chinese? Oh, around 11,400. While illegal immigrants from Asia make up 9% of all illegal immigrants and Europeans/Canadians make up 6%, can you guess which region constitutes a larger proportion of the world's population? (Hint: the world population is 6.5 billion people and there are 3.9 billion Asians.) So why do the most indelible images of illegal immigration involve dark foreigners streaming out of dank containers like so many cockroaches from beneath the kitchen sink?

I'll answer in plain English so that no one misses my point. Racism. White media bias. The hobgoblin of little minds.

The mainstream press loves Jack Nicholson's Chinatown, *where inscrutable Asians conduct nefarious business right beneath our noses. They peddle human organs, import sweatshop workers, and still manage to dry-clean our clothes and beat their wives. No matter how long and rich our history is in this country, Asian Americans are perpetual foreigners. We are reminded of this by the Chinese Exclusion Act of 1882, the Japanese internment during World War II, and the persecution of Wen Ho Lee during the Clinton Administration.*

The Irish may have been ridiculed, but they were never legally excluded from immigrating. Italy and Germany were our enemies in World War II, but their descendents weren't sent to American concentration camps. And don't get me started on how losing computer files isn't a federal crime unless committed by a Chinese American. Just as our persecution is cyclical, so are the media stories about us.

Do I think the suffocation of Chinese migrants aboard the MV Meriwether is reprehensible? Of course. But there's a reason why we don't raid Microsoft to apprehend Canadian programmers and the economics departments of American universities to weed out Scandinavian grad students. There's a reason why we focus on how Chinese orphanages obtain infants but ignore the Ukrainian ones. Color. As Chris Rock says, "if it's all white, it's all right."

Normally I would let the mainstream media have its feeding frenzy. There are too many good things happening in our community to indulge in dominant society's fetish for the dark and deviant. But it's my duty to report on the MV Meriwether to correct the "official" accounts about the smugglers and to ensure a charlatan's efforts to set himself free are not successful.

*First, I have it from a source close to the investigation—*very *close to the investigation—that the Chinese triads are* not *the primary suspects in this case. Who is? The domestic pornography industry, America's homegrown mafia, the dons of which (surprise, surprise) are white males. Anyone who has perused adult DVD titles will not be surprised to find an abundance of films featuring Asian women. Behind this insatiable desire for new dragon ladies is a lesser-known fact: cheap Asian labor—as gaffers, cameramen, sound technicians—creates cheaper movies and higher profit margins. Why haven't the major dailies reported this? Need I be redundant?*

Second, it was only a matter of time before a certain "protest" became known to the general public. A few stalwart Christian souls have begun to organize in support of a Chinese migrant who has up to this point refused to speak to government attorneys. This migrant's unequivocal silence has, in fact, made him a hero inside the detention center. What started as one detainee's silence became an entire cellblock's, and then an entire facility's, until detainees in places as far flung as Texas and Connecticut have started to refuse answering the simplest yes or no questions.

As my readership knows, I am the first person to speak out against the excesses of governmental power. I organized protests against the Clinton administration's treatment of Wen Ho Lee when others suggested it would be more prudent to remain silent. I pressured the city and powerful private parties to provide mitigation funds to the International District after it bore the brunt of the traffic and gained little of the business from the stadium projects. Normally, I would be behind my Asian brother's "silent protest" against Homeland Security's heavy-handed treatment of him, which has included months of solitary confinement.

But the circumstances here are anything but normal.

My source informs me that the Chinese migrant leading this "silent protest" is a puppet for the white gang behind the trafficking scheme, thereby leaving intact the implication that this is yet another inscrutable Chinese plot. What evidence does the government have? Cell phone records. Tax records. Fake visas and passports. Illegal immigrants on the payrolls. Everything necessary for a conviction except for one thing: testimony from the "victim."

The so-called victim either fears retribution or is himself benefiting from the trafficking scheme. That is, at the most charitable, he is a coward who refuses to assist the government in bringing murderers to justice. More likely he's "on the take:" a low-level criminal sealed into the container to keep the other migrants in line. An overseer. A traitor.

If this migrant's actions were a political statement, I would be behind him 100%. But a political dissident has political views, and this one has none. If he remains silent he does so because he fears a fate worse than imprisonment and deportation. He is saving himself by betraying the real victims.

The smugglers engineered an intricate hoax, one involving a falsified journal that could not possibly have been written by a Chinese immigrant. In it, the smugglers besmirch the name of a trans-

national businessman, a "foreigner" only in the technical sense. He has invested in revitalizing our community even though he wasn't reared in it. He is a believer in an Asian community that extends beyond borders, and his investments will pay dividends long after the MV Meriwether becomes a historical footnote.

If the falsified journal were not enough to reveal the "victim" for what he truly is, then there is this: his "silent protest" hurts those it purports to help. A Cambodian youth, here since the age of two, was deported though he'd stopped gangbanging and became a youth counselor. A Ghanaian woman refused to inform detention officials she was suffering from an asthma attack and died. The list of true victims grows longer by the day.

I attended the Chinese migrant's detention hearing. He showed not the slightest remorse as a pillar of the Somali community sold himself down the river in silence. Instead he played to the audience, pausing upon his exit for an oh-so-dramatic glance backward.

Enough is enough.

I'm sure the white liberal establishment is ready to rush to this Chinese migrant's assistance based on his harsh treatment at the hands of detention officials. They will see the "silent protest" as an opportunity to highlight the abysmal human rights records at detention facilities and the kangaroo-court nature of the immigration hearings. Normally I would encourage our community, shoulder to shoulder with other communities of color, to join this struggle to ensure we are the actors and not the acted upon.

But these are not normal times.

A migrant who uses other migrants for his own personal gain is not entitled to the full protection of our laws. If the government can extract from him the information it needs to protect the lives of countless migrants—here in detention facilities and overseas—then our community and our nation as a whole will be better for it. No longer will society be able to point to freakish "others" victimizing their own; wider white society will discover that the victimizers look a lot like themselves.

I'm not saying the ends always justify the means. But they do here.

Most people wrap fish with the *Seattle Asian Herald,* but its readership apparently extended to leftward leaning civil rights organizations. A week after Norene's editorial appeared, an attorney from the Center for Civil Liberties visited me. Ander Andersson must have been in his thirties, but his delicate features and 8 a.m. enthusiasm suggested youth.

"No, no," Ander said. "Don't talk. I didn't ask the guards to leave so you would violate your vow of silence. I wanted to explain how we're going to nail the administration to the wall."

Ander brought his own interpreter, a young Chinese woman with a nose stud and the ends of her hair dyed red. She didn't remove her iPod earbuds.

"It's delightful to be here," Ander said. "Your incarceration and protest movement are a tremendous stroke of luck. The Center looks for promising test cases: shoplifters sentenced to life, female military officers who need third-trimester abortions, and now you.

"The ninety days Homeland Security had to remove you from the country have passed. Under *Zadvydas* and *Martinez*, they now have six months to effectuate your removal. If they can't, they have to release you…except in your case, they're claiming upfront you're a flight and security risk that justifies indefinite detention.

"The government plans to imprison you until you implicate someone in the smuggling scheme. They've even taken the unusual step of having the Chinese embassy submit a letter saying that China has no interest in repatriating a person who refuses to admit to Chinese citizenship. Technically you've never 'entered' the country because you were caught on the high seas, but you can't leave because no one will take you. Indefinite detention, inadmissible aliens, the constitutionally infirm 'national security' exception, this case has it all. Stupendous!"

I mouthed a protest. Ander put a finger to his lips and reminded me about the detainees who were relying on the integrity of my silence. Despite the handcuffs, I reached for Ander's fountain pen. Ander danced backward and pushed the panic button. The guards arrived to press my nose into the table until I nodded to the question, posed in English and Chinese, of whether I would behave.

Ander explained to the interpreter that dealing with hostile people was part and parcel of establishing landmark rulings. "It's the principle," he said, "not the person." The more I shook my head, the more delighted Ander became, his hand jabbing the air as he described how my case would transform the landscape of the law.

"Initially, I thought the best course of action was to wait out your six months," Ander said. "Six more months of complete silence and the news outlets would be compelled to carry clips of the charter planes being hired to ship you all out of the country. If we got lucky, they might focus on a pregnant woman or a child. Then two factors suggested we should strike now, while the iron is hot.

"First, of course, is the pressure the private detention centers are putting on Congress to stem this mass exodus. There are 27,500 immigrants in detention every single night. That's a 25 percent increase from last year. At $95 a night, that adds up to $1 billion spent annually on detaining immigrants, 20 percent of which is pure corporate profit. Migrants are their bread-and-butter, the reason they've enjoyed double-digit growth since September eleventh. The silent protest is a disaster for private prisons. They can't fill their beds!

"Second, in response to Congressional pressure, the U.S. Attorney came forward with a bizarre settlement offer. They wanted to release you with no restrictions pending your deportation so long as you disavowed any political motivations. Given China's refusal to recognize you as a national, this amounts to a free pass to stay in the United States forever. Can you believe that? They even offered to arrange a conditional work visa for you."

I leaned forward, which caused Ander to lean backward. His eyes flickered toward the panic button.

"Of course I refused the government's offer," he said. "They can't buy their way out of the silent protest. Their offer is anathema to the sacrifices that you and countless other illegally detained immigrants are making to highlight the unconstitutional and inhumane private prison system. We're going to file a habeas petition to get you out in a way that changes the law, not just conditions for individuals. You're your people's Aung San Suu Kyi: you'll endure torture and isolation until everyone is free. The appeals alone might take years. Let's take it all the way to the Supreme Court!"

For Ander, my slumped shoulders acknowledged the heavy weight I bore as the silent rebellion's leader. He pointed out that the more I suffered the more compelling my case would be. Then he ignored me and fretted aloud about the selection of the judge, hoping for a liberal judge but not one who was too liberal to be taken seriously. The outside world was starting to pay attention. The Asian community was calling for my criminal prosecution. Immigrant advocates were calling for my immediate release. There was even a nut job who claimed I was her ex-husband.

The last comment caught my attention. I had presumed Tanya would be working too hard at the firm to indulge her interest in Asian American issues that began shortly after she adopted my surname. She was flattered when white people asked her for Asian-restaurant recommendations; she voiced ethnic pride in outfielder Ichiro Suzuki's success. Tanya could save me. I would no longer languish in my cell as the lonesome poster child for civil liberties.

It wasn't to be. No one but Rajiv Patel and his interpreter visited me for six weeks. But five days before my federal hearing, after more than four months in detention, I woke to a welcome surprise. I could whisper.

CHAPTER 39

The first day brought whispers and the second, vocal hiccups. The third day brokered a strained rasp. My vocal cords should have withered and died. Instead they'd been pickled by Kolling's pharmacological poisons—immobilized like the Botoxed eyelids of an aging, Las Vegas lounge singer, quivering to life for a final curtain call.

But the ability to speak differs from having anything to say. Who would believe me? Kolling would deny the truth. The Asian American community would back him; my former law firm and my ex-wife would join them. Bruce would sic his Polynesian hooligans on me. The immigrant detainees who'd sacrificed themselves to share my solitude would see me for what I was. A privileged, self-centered fraud.

The night before my federal hearing, I couldn't sleep. Then I heard it. Or rather, I heard him.

Melody is context, a relationship not just between musical notes but between song and listener. Whistling in a park on a summer's afternoon is cheery. Whistling within the bowels of an empty prison block at 3 a.m. is eerie.

There was no good reason for the guard on duty to approach my cell. Was it a final attempt to beat sound back into me? Had Bruce paid someone to knock me off? Would the government transport me to a country where they could torture me with impunity? It wasn't until the Andes mint slipped beneath the door that I recognized the tune. *Dum, da da dum, duh duh duh duh duh dum.* It was what played at the opening and closing of Troy Bobbins's audio seminars: Troy's theme song.

The guard sauntered away, his hands clasped behind him. He was rounder than he should have been, and his hair had grown out into a ducktail, as if he'd recently returned from the Puyallup Fairgrounds. I pounded on the door. He paused, then returned to wave his key fob over the electronic sensor. The door slid back. Before me was the sturdy frame of a man who'd been fit but had let himself go. His oversized horse teeth were the same.

"G'day, mate," he said.

"Troy," I said. *Australian* Troy. "Is that really you?"

"It's Terry, actually. We haven't got time to dillydally. Follow me. Swing shift starts in two hours and you've many people to visit."

The last time I'd seen Troy he'd worn three days of stubble and reeked of whisky. By now, his Perma-tan had faded and his midsection suggested a fondness for meat pies, but at least he was sober.

We passed through the slumbering cellblocks until we entered the administration building. Troy rolled away a chair behind the reception desk. Beneath, flush with the floor, was a hatch. We each grabbed a handle and swung the portal open. Before us was a staircase that led downward into a brighter, whiter place.

"After you, mate," Troy said.

"No, please. After you."

"Aren't you the suspicious one?" Troy said. "I'm not on Kolling's side, if that's what you're thinking. I won't be on your side either if things get sticky. But I miss being of some use. It's my nature."

The lower floor was indistinguishable from the one above except no one manned the security booths or walked the floor. The detainees hadn't read the memo about the silent protest: they talked and laughed the way normal people should. Three dormitories were filled to overflowing with orange-clad Spanish-speakers who'd pounded a chrome picnic table into a makeshift fire pit. A table leg served as the spit for a roasting hen.

"*Mariel* Cubans," Troy said. "Castro's reanimated corpse has a better chance than these poor sods of making it out of here."

The detainees in the Chinese cell block were skinny and young. An old man was curled up on a bottom bunk, asleep with a pillow between his knees. His limbs disappeared into the folds of the baggy, orange pajamas. A tall slender boy called out a greeting in Chinese. He approached to utter unintelligible words.

"What'd he say, mate?" Troy said.

"Christ, Troy," I said. "What makes you think I speak Chinese?"

"Chinese, Japanese, what's the difference? Ah well, let's push forward, shall we? The lower floors can get a bit depressing, but that's the benefit of rubbing elbows with the poor: the ability to look at someone else and say, 'Thank goodness I have more than he does.'"

We exited the group dormitories. A metal staircase and a catwalk connected two levels of individual cells. In the common area, detainees milled about, clad, like me, in red. At the center table a man and a boy shifted white and black stones on a board. No, the short one was too stout to be a boy. He was a midget with a scar on his neck in the shape of a human mouth.

Milton swept his forearm across the board, sending the stones bouncing across the floor. "You cheated again, you son of a bitch."

John Smith shook his head, a patronizing smile on his lips. "Skill doesn't constitute cheating. 'Go' is the mother of all strategy games, its permutations more complex than those in chess. Your problem, Mr. Schwarzer, is that you lack a strategic mind. Anticipate not just your opponent's next move, but his next five moves."

Milton glowered. "Look where your strategic thinking landed you."

"Oy!" Troy said. "You've got company!"

Smith grinned. His teeth were as white as Troy's but proportional to his mouth. Milton continued to glare.

"Mr. Watanabe," Smith said. "I had considered investing in the private prison system before your silent revolt. It's an industry that flourishes in a recession. I should have anticipated that people with nothing to lose would find ways to muck things up."

I'd heard reports of Smith's demise, but I'd never seen his corpse. I could write off Sha Long and the boys as denizens of an alternative universe where Balthazar Salgado occupied a suite at the Ritz Carlton. But Milton...I'd held his hand while his blood turned cold.

"Milton." My throat caught. "Her only crime was that she idolized Luba. She wanted you to save her."

Milton snorted. "If you're going to cry, do it somewhere else. She was a stripper. You knew her for ten minutes. Millions have suffered more; millions have suffered since. I don't see you blubbering about them. If you're looking for an apology, you've come to the wrong place."

"Sheila's turning tricks to support her drug habit," I said. "Kolling owns *Das Puppenhaus*. A container of people suffocated like butterflies in a jar. Kolling was our enemy. If you could have focused your hatred on Kolling instead of on an innocent girl, neither of us would be here now."

"Collateral damage," Milton said. "Hate isn't a wrench used to tighten a screw. Hate is a force of nature: a motivation, a means, an end. Hate is altruism and self-sacrifice. What happens to you or to me doesn't matter. Hate cleanses us all."

"I hate you," I said.

"If you did," Milton said, "you wouldn't be whining about unfairness. And you would know exactly what to do now."

I looked at Troy for clarification, but he contemplated his fingernails, which were long and dirty.

"Grow some *cajones*, Watanabe," Milton said. "Remember the people who've betrayed you. Your ex-wife and her lover. The Japanese girl. Sheila. Kolling. Me." He angled his chin toward Smith. "This smug bastard. Don't question what's right or wrong. Strike back."

Smith cleared his throat. "If I might interject. Mr. Schwarzer's 'plan,' or whatever you want to call it, is ridiculously shortsighted. Vengeance is one goal. But the best revenge is to live a good life. Once the media discovers the government has tortured and imprisoned a U.S. citizen, you'll be paid a pretty penny for your silence. Purchase a beach house. Mail-order a Filipino bride who looks like Megumi. Comfort will heal a bruised ego."

"Are you saying I should say only enough to get myself out of prison," I said, "but not enough to jeopardize my negotiation position for a huge government settlement? What about the detainees who've sold themselves down the river to join the silent protest?"

Smith scratched his sandy-blond hair. He looked good even in detention clothing, his hair carefully mussed, an actor playing the part of a prisoner. "It's essential not to let emotions jeopardize your bargaining position. I knew KGI's new business strategy was a mistake. If Mr. Kolling continues his present course, the company will be bankrupt within two years. I should have started a competing karaoke business long ago; instead I kept trying to change his mind. Look how I've been rewarded for loyalty."

Troy touched my elbow. "It's time we got a move on, mate. We're running out of time and a few ladies are waiting to see you."

The women's dormitories weren't as crowded as the men's were. Unoccupied bunks were littered with photographs, hairbrushes, and the like. Troy led me to a cell beneath the staircase. The woman on the bottom bunk was wrapped in a blanket and faced the wall. The one on the top bunk dropped her *People* magazine and sat up.

"Wait a second," she said. "You look familiar. And I'm not just saying that."

Her hair was a washed-out brown and cut into a boyish mop. Her face was exceedingly plain, but her complexion was unblemished and smooth. She ignored the ladder and swung down from the top bunk with a showy swirl. She embraced me and the scent of baby powder assailed my nostrils. An arc of discolored flesh ran across her throat from ear to ear. No doubt there were other scars hidden beneath her prison-issue orange togs. The police Polaroids had detailed her wounds.

"Chandra," I said.

She stepped back. "You're not a friend of my parents, are you? I thought we knew each other from, you know, somewhere else."

I willed myself into composure. "When we met, you introduced yourself as 'Luba.'"

Chandra smiled and ran her fingers through her short hair. "That's what I thought. I never forget a face. I've run into customers at Taco Bell, in the library, wherever. Most men run away before I can say hello. You're different."

474

To how many men had she handed that line? Inside the velvet darkness of the Fantasy Labyrinth, I would have believed her. But here, in a sterile, brightly lit cell, I couldn't. She wasn't an object of desire. She was a teenager who'd washed up for bed.

"What are you doing here?" Chandra said.

"I'm trying to figure out what I'm supposed to do next," I said.

Chandra nodded. "I *totally* know what you mean. I'm trying to figure out what to do with my life too."

Chandra gestured toward the chair in front of the chrome writing table. Once I was seated, she draped an arm over my shoulders. Troy remained outside of the cell, eavesdropping but pretending not to.

"I'm not really enrolled in college," she said.

"Oh?"

"I mean, it's not a total lie. I took a few classes at a junior college and meant to transfer. That's why I got a job dancing. I tried to save money but, you know, things happen. I'll go back as soon as I know what I want to study. I mean, I have friends who study English, but what do you do with an English major? I'll return once I've gained more life experience."

Chandra stretched her arms over her head and did a side bend, impressively limber. "I've had some offers, you know, for photo shoots and what not. But what's the future in that?"

"I agree," I said, knowing she was looking for support rather than discussion. Chandra babbled about what a drag her parents were, how she needed a new car, how her friend moved to LA and was temping at a Jewish school while auditioning for television commercials. The girl in the bottom bunk had extricated her torso from the blanket. Her hands obscured her face, but she appeared to be peering at us.

"I wish they put me in here with someone who spoke English," Chandra said. "Or at least with somebody who wanted to learn." She lowered her voice. "All she does is lie there all day and cry."

"Has she been here long?" I said.

"A couple of months. She was one of those illegals who came in a shipping container. Can you imagine doing that just so you could work as a nanny? It makes me feel so lazy."

Chandra prattled on. When I stood to leave, she took my hands into hers.

"You'll come back to visit, won't you?" she said. "I'm sorry I talked so much about myself, but I want to learn all about you. We could really get to know each other."

I said something noncommittal and pulled away. At the door, I glanced back over my shoulder. Chandra slouched in the chair I'd vacated. The girl on the bunk had turned to watch me depart. Yes, it was her, face swollen from crying. The front of her pajama top was dampened in two moist medallions.

Troy suggested that we take a break in the employee lounge. He purchased a pack of peanut M&Ms from the vending machine and shared them with me. If he wanted to get back into shape, he should start snacking on fruit while working the night shift.

"Troy," I said. "You've got to help me out because I'm confused."

"I wish you would stop calling me that. The name's Terry. Terry Stottart."

"Fine. Terry. According to *Lesson 10: Think Selflessly, Act Selfishly, A Self-Centered Spiritualism that Will Save the World*, you advocated acting entirely within one's own self-interest, assuaging one's guilt through publicly recognized good deeds carried out with no greater than 5 percent of one's net proceeds. In other words, bad deeds could be balanced out by good deeds, and vice versa, like a karmic checking account. You said the cardinal rule was never to jeopardize one's own position because 'if you're gone, who's left to help?'"

Terry sighed. "That was a past life. And besides, I'm contractually prohibited for three years from discussing my former business."

"That's overreaching," I said. "They can stop you from competing for business or from helping someone in the same line of business. But they can't keep you from having conversations. You're not selling me anything. You can dispense free advice."

Terry winced. "I suppose you're right, mate, though it hurts to give out free what I used to charge at a thousand bucks an hour. But I said I'd help you, so go ahead."

"I'm an American citizen," I said. "I could care less about whether detention conditions improve or immigration law becomes more humane so long as my lifestyle isn't affected. What would you think if I took Smith's suggestion, called off the habeas hearing, and sued the government for millions of dollars?"

"Spiffy," Terry said. "That's a ripper of a plan."

"It would mean, of course, that I would lie to the government about how Bruce financed my attempt to steal

Megumi from Kolling. But it would be a white lie since he doesn't traffic Asians to the United States. He may traffic eastern Europeans, but not Asians." I paused. "Wait a second...didn't he just import a Malay man who's using my identity?"

"That's a beaut," Terry said. "Say whatever you need to say to make things right."

I sighed. "But what about the people who died in the container? Six people, plus a brain-damaged seventh. What about the immigrants who've joined the silent rebellion to help people they'll never meet? Am I supposed to pretend they never existed?"

"Pretend away, mate."

"And there's Kolling," I said. "He's responsible for the demise of your company, the death and servitude of countless others, Megumi's misery, my imprisonment. He should pay for what he's done."

"That's the spirit, Guy. Tear the boomer a new clacker."

"Troy...I mean, Terry. Is there anything I can say that you *won't* agree with?"

Terry shrugged. "Life's a funny thing, Guy. One day you're taking bubble baths with Playboy bunnies and the next you're moonlighting as a guard at a private prison. All that matters is your self-regard. If you want to set yourself up with a posh pad, then more power to you. If you'd rather be a martyr for the dark masses who wash up on our shores, then go full-Gandhi. That seems like more effort than it's worth since suffering will exist whether you plunge into it or ignore it, but this is a free country.

"You want to put Kolling's head on a pike? I'll put you in touch with some friends who'll take a crack at him for the right price. Want to run away and hide? Convince your-self that you're better than he is by taking the high road. Everything's relative. You're happy or not, successful or not, based on who you compare yourself to. Being born Ameri-can, you're in the top percentile of affluence even if all you do is watch television and drink beer.

"I didn't get rich by teaching people to become better. I made a fortune by teaching people to *feel* better. Why wake up to say, 'I'm a white-collar slave chained by my mortgage to a desk,' when you could say, 'I'm a winner'? What you win doesn't matter. What matters is that you feel entitled to winning. There's no such thing as right or wrong. That's the beauty of free will. All you have to do is remember one inviolable rule."

"What's that?" I said.

"Tell the truth or lie," Terry said. "Kill Kolling or pro-mote his new karaoke Shangri-La. Campaign against Third World sexual slavery or bed a Thai whore who shoots ping pong balls out of her Michael. Do something, do anything, just don't give it away. This is life. There are no substitu-tions. Even the biggest whacker in the history of man has to play both halves full speed."

I slept no more than an hour. I woke with the aftertaste of chocolate and peanuts on my tongue. There were no mes-sages hidden on my breakfast tray; there was just an empty candy wrapper crumpled in a corner of my cell.

CHAPTER 40

A federal hearing resembles a wedding ceremony. The guests, bisected by a center aisle, are dressed in their Sunday best. All eyes turn toward you as you enter in shackles. You may not know everyone, but everyone knows you.

If I remarried, I would invite Tanya to the ceremony, if only to prove that I too had moved on. I'm glad she made it to my habeas hearing. She called out my name, syllables blurted out in the midst of a swim stroke, but Jay Weed restrained her with a hoof on her forearm. Gracie repeated my name at increasing decibel levels until a federal marshal threatened her with expulsion. She brought a date too, a twenty-something Asian American girl with blond highlights who looked a wee too comfortable in her beige pantsuit.

Carolyn, the firm's perky, career receptionist was there, looking lost without her headset. So was the staff of the defunct Lily Pad, except for Ricardo and Jaime, who must still be in southern California, and Mori, of course, who was living out his twilight years with Irma at a beachside karaoke resort. Jimmy's time away from the DJ stand had not been kind. His sideburns had grayed, his belly protruded from his Goodwill-rack blazer. In the back, Sheila wore a sleeveless blue dress. She was dwarfed on either side by the Polynesian brothers, Lopeka and what's-his-name, tropical reminders to keep my vow of silence.

Should I have invited Sunny? Surely she'd forgiven me for insulting her life's work. But nothing kills romance faster than the appearance of desperation; nothing says desperation like a grown man in red pajamas and handcuffs. It would have been nice to see Billy, but he must not stock the *Seattle Asian Herald* in his boat shop. He would have felt at ease among my other supporters, geriatric Christian activists. The group took up the front two pews, their black sweatshirts emblazoned with a Bible citation: "[T]he truth will set you free. — John 8:32."

Was that why we were assembled? What was the truth for Norene, who'd conscripted a busload of elderly Asian immigrants to voice the community's sentiments? The old folks from International District senior housing couldn't speak English, but if Norene put her thumb down, they booed. If she put her thumb up, they cheered. Otherwise, they appeared puzzled, or sleepy, or disoriented by the confiscation of their shrimp chips and satchels of Capri Sun.

What was the truth for the men in checked work shirts and tractor caps who yelled, "Close the borders!" and "Stop taking our jobs!"? They'd caravanned over in their raised pickup trucks from eastern Washington. Had the influx of cheap Mexican labor trashed their children's futures as strawberry pickers? Had they been turned out from their jobs as busboys, maids, and slaughterhouse workers? Would my continued imprisonment and eventual deportation help them to sleep better at night?

Monolingual Asian immigrants sitting cheek-to-jowl with border vigilantes, cheering for the same side. Christian strangers supporting me and thousands of faceless migrants, regardless of our past and present sins. Hope is a renewable resource in America.

I absorbed the spectacle with the dispassionate acuity of an elite karaoke performer. Thought is the enemy of action. Reflection kills spontaneity. Call my federal hearing what you will—wedding ceremony, political spectacle, or legal contest—but the video was rolling and the music was playing. It was time for me to sing.

"All rise," the courtroom deputy said. She was a stocky woman with a dour expression. "The United States District Court for the Western District of Washington is now in session, the Honorable Marina Clark presiding."

The judge was a diminutive woman with a large presence. She set down a binder next to a stack of paper. At her elbow was a laptop computer. She took her seat and peered directly at me over her spectacles.

"You may be seated," she said into the microphone. "I would prefer if the audience did not boo petitioner."

At the counsel table, Ander Andersson's leg jiggled in excitement. Next to him were three law student interns for the Center for Civil Liberties, two young women and a man, all two years removed from hitting up their parents for milk money. The government was represented by Homeland

Security attorney Rajiv Patel and a sandy-haired man in a bow tie roughly the same age, in his early or mid-thirties.

The judge read off the name of the case and called my counsel to the lectern. Ander introduced himself but didn't get any further.

"Before we begin, Mr. Andersson," the judge said, "I would like you to explain why you joined the government's opposition to the *amicus curiae* brief by an American citizen who claims the detainee, your client, is, in fact, an American citizen with the right to be released immediately. Wouldn't that be a beneficial outcome for your client? That he be set free?"

Ander Andersson smiled at this softball. "Your question goes to the heart of who my client is and what he stands for. My client is the leader of a massive detainee rebellion, the likes of which the Department of Homeland Security has never seen. At great personal risk to himself, he defied governmental tyranny and the abusive practices shielded by the scrim of privately run prisons. His silent protest has been joined not just by detainees throughout the United States, but also by domestic inmates, who say more through their act of civil disobedience than could be said in a thousand newspaper articles or legal treatises. The man who stands before you—"

"Hold on, counselor," the judge said. "I promise you ample time to mount your soapbox. Right now, I want to know why you would oppose the acceptance of a position, which if true, would liberate your client."

One of Ander's interns, a girl with long, straight hair swept over her left shoulder, scribbled furiously on a scrap of paper. She handed it to him.

"Pardon me, your honor," Ander said. "I've let my passion for justice get in the way of answering simply. We oppose Ms. Watanabe's *amicus* brief for two reasons. First, neither my client nor the government has disputed my client's national origin as Chinese."

"The Chinese government has," the judge said.

"The Chinese government will not accept a detainee who refuses to acknowledge his own identity. That refusal is, however, my client's way of protesting the U.S. government's indefinite detention of him in substandard conditions."

"Okay," the judge said. "Proceed with your second point."

"Second, your honor," Ander said. "If we accept Ms. Watanabe's account as true for the sake of argumentation, she has no standing to assert Mr. Watanabe's rights. Though Ms. Watanabe has kept her surname, she is, in fact, Mr. Watanabe's *ex*-wife. She has no more right to speak on his behalf than a street mime would. If, of course, street mimes could speak."

"There's a difference between dispositive," the judge said, "and tremendously enlightening, isn't there, Mr. Andersson? Ms. Watanabe attached wedding photographs taken in front of the Seattle Center. That would seem to contradict the stipulated facts that petitioner was apprehended on the high seas and has been in government detention ever since."

"If I may interject." The government attorney in the bow tie stood up. Patel remained seated, an impassive expression on his face.

"Ah, Mr. Lassiter," the judge said. "Congratulations on your recent appointment as U.S. Attorney. Your predecessor had a sterling reputation for fairness and candor. His dismissal came as a shock to all the members of this district. I would love to hear the government's present position, given that the letter briefs you faxed over this morning contradict the government's prior position and, at times, common decency."

Mr. Lassiter adjusted his bow tie. "Your honor, the claims made by Ms. Watanabe née Dullard concern sensitive security issues that cannot be discussed in court. The Department is obliged to say only that the detainee represents a significant risk to the community. Drawing any conclusions about the verity of Ms. Dullard's claims would encroach upon the executive's investigative prerogatives and would, therefore, violate the separation of powers."

"You're saying that the court should not address Ms. Watanabe's claims," the judge said, "because the government believes the court hasn't the power to do so?"

"Precisely, your honor."

The judge tapped on her computer keyboard. "That logic would swallow this proceeding, wouldn't it? If the court can't address her claims, then the court certainly can't address *his* claims. Petitioner is the source of the security risk."

"That's correct, your honor. Whatever the government does with petitioner cannot be reviewed here. The Military Commissions Act strips this court of jurisdiction to hear cases involving terrorists and other enemy combatants. Petitioner must seek relief from the Secretary of Defense."

The judge lifted her fingers from the keyboard. "Are you telling me, Mr. Lassiter, that the government now asserts that petitioner, the sole conscious survivor of a tragic voyage, is, in fact, a terrorist? I haven't seen a shred of evidence to support this assertion."

"Your honor," Mr. Lassiter said. "The government cannot present its overwhelming evidence of petitioner's ties to known terrorists because doing so would jeopardize ongoing investigations. The court must accept as true this assertion from a co-equal branch of government. Anything less would embolden our enemies."

"I see why you have risen so fast within the Department of Justice." The judge brushed her bangs from her eyes. "Here's a solution. Present the evidence to me *in camera*. It won't be placed in the official court record. I'll dictate a notation that such evidence exists. We can recess right now for that purpose."

Mr. Lassiter shook his head. Next to him, Patel remained stone-faced. "Again, your honor, the court doesn't have the authority to review this evidence. It would be an encroachment on executive prerogatives."

"Your honor," Ander said. "You see my client's predicament, don't you? Even before Mr. Lassiter was appointed as U.S. Attorney, the government refused to share any evidence about my client's supposed danger to the community. We learned through a newspaper article about a journal my client allegedly handwrote during his voyage."

"The government need not exchange exculpatory evidence in a civil proceeding," Mr. Lassiter said. "And particularly not in a case that should be tried by a military tribunal."

"The sole charge against my client is illegal entry," Ander said. "How can the government wave its magic wand and turn this into a terrorism case? Even if it could, how could it refuse to provide my client *or* the court with evidence of danger. The government offered my client's immediate release into the community if he broke his silence—"

"I object, your honor," Mr. Lassiter said. "That was a confidential settlement offer. It can't be discussed in open court and the reference should be stricken from the record."

"Stop," the judge said. "I've heard enough. The government says petitioner is a terrorist but refuses to provide evidence to support that assertion because the executive cannot trust the judiciary with sensitive materials. Petitioner's attorney says the court shouldn't consider evidence that petitioner is an American citizen because there are detainees counting on his leadership. You two have tied legal doctrines into knots that Justice Cardozo couldn't unravel."

"Thank you," Ander said.

"Thank you, your honor," Mr. Lassiter said. "I would add that were petitioner an American citizen, we would still have the right to detain him without judicial intervention."

The judge sighed. "Attorneys like you are chasing me into retirement. I am tempted out of sheer frustration to release petitioner into Canada. Instead, I'm going to let this hearing proceed over the duly noted objections by the government. Mr. Andersson, you're on the clock. Please don't repeat what you've already discussed in your briefs."

What followed was forty-five minutes of each side repeating its arguments in novel, yet more tedious, ways. Ander: "Substandard conditions; government secrecy; silent protest; blah, blah, blah." Mr. Lassiter: "Executive privilege; secret evidence; danger to the community; military tribunals; blah, blah, blah." At the outset, the audience cheered or jeered with approximate accuracy. The judge tired of reigning them in. As our precious few moments on this earth were, however, sucked into the maw of oblivion, the audience whispered amongst themselves, or stepped out for restroom and cigarette breaks. The judge pulled her laptop computer closer and continued to type: e-mails, I suspected, about dinner plans or upcoming vacations.

Throughout, Rajiv Patel kept his eyes on me. I ignored him at first but couldn't help but notice that his expression had changed. When he'd visited me in lockup, his face had been enflamed by righteous indignation. Now his expression had softened, though it remained intense. I shook my head as Ander launched into a speech about how my courage had inspired guards and nurses to report the abuses they'd witnessed. I put my hand over my ear to muffle the prattle emitting from the Chinese interpreter's mouth. Patel raised his eyebrows. I nodded.

Patel rose to his feet. "Your honor," he said in the middle of one of Ander's dramatic pauses. "I think this hearing could be resolved quite quickly if we simply called Mr. Wata—petitioner—to the stand."

Ander objected. "My client has not, as a matter of principle, spoken to his own attorney. The government's attempt to compel him to speak or be held in contempt of court is a ploy designed to waste the court's valuable time."

I stood up. Behind me, the audience went silent. It took several beats for Norene to signal her senior citizens to boo me in a desultory fashion. Ander and the interpreter motioned for me to sit down. I shook my head.

"It appears that your client has more to say than you are suggesting," the judge said.

Patel and Mr. Lassiter whispered to one another. Patel jabbed his finger into his palm for emphasis. Mr. Lassiter fidgeted with his bow tie and stepped aside. Patel told the judge that he would examine me.

Ander implored me with his eyes. I ignored him. In the witness box, I raised my right hand and nodded at the oath.

"Let the record show," the judge said, "that the detainee, without the benefit of translation, has nodded his assent to being sworn in."

Rajiv Patel looked sharp in his suit, which was almost iridescent. His diamond ear stud glinted and his closely cropped hair carried a wet hairspray sheen.

"Sir," Patel said. "Would you please state your name for the record?"

"My name is Guy Watanabe."

Exclamations burst forth from the crowd. Several Asian seniors booed reflexively while their friends started to cheer. It took the judge a dozen gavel strikes to quiet the audience.

"Would you please state your nationality?" Patel said.

"I am an American," I said.

Patel nodded. "Mr. Watanabe, please recall that you have sworn to tell the truth, the whole truth, and nothing but the truth. To do otherwise would be to commit perjury, a crime for which you could be prosecuted. Please consider this question carefully before you answer. Why have you chosen to appear before us today?"

"I am here," I said, "to speak out on behalf of my brothers and sisters in bondage who have no voice."

Okay, so I lied. But I tell you what: I played that courtroom like Charlie Daniels played his fiddle in "The Devil

Went Down to Georgia." When I finished describing the Chinese factory encampments, the girl with the baby on her hip, and our inexorable suffocation, there wasn't a dry eye in the house. Who better than a karaoke champion to sense not only what the audience *wanted* to hear but what they *needed* to hear?

It wasn't all an act, of course. I cried when I described how my fingers lacked the dexterity to cover Sha Long's body in cardboard. And what it was like to wake amongst corpses, pleased that their deaths meant more air for me.

But I made up whoppers to keep Bruce off my back and preserve facts known only to me. According to the authorities, Megumi Tanita had died within the container. I knew the corpse that carried her passport was someone else. As for Kolling…I couldn't attack him directly. That would alert his army of attorneys, his public relations firm, and his allies within the Asian American community. I would have to take him down some other way.

CHAPTER 41

Troy Bobbins would have been proud of me. Maybe not New Troy: chubby, racist, alcoholic, moonlighting-as-a-prison-guard, Aussie Troy, who binged on chocolate and lacked direction in life. That Troy would have spouted relativistic crap about whatever I did being fine so long as I *felt* fine about it.

I'm talking about Old Troy, Real Troy, the one who knew there was a way to reconcile Smith's pragmatism, Milton's thirst for vengeance, and my guilty conscience.

"Those who say success is an illusion have been smoking too much hippie lettuce," Troy instructed. "The real illusion is sacrifice. Who needs it? Every situation is a win-win for the enlightened man. You can do good *and* do well."

Advice shouldn't be doubted because it's cribbed. Why do acne sufferers order Proactiv® Solution when the same active ingredient—benzoyl peroxide—costs a fraction of the price at Bartell Drugs? Because substance doesn't matter as much as packaging, charisma, and an effective distribution network. But the truth doesn't mutate; our confidence in it does.

I did what I could to help myself and the deluded souls who'd joined my inadvertent protest movement. The truth set me free, but lies kept me from being kneecapped by Bruce's henchmen and preserved a payday from the government. So what if I made myself look better? That wasn't vanity but a tool. Popularity is power. What better way to represent the migrants' interests than to serve as their more articulate voice?

Norene Wong ate up my story about how the search for my Chinese roots led me to help factory workers organize a strike against their American corporate overlords. She ran a front-page article in the *Seattle Asian Herald* suggesting that Nike, Liz Claiborne, and Coach—with the backing of covert CIA operatives—had conspired to ship me and other troublemakers out in a floating tomb. The *Seattle Post-Intelligencer* ran a profile of me on July fourth and *60 Minutes* broadcast a five-minute segment entitled, "Guy Watanabe: The Color of Patriotism." (John Stossel broadcast a response on *20/20* entitled, "Guy Watanabe: Friend or Fraud?")

The government didn't really mind if I exposed mistreatment of immigrant detainees. That "secret" was detailed in books, newspaper articles, court depositions, and United Nations human rights reports. I was a hit at fundraisers for the Center for Civil Liberties, the Immigration Alliance, the Asian American Museum, the Northwest Asian American Theater, and STOP! Racism; raked in dough as the grand marshal of the "silent auctions;" brought the audience to tears long after my own were simulated. I stood next to the governor and Asian American legislators as they announced a state-federal task force to examine how to assist victims of human trafficking. The only problem was the general public simply didn't care.

Once I began speaking, the protest died the way it began—silently. The private prison company transferred the Tacoma warden to Louisiana, the Louisiana warden moved to Tacoma, and the government claimed that the abuse it hadn't committed had been rectified. Complaining detainees were transferred to facilities thousands of miles away from their families and pro-bono attorneys. Homeland Security fired Rajiv Patel, called my inability to name the human smugglers trauma-related amnesia, and negotiated a big fat settlement check. The overflowing detention centers attested to the government's tough stance on crime, terrorists, and foreigners. Humdrum normality returned, ranting from the radical left be damned. Surely I couldn't be blamed for Newton's First Law of Motion, that every body continues in its state of rest unless compelled to change by forces impressed upon it.

From time to time, I volunteered with elderly Catholic activists who tracked the immigrant detainees passing through the Tacoma detention center. I helped to update their ancient database, moved boxes that might have resulted in broken hips, and repackaged bulk gold crosses into cellophane envelopes. I became especially close to Marjorie and Benjamin, the couple who'd shown up to my first detention hearing. As we walked out to the church parking lot one night, I asked why they helped faceless migrants who disappeared without a trace.

Benjamin shrugged. "My father once told me that the world is a sinking ship. If you expect to raise it out of the water and get it to fly, you'll be forever disappointed. But if you dedicate your life to ensuring that it will sink no further, perhaps you'll be pleasantly surprised."

I sometimes hung out with Ander Andersson and the Center for Civil Liberties staff, who operated out of an office shared with a naturopathic pet store. I played second base for their softball team, which was always short of able bodies. We got killed by the private attorneys, whose stream of summer interns with former college experience trounced our interns, half of whom sniffed about the patriarchal nature of competitive sports.

"Nothing's changed," I said. Ander and I were sitting on the artificial turf, the cooler between us. We drank herbal iced tea blended with organic cane sugar. The other side had beer.

Ander fiddled with the brim of his cap. "Do you ever wonder what might have happened if you'd remained silent? You know, taken one for the team?"

"I can't turn the clock back now, can I, Ander?"

Ander looked embarrassed that he'd asked. "You told the truth. That's the important thing. When it was revealed that you weren't really an immigrant, the appeals court would have vacated the case anyway. You saved us from a pyrrhic victory. Not all of us are Mahatma Gandhi. You should be happy to be Guy Watanabe: an American, not an illegal immigrant."

You see? A true believer like Ander Andersson admitted that, excluding martyrs, I'd done the best a man could do. Merely mentioning my name scared city officials into appointing more Asian Americans to committees. I was paid honoraria to address university students. Liberal white women flirted with me; radical black men bumped my fist in solidarity. I would soon be a millionaire living off the earnings of my suffering. What more could I want? What more did I need?

Aussie Troy would say to compare myself to the poor sods who'd been deported penniless and to rejoice in my good fortune. He was wrong. My dissatisfaction had nothing to do with perspective. There was an objective source for my sorrows. Horatio Kolling was the reason I felt empty inside. He'd expanded his karaoke empire by stealing something precious, something essential, from me. I wanted it back.

Like life, November in Seattle is rainy, cold, and dark. That's why I welcomed Billy and May's arrival for Thanksgiving. It's physiologically impossible to suffer from seasonal affective disorder while trying to keep a hyperactive child from breaking your remote control and rearranging your music collection.

May's mother Lizzie had gone missing for a month, resurfacing only after she was arrested for DUI in Arizona and was court-ordered to call Washington state Child Protective Services. She told Billy that it was time to make a "fresh start" and supported his adoption application. Besides, her new beau, an ultimate fighting promoter, didn't like kids.

Billy woke hours before I did to buy fresh pastries and cook breakfast. Enjoyment of his gourmet talent was counterbalanced by May's moodiness. One moment, she would ask me in the sweetest voice to read to her. The next, she would writhe like Linda Blair on the kitchen linoleum. I suggested we slip a few tranquilizers into her cereal. Billy wasn't amused. So I called for backup.

The day after Thanksgiving, Gracie and her girlfriend Paula joined us at the Children's Museum. Later, we climbed Queen Anne hill to drink *café con leche* at a Cuban café. May was enamored by everything about Paula, from the frosted tips of her hair to her double-jointed arms. Yes, May nearly strangled her by trying to steal Paula's beaded necklace. But Paula never raised her voice. She whispered in May's ear until the girl stopped baring her teeth. Dating Gracie must have honed Paula's conflict resolution skills.

Gracie wouldn't stop criticizing my plan to sue Horatio Kolling for possession of my karaoke medallion. Several weeks before, the Karaoke Group International's Karaoke Xanadu had opened in the foothills of Leavenworth to rave reviews. Since that time, Horatio Kolling's face had been everywhere: billboards, newspapers, magazines, tourist guides. I was watching a freaking Sonics game and his smug mug appeared, inviting viewers to "Live the life of royalty at Xanadu." Everywhere he was pictured with my medallion dangling from his neck. Everywhere he, not me, was referred to as the "Karaoke King." King County had sold KGI the rights to the appellation. I had been the first and the last Karaoke King, and thereafter the title reverted to a man who'd neither earned it nor deserved it.

"Would you move on already, Guy?" Gracie said. "Did Kolling Botox your vocal cords or your fucking brain?"

"Whose side are you on?" I said. "His or mine? I thought you'd have my back. Fuck, Gracie!"

"Let's go play with a puzzle," Paula said. She led May by the hand to the other side of the café. The barista looked perturbed, but, shit, Gracie had raised her voice first. Billy stroked his mustache meditatively.

"I'm not sure I understand," Billy said. "If these karaoke bars promote prostitution, why can't they just be shut down?"

Gracie rolled her eyes. "Geez, Billy. That's like asking why Darwinism didn't kill God. People have sex. People make money. But it's illegal to have sex for money? Prostitution's illegal everywhere but absent nowhere. Outlaw God and churches go underground. Outlaw sex and it goes underground. You can't exterminate human desire."

I shook my head. "How libertarian of you, Gracie. The real reason Kolling won't be shut down is because of friends in high places. He and his employees have donated to the campaigns of nearly thirty elected officials. The state Attorney General spent the entire weekend at Xanadu. If the hostesses' visas are in order, no one's going to touch a Kolling business. It's just 'coincidence' that KGI hires attractive Asian girls in their twenties."

"Hello, Mr. Conspiracy Theory," Gracie said. "There's no crackdown because law enforcement has better things to do than lock up pot smokers and prostitutes. You're such a prude! What do you think should happen, Guy? Throw those girls in jail and then deport them so they can work in Chinese brothels for a buck a day?"

"It's still exploitation," I said. "Look what Kolling did to Megumi. Have you forgotten what happened in that container?"

"How could I forget what happened in the container?" Gracie said. "I can't go to a fricking fundraiser without people dissolving into tears over their salads. I'm not saying Kolling shouldn't be punished for what he's done. But attacking Kolling on prostitution isn't going to work."

"I know that. I'm suing him for trademark infringement. I'll get a court order to compel him to return my medallion and cease-and-desist from referring to himself as 'Karaoke King.'"

"The cease-and-desist order won't fly," Gracie said. "He paid for that title."

"I think I'm the one who asked about the prostitution charge," Billy said.

"Did you?" Gracie said.

"Why won't it fly?" I said. "The county may have sold him the title, but the rules haven't changed. The throne is determined by competition. Kolling never competed for the crown, *ergo*, he's no Karaoke King. He's a Karaoke Usurper."

Gracie flared her nostrils. "Who said kings can't take their crowns by force? He toppled you, unfair and square. Move on. Your fixation on that prick is borderline creepy."

"What if I told you his flourishing business and my inability to move on are related?" I said. "What if I told you I can't live without that medallion?"

Gracie pushed away her bottle of mineral water. On a health food kick, she'd stopped drinking caffeine and dairy products. "What are you saying, Guy?"

I motioned for Gracie and Billy to lean closer. "What if I told you that when Kolling took my medallion, he stole my soul?"

Gracie and Billy looked at me, then looked right through me, as if I'd turned transparent and they were adapting to the view through my skull.

"Brother's losing it," Gracie said to Billy. "You talk to him." She walked across the room. May wasn't pleased to share Paula's attention with Gracie, but Gracie was in such a foul mood, even May was cowed.

Billy and I sat for a few moments in silence, draining the dregs in our mugs. "I've gone over this again and again in my mind," I said. "It all makes sense. Everything bad that's happened to me took place after I lost the medallion."

"You've been traumatized," Billy said. "It takes time to get past the bitterness."

"I don't need to be psychoanalyzed," I said. "I need your support. Everything could have turned out so much better. Don't you ever feel that way?"

Billy looked over at May, who was lying across both Gracie's and Paula's laps, dangling her head backward and giggling. "I do. Of course, I do. And then I wonder whether things may have turned out better than I could ever have planned."

Tanya wouldn't have invited me to lunch at McCormick and Schmick's without having an ulterior motive. No one dines there unless they're entertaining guests or caught in a new city with no other place to spend a per diem on bad, expensive seafood.

Our relationship had benefited from my time in the container. I couldn't help but feel tenderness for her efforts to liberate me. She'd asked Jay Weed to pressure his powerful acquaintances on my behalf. She and Jay were horrified to learn about Kolling's possible involvement in the human slave trade. "Possible" involvement because they found, after extensive investigation, that there were no links between KGI and the human cargo. The shipping company was a subcontractor to a subcontractor that was a subsidiary of a Marianas Island subsidiary of an international conglomerate that owned, among other things, an environmentally friendly hand soap and a line of gourmet dog food. Tanya and Jay admitted that KGI may have been duped by a business partner's subsidiary, an inevitable result of our "increasingly interconnected world." They continued to represent Kolling and KGI in their extensive land and business deals.

Tanya looked good. Svelte. But she also looked bad, and I say that without lingering resentment. She had that half-starved, triathlete hollowness to her cheeks. Tanya ordered a Caesar salad and a Diet Coke. I congratulated her for acing her law school exams. She basked in my praise, then introduced the topic of my lawsuit. She said my legal theory made no sense. If King County had, indeed, sold all rights and privileges to the title of "Karaoke King," then the manner in which one attained the title could be changed by the successor in interest.

"You're forgetting," I said, "that in every press photo, Kolling is wearing a medallion imprinted with my name. If he wants to mint a new one for himself, more power to him. But he's wearing a stolen item. I'll concede he might have the right to call himself the 'Karaoke King,' but he's definitely not 'Guy Watanabe.' This civil suit is a courtesy. I could report him to the King County Prosecutor for theft."

"Mr. Kolling says he received the medallion as a gift," Tanya said. "And the person who gifted it to him received it as a gift from you. If that's true, he couldn't have stolen it."

"And Kolling knows that the person who gave him my medallion died in a container with six, now seven, other people. It's his word against mine. I'd like those words to be recorded in open court."

"Is it about the attention, Guy?" Tanya said. "Are you so addicted to the limelight that you'll take down a man who generates thousands of jobs here and worldwide?"

"If he returns my medallion, he won't hear another peep out of me."

Tanya sighed. She reached for her attaché case and pulled out a binder-clipped document. She slid it forward.

"What's this?" I said.

"A settlement offer," she said, "in the form of a karaoke competition. If he wins, he keeps the medallion and the title. If you win, you get the medallion and he'll renounce the use of 'Karaoke King' in his promotional materials."

"Does Kolling also offer to raise the dead?" I said.

"It's easy for you to sit on a moral high horse," Tanya said. "But with a business as large and diversified as Mr. Kolling's, he's bound to deal with companies with fewer scruples than his own. He didn't have to make this settlement offer. He wanted to. It gives you everything you want: a competition for the title in front of a huge crowd in his state-of-the-art facility. Xanadu is amazing. I've never seen a more breath-taking entertainment complex."

I didn't read the settlement offer until I returned to my apartment. It was straightforward: Kolling and I, head-to-head, on Xanadu's main stage. Three rounds, the winner determined by an amalgam of computer and audience scoring. There was a handwritten notation in the margin of the last page. It wasn't legible until I turned the page side-ways and reflected it in a mirror.

The message said, "She may have chosen you, but I still own your soul."

CHAPTER 42

The competition's official name was "Horatio Kolling Presents the Karaoke Group International's 'Crowning of the Karaoke King.'" Its popular moniker was the "Mambo in Mongolia." Tickets sold out shortly after the event was announced on the International Channel and in the Asian American press. The Seattle Channel outbid TVW for tape-delay rights.

With the Lily Pad gone, I chased karaoke nights at bars in every Seattle neighborhood from Greenwood to Georgetown. From 9 p.m. to 2 a.m., six nights a week, I trained. On my off day, I spoke only when spoken to and avoided second-hand smoke. Jimmy kept me on a strict song count to preserve my vocal cords. It was just like old times and, truth be told, I was a better singer than before. I no longer faked emotions on songs about lost hopes and dreams. I had suffered for my art and deserved to win, even if the International District odds makers thought otherwise.

"What do you mean twenty to one?" I said. "It was ten to one five days ago. How could my chances be getting worse?"

Jimmy was on break from ladling udon into Styrofoam bowls. He wore a red apron, a bundle of disposable chopsticks protruding from his pocket. His lazy eye, angled at the ceiling, quivered. "Home court advantage, Guy. His house, his equipment, his rules. Tickets too pricey for regular people. What do rich people know about karaoke?"

It was odd to hear Jimmy use my given name. Though he was my trainer and most enthusiastic supporter, he had ceased referring to me as the "Karaoke King." He was preparing for the worst, but I knew something the invisible hand didn't. Even in my oxygen-deprived stupor, I recalled every word that Megumi had uttered through the quarter-sized hole in the container. Her last ones were these: *No matter how much he practices, he sounds like a tortured animal.*

"Listen, Jimmy," I said. "When the odds are the widest, right before they turn off the line, put every last cent on me. I'll bring home that crown. I promise."

Jimmy shrugged. "Got to get back to work, Guy."

"This isn't bravado. It's a guarantee you can bank on."

"Jimmy never got tortured by the government," Jimmy said. "He needs to earn his daily bread."

Jimmy waddled off to the noodle counter. How had a man who never ate gained so much weight? Had creases of worry always lined his face?

Would she be more receptive to my invitation while standing in front of the karaoke screen where we'd flirted or in front of the Casio keyboard where I'd trashed her compositions? I waited until the very last moment to call, three days before the competition, when I knew I'd have to pay a huge penalty for booking her flight. What did a little more consumer debt matter once the settlement check arrived?

"Hello?" she said. "Hello? Is anyone there?"

Her voice was huskier than I'd remembered. I'd waited until 11 a.m. to call, but she sounded as if she'd just woken up.

"I can hear you breathing, you creep," she said.

"Sunny?" I said. "I've got a bad connection or something. Oh yeah, that's better. This is Guy. Guy Watanabe. I don't know if you remember me."

"Guy? You're so famous, I couldn't forget you if I tried."

There was an awkward pause. "Oh yeah," I said. "The whole container business. That seems like a lifetime ago, all that suffering and dying and imprisonment and stuff. How are you? What have you been up to?"

I'm horrible at small talk, but Sunny made it easy. She told me that she'd taken my advice about song selection and diversified the song list at Choi's Club. People other than Jorge took the microphone now and then. She was thinking about applying for a small business loan to purchase a new sound system. She would have to wait to upgrade the video screen. Her dog Henry had torn his ACL. It wasn't the athletic activity as much as his weight. She put him on reduced-calorie kibble and stopped feeding him table scraps (unless he begged). A surprise immigration raid had scared away her clientele. She'd closed down for two weeks and was still operating at a loss.

"Sunny," I said. "I don't know if you've been paying attention to the karaoke competition world, but there's a pretty big one coming up."

"You mean the *Mambo in Mongolia.* That's Saturday. My relatives in Korea e-mailed to see if there was any way to score tickets. Do you know Asian travel agents are selling 'Karaoke King' tour packages? Everyone wants to see Xanadu. It's become the Asian pilgrimage to Mecca. I've heard the video screen is three stories tall. Is that true?"

"It may be," I said. "I haven't really seen it yet."

"Don't you think you should? You know, from a competitor's standpoint. You don't want to be overwhelmed on the night of the competition. You've got to be able to block all of that stuff out."

"That's a great point," I said. Except that would entail contacting Kolling's people, which I refused to do.

"This is the karaoke contest of the century," she said. "You must be getting six figures to put your reputation on the line against that corporate clown. How can he call himself the Karaoke King? He doesn't even sing on his own commercials. What do you get if you win? A contest in Sri Lanka gives away Corvettes. KGI's contest is sponsored by Toyota, right? Those FJ Cruisers are sweet! You've got to push for one of those."

I cleared my throat. "Actually, the winner gets the title, Karaoke King. And my karaoke medallion. The medallion I won the first time around."

A pause ensued. "Do you know tickets to the competition are being sold on eBay for five hundred bucks?"

"Um, yeah," I said.

"Do you realize how much money KGI has is making in ticket sales, free advertising, television rebroadcast rights, and sponsorships?"

"I think it's better this way," I said. "A more pure competition. You know, just me and Kolling, *mano-a-mano*."

"How is it pure if he gains millions of dollars, win or lose, while you gain nothing, win or lose, except for a title you already carry and a medallion you already own?"

I had no answer for that. I changed the subject. "I called to see if you wanted to attend the *Mambo in Mongolia* as my special guest. I've been allotted six seats, and I was hoping you might consider it. If you're too busy, I understand. I'll pay for airfare, of course, and accommodations. I know this is short notice, but—"

"You have six tickets?" she said. "You're the main attraction and you secured six, zero-six, complimentary tickets for yourself? I don't mean to be critical, Guy, but I think you need to hire a business manager."

"I think you've made that point painfully obvious," I said. "But for right now, I was wondering if you might consider coming to the competition as my date."

Another long pause. "Sunny?" I said.

"Shit," she said. "Shit, shit, shit. My mother's sixtieth birthday is this Saturday. She's been planning it since she turned fifteen. We've got relatives flying in from Korea. I'm in charge of everything—the food, the entertainment, photographs—because my good-for-nothing siblings never organize anything. For Koreans, the sixtieth birthday is a big deal; so big, they keep on celebrating it for three years. If it was any other weekend…"

"No, no," I said. "It's my fault for giving you so little advance notice."

"I'm flattered you asked me. I'd rather hear you sing than mingle with relatives I've never met. I would love to see you pound that Johnny-come-lately into the ground. But I can't shirk my responsibilities."

"Sixty. Wow. Your mom must have had you when she was really young."

A short pause. "You're short on tact, aren't you, Mr. Karaoke King?" Her voice was tinged with mock rage.

"Oh yeah. Sorry. I'm disappointed we won't be able to see each other."

"You know, Guy, this competition may be huge, but it doesn't mean the world ends on Saturday. They'll be other Saturdays. Invite me up to Seattle again, and I might say yes. I'll even pay my own way up. It's not like I'm poor, you know. I do run my own business."

I should have ended the conversation right there, on a high note. She'd forgiven my former indiscretions. She'd hinted at lingering romantic feelings. Instead I made the mistake of asking one last question.

"Would you say yes to me even if I lost the competition?" I said. "If I was no longer the Karaoke King. If I was just plain, old Guy Watanabe?"

"What kind of question is that to ask three days before battle?" Sunny said. "Stop thinking like such a loser! Win the competition, then we'll talk."

CHAPTER 43

Xanadu's entrance and accommodations were aboveground, but the performance auditorium had been hollowed out of the earth. Visitors descended by escalator three stories into a grand cavern illuminated by a thousand jeweled stalactites refracting the rays of an indoor sun. The stage wasn't on one end of the hall but in the middle, a disk rising like an obelisk above the heads of the patrons, fit for U2 during its *Joshua Tree* heyday but itself dwarfed by the video screen. Its digital image of a river was so sharp that every filament of moss on the rocks was distinct. The sound of water surrounded us, though the speakers were invisible.

Xanadu was more than a karaoke ideal; it was a karaoke paradise. Or was it a Karaoke Valhalla—the final resting place for slain karaoke champions?

"Breathe, Guy," Gracie said. "When you take that microphone, all the glitz in the world doesn't matter. Everything you need to win this competition is right here." She tapped my sternum. "Don't let him get in your head. Don't lose the contest before it starts."

"It's beautiful," Jimmy said. He searched for other adjectives, lips moving soundlessly.

Billy said something, but it was drowned out by waiters calling for their orders. Six measly tickets and Kolling had placed my party next to the kitchen and the restroom, the scents of prime rib and cleansing detergent creating an unsavory mélange. Billy repeated himself.

"I said I don't like it. It's fancy but superficial. Once you've seen it, why come back? Especially with prices like these."

Gracie had borrowed Whitney Houston's dress from the eighties video "How Will I Know?" She might dis other women's fashion choices; that didn't mean she'd developed her own style. Clingy materials are a no-no for thick women. Paula, on the other hand, looked out of this world, her strapless dress accentuating her broad and shapely swimmer's back.

"I think I agree," Paula said. "Even if Xanadu were in Seattle, I wouldn't meet my friends here after work. Why drive two hours for a simulated cavern of ice?"

"Hello!" Gracie said. "Las Vegas is in the middle of a desert and it's doing fine. If you build an expensive place, Asians will come. The more exclusive the better."

"Las Vegas is the exception, not the rule," Billy said. "Washington's got casinos, but no one travels here for them. Washington casinos attract Washington addicts. I'd take Mr. Frog's over Xanadu any day. Too bad Mr. Frog's is gone."

"See?" Gracie said. "Neighborhood bars like Mr. Frog's and the Lily Pad are going the way of the local bookstore. Xanadu is the wave of the future. Stop moaning and get used to it."

"I feel nauseous," I said.

The brilliant white light reminded me of the permanent daylight in solitary confinement. The utterances of the excited crowd echoed off the cavern walls. The stereophonic river leaked into my head. I'd been to Xanadu before—in the lonely space between lying down and falling unconscious. I was tumbling into that abyss again.

Win the competition, then we'll talk. Had Sunny meant that as encouragement or ultimatum? Training for this night, I'd visualized how I would feel if I won but hadn't plumbed the disgrace of losing. What if I laid everything on the line and humiliated myself? Until now, Kolling's ownership of my soul had been speculative. Was I prepared to learn he was right?

Three rounds of five songs each, each round scored separately, each round carrying the same weight. Win two of three and the competition was over.

Fifty percent of the score would be objective: a computer would measure pitch against the accompanying music and determine a number from zero to one hundred. Fifty percent would be subjective: crowd appreciation, measured by applause, of course, but also by "physically visible indicia of engagement," that is, body language, facial expression, breathing, and even the marginal increase/decrease in room temperature. It was a Scandinavian evaluative tool meant to assuage my concerns about Kolling's clearest advantage: the home crowd. The technology was a karaoke audience polygraph. It could tell the difference between real and simulated enthusiasm.

Hogwash. You don't have to measure the *truth* of a karaoke crowd's reaction. Alcohol took care of that. What mattered was who they were and what they liked. This was a crowd filled with rich, Asian men. They'd managed to work their business trips around the competition so their companies could pick up the $400 to $2,000 per night tab at Xanadu. They reveled in the attentions paid to them by the "hostesses," all of whom were gorgeous and dressed in form-fitting *cheong sam* dresses slit up to their hips.

When I was introduced, the applause was polite. As Jimmy had surmised, they had no true appreciation for my accomplishments, whether in the karaoke or protest worlds. That's why I planned to let the audience score fall where it may. Not so long ago, Kolling couldn't sing. No matter how many vocal lessons he'd taken, he couldn't have advanced to my level. Break even on the audience, win over the computer, win the war.

I felt better onstage. Yes, it was daunting to have every button on my shirt and blemish on my face broadcast on a gigantic overhead screen. No, I hadn't expected that my "lounge," where I waited onstage while Kolling sang, would be furnished with a divan, a coffee table, and a hostess in a low-cut dress serving me Vodka Collins from a chilled pitcher. She was six feet tall with a bosom to match, a creature cooked up in an evil Communist party experiment to counter the influence of Danish erotica. I looked like a dwarf seated next to this Asian Amazon. Kolling wanted me to look absurd but, in the end, the truth would be revealed with a microphone in my hand. No matter your wealth or your power, you can't win if you can't sing.

Kolling arrived to his own theme music, a hip-hop riff mixed with an Indian sitar. It sounded like Panjabi MC with Jay-Z rapping over the top.

Beware! Beware! Yeah, yeah.
His flashing eyes, his floating hair!
This is your boy! This is your boy!

The crowd stood and cheered. Why not? Here was the man who'd built this pleasure dome, populated with pleasure drones, where the alcohol flowed more swiftly than did the sacred river Alph. If Kolling wanted to be introduced as the Karaoke King and throw off his cape to reveal a rhinestone-studded blue suit, who would question his taste? Kolling opened his arms and basked in the adulation. His guarded expression was gone. In its place was childlike glee. A blissful innocence. The joy he'd stolen from me had transformed him.

The master of ceremonies was Robert Louie, Seattle weatherman, best known for his reports near fallen power lines in the midst of hailstorms. The video of him stepping on a live wire and being launched across the street became a YouTube favorite. He looked fifty pounds lighter without his parka but clearly spent too little time indoors. As if trying to overcome gusting winds, he yelled an abbreviated version of the rules into the microphone. He noted that the video screens would broadcast the official scores in real time.

"RED means computer score, people!" Louie's voice was already hoarse. "BLUE means audience score. So if you like what you hear, MAKE NOISE! The audience score can't be tabulated until two-thirds of the way into each song. TWO-

THIRDS! This is a winner-take-all showdown for the karaoke crown. MAY THE BEST MAN WIN!"

Singing position is important. If you're bad, go first so
there's no basis for comparison. If you're the superior talent, go last—leave the final impression. I won the coin flip
and elected to go last. That meant I was second in rounds
One and Three, and first in Round Two. If it came down to
a Round Three, I would pull out all the stops on my final
song.

I shook that bastard's hand in a false show of sportsman-
ship. I wasn't counting on the vote of this undiscriminating
crowd, but it did me no good to antagonize them.

"I wish Megumi could have been here tonight," I said,
"to see me pummel you into submission."

Kolling's grip tightened. "The girl never understood the
meaning of gratitude. She got what she deserved. As will
you."

This amateur thought he could take me? He wouldn't
have his yes-men to nod their approval for every pathetic
yelp. When I was through with him, he'd wish he was back in
the boardroom, buying out punks like Troy Bobbins. Bend
over, Horatio Kolling, because your ass is mine.

The Asian Amazon poured me a Vodka Collins that I
immediately drained. The lights went down and the spotlight went on. Kolling's visage appeared on the monster
screen and the monitors that surrounded us like honey-
combs. Kolling's first song cued up: "Sweet Caroline" by
Neil Diamond.

That was the only way Kolling would stay close, by singing cupcakes. Yeah, okay, he sounded good. He sounded,
in fact, like the Neil Diamond LP. I've got the vinyl. If I

weren't watching his diaphragm straining and the perspiration beading on his face, I would have thought he was lip-synching. But the vocal timbre was all Kolling.

I kept my eyes on the scores. The red numerals, indicating the computer rating, flickered between 95 and 97. That was the key to the computer score, wasn't it? To sound as close to the original as possible. Did that mean the computer couldn't tell the difference between a misstep and an improvement? I waited on the audience number. There it was. A 97. Christ Almighty. The audience cheered the indicator of its own enthusiasm. The final tally was Computer: 96; Audience: 97. Kolling flared his nostrils in my direction.

Focus, Guy. You're the superior singer. Take one song at a time. The truth will out.

My first song was "Tutti Frutti," but Pat Boone's version, not Little Richard's. Pat Boone of the sweaters and white buck shoes. The song was easy but boring. No matter how white-bread I tried to sound, I could go no higher than a computer 92. How could I make up ground with crap like that?

People rose to go the restroom and order drinks. I added vocal flourishes and my computer score dipped. 85. 82. The audience murmured disapproval. They were watching the board as closely as I was, their tastes were being shaped by the scores instead of shaping them. I raced back to the straight-and-narrow. My computer score bumped into the high-eighties. The final tally was Computer: 88; Audience: 71.

A B+ and a C- versus Horatio Kolling's two As? The competition wasn't supposed to kick off this way. I was a better singer than that, wasn't I? Had Kolling stolen my voice along with my medallion? Jimmy said I sounded good, but could his opinion be trusted now that he'd been out of the karaoke world for so long?

The hostess poured me another drink, her face showing not a hint of emotion. I drained my glass. She refilled it. I drained another one. The lights onstage were too bright for me to see my table of friends, tucked away behind a pillar in the back of the room. I was fighting this battle alone.

Four songs later, Round One was over. Kolling had decimated me. I'd kept up as best I could, singing bland song after bland song as blandly as I could. But I couldn't match his computerized score, and the audience was turning against me. Unless the songs increased in difficulty, I would lose. And what if the computer was right, that Kolling was better? I'd been outgamed, yes. But worse, far worse, I'd been outsung. Had Megumi's final betrayal been to lie about Kolling's karaoke prowess?

We took a five-minute break. I stumbled over to my friends and avoided eye contact with the audience, who by this point must have been mocking me. My only relief had been found in vodka. If I kept up my drinking pace, I'd pass out before I lost.

"Would you stop watching the score?" Gracie said. "You look like a deer in the fucking headlights. I've heard you sound better with strep throat. What the hell's going on?"

"If I sing a song the way I want to, the computer dings me," I said. "The crowd doesn't like me. Screw them. If they want to crown Kolling, let them crown his ass."

Gracie threw ice water in my face. "Have a freaking breakdown after the competition. He won Round One, but

Round Two is a new ballgame. It's nil-nil. Stop whining and start focusing. I've never heard such boring karaoke sung by so-called elite singers. Everything's on-tune and ho-hum. Spice it up. Don't sing to the computer. You're Guy Watanabe. Sing like him."

"That machine's awfully good," Jimmy said. "Too bad Jimmy can't afford one."

What was he yammering about? Panic seized me. "You didn't put your money on me, did you, Jimmy? Tell me you didn't!"

"They laughed when Jimmy said a man could beat a machine." He shook his head sadly. "In the end, the machine always wins. We're flesh and bone, Guy. Weak."

I felt as if I'd been shot in the gut. What if Jimmy lost his life savings because he believed in me? Billy wrapped his arm around my shoulders and led me back to the stage.

"I can't win," I said. "Kolling outmaneuvered me."

"Better to lose as yourself," Billy said, "than to win as someone else."

Damn you, Billy—what the hell do you know about competition? This was *war*, not home economics. But my only alternative was to lose boldly.

Round Two, Song One, the Challenger: "Shout," by Tears for Fears. Oh yeah. You know I let it all out. The computer score started in the nineties, but as I warmed to the tune, it dipped into the low-eighties. Fuck the computer. Or as Jimmy called it, "the machine." I encouraged the crowd to stand up and raise their arms. Half of them did, bouncing up and down. That's right, dance like it's morning calisthenics.

Computer: 83; Audience: 95.

Whoa! That was a hell of a lot better than I'd done singing for the computer. The crowd actually looked like it was enjoying itself. Their emotion had a negative spillover effect on Kolling. His next song garnered a Computer 93 and an Audience 82. He looked stiff and unnatural doing anything other than standing at the microphone and singing like a marionette. Once the crowd had tasted the real thing, aspartame left a sour taste in their mouths.

Kolling was singing neither better nor worse than he had in Round One, but it's all a matter of expectations. Sing at the same, uniform level of excellence and it becomes tedious. Whether a man visits too many cathedrals or eats filet mignon one too many times, he grows insensitive even to the most visceral pleasures. Humans need variety; they need change; they need excitement. Kolling's audience score kept declining. Why pull for the favorite when the underdog is surging? And pulling ahead.

Score Round Two to the Challenger, Guy Watanabe.

Kolling no longer looked at ease. He scowled in my direction. I raised my hands into an open triangle I placed over my bangs, hair protruding.

"Puss boy," I mouthed.

My posse was amped, crowding me during the break.

"Attaboy, Guy," Gracie said. "Don't pull the boot off his neck. Plunge the sword straight through his heart."

"You're coming through loud and clear," Billy said. "Singing isn't just mechanics, it's emotion. Kolling is dipping into a dry well. It's not about the head; it's about the heart."

I was five short songs away from regaining my kara-oke throne. I couldn't wait to watch the Seattle Channel rebroadcast. I hoped they had close-up reaction shots of Kolling when, left for dead, I blew him out of the water.

"Do you think the machine can learn emotion?" Jimmy said. "Does the machine understand there's something more than perfection?"

"We don't need to worry about the computer score," I said. "We've switched strategies. The computer can't under-stand what the audience feels."

Jimmy shook his head. "Not the computer." He pointed to his throat, then held up an imaginary microphone. "The machine. The singing machine."

Gracie and Billy hustled me back onstage, but I pondered Jimmy's question. The "machine" to which he referred was different from the "computer." I recalled something Jimmy told me long ago about KGI's purchase of the Lily Pad. It was to become a membership club, replete with high-tech karaoke machines. Those karaoke machines eliminated the need for a human DJ by having the performer cue up the song by uttering the title. They would also allow anyone to sing on-tune.

Kolling was up first in Round Three, moving through Willie Nelson's "On the Road Again" with a workmanlike mimicry. And finally, I saw him for what he was. A charla-tan. A cheater. He'd tried to beat me using a lip-synching machine, but he'd failed. And that was more pathetic than losing to me for real.

It's important to relish moments of victory so that, in the future, they can be recalled vividly and with great satisfaction. I plucked the orange umbrella from my drink and handed it to my oversized hostess. I drained my delicious drink, then hurried to the microphone before Kolling had finished his song. I heard what the audience, far below us, could not. Up close, Kolling's voice could best be characterized as the bleating of a sheep with acid reflux.

"I know your secret, you dickwad," I said when he came off the stage. "You must feel like shit knowing that you cheated and you're still going to lose." My throat felt uncharacteristically dry.

"Is that so, Mr. Watanabe?" Kolling said. "Perhaps you should have brought your own supply of bottled water."

Round Three, Song One, the Challenger: "Shit, Damn, Motherfucker," by D'Angelo. That's a song you don't see too frequently in karaoke bars. But it was oh so apt here.

How many times did I need to be drugged, beaten, and cheated to know not to trust his drinks? I made it through the first third of the song in reasonable fashion, but by the halfway point my tires were flat and my radiator steaming. My throat closed into a narrow reed and frog-like croaks emerged in place of the lyrics. *Sht. Dm. Mth fkr.*

I passed it off as best I could, dancing sometimes in place of singing. But the crowd noticed the difference. A mob can turn on you in an instant, and this was longer than an instant. I struggled through four more songs that way, unable to reach the high notes, chirping and chirruping along like a cane toad that had licked its own skin. At first, the audience greeted me with silence. Then with laughs. Then with jeers.

My scores? Best not to print them. Needless to say, I was wrong about the logistical impossibility of scoring zero.

At the end of the night, as confetti rained down from the heavens and champagne corks popped, Horatio Kolling stood alone at center stage, hoisting my karaoke medallion overhead. He looked supremely satisfied. He looked like a man in control of his own destiny. He looked like, and he was, the Karaoke King.

I slunk off into the night, unheralded and unnoticed, with my small group of forlorn friends. I had lost. Guy Watanabe was a loser.

I knew better than to mention the whole "Kolling ate my soul" business during the long weekend we spent in Chelan. Gracie would have labeled me a superstitious idiot. Billy would have said something borderline Lao Tzu, like "only when you're an empty vessel can you be filled up with the present." My only consolation was that Jimmy hadn't bet the farm on me—just a bubble tea with an Uwajimaya cashier.

Oh, they tried their best to cheer me up, and on occasion they succeeded. On an unseasonably warm, spring Sunday, Billy took us out on a boat to where it seemed all the cherry blossoms had bloomed at once. May drew uncharacteristically cheery portraits, where I was no longer a sadistic frog stabbing a multi-eyeballed monster but a man, a stick-figure man, sitting by the fire with a group of friends.

We ate well. We slept well. We took long walks along the lakeshore. I discovered that Chelan wasn't the hick town of my imagination, but a community filled with artists as well as mechanics, doctors as well as deacons. I could see why Billy'd never left it for the caffeinated, double-income-no-kids neighborhoods of Seattle.

But when the lights were out and I was alone with my thoughts, I felt the loss of my soul acutely. Was it possible for a man to regenerate his soul the way a lizard grew back a severed tail? Would I ever be anything other than a loser?

"You know John Henry lost to a machine," Billy said over multi-grain, pecan waffles. "There's no shame in it. And who do we remember more fondly, the man or the machine?"

Yeah, yeah. Take your advice to a Quaker Oats commercial, Billy. What we remember is that John Henry lost. He lost.

THE END

EPILOGUE

My story should end there. But it doesn't. Few of us die with a hammer in our hands. The rest of us plod along until we keel over from clogged arteries at the age of seventy-eight. We all want to be winners. But most of us are losers.

I didn't deserve to lose the karaoke crown. But lose I did. The *Seattle Asian Herald* ran a half-page photograph of Kolling holding up my medallion. Beneath it is a smaller photo of me. Tears stream down my face and my hands press against my pharmacologically-challenged throat. The caption reads: "Wa-ta-NO-be chokes."

I didn't deserve a multi-million-dollar settlement from the government. But I took it. I would like to say the first thing I did was donate the entire sum to immigrant rights causes. That would be a lie. I bought a Porsche Cayman S for my father, who showed up wearing driving gloves at 7 a.m. on the day after the government check cleared. Next I purchased a 62 inch LCD HDTV, an Xbox 360, and a Toyota Prius (in Seattle, the ultimate symbol of doing good *and* doing well). A distant third was establishing the Center for

Civil Liberties and Marjorie and Benjamin's kitchen-based mission as the administrators of a trust that funded projects for immigrants—legal, illegal, and somewhere in-between. Money can't make a sinking ship of state sprout wings and fly, but maybe it would bail some water. It wasn't fair to be paid so much for so little, while scores of detainees were paid nothing for suffering unspeakable brutalities. Then again, they didn't endure three non-profit fundraisers a week. I hope Congress will consider a guest-worker program to help alleviate my burden.

Regardless of desert, life goes on. Tanya and Jay's wedding reception was catered by Tom Douglas of Dahlia Lounge. Gracie and Paula decided that if they couldn't be "married," they didn't want state ratification of their union at all. I sang at their rocking commitment ceremony. Sheila and I talked on the phone a few times—she told me she'd enrolled in community college—but we lost touch. Since she lived in southern California, which I visited frequently, she could have met Sunny and me for lunch. But Sheila always bagged at the last moment. Some relationships wither away. And some flourish.

Sunny didn't, as I'd feared, refuse my telephone calls once she learned that I lost the karaoke title.

"How shallow do you think I am?" she said. "You're the one who said *I* have no talent. This puts us on even footing."

I can't say I understand my attraction to her. Sunny not only has bad taste in music, she can't appreciate good music. I'll put on, say, a Ben Harper CD, and the first thing she'll ask is, "What the heck is this?" Then, "This sounds too weird." A few seconds later, "Would you turn this off?" We take eight-hour road trips and do nothing but talk because we can't agree on what music to play.

I *think* Billy likes her, though he nearly fainted when she poured Tabasco Sauce on the artichoke frittata he had so lovingly seasoned. They hadn't known each other for an hour before she said that May needed more "discipline and boundaries." When Billy soothed May out of a tantrum, Sunny told him he was encouraging bad behavior. "You've got to stop being such a doormat, Billy," she said. "If that little girl walks all over you now, just wait until she's fifteen and her hormones are popping."

Sunny has strong preferences. If I help around the office, she watches for five minutes before pushing me aside and doing everything herself. She tells me she could never live in Seattle because of the crowds, though she knows I can't live in the arid wasteland she calls her home. The desiccated air gives me nosebleeds and makes my eczema flare. We argue all the time, especially about karaoke.

Granted, Sunny is a whiz with finances and mixed drinks. But she knows nothing about being a karaoke proprietress. The microphone is for the customers, and Choi's Club sees more customers than ever now that I've expanded her song library. But the longer the line of singers, the more songs Sunny reserves for herself. If she wants to cue up the songs, she has to learn not to be a microphone hog.

I wonder sometimes what life would have been like as Megumi's husband. I picture her pale, lithe body in a bikini, lounging beneath an umbrella on a Third World beach. Then I hear Sunny mangling a perfectly good song on her Casio keyboard and am jolted back into reality. But reality has its own allure.

I was more surprised than anyone when the Karaoke Group International filed for bankruptcy. They folded overnight, little over a year after Xanadu's Grand Opening. And it wasn't just Xanadu that closed and sold its assets and equipment at auction. It was the worldwide network of KGI-owned karaoke facilities. The late John Smith had been right. KGI's One Karaoke Establishment strategy was unsustainable.

The *Wall Street Journal* wrote the business obituary, entitled "Why KGI Was Not the Next Starbucks." According to the *Journal,* the overseas Asians who constituted Xanadu's initial customer base decided they could find the same product cheaper at home or in the developing countries of Southeast Asia. A graph illustrated how investment in karaoke technology had negligible effects on repeat patronage. In Calcutta, KGI's membership bar was outperformed by a karaoke shack, where the owner pushed play on a cassette tape recorder and tapped a tambourine.

"You want to go where everybody knows your name," a Bengali postman explained.

In a *Seattle Asian Herald* editorial, Norene Wong disagreed. She said Horatio Kolling had angered the white establishment by not paying obeisance to the stock market. Kolling kept tight control over KGI's operations in order to nurture karaoke's Asian essence, "to keep it from being killed by the thousand cuts of acculturation." Why, she asked, would Americans embrace coffee but not karaoke? Racism.

I can't help but wonder if Kolling, by swallowing my soul, actually weakened himself. KGI enjoyed record profits and expansion before Kolling met me. Under the Neighborhood Karaoke Strategy, KGI's franchisees did all the work and KGI reaped all the benefits. Why did KGI take on unsecured debt to buy out Troy Bobbins's self-help empire? If KGI wanted to fund its own restructuring, it should have chosen an industry synergistically related to karaoke.

Kolling will rise again. Look at Troy Bobbins—I mean, Terry Stottart. He has a new infomercial out for a product called the "Ab Annihilator." It's a machine that employs gravity and electric shocks to stimulate your stomach muscles while you sleep. Terry's flab is gone and you could grate cheese on his six-pack. If Terry can reinvent himself, surely Kolling can too.

Meanwhile, the state of Washington is negotiating with a consortium of Native American tribes on a land swap: reservation land for Xanadu. If it goes through, the tribes would have the largest casino west of Las Vegas. The move is opposed by non-Indian casino owners and the Muckleshoot tribe, which owns the largest casino in Washington. The litigation will continue for decades.

A non-profit developer took over the KGI facility that was supposed to supplant the Lily Pad. With support from the city and the Gates Foundation, it became an early-childhood learning center. First-generation immigrants and their toddlers stream in and out of its air-conditioned environs. It has broadband access, interactive games, and multi-media displays that rival those at the South Visitor Center of Salt Lake City's Temple Square.

Jimmy works there as a docent. He leads tours, schedules parenting classes, sorts mail, and provides general good
cheer. That's how I received a letter that would otherwise
have gone into the trash. It was addressed to "Guy Watanabe, Ex-Karaoke King" at the Lily Pad. There was no return
address.

I took the letter to Gossip and ordered a bubble tea.
I ignored the teenagers who pointed and made choking
sounds. The handwriting was neat and familiar.

Dear Guy,

I don't know if you'll receive this letter, but
I think you're not the kind of man to move
very far. It would have been simpler and
safer had you died, but I'm glad you didn't.
After all that time with no air, it's good that
you didn't end up like my cousin Rong, who
drools and lives at home.

I am happy you still have a brain, and you
still like to sing. You sing beautifully. I know
Horatio cheated. He always does. That's why
he's a winner. You didn't deserve to lose
everything, but sometimes that happens.
Good people suffer and bad people profit.
Life is unfair.

I wanted to tell you I didn't run off with another
man. I ran away with myself. I wanted to find

a different person—not Megumi, not Pon, but someone I could be proud of. I am living in a small, flat town. It has two gas stations, a discount mall, and now, a Thai restaurant.

You will be happy to know I've invested my money wisely. I thought to myself, "What do I like?" The answer is food. No, I don't like to cook. I like to eat. But I have good management skills. There are many workers here without papers who are cheap to hire and fear deportation. They work hard and make no trouble. Restaurant work is easy: I smile, run credit cards, and put fortune cookies on the tip trays (Americans <u>love</u> fortune cookies!). It's more fun being an owner than it is being a worker.

When we traveled the southwestern desert together, I discovered this: America is a vast, open space in which every person can disappear. Like the dunes of white sand you adored, the winds can blow and all traces of our past can vanish.

Sometimes at the end of the night, after I've stored away the money I don't record, I can't help but think of you. I think I may miss you. It would make me feel sad if you disappeared.

But don't look for me. I would be angry if you surprised me again.

Do you still sing every night? Be careful. Older men who drink a lot get fat. Fat is not handsome.

Goodbye,

Jade Sin

Maybe Milton Schwarzer was right all along. Maybe the only trustworthy relationship is *quid pro quo*.

Sunny has something I need: a head for business and mad bartending skills. I have something she needs: musicality, decorum, and enough capital to turn an abandoned karaoke bar in Chelan into something special. I told Billy to keep tabs on the former Mr. Frog's, and to put in a high bid on my behalf if someone else showed interest. That went on for months before Billy, the man Sunny refers to as "spineless," said he was fed up with my indecision.

"It's time for you to pop the question," he said.

He was right. I kept waiting for the perfect time, but the truth is that time itself is impartial. We make time perfect or imperfect, right or wrong.

Sunny and I spent Christmas in Chelan. We stayed at a bed-and-breakfast to keep Billy from waiting on us hand-and-foot and May from peeping in on us in the middle of the night. The day broke bright, clear, and cold with a light sprinkling of snow on the street. We walked past the gift shops, coffee bars, and real estate agencies until we reached a boarded-up storefront.

Sunny has faint pockmarks on her face. She has the kind of high, broad Korean forehead I used to make fun of as a child. She nags me about eating second servings while she stuffs her own face. And the only thing worse than her taste in music is her taste in movies. Regardless of her flaws, and regardless of mine, I've fallen hard for her. I don't want to share solitude with her. I want to share life.

That's why Milton's advice that *quid pro quo* is the only relationship to trust isn't wrong. It's incomplete. Love is inherently untrustworthy. It's unpredictable and irrational. The person you *should* love isn't the person you *do* love. A man can control when he wakes up, what he does during the day, and when he goes to bed. But he has little control over his own heart.

Thank God.

Sunny and I shivered in front of the storefront. There was graffiti on the windows. The roof was bowed by the weight of ice. A rat hole was chewed into a corner of the door. But the alley led to a spacious parking lot, and I knew from experience the main room was larger than the entrance suggested.

"Why did you bring me here?" Sunny sounded uncharacteristically demure.

I took her hands. "What do you think about the two of us owning a karaoke bar together?"

ACKNOWLEDGMENTS

There are men and women
so lonely they believe
God, too, is lonely.
—Carl Sandburg, 1928[1]

Few endeavors require more solitude than completing a novel. I wish those empty spaces had been filled with the awe I felt while hiking alone in Arches National Park during my journey to trace Guy Watanabe's meanderings through the southwest. Bathed in the light of a sandstone sunset, I was content to be small and insignificant, dwarfed by the vastness of that warm, lunar landscape. More typically, however, I encountered the solitude of a schizophrenic unable to silence disparate, desperate voices. Being an author, creator of worlds, can be lonely. Thank goodness I shared solitude—and coffee, camaraderie, and joy—with so many kind individuals.

---

1 "They Ask: Is God, Too, Lonely?," reprinted in *The Seashell Anthology of Great Poetry*, ed. Christopher Burns (Edgartown: The Seashell Press, 1996).

Thank you Soaring Meringues—Daniel Becker, Stacey Bennetts, Lynn Dixon, Michelle Furtado, Betsy Herring, Marschel Paul, and Carla Saulter—fine writers and friends all. My novel may not be svelte, but it is shapely only because of Betsy's discerning eye; Marschel, your faith in my karaoke opera pales in comparison to my belief in your gorgeous, historical novel. Thank you Lyn Coffin, JT Stewart, and Corry Venema-Weiss for your advice, integrity, and creativity. Thank you Skye Moody for your early and enthusiastic support for Guy's forlorn intransigence. Thank you John Chun, Lynn Hall, and Sung Yang for being the first impartial readers of a manuscript that didn't look or sound like anything you'd expected; and Mark Wittow for volunteering to review *pro bono* my contract and those of countless other artists. Thank you Susan Rich for being an exquisite poet, an artistic confidante, and a generous and compassionate soul. While writing this novel, I lost a dear friend, SCK, to suicide: her fictional self lacked the capacity to appreciate the beauty of her true self.

Thank you to the amazing team at AmazonEncore: Senior Editor Terry Goodman (did *no one* question your sanity and/or taste?); marketing maven Sarah Tomashek; überpublicist Kimberly Burns; Author Relations Manager Jacque Ben-Zekry; enigmatic, literary "carer" (to borrow Kazuo Ishiguro's term) Jenny W.; and the designers of the Karaoke King's "look." Thank you Artist Trust for financially supporting my second novel long before my first one found a publisher; Nirmala Singh-Brinkman and everyone involved with the Artist Trust EDGE Program for helping writers to thrive artistically and professionally; Richard Hugo House for being a "big tent" for Seattle writers; and the Yale Law

School Career Options Assistance Program (COAP) for enabling graduates to chase different dreams.

Most of my novel was written in two West Seattle cafés: C & P Coffee Company and Coffee to a Tea. Thank you Cameron, Peter, George, and Jodi for providing strong coffee, tasty eats, and beautiful spaces for local artists, community activists, and creatures big, small, and sometimes four-legged.

I am indebted to a number of writers and their works. Like Huckleberry Finn, Guy drifts through many lives and locations, except Guy is carried along by an impersonal stream of transnational commerce; Guy, Megumi, and Horatio engage in an alternating chase through American motels on a trail that was blazed by Humbert, Lolita, and Clare; several characters draw their names or inspirations from *Do Androids Dream of Electric Sheep?*, including Troy Bobbins and his self-help form of Mercerism; and Guy attempts to maintain his equanimity during a lap dance by butchering Theodore Roethke's poem "I Knew a Woman." I hope that Karl May's garrulous, existential cowboys would have approved of their creator's reincarnation as a hirsute, gay German biker who shoots amateur porn. On a more serious note, I recommend two books for those interested in exploring the issues of contemporary slavery and the involvement of private prisons in the warehousing of immigrants: Kevin Bales, *Disposable People: New Slavery in the Global Economy* (Berkeley: Univ. of Calif. Press, 2004); and Mark Dow, *American Gulag: Inside U.S. Immigration Prisons* (Berkeley: Univ. of Calif. Press, 2005). I have had the privilege to serve with a number of legal heroes of every political persuasion. EAW, Barbara R., Jerome F., James R., Mary Alice T., James D., and

Brian T. are my exemplars of intellect, practicality, and compassion. Thank you judges and clerks of every stripe: Guy would have escaped the legal labyrinth within hours had he landed in the true Western District of Washington.

Finally, I must express gratitude to my family for their unwavering—okay, well, not always skeptical—support for an unconventional novel that took forever to wobble off on its own two legs. Although my parents (through birth and marriage) would have preferred to brag about their son the law-firm partner, they can at least stop running away from friends. Thank you San Lin, Xiao Wei, Joy, Nick, Rick, Paige, and Baby Taylor. Thank you Chris Hong, Brian Surratt, and Maya H. Surratt: I can't imagine any place warmer than our extended family household. Thank you to my wife, Katie Hong, for teaching me that while love's path may be fraught with mundane obstacles, passion need not be ephemeral. And thank you Khalil and Ariadne for entering our lives at just the right time. Please don't read beyond page one before you turn eighteen. Just know that the little lost boy found his way home.

ABOUT THE AUTHOR

Photo by Nubar Alexanian, 2005

At Harold Taw's birth, a Burmese monk prophesied that if he fed monkeys on every birthday, his family would prosper. For forty years, the author has complied, and his achievements are many: Graduating Phi Beta Kappa from the University of California at Berkeley; being a Fulbright Scholar in rural Thailand, where he studied the spread of AIDS; earning a degree from Yale Law School; serving as law clerk to federal trial and appellate judges; and working as a corporate attorney. An Artist Trust GAP Award allowed him to travel to Thailand and Burma to research his second novel, *Saturday's Child*. Taw earned recognition from the 2010 British Feature Screenplay Competition, the 2010 Beverly Hills Film Festival, the 2010 Canada International Film Festival, and more, for his screenplay *Dog Park*. *Adventures of the Karaoke King* is the author's debut novel.

/